COSTLY LESSONS

"I will teach you how to train your people to fight. But I must warn you, such lessons do not come cheaply," Kane said as he looked at her, his eyes narrowing intently.

"I did not expect them to. The golden hawk is worth a great deal. 'Twill more than compensate you for what time you will spend."

Kane drew back, staring. "The golden hawk?"

" 'Tis literally that. Gold." She held out her hands to measure an astonishing size for what she spoke of. " 'Tis that large, and it is also the heart of my people."

"The golden hawk," he said again, this time stifling a chuckle. "You are an innocent, aren't you? I have no wish or need for your precious golden hawk. I do not covet such things."

Distress darkened the blue of Jenna's eyes. "But then what will you take? All we have is the Glade, and what is the difference between giving it up to you and losing it to the warlord?"

"I do not want your land, either."

"But then . . . what can we offer?"

"I care for nothing from your precious people, Jenna of the clan Hawk." He rose then, and went to her. He crooked a finger beneath her chin and lifted her head. "But you . . . you can offer me something I want. . . ."

A SPECIAL HOLIDAY TREAT!

Justine Dare again delights readers
with a marvelously romantic and
evocative story of the joy of Christmas
and the promise of the New Year in an
exciting new anthology—

*A Stockingful
of Joy*

by

Jill Barnett

Mary Jo Putney

Justine Dare

Susan King

On Sale in October 1997 from Onyx.

FIRE HAWK

Justine Dare

A TOPAZ BOOK

TOPAZ
Published by the Penguin Group
Penguin Books USA Inc., 375 Hudson Street,
New York, New York 10014, U.S.A.
Penguin Books Ltd, 27 Wrights Lane,
London W8 5TZ, England
Penguin Books Australia Ltd, Ringwood,
Victoria, Australia
Penguin Books Canada Ltd, 10 Alcorn Avenue,
Toronto, Ontario, Canada M4V 3B2
Penguin Books (N.Z.) Ltd, 182–190 Wairau Road,
Auckland 10, New Zealand

Penguin Books Ltd, Registered Offices:
Harmondsworth, Middlesex, England

First published by Topaz, an imprint of Dutton Signet,
a division of Penguin Books USA Inc.

First Printing, July, 1997
10 9 8 7 6 5 4

Copyright © Janice Davis Smith, 1997
All rights reserved

 REGISTERED TRADEMARK—MARCA REGISTRADA

Printed in Canada

Once again for Hal, whose songs are as timeless
as the place in this story—
With thanks for the wisdom, the magic . . . and the music.

Some say the magic is gone. Dead, buried amid the concrete, glass, and smog of our world.

Some say the magic never existed, that it was dreamed up by people who couldn't explain their world any other way.

But some know. Some know it still lives. Some know that it can be found in those moments of sunset that paint the sky with colors that can't possibly exist, in the whiff of wildness on the wind, in the achingly familiar sound of a song never before heard—and heard a thousand times.

They know. And it is they who will find the old man in the forest—and their own miracle.

Chapter 1

Before Arthur was King, in a place out of time . . .

She'd never wanted to kill before.

Jenna stared down at the freshly turned earth, watching the rain turn it to mud, wishing she could cry as the sky did so freely. But she had no tears. She had had nothing left but anger for a very long time. There had been too many burials. And too many of those had ended, like this one, with a stone set at the head of the grave that bore the symbol of the Hawk. She had never wanted to kill, but she knew now that she could learn. With pleasure.

"Jenna—"

Jenna ignored the soft voice of Evelin the healer; the woman could say nothing she had not heard before. She turned away from the freshly turned earth. Justus had been her brother, and she had loved him. Idolized him, with his gentle good humor, his quiet ways, and the quick, sharp mind that had helped her hone her own to a sharp edge.

None of it had done him any good. The very things that had made the clan prize him had been his downfall; he was a man of peace, not war. He hadn't known how to fight any more than any of them did. And now he was as dead as if he'd been a helpless child, not the pride of his people, the heir to the golden Hawk. And she was alone. Alone with her fears. Alone with her duties. Alone with the weight of generations of responsibility on her shoulders.

Alone with her anger.

It bubbled up in her again, fierce and relentless. She was soul-deep weary of feeling so utterly helpless. The last time the yearly rains had come, she'd had a family. She'd had a mother who, despite being the hereditary head of the clan since Jenna's father's death shortly after she was born, had always had time for her children. She'd had a sweet, loving brother, who had born the Hawk title with a solemn sadness after the death of their mother.

And now she had no one.

No one but an entire clan, all looking to her to do . . . something. To help them. To save them. And she didn't know how.

Neither had her mother. Or her brother, in the short time he'd lived to hold the Hawk. They knew nothing of war, and she was as ignorant as they. The closest any of them had ever come to fighting was hearing of the exploits of Kane, the mythical warrior of the mountains, stories told to entertain children.

None of them knew how to fight, yet they expected her to acquire the knowledge that would save them.

"Jenna, it is time for the ceremony."

"My brother is barely cold," she snapped at Evelin, even though she knew it was tradition and not the kindly healer herself who demanded it.

"Which is why it is time," Evelin said, ever reasonable even in the face of Jenna's temper.

Yet moments from now, Jenna mused as she shoved the long mass of her hair back from her face and reluctantly followed the elderly woman, such a show of temper from her would cause much obsequious bowing and apologizing. She would be the same

woman she was now, the people would be the same.
The only difference would be she would have the precious golden Hawk, the emblem of her new and unwanted rank. The emblem she had never expected or desired to hold.

She stood miserably in the rain as the ragged clan of less than one hundred, all that was left now after months of a battle that was so one-sided as to be hardly deserving of the name, gathered around her in the clearing. Evelin, as the oldest clanswoman still living, began the melodic chant. Rising and falling, an evocative mix of mourning for the fallen leader and celebration of the new one, the chant had been a part of Hawk clan tradition for generations. She'd been too young to pay attention to it when the Hawk had passed from her father to her mother upon his death. But she remembered it far too well from the ceremony that had turned it over to her brother, remembered it because it had been mere months ago. Not even five cycles of the moon had passed since Justus had stood where she was now.

She glanced at the gathered clan. They were all gazing respectfully at Evelin, as was expected. Only Cara, her dear friend Cara, looked at Jenna. There was such warm sympathy and understanding in the young woman's eyes that Jenna felt the fierce anger inside her ebb ever so slightly. But still, when Evelin held the precious statue out to her, she wanted to scream her refusal, wanted to cry to the weeping heavens that this was not right. But she had no time now; grief was a luxury she could not allow herself. She had had to keep going after her mother's death, and she had to keep going now, after Justus's death. She had to, for the sake of the clan. She had to, and she would.

She took the heavy golden bird. A lifetime of inculcated traditions were not set aside so easily.

The chant went on, the low words in the ancient

language no one spoke any longer, the words that gave
to Jenna the power she'd never wanted, the power
she'd thought herself saved from ever having to wield
by the good fortune of having an older brother.

A movement on the edge of her vision caught her
attention. She looked toward it. Cara was not the only
one who was breaking with tradition and looking at
Jenna rather than the healer conducting the ceremony.
The old man who had come to them out of the forest,
a refugee from the brutal attacks, was watching her
intently. His eyes, sometimes the green of the misty
wood, sometimes nearly as gold as the Hawk whose
weight was already tiring her arms, were fierce with
an intelligence tempered by an unerring wisdom. Despite his intimidating demeanor, Jenna had often gone
to him to hear the amazing stories he could tell, of
times and places never imagined, of things that could
not be, yet came alive in his telling in a way that never
failed to fascinate her.

And now, the old, silver-haired man with the dark
brows, known only as the storyteller, sent her a look
not of sympathy and understanding as Cara had, but
of strength, and a support so strong it was almost tangible. So powerful was the surge of it within her that
Jenna blinked, startled. As if her involuntary reaction
had been a sign of a message received, the old man
looked away, glancing up at the clouds that had been
pelting them for nearly a full night and day.

Evelin began to walk around Jenna in the traditional way, tossing handfuls of her precious herbs
down onto the muddy earth, herbs mixed in a way
known only to the clan's healer, and handed down by
each healer to the next.

As if responding to the ancient invocation, the rain
began to slow. Jenna saw the people glancing skyward,
much as the storyteller had, as the ominously dark
gray skies began to lighten.

Evelin drew out the traditional dagger, with its hilt carved in a replica of the Hawk, at last beginning the final chorus of the chant, the words meant to call blessings down on the new Hawk, the holder of the golden symbol of the rank of leader of the clan. The rank had been in Jenna's family for generations, since the only reason for change was misuse of the power it bestowed.

She wondered idly if not using the power at all fell under that dictum.

Evelin's last words echoed, and silence fell upon the group. From the corner of her eye Jenna saw the storyteller nod sharply, as if in approval of Evelin's performance. *You'd think the old man wrote the chant himself,* she thought, *as pleased as he's looking.* A gust of wind blew rain into her eyes, and her vision blurred for a moment. When she blinked them clear again, the rain had stopped and the old man was gone. Another one of his eerie disappearances that brought on the rumors among the children that the man was a warlock, or worse.

Evelin reached out and slid the ceremonial dagger into the sheath at Jenna's waist. Then the healer turned to the gathered clan. "I give you the new Hawk."

A cheer arose, with more enthusiasm that Jenna ever would have expected; she didn't think they had that much left in them. She wondered what it was for, that enthusiasm. She wondered what difference they thought a new Hawk would make. She wondered what lies they were telling themselves.

She wondered what in the name of the heavens they expected her to do.

"I've been expecting you."

Jenna's breath caught as the low voice came out of

the shadows. She should be used to it by now, she thought; no one ever surprised the storyteller.

Involuntarily Jenna shivered. The fire in the center of the small hut had gone out, and she wondered that the old man's bones could tolerate the damp and cold.

"Sit down, Jenna."

She saw only the swirl of his robe in the dim light as he stepped forward. And then she saw his face, wide jaw, dark, heavy brows beneath silver hair, and always those eyes, fierce, penetrating, the fire from within burning as brightly as the fire reflected in them—

Fire?

She glanced downward, only now realizing that the fire she'd thought lacking even any lingering embers was burning steadily, providing the light she'd needed to see him, and warmth enough to take away the chill of the damp air.

"Or perhaps I'm being too familiar? You are, after all, the Hawk now."

Jenna wrinkled her nose. "Mercy, not you, too."

The man's mouth quirked upward at one corner. "Had enough of it so soon? Most would enjoy the fealty of an entire clan."

"The fealty is fine," Jenna said wryly. " 'Tis the expectations I find difficult."

The storyteller chuckled. Jenna smiled despite her worries; she alone had always managed to make the mysterious man smile. He had come to them weighed down by a darkness she sensed was deep and long-standing, and it had given her a special sort of pleasure to be the one who could brighten it for him. And it seemed a small price to pay for the wondrous tales he spun, holding adults and children alike enthralled.

But it was not stories she'd come for now. She wasn't certain why she had come, really. Perhaps she had some crazy idea that because the man sometimes told tales of faraway battles he at least knew *something* about fighting. More than she did, in any case.

She took the seat he indicated, a low stool that bore the marks of Latham, the clan's woodworker. The storyteller dropped to sit cross-legged on the ground before the fire, his only cushion the bear pelt that passed from storyteller to storyteller. It had lain unused, this hut unoccupied, since Gillan had died in one of the first attacks.

Jenna noticed, not for the first time, that the storyteller moved with a limberness that belied the gray of his hair. It was odd, she thought, also not for the first time, that no one had ever discovered much about the man's past; the clan was generally a curious lot when it came to newcomers. Odder still that she, the most curious of them all, hadn't tried to pry his own story out of him, hadn't even charmed his proper name out of him. But he had come here and taken Gillan's place almost without question; his skill at storytelling had rendered questions seemingly needless. And no one had really felt up to the task of asking, not when it meant looking into those fiercely intelligent eyes.

"Why did you expect me?" she asked.

"Because it is time."

Jenna sighed. "Must you always be so mysterious?"

A delighted expression crossed his face. "Have I succeeded, then? Good."

Jenna found herself smiling despite her worries; it was difficult not to when that rare grin lit up the storyteller's expression. For an instant she thought she saw something change in his eyes, some flicker of a reality hidden behind a mask, but it was gone so swiftly she could not be sure.

"That's what I was hoping to see," he said. "You smile too little of late."

"There is little to smile about," she retorted. "You

know that better than anyone. You must know that
I—"

She broke off. Did she dare confide her fears, even
to him? Did she dare admit how frightened she was,
how helpless she felt, how terrified she was that she
would not be able to save the people who depended
on her?

"You will not let them down, Jenna."

The uncanny accuracy of his guess, and the unshakable certainty in his voice, sent a shiver down her
spine. Who *was* this man?

Her fears, pressing now, churning, overcame her
doubts, and the words came from her in a rush. "How
can you say that? We've had no fighting here for generations. How can I help? How can I save my people,
when I know no more than they do?"

"You will find the way." His eyes had gone distant,
unfocused. His voice had changed, taken on the softly
compelling note it held when he was telling one of his
wondrous tales. "You will go far from here, from your
home. Face dark trials. The serpent's tongue, the
lion's roar . . ."

Jenna stared, holding her breath as his voice trailed
off. The silence spun out, as taut as the strings of
Cara's harp. The storyteller continued to stare, as if
at something only he could see. Finally the strain was
too much for Jenna, and she had to break the stillness.

"But why? Where am I to go? What am I to do? I
know nothing of war!"

He sucked in a short breath, and that quickly was
back with her, his eyes again focused and intent.

"Then you must find someone who does."

Her mouth twisted at one corner, and she looked
at him pointedly; despite the oddness of his ways, and
the fact that many of the clan were intimidated by
him, Jenna was not.

"I did. I came to you."

The storyteller blinked. "Me?"

It was the first time she'd ever seen him startled, but she couldn't spare time to dwell on her small victory. "You at least speak of battles. It is more than anyone else."

He smiled, but shook his head. "You flatter me, child. They are only stories."

"But the battles were real, were they not?"

"Yes. But still—"

"Your stories are as detailed as if you were there yourself."

"They are very good stories," he allowed, his smile widening.

"But you have known such things, or known of them," she insisted. "Surely there must be some plan to be drawn from those tales, some method by which such things are done, such battles are fought? Surely you must have one tale, amid all your tales, of a small force who defeated a more powerful one? Or at least held them at bay?"

"I have many," the storyteller said. "Some that will ring in history forever, some yet to come."

Jenna grimaced; she'd lost patience with his enigmatic allusions to other times and places. "I will be content with one that will help us here and now," she said a little sharply.

The storyteller laughed. "Ah, Jenna, you are truly fit to be the Hawk."

His approval warmed her, but she felt it was undeserved. "I don't feel fit. And unless you can help me, I shall be proven right."

The weight of responsibility seemed crushing now as she thought of the inevitable end if things continued as they were. Those few who had survived until now would be slaughtered like so many pigs. Her friends, and the children, would end with throats cut, sightless eyes staring at the heavens, up to the gods who had apparently forsaken them and left them to the bloody hands of a warlord who had set his evil sights on their quiet glade.

"I cannot," he said.

Jenna's heart sank. She hadn't realized how greatly she had counted on his help until now, when he denied he could provide it. But something else he'd said prodded at her, and she lifted her head, marveling anew at how much effort it took to simply meet his gaze.

"You said I must find someone who does."

He nodded, and she saw that light of approval still lingering in his changeable eyes, eyes so different from her own, which were always, ever blue.

"Who?" she asked.

He shrugged, as if it were common knowledge. "There is only one who can help you."

"Who?" she repeated.

"Kane."

Jenna's arched brows shot upward. "Kane? He's a myth! A legend, a story told to children—"

"So they say."

"But everyone knows he's not real, any more than the beast of the lake."

The storyteller shrugged again.

"You're saying he is real? That he lives?"

"He exists."

Jenna wondered at the choice of words in the storyteller's quiet confirmation, but the entire idea was so absurd she could only shake her head.

"But everyone—"

"Before I came here," he interrupted, in such a mild tone it took her a moment to realize he might truly be imparting some bit of his hidden past, "I passed through a land where there was a legend of a distant place, a glade in a magical forest that provided safety for all the souls that resided there, where all wants were met, peace had reigned unbroken year after year, and where the leader was marked by the possession of a golden hawk. All knew it was merely legend, all laughed at the idea of ever setting out to find such a place, for it was only a myth. Everyone knew that."

Jenna opened her mouth, then closed it again. Her mouth quirked; she'd been through this before with this puzzling, very curious man. "Another lesson hidden in allegory, sir?"

He smiled, that gentle, approving smile that seemed to lighten even her heavy burden. " 'Tis often easier that way, is it not?"

"Especially for those too stubborn to see?"

"You are never too stubborn," he said. "But sometimes you are too close."

For a long time, Jenna sat there looking at the storyteller. She wondered if she had sensed from the beginning that he would somehow hold the key to their survival, wondered if that was perhaps why she had never questioned his sudden appearance, or his right to the position of storyteller to the clan.

He merely endured her scrutiny, as if he'd said what he had to say, and it was now up to her.

As, she supposed, it was.

At last, her fears still present but quieted somewhat at the prospect of doing something—anything, no matter how preposterous—she let out a long, compressed breath.

"What must I do?" she asked simply.

The storyteller smiled.

The man who was only a myth sat by the fire, staring into the darkness. It would be more natural to stare into the dancing flames, but old habits died hard, and the warrior buried deep within him could not relax enough, even after all this time, to let his night vision be destroyed by staring into the light.

He wondered if he would ever relax that much. If, perhaps, after a decade or so of peace in these high mountains, the warrior might truly give way to the man of peace he'd fought so hard to become. A man who did not see the potential for ambush in every narrow pass, a man who did not hear the approach of an enemy in every footfall, a man who did not wake every morning and search anew for any sign of treachery in his small domain.

He wondered if he would ever be as other men, then laughed at his own foolish fancy; Kane was Kane, and such would he always be. He had done it to himself, with his own blindness, and it was only right that he pay for it with the rest of his life.

Almost absently his hand stole upward, to trace the scar that ran from his right temple down to his jaw. He'd heard many versions of how he'd received the mark, from a heroic battle against a dozen men to the clash with the fierce lion whose skin now warmed his shoulders against the mountain cold. Only he knew the truth behind the slash that had left him carrying the narrow, oddly straight line of whitened flesh. He didn't dwell on it, was merely thankful it hadn't taken his eye as well as disfigured his face.

He pushed raven dark hair back from his forehead. The unaccustomed length of it, falling past his shoulders now, was a constant reminder of the vow he'd made never to don a battle helm again. He would never again shear it short for that purpose. He would never—

His thoughts ended abruptly as the faintest of sounds, a mere whisper, like that of a feather pushing against the still air, gave him warning. A moment later a glistening shape came out of the darkness, the sheen of its body the only difference between it and the black of the night.

The raven landed on the log across from him, cocking its head as it looked at him. A wry smile curved his mouth.

" 'Tis as well you sent your emissary ahead, Tal," he said into the darkness. "I'm a bit edgy tonight."

The laugh that came back at him seemed too sweeping to have come from any human, but Kane had always had his doubts about Tal on that score anyway.

A second shape emerged from the blackness, with even less noise than the bird had made. Kane looked up at the one man he called, if not friend, at least not enemy. Although Tal was slightly shorter, Kane knew he had a wiry strength and quickness—and some unique talents Kane hadn't quite figured out yet—that rendered the difference unimportant. Tal's hair was almost as dark as his own, but the flash of silver at the temples—at odds with the young face—and its slightly shorter length, just above his shoulders, ended the similarities. He wore a simple tunic and leggings of soft leather much like Kane's own, and moved like a man utterly at home in his body.

"And when are you not on edge, my friend?" he asked.

"When I'm asleep?" Kane suggested wryly.

The laugh came again. "Not even then, Kane. Not even then." He sat on the log beside the bird, who looked at him expectantly. "Be off with you. Make your hunt. You've been patient enough."

The raven squawked something that sounded remarkably like "At last," and took flight, making no more noise in departure than it had arriving.

"You keep strange friends," Kane observed.

Tal lifted a dark brow. "This from you?"

"Precisely," Kane agreed dryly, not missing the implication that he was among those strange friends.

Tal chuckled, and Kane found himself smiling. Somehow the man always did that to him, lightened a burden carried so long he'd become almost numb to it. He'd been more than wary when he'd first encountered Tal; he was wary of any stranger, and more so one who seemed to materialize out of the mist with no more warning than the bird that seemed to be his constant companion. And in recollection, it was nothing short of astounding that he'd come to trust the man as quickly as he had, but he had to admit the man had a way about him. Even the animals trusted him, merely glancing at him when they would have slipped away from Kane's approach.

It was something in his eyes, Kane had once decided. Something in those changeable, intense eyes.

"You are feeling a bit edgy tonight, aren't you? Why?"

Kane shrugged. He had no answer for that. It was just an odd feeling that had overtaken him today, a feeling of . . . anticipation. As if something were about to happen. It was not quite like the feeling he used to get on the eve of a battle, knowing what the morrow would bring, but that was the only thing in his experience he could liken it to.

Tal glanced around as if he'd heard something. Or as if the woods held the answer. And for him, Kane had often observed, they did.

"Is it the feeling of waiting?"

Kane stiffened. Really, sometimes the man's uncanny guesses were too much to be borne. If Tal hadn't denied it while steadily meeting his gaze, Kane would have believed him a mind reader, a diviner of the sort careful men looked askance at. As it was, his observations were enough like prophecy—and came true often enough—to be thoroughly unsettling.

"The forest is rife with it tonight, is it not?" Tal said, as if he hadn't noticed Kane's reaction, when Kane knew the man never missed such things. Tal looked back at him once more, holding his gaze levelly. "After all this time, you still don't trust me? Do you think I cannot feel what you feel? I lived in this forest long before you came here, and I'll be here long after you're gone."

"I will die here," Kane said. "Will it be that soon? Or are you that much younger than I, then, that you will be here so long after?"

"No," Tal said, with no clarification of which question he was answering. Kane knew better than to ask; Tal wasn't in the habit of explaining himself, and Kane had too many secrets of his own to pry into another man's.

"Where have you been hiding these last weeks?" he asked instead.

Tal gestured vaguely, a motion that took in far too much area with only one common characteristic, which he then spoke in a tone as vague as the gesture.

"Down there."

Kane's mouth quirked. "Oh."

That got Tal's attention. "It's getting . . . quite ugly down off the mountain."

Kane went still. "It has always been ugly down there."

"But it is worse now. The warlords are slaughtering innocents as well as each other. People who have lived in peace for countless years. Who know nothing of fighting."

"What the warlords—all of them—do," Kane said, enunciating carefully, "means nothing to me."

"And why should it?" Tal said easily.

"Precisely." It was flat, unequivocal.

"Nothing happening down there means anything to you."

"No."

"What happens here on your mountain is the only thing you care about."

"Yes," Kane agreed, but he was looking at Tal suspiciously; he had learned to recognize when he was being led by the too-clever man. "Why?"

Tal shrugged. "No reason," was what he said. But Kane distinctly heard *You'll find out.* He stared at the unlikely man who had become, even more unlikely, his friend. He supposed he had to admit that. Tal was not merely not an enemy, somewhere along the way he had indeed become a friend.

But Tal's barely disguised smile did little to reassure him. In fact, it made him more edgy that he already was.

So edgy that when he heard the rustling sound behind him, he whirled and reached for a sword he'd quit carrying years ago. And straightened up as the maker of the sound staggered out of the dark and collapsed at his feet. He stared down at the woman crumpled in the dirt, strands of fiery hair escaping from the cloth that tied it back.

"Damnation," he muttered. "Who are you?"

He looked over his shoulder at Tal.

He was gone.

But Kane could swear he heard laughter from out of the darkness.

Chapter 2

Jenna snuggled deeper into the warmth, seeking to pull the sweet tendrils of sleep back around her. The movement sent pain shooting up from her right ankle to her knee, and she came sharply awake. Her involuntary recoil from the pain in her leg caused another sharp jab of pain in her left shoulder. Her breath caught, and she stifled a moan.

"You'll regret it less if you stay still."

Her head whipped around and she sat up, her eyes searching the shadows for the source of the deep, rough voice. She did cry out then at the sharp pain that seemed to stab from both her leg and her shoulder.

"As you will, then," the voice said.

Instinctively she pulled the roughly woven, heavy cloth blanket closer around her. Vaguely she realized the ankle she had twisted had been bound, and that some sort of balm had been smoothed over her bruised shoulder, but her attention was fixed elsewhere. She stared at the man who sat beside her, illuminated only by the single tallow light that sat on a short, wide, upended log apparently serving as a table.

Kane.

There could be little doubt. He was as the legends described him, tall and broad and strong, a long mane of hair as dark as night, cold eyes of an odd, smoky gray. In only one way did the legends lie; they'd called his countenance menacing, frightful, said that his face was twisted into ugliness by a wicked scar. The scar was there, but it was as neat and tidy a mark as she'd ever seen, given what must have been the viciousness of the wound that had caused it. And she found his face not in the least ugly; his features were strong, he looked stern and forbidding and more than a little intimidating, but hardly ugly. Scar or not.

"You *do* exist," she whispered.

"Obviously," he said, his tone biting. "The question is, do you?"

She blinked. "Me? Of course I do. I'm here, aren't I?"

"So it would seem. Unless you're something Tal conjured up out of that wicked imagination of his."

Jenna had no idea who or what he was talking about, but hastened to speak. "I assure you, I'm quite real."

"Then you won't mind telling me who you are and why you have intruded upon me." His tone lowered ominously. "And how you got here."

Jenna chose the simplest question to answer first. "I walked."

His eyes widened, then narrowed. "Walked? Up this mountain? From where?"

"My home. At the foot of Snowcap."

He went very still, and she saw he knew just how far her mountain, known for its permanent cap of white, was from his own mountain abode.

"You walked . . . from there?"

She nodded. "And an unpleasant ten days it was. The storyteller was right. All manner of fierce creatures, fanged serpents . . . I did not encounter the lion he predicted, but enough other things bent on having me for supper to make up for it."

She knew she was chattering, and realized she was indeed intimidated. But then, who would not be, sitting two feet from a legend? And he looked nothing less than mythical in the flickering light of the tallow lamp, which cast mobile shadows on the walls of what appeared to be a small cave; when they said Kane never left his mountain, she hadn't realized he actually lived *in* it.

She was very conscious of his eyes on her. There was a grudging respect in the gray depths as he looked at her, his gaze sliding over her body as if noting all the bruises, cuts, and scrapes that adorned it as a result of her arduous journey.

"Who are you?" he finally asked.

"My name is Jenna. I'm of the clan Hawk, holders of Hawk Glade."

His brows lowered again. "Hawk Glade is a myth."

The irony of it caught her off guard, and she laughed. He drew back slightly, as if startled—or stung—by the sound.

"No more than are you, sir," she said. "If I can believe you are the mythical warrior Kane, then surely you can believe in something so much simpler."

"The Hawk Glade I was told of is a place of peace and magic, of fruitful life and happy people. Something I find very much harder to believe in."

Jenna's expression changed as the sadness flowed back, erasing all traces of her earlier laughter.

"It was all of those things, once."

Emotion tightened her throat and she fought it back; this was not the way to approach this man, she was sure. Kane was reputed to be as hard as granite and as cold as Snowcap's glaciers; tears would not move him.

But she had to move him.

She swiped at her eyes angrily, and the quick mo-

tion brought tears of another kind to her eyes, tears
of pain as her bruised shoulder protested.

"Rest."

It was an order, given by a man clearly used to the
process. Still, Jenna shook her head.

"I must speak to you. It's why I came."

He let out a harsh breath. "I cannot stop you from
speaking. But if you wish me to listen, you must rest
first. I have no patience to deal with a rambling dis-
course on whatever fool's errand has brought you
here."

"It is not a fool's errand. Desperate, I will allow,
but—"

"You have come a long way. You have survived a
journey that would have defeated many. For that, I
suppose I must let you say your piece. But I warn
you now, it is useless. Whatever you wish from me, I
cannot give."

Jenna fought her trembling; was she to be denied
without even a chance? She forced her chin up.

"Or will not?" she said, her fear putting an edge in
her voice even as she realized it was no doubt unwise
to provoke the man she'd come to seeking help for
her people.

Kane looked startled at her temerity, then shrugged
as if it meant nothing. "As you will."

He stood up, and Jenna caught her breath as he
towered over her; he was indeed as tall as legend had
claimed him. And as broad. And as strong, she
guessed, judging from the powerful lines of his body
in the soft leather tunic and leggings he wore. The
laces at his throat were loose, as if his chest were too
broad to be covered easily, and the sleeves of the
garment clung to powerful and supple muscles as if
they were his own skin.

He turned his back to her, and Jenna searched her
mind for some word, any word, that would make him

stay and listen to her. But her mind suddenly seemed
to lose the capacity for coherent thought; her observation of his clothing had brought abruptly home to her
that she herself was somewhat lacking in that area.
She nearly gasped as she realized she was clad only
in a shirt of some finely woven white cloth, fine
enough to have belonged to the wealthy highborns the
storyteller had told her of, those who lived so far away
and had such strange ideas about people and ruling.

A man's shirt. A shirt that swam upon her slender
frame so loosely that it could well have belonged to
a man the size of Kane.

The fact that it probably did took what remained
of her breath away.

She had walked here.

Kane supposed, out of everything, that was what
amazed him the most. This woman, who would barely
come to his shoulder on her feet, had endured a journey that most men he'd ever known would hesitate to
undertake on foot. As if the pure distance weren't
enough, the going was treacherous; not only the pred-
ators she'd mentioned, but countless other hazards,
swift-moving rivers, swamps hiding lethal, shifting
sands, thick, scratching underbrush too often dotted
with poisonous plants. And all of that was nothing
compared to the task of scaling the mountain itself.

But she had done it. She had walked that distance,
through such perils, and then had had the courage left
to risk the dangers of the mountain. Apparently, with
him as her goal. He supposed he must admire her
tenacity; this haven was not a place easily found or
reached.

Which brought him to the most interesting of the
questions her presence gave rise to: how had she
found him? In all the years he'd lived here, only Tal
had found him, and Tal knew these mountains like no

other. No one else had ever done it. Men had come hunting him, yes, but he'd managed to avoid being seen by any of them. Sometimes he wasn't quite sure how; once he and Tal had been caught in the open by a group of armed men, yet they had somehow never spotted them, even though it had seemed they were looking right at them. So much so that Kane had been certain they would die, and regretted that Tal would die with him, yet another soul tallied to his bloody accounts.

He shoved aside the memory and turned back to the complication at hand. Regardless of how she'd found him, regardless of the impossibility of the journey she'd made to do it, she was here, and he had to deal with it. With her. And it had been far too long since he'd had to deal with his fellow man, other than Tal, who was different enough to not be counted. And longer still since he'd had any dealings with a woman.

And she was most definitely a woman.

He spun on his heel and began to pace before the fire. He'd had no choice. He'd had to tend her injuries, or they might well have festered, she would have died, and he'd have yet another death on his conscience. There had been nothing carnal in it, he wasn't fascinated by the bright, rippling waves of her hair, he'd barely seen the womanly curves of her body as he stripped her, hadn't acknowledged that the soft curls at the juncture of her thighs were a shade darker than her hair, hadn't noticed at all the way her soft, rose-tipped breasts made his old shirt peak in the most interesting way. That part of him was long dead, and the tightness he'd felt in his lower body merely an instinctive response to the memory of a time when he'd taken his fill of womanly companionship at his whim.

He spun on his heel again, and started back in the other direction. Damn Tal; he'd disappeared as swiftly and completely as that raven of his, just when he might have been of some use. He could have tended the woman, and much more proficiently; he had the knack, while Kane's medical skills were of the crude, rudimentary kind learned on a battlefield.

And he doubted Tal would be wrestling with such ridiculous thoughts about the woman; he'd told Kane once that he was dead to such things, and he'd found the freedom from such urges quite liberating.

At the time, Kane had heartily agreed, thinking himself in the same situation. But Tal had shook his head, and observed in that maddeningly confident way of his that Kane's heart wasn't dead, merely in a long sleep, as the bears of the mountains did in the winter, and that someday it would awaken and be ravenous. That someday the right lady would lay a fair hand at his door, and he would let her in. Kane hadn't much liked the idea, and had scoffed. Tal had merely smiled and let the subject go.

Again Kane turned, only vaguely aware of the speed of his gait. He would let her stay until her ankle was strong enough to support her again, he had little choice about that. He could hardly cast her out as she was; either the mountain would kill her or its more brutal inhabitants would, as she'd said, make supper of her.

That the old Kane would have turned her out without hesitation was a fact that wasn't lost on him. If she were of no use to him, he would have left her to her own devices, caring little if she survived. He might have sampled the tempting sweetness of her body first, but even that, as everything in life, was transitory, and only of passing interest.

But that Kane was dead. At least, to the world he was dead, a man relegated to the status of myth; Kane himself was resigned to the fact that he would carry some piece of that brutal, vicious man inside him until the day he died. The day he had realized that, he'd been tempted to walk down from his mountain and put the prophecy he'd been given to the test; he wasn't sure he still wouldn't welcome the death that had been promised should he leave this place. Surely the world would be better off.

"I see you've slipped beyond edgy into plain surly."

Kane spun around, barely stopping himself from again reaching for a weapon that no longer hung at his side. He swore under his breath, low and harsh.

Tal put up his hands, palms outward. "No, thank you," he said to Kane's muttered suggestion. "I've been there, and I don't care to go back."

"Where's your familiar?" Kane asked, still peeved. He wasn't used to being taken by surprise, and now it had happened twice in one day. Tal he'd almost grown accustomed to, but that a woman had done it . . .

Tal's mouth quirked. "I do wish you'd stop that. You know people don't take kindly to that kind of thing these days. I have no desire to be hanged for being suspected a wizard."

"Then quit acting like one."

"Me?"

Tal's look of innocence was so overdone, Kane couldn't help smiling wryly. And had to admit, were it not for Tal, he would have been mightily lonely up here on this mountain all these years past.

"Where *is* the winged hunter?"

"Maud?" Tal shrugged. "Off hunting."

"And where did you disappear to in such a hurry?"

"Off hunting," he repeated, and lifted one hand to reveal the results, a sizable rabbit and equally plump pheasant Kane hadn't even noticed he held. "I thought you might not have time for a while, what with your . . . guest."

"You seem awfully sure she'll be here awhile."

"Won't she?"

"Only until she's well enough to walk," Kane said firmly, while inwardly acknowledging that he doubted the woman would be up and moving for several days.

"Of course."

Kane eyed Tal warily; whenever he agreed so easily with something Kane himself was wrestling with, Kane knew he was in trouble.

"She's quite . . . striking in appearance, is she not?"

"If you like hair that color." *A color that made you think you could warm your hands at its fire.*

"The color of a sunset? Some do, I hear." Tal looked thoughtful. "Her eyes?" he asked.

Kane blinked. "I didn't . . ." His words trailed off. He'd been about to say he hadn't noticed, but it was a lie; he had. How could you not? "Blue," he said abruptly. And it seemed a poor word for the intensity of the color; even in the shadowy light of the cave, they'd been bright, vividly blue.

He wondered how long he'd been standing there like a fool, contemplating the color of a strange woman's eyes, when he came out of his reverie and saw Tal watching him with obvious amusement.

"What difference does it make?" he snapped.

"None," Tal said. "None at all."

"Stop agreeing with me. It makes me nervous."

Tal laughed. "I'll be off then, to round up that unruly bird."

"You mean you can't just whistle?"

"I can. But Maud is like any woman; she'll respond only if she's already of a mind to."

"I didn't realize you were so well versed."

"A wise man should always know as much as is possible of those around him. 'Tis merely a matter of seeing patterns others miss."

"I thought you said it was impossible to truly know a woman."

Tal raised a dark brow. "I was speaking of birds."

Kane flushed. Tal grinned, lifted a hand to his forehead in a mock salute, and disappeared into the forest.

There was no questioning that he was angry. And little doubt that it was directed at her. Yet he tended her with gentle care, a care much at odds with his fierce looks. And even more at odds with his widespread, lethal reputation. A reputation so vast he had become thought of as a mythical being, because it seemed impossible anything less could have amassed it.

Jenna had barely felt the pain as he rebound her ankle. It had been slightly less swollen, but she wouldn't have noticed anyway; she was, she admitted ruefully, far too fascinated by the man bent over her foot.

For two days she had seen little of him, except when he brought her food, tended to her injuries, and assisted her with more personal needs with a brusqueness that made the embarrassing process remarkably less so. He never spoke more than two or three words, and if she tried to begin a conversation he merely walked away. She spent her time testing her recovering body with occasional efforts to move, and contemplating her surroundings.

For a cave, it was almost comfortable. She lay in a small alcove off what appeared to be a larger chamber, a room large enough for even a man of Kane's size to stand upright with room to spare. There were niches hollowed out of the walls that contained what apparently was a winter's worth of foodstuffs. She lay on a bed of soft fur, and the cave walls were hung with various pelts for warmth from the cold stone. And there was a place across from her that showed signs of being used as a hearth.

She had been curious when she'd spotted that, wondering what kept the cavern from filling with smoke, then noticed the shape of the roof of the cave above the spot streaked with soot. There was a chute grooved into the stone, a perfect, natural channel for the escape of smoke. She would bet, with a fire going to heat the stones around it, the cave would be comfortable even on the notoriously cold nights of winter in these mountains. Kane had chosen well; if you had to live in a cave, this was probably one of the best to be had.

Why he had chosen to live in a cave at all was another question. And she doubted if she would ever get an answer to it. Not that it mattered. Nothing mattered, except getting him to help her. If she couldn't do that, there was nothing left. Her people would die. And if it came to that, she would die with them. Not just because it was her place as the Hawk, but because the clan was her entire life, she was connected to them in ways she'd never realized until the attacks had begun and she was faced with losing it all.

She shivered, although it wasn't cold. She had to get Kane's help. She simply had to. The alternative was unthinkable. And she couldn't wait any longer. They had rarely gone a week without another attack from the warlord, and only the magical protection of the glade had kept them from being wiped out already. People were dying while she lay here coddling herself.

Today she had progressed to sitting upright for a long period, and while she was happy at that amount of success, she was anxious to go further. Anxious to get back on her feet. Anxious to get on with her mission.

She had to talk to Kane, and he refused to stay with her long enough for her to do it. So she must, it would seem, go to him.

She managed to get to her knees, then braced her

uninjured foot beneath her. She stood, carefully, uncertain of her own stability. And even less certain about venturing forth clad only in this shirt; although it covered her from neck to well below her knees, she was very conscious that she wore nothing beneath it.

Her eyes told her she was no more revealed than in her own soft leather leggings and the rough-woven cloth tunic she had worn on her journey. And logic told her that Kane must have seen all there was to see of her already; someone had undressed her and put this shirt on her while she lay senseless, and Kane was the only one here.

This realization sent blood rushing to her cheeks, and she wobbled slightly on her feet.

It's over and done, she chided herself. *You cannot change what happened, that you were so weak you tumbled in a senseless, useless heap just as you reached your goal. Let it go. He obviously will not speak of it if you do not.*

"If he will speak of anything at all," she muttered to herself. He would, she thought fiercely. He must. She would make him listen, make him help. Somehow. There were no other options. She would do whatever she had to. Starting right now.

She steadied herself, testing her ankle with a slight bit of her weight. It protested, but she thought she could walk. She turned her head and listened, hoping to hear a sound from outside that would tell her he was there. She heard nothing. But she did spy a small pile of clothing at the foot of the pallet she'd been lying on; her own clothing. Looking tidy and freshly cleaned.

Kane, the mythical warrior, acting as a washer? For a woman he did not even know? It hardly seemed possible. Yet there her clothes were. And welcome, she thought as she reached for them.

It took her much longer than she would have liked,

yet less than she had feared, to get dressed. And only partly because of the lingering stiffness of her body; she spent far too long trying to envision the fierce warrior washing her delicate shift with his big, scarred hands. It was an image that made her shiver in the oddest way as she pulled the garment on; she wore it beneath the rough cloth tunic to prevent her skin from being rubbed raw. It was her one costly piece of clothing, and her only indulgence.

After considering the still swollen condition of her ankle, she decided against her boots; they looked so sadly battered by her trek she wouldn't be surprised if they fell to pieces should she pick them up. And she would not be walking far anyway; it would be enough test of her injury simply to make it outside.

She hadn't thought the cave truly so dark, the cloth hanging at the entrance was pushed back to allow daylight inside, but still she found herself blinking as she hobbled into full light. She stopped, not daring to risk a misstep until her eyes had adjusted. She didn't want to—

"What are you doing?"

It was short, sharp, and angry. That alone would have told her the source, even if the rough, low timbre of the voice had not already done so. She turned toward him, squinting against the bright sun as he towered over her.

"Trying to become less of a burden," she said in the sweet, meek voice her brother had always called wheedling.

"If that was truly your concern, you wouldn't have come here."

So much for wheedling, Jenna thought. Just as well; she couldn't sustain it for long anyway; meek, Justus had always said, she was not.

Justus.

She suppressed a shiver as grief rippled through her

once more. She had no time for such luxuries as griev-
ing, she reminded herself yet again. She had time for
nothing except making this fearsome man agree to
help her people. Now, with him towering over her, it
seemed a much more hopeless task than it had as
she'd lain contemplating it.

"You should not be up. Your ankle—"

"Aches, but it is bearable. And it seems a small
cost, compared to being wrapped in the coils of a serpent as long as you are tall."

Her eyes adjusted now, she could see the bemused
expression that flitted across his face. She doubted it
was at her tale of woe, and suspected it was because
he was not used to being interrupted.

"I doubt it would take a serpent that length to wrap
around such a tiny morsel."

Stung, she drew herself up to her full height.
"Among my clan I am near the tallest of women, and
taller than some of the men, as well!"

"I thought this wondrous Hawk Glade supplied all
the needs of its holders. Does it not supply enough
food to grow full-size men?"

Anger shot through her as she remembered the
bravery of those men Kane was belittling, men who
knew nothing of warfare or even self-defense, but
tried to defend their home and loved ones anyway,
even knowing they would die by the score.

"We are more concerned with brains than muscle,
with heart and courage than blind force," she exclaimed. "And you will not find better men for those
qualities in any place in any land than you will find
among my people."

For an instant she saw satisfaction glint in his eyes,
although she could not guess at the cause. What had
he to feel satisfied about? That he had provoked her
to anger, when she meant to supplicate? That he had

prodded a wound still so raw that it managed to deflect even her consuming grief?

She had the flickering thought that that might have been his intent, but she could deduce no reason for him to care if she grieved, so she discarded it swiftly. And chastised herself fiercely for having spoken so sharply to the man from whom she had come to beg help.

"Sit down," he said abruptly. "Before you fall."

"I won't fall," she said, although she wasn't at all certain of that. It just didn't seem wise to let this man know just how weak she was feeling.

"And I won't catch you if you do," he warned.

"I did not ask you to," she retorted, wondering if it was her weakened state that made her so irascible this day. She smoothed her hands over the rough cloth of her travel tunic. It hung loose without her belt—

Her belt. And the dagger that was sheathed in it. Neither had been in the neatly folded pile of her clothing.

"I thank you for cleaning my clothing," she began.

"They would have been unwearable had they waited for you to do it."

"I thought perhaps . . . is there someone else here who . . . does for you?"

He gave an inelegant snort. "The only person who frequents these heights is a rapscallion who disappears whenever the spirit moves him. Which means whenever there's something he'd rather I deal with."

Despite the words, there was a rueful affection in his tone; although legend held him a man who walked alone, Kane the warrior had at least one friend, it seemed.

"Then you will be the one who knows the whereabouts of my dagger?"

He gave her a long, silent look. "An interesting

weapon," he said, answering yet not answering her question.

"It is . . . important to my people."

"You were to use it, I presume?"

Jenna blinked. "Use it? For what?"

Kane shrugged. "To kill me, of course."

Chapter 3

"Kill you?"

Her startled exclamation seemed genuine.

Or perhaps, Kane thought, she was simply very good at playing her part. She certainly wouldn't be the first woman to be very good at such things. Nor the last. He'd met a few, in his other life. And he doubted that much had changed since he'd last dealt with women.

"That is why you're here, is it not?"

She sat down at last, on the log beside the stones ringing the outer fire. He saw her tremble, whether from fear or weakness from her injuries, he didn't know. She stared up at him.

"By the heavens, why would you think that?"

He shrugged negligently. " 'Tis the usual reason people look for me."

"I'm surprised anyone would have the courage to even try to kill Kane the Warrior."

"No one has, since I've been here." He eyed her coldly. "No one has made it this far."

Her effort to divert him from that subject was immediate. "Have you made so very many enemies, then?"

He felt the old weariness begin to steal over him, the lassitude that had so often tempted him to offer himself up for the killing, just to be done with it. A simple walk out of these mountains, a calling in of the promise that should he leave them, he would cease to be, had never seemed more tempting than at this moment. He resisted the urge to do it right now, to turn and walk away, and never come back to this place that had become his only haven.

" 'Tis all I have made in my life," he murmured.

He shook his head, trying to fend off the ugly feeling. He found the woman called Jenna watching him, her eyes so wide and vividly blue it put him in mind of the mountain sky in summer just before dusk, when it darkened to a blue never seen in any other place. Until now.

There was something in those eyes that made him uneasy, some trace of something soft and warm, something that was somehow threatening to him. More threatening perhaps, than even the razor-sharp blade she had carried.

"I have no wish to kill you," she said quietly. "Quite the opposite."

He went still, every warning instinct he possessed clamoring to life. He'd learned long ago that people who approached him voluntarily, if they did not have his death in mind, had only one other reason.

They wanted him to bring death to someone else.

As swiftly as a hawk's strike, he felt the coldness sweep through him. The icy calm, the assessing aloofness that he'd thought himself done with forever. It was so very strange, he thought, this being able to look at himself as if from a distance, to analyze, to poke at what should be painful and feel nothing.

He'd been here in this place for years, trying to rid himself of this, of this coldness that separated him from others, that enabled him to look at them with such dispassionate calculation. Were they to be asset or hindrance? Would they help him achieve his goal, and thus deserve to live, or would they be in his way, to be killed and tossed aside without a second thought? For a lifetime that had been his credo, the principle by which he'd lived, driven into his very soul by the man who had perfected it.

For years now he'd hidden out here in these mountains, searching for a healing. And now this red-haired, wide-eyed woman had, in the space of a moment, shown him there was no healing for the likes of him. With a single utterance she had reduced his hopes, his conviction that he had, indeed, come a long way from that vicious, brutal man, into dust.

He was Kane, and so would he ever be.

He turned his back on her and walked into the woods, knowing even the warmth of the morning sun was not enough to save him from this chill.

Jenna sat on the log, shivering. It wasn't cold, here in the sunlight, yet she shook as if she sat atop Snowcap.

There was a coarse blanket on the ground beside the fire; she reached for it and pulled it around her. She caught a scent, faintly wild and male. And only then realized this must be where Kane had been sleeping; she had literally put him out of his bed.

There were men who would not have allowed that, she thought. And of late she had learned there were men who would not have cared that she was unconscious; she was female and of only one use, and her participation was not necessary. Kane apparently fell into neither of those categories. But she was no closer to knowing what one he did fall into. No closer to understanding him at all. In fact, she was farther from it than ever.

What had she said that had put that look in his eyes, that cold, vacant, dead look? She'd seen too much of death of late to use the term lightly, yet there seemed to be no other; Kane's clear gray eyes had gone flat and empty, as if she'd somehow killed the soul inside the man.

And she didn't know what she'd done. She'd not even begun her entreaty, had not yet said a word about why she had truly come here.

Panic gripped her; what if he didn't come back? He had looked, in that moment before he had turned and walked away, like a man who could easily do just that. He looked like a man who had lost all of value to him. Or like a man who had never valued anything, including himself. Who could walk away from everything without even a glance back over his shoulder.

The storyteller had warned her it would be difficult to deal with Kane. More difficult, in fact, than if he had been the myth some thought him. Myths were immune to human failings. Kane, he'd said, was not. "Some wounds never heal," he'd said in that sometimes infuriatingly vague manner. "And he carries many."

She knew that to be true, now. There had been pain in Kane's face, in his voice, in his posture when he'd spoken of enemies. But when he'd left her just now, there had been nothing. No pain, no anger, no emotion at all. It was, she thought, coming back to it again, a dead man who had walked away.

She would have preferred his anger. She had disrupted his life, she knew that. If nothing else she had noticed that about this place; except for the occasional call of the wild things and the whisper of the breeze, it was the quietest place she'd ever been. She imagined days could pass, one after the other, with a mind-numbing sameness that could, to an uneasy mind, pass for peace. Perhaps it was that which she had taken away simply by coming here, perhaps it was that loss that had provoked him to anger.

But what had caused that total extinguishing of the light from within?

She thought of going after him, but she doubted she could manage much distance. And if she found him, she had no idea what she would do. How could she, when she had no idea what she'd said that had sent him into the shadowy forest?

He would come back, she told herself, trying to think logically. Where else would he go? He didn't seem to have many possessions, surely not enough that he would take their loss lightly. She herself had few things that were of value to her—and her idea of value no doubt differed from many—but those she had, she treasured. From what she'd seen, Kane had even less, so little that what he did have must be important to him, she thought.

Or did the sparseness of his possessions only mean it would be easier for him not to come back? The storyteller had come to them with little, a few belongings in a sack, no more. He had said he preferred to travel lightly; possessions tied you to a place, kept you there when it might be better if you moved on.

She'd been afraid then that her people would lose the one small joy remaining to them, the joy of listening to the storyteller around a fire, spinning his tales in that mesmerizing voice, been afraid he would move on when he realized how little safety they could promise him. As if he'd read her fears, he had smiled gently and assured her he would be there as long as he was needed.

She wished he was here now. He could be so maddening, yet she always felt better when she talked with him. He always seemed to ease her fears, and often in his seemingly innocent tales and allegorical stories she found an answer she hadn't even been aware of seeking.

But she could find no answer now. Nor could she

physically go after Kane. Nor did she know what she would do or say to a man who looked like the walking dead.

She had to assume he would return. Whatever she'd said or done, she simply could not believe that a single woman had, with no effort at all, driven away a warrior with Kane's reputation. He would come back.

He had to come back.

"I've seen more cheerful faces at burials."

Kane stopped walking. It was his only reaction to the voice that came from above him; he seemed beyond anything else. He was almost sorry it was Tal. Had it been one of the men from the warlord who hunted him, he could have brought this miserable existence to an end once and for all.

He heard a rush of sound, and Tal dropped down beside him, from whatever tree limb he'd been perched on, no doubt looking at the world with that faintly amused smile.

"Forgive me, my friend, but you do seem a bit grim this fine morning."

"If you want to beg forgiveness, it should be for disappearing like the wizard I'm half convinced you are."

Kane had tried for the bantering tone they usually adopted, but it fell short. He avoided looking at his friend, but sensed Tal's eyes narrowing, knew they were taking on that piercing intensity that made Kane think he was seeing through to his soul. It usually made him uncomfortable; his soul wasn't one that could stand up to the kind of scrutiny Tal seemed able to perform. But today he felt nothing.

"What has she done?" Tal asked softly.

Once Kane would have parried the question with a denial, or a question in turn, asking the man what made him think the only "she" he could be referring to had anything to do with it. But he'd learned in short order that when fixed on something, Tal would not be gainsaid, and dissembling was useless; he saw everything with those fierce, changeable eyes. And often saw patterns where Kane saw only chaos.

"Nothing. Yet," he said, his voice a dead-sounding thing even to himself.

"Yet?"

He looked at Tal then, knowing the man would see, knowing it would save him much in the way of explanation.

"She's come to ask me to kill for her."

Tal's dark brows lowered. Kane withstood his gaze like a man on a rack, his jaw set, his eyes never wavering as the other man's searched, probed.

"Are you certain?" Tal asked, his voice low.

"You know as well as I there are only two reasons people search me out. I do not believe she is a murderess."

"She is not," Tal agreed, with that certainty that Kane usually found irritating; this time it was strangely comforting. "But are you assured that is her aim?" he asked again. "Perhaps she wishes something else from you."

Kane smiled, a smile he knew was humorless and cold. "What else have I to offer anyone?"

Tal's eyes shifted, from the fierce gold of a predator to the misty green of the forest around them. "More than you know or would ever believe," he said in an oddly distant, quiet voice. Then, before Kane could react, he added in normal tones, "What will you do with her? Send her away without listening to her?"

Kane took in a breath. The coldness was, to his surprise, receding. Or perhaps he shouldn't be surprised; Tal often had a most unsettling effect. It was difficult to describe, but he'd encountered it often enough to have given up trying to deny that it happened.

"It's what I would like to do," he admitted.

"But?"

Kane sighed. "She's come a long way from her home. Further than anyone ever has. She's endured much, she who looks too fragile to have ever withstood such harshness."

"And it hardly seems fair to turn her away so coldly, does it?"

"What does Kane care of fairness?"

Tal smiled suddenly. "When you begin to speak of yourself as if you were someone else, I know you have reached the end of your arguments."

Kane's mouth twisted. "What would you have me do?"

"Whatever you can live with, my friend."

It was lucky, Jenna thought, that roasting a pheasant over a fire was a simple task; preparing food had never been a talent of hers. She knew the rudiments of the task and had managed to find some herbs with which to rub the bird's skin, and some edible tubers to bake in the coals, but even that had taxed her skills. Justus had been the adventurous one when it came to that, always trying new foodstuffs, delighting when they met with accolades, and laughing good-naturedly at the rare failures that made his guests discreetly fill up on large chunks of bread.

It swept over her like the wind rushing down from Snowcap. She would never hear that laugh again, just as she would never feel the warm comfort of her mother's embrace. Nor would she see the antics of Jack the miller, whose silly faces had made the children laugh, nor would she hear Kayla's beautiful voice raised in song.

She resisted the urge to call their names, the seem-

ingly endless list of the dead. But it took all her fragile
strength, and she had none left to stop the shudders
that gripped her. She refused to weep, but she could
not stop the shaking. She told herself it did not matter,
there was no one here to see, no fierce warrior who
would no doubt glare in disgust at her weakness. And
perhaps there would not be; he had been gone a very
long time. Perhaps her long, harsh journey had been
for naught, and she was truly defeated before she
began.

Perhaps it was a fruitless effort already. Hawk
Glade could well have been overrun by now, its protection broken through at last, although the warlord
Druas seemed content for the moment with weekly
raids on anything and anyone found moving outside
the glade, doubtless to weaken them for an easy kill.
Even if she were to survive the journey home, there
might be no home still standing when she arrived. And
if she returned empty-handed, that would be the end
result anyway, and she would have the deaths of an
entire people on her conscience. She would not even
be able to face her own inevitable death with dignity,
not with the shadow of having to answer for her failure hovering.

She hated this feeling, of having her fate in another's hands. She'd hated it when the attacks had begun,
and they'd realized they were at the mercy of the warlord. And she hated it even more now, when she could
do nothing but helplessly wait for a man who might
never return, and who might not even listen to her if
he did.

But most of all she hated this sense of desperation.
And the more time that passed, the deeper it became,
until she felt she was going to fly apart.

She leapt to her feet, wobbling as her ankle
protested.

"It will never heal if you don't stay off of it."

She stifled a yelp and spun around, barely remembering not to do it on her injured side.

"It is not fair," she muttered, "that any man your size can move so quietly."

"I'm surprised you did not hear the rumbling of my stomach."

Jenna drew back, startled not so much by his words as by the wry glint of humor she thought she saw in his eyes. But it was gone so quickly she couldn't be sure.

"I . . . I hope you're not angry, I found the bird . . ."

"Angry? At eating something I have not had to cook myself? Unlikely."

Jenna couldn't help staring at him. What had happened to the laconic, almost curt man who had left here this morning? Hope surged in her, but she couldn't help being a little suspicious of the change.

He said no more, but ate his portion of the meal with a certain relish that made her feel oddly pleased. When it was done, she sat in silence for a long moment. She had been concentrating so hard on willing him to come back, she hadn't really dealt with what she would actually say if he did.

And then he stunned her by taking it out of her hands.

"Begin, Jenna of Hawk Glade. Tell your story so we may get this over with."

It was less than she'd hoped for, but more than she'd expected; at least he would listen. She pondered for a moment where to begin, then decided. She must convince him of why the Hawk clan should be saved, before she asked him how to go about doing it.

"What you have heard of Hawk Glade is true. It is a place of peace and magic, of fruitful life and happy people."

"Nothing less than a miracle," Kane said dryly.

Jenna refused to let him sway her from her task.

"My people had fled a bloody, ancient war, had jour-
neyed far and endured much before they were led
there. Perhaps they deserved a small miracle."

"Perhaps. Led there?"

She nodded. "They were weary, ready to give up.
Then a bird appeared, circling overhead. It came low
in the sky, then cried out and flew toward the setting
sun. Moments later it returned, and did so again. And
again. My ancestress took it as a sign, and led her
small band west."

Kane's mouth quirked, and Jenna spoke quickly to
forestall the laughter she was sure was coming; what
other reaction could she expect from this hardened
warrior whose cold ruthlessness had elevated him to
the status of legend?

"I know it sounds odd, to take a wild bird as a
messenger, but—"

"No."

She drew back a little, surprised.

"No . . . what?"

"I don't think it odd, a bird as messenger. But most
would. They followed this . . . ancestress of yours? On
such a fool's pilgrimage?"

Jenna drew herself up straight. "Marrifay was a very
wise woman. It was only due to her leadership that
they had survived thus far. Of course they followed
her."

"And she was your . . . grandmother?"

"No, this was much longer ago than that. She was
the grandmother of my grandmother's grandmother."

Kane's mouth quirked again. "So that is . . . seven
generations?" Before she could answer, he went on.
"Impressive. Not many can know their lineage back
so far."

Something in his voice made her uneasy, but she
could read nothing in his face in the rapidly fading
light. Nothing except the sternness that seemed his

usual expression. She wondered that he dwelt on such unimportant things, then, with sinking heart, wondered if all she was saying was unimportant to him. Wondered if he had no intention of bestirring himself to help her, and therefore nothing she told him was of any consequence.

It could not be so. She could not let it be so. She went on determinedly.

"They soon came to a thick forest that ran rich with game and was dotted with clearings full of harvestable plants. It was, as you say, a miracle. The clan wished to stop right away, but Marrifay made them continue. At last she came to the largest clearing they had yet encountered, and she declared them home. For there, the bird sat waiting."

She waited then, again expecting laughter at the least. Instead, he merely nodded.

"I see. The bird was a hawk. Hence Hawk's Glade, and the Hawk clan."

"Yes."

She was pleased that he had guessed the rest of the story, and seemingly accepted it so easily, but it was that very ease that worried her; he did not seem a man to take well to such things. And she had more of the same to tell him, and she was certain he would laugh before she was through; to an outsider the tale could sound nothing less than absurd. To accept it would be to admit belief in inexplicable things, a belief that could cost one dearly were it found out by those many who looked upon such things as coming from demons, or worse. But she had no choice; he must know what they were dealing with in order to help them.

And he must help them. He must.

"It was not until they had been there some time that it became obvious this was no ordinary forest. Not only did it abound with game, but even after months of trapping the number did not seem to lessen. The crops flourished beyond anything anyone had ever seen, yielding so much there was abundance for all. There was the perfect amount of rain, and sun, and it was never too cold or too hot."

"Paradise indeed," Kane muttered. "I'm surprised you were not overrun with folk eager to partake of such bounty."

"That was yet another way in which the forest was . . . unusual. On the few times when outsiders approached our village, even though they passed close by, they never stopped, as if they had never seen the village at all, though they must have."

Kane's brows lowered, and she felt his suddenly sharpened gaze as if it were a physical thing. She sensed it was not just the Hawk story that had caused this sudden intentness, but she didn't know what else it could be. Perhaps he'd decided she was crazy, or worse, a witch or sorceress of some kind, and was even now wondering if he should kill her. She went on hastily.

"The Hawk clan has lived in peace since that time. There were minor disputes, as there always are among people living in a small place, but they were quickly resolved. Yes, like any other clan, we have the occasional outlaw, but they soon depart for other climes. We have little worth stealing, except that which cannot be stolen."

Jenna tried to concentrate on what she should say next, but found it difficult under the steady gaze of those gray eyes. All she could do was remember how flat and dead they had looked. And she wasn't sure she liked what she saw there now very much better. He looked away then, tossing a piece of wood on the cooking fire that had nearly died out. A shower of sparks arose, and a few moments later there was a series of loud snaps as the resin in the log heated and popped.

He lifted his head to look at her. "Why you?"

She blinked. "What?"

"Why were you sent to . . ." He paused, then lifted one shoulder, causing the pelt he wore to gleam in the last rays of sunlight. "To approach the lion?"

The lion. It was a lion's pelt he wore slung over his shoulder.

The serpent's tongue, the lion's roar . . .

The storyteller's words echoed in her head. So he'd been right all along. As he usually was. She had indeed heard the lion's roar, it simply had not been in the way she'd anticipated. She nearly smiled.

"Jenna?"

She shook her head, as if the action would somehow release her from the odd sensation that seemed to make her senseless whenever he spoke her name.

"Why you?" he repeated.

"Because it is my duty. As the Hawk."

"As what?"

"The hereditary leader of the Hawk clan."

He seemed to go very still. "So that explains why you refer to them as 'your people.' You're . . . the leader of this clan?"

She took in a deep breath. "Not . . . by choice. The Hawk was to have gone to my brother."

"The Hawk?"

"It is the badge of office. A golden Hawk, that is passed from leader to leader. My family has held it since the beginning. They voted Marrifay as the first Hawk, and it has passed down directly to her descendants."

"And now you hold it?"

"I do. My father became the Hawk after my grandfather died. It passed to my mother when my father died."

"It passes out of the direct bloodline?"

He sounded merely curious, not critical, so she answered him evenly. "With the understanding it will pass to the children of the bloodline in turn. But while she held it, my mother was the Hawk as much as my father was, and so she was treated."

"Interesting."

Jenna shrugged. "When you marry a Hawk, you become one as if by blood, in the eyes of my people."

"What happened to your brother?"

The anger burst through her, catching her unaware; it had driven her to complete her journey, but she'd been too weak for the luxury of it until now.

"He was murdered," she ground out. "Just as my mother was before him. By a bloodthirsty, evil man who wishes to steal what must be given. And is willing to slaughter an entire people to get what he wants."

She could see his face more clearly now, thanks to the firelight. Kane looked as if he'd just received an answer to a question that he had been carrying for some time.

"And what is it he wants?"

"Our forest. It is in his way, and he must go through it, to make his way north, or go a very long way around, since our forest is at the base of Snowcap." Her voice was still full of anger. "He will kill us all, for a shorter path."

"And now you wish revenge?"

"Of course I wish revenge," she snapped. "But 'tis a luxury I cannot afford." And then it struck her what he'd meant. "You think that is why I came here, to seek your help in avenging my family's death?"

"Is it not?"

"It is not!" She rose abruptly, ignoring the twinge she felt in her ankle; she'd pampered herself long enough. "There is far more at stake here than my own pain or heartache. Yes, I wish revenge. They have taken from me those I hold most dear and left me alone. But my pain is insignificant next to the pain of my clan. They are dying, Kane. There are already so few left we may not survive. We know nothing of fighting. Nothing of war. We never had to learn."

"Does not your magic forest protect you?"

She searched his face for some sign of sarcasm, but found only a coolness that reminded her just who this man was. "It protects only the glade itself, where the village is. Anyone who sets foot outside it, to check the snares, or harvest crops, is vulnerable."

She paced before him, between the log he sat upon and the fire, thinking irrelevantly that the heat radiating from the man was nearly a match for that radiated by the fire. She put her right foot down solidly, ignoring the pain despite the fact that it was threatening to make her queasy.

"It is not for my family that I am here. It is for something much larger, much more important."

She turned then, turned to face him, knowing this moment was crucial to her quest, that she must convince him now, and that she must not show the slightest sign of her terror that she would fail. "He values courage," the storyteller had told her. "It will move him where little else will." She hadn't questioned the old man's knowledge; by then she was already committed to what might yet turn out to be a fool's errand.

"Can you see that, Kane? It is not my family, nor even my friends that have driven me to you. It is so much more. It is Hawk Glade and all it represents. Generation after generation living in peace, of people safe in their homes, of elders living to ripe old ages, their wisdom treasured, and children running happy and safe, and free to grow up to become whatever they wished to be. Of people freed of daily cares, and able to turn their hearts and minds to wondrous things, to paint, to tell stories that will forever be

passed on, to make music so sweet and beautiful it
squeezes your heart."

"How," Kane said, "are you certain you are alive?"

It took her a moment, then she smiled sadly. "Is
that truly how you judge your life, Kane? By how
much pain you experience?"

"Or how much I can inflict."

The words were harsh, his voice bitter, yet there
was something in his eyes, something she felt to the
depths of her soul, a certainty that those cold words
had been a cry of pain in themselves.

"Kane—"

Something of what she'd felt must have echoed in
her voice, because he recoiled as if she'd offered
him pity.

"I cannot help you."

Panic seized her. "But—"

"I cannot," he repeated, and stood. He towered
over her, but her desperation made her hold her
ground.

"But you must."

"No."

"If you do not, my people will die!"

"Then they will die."

He once more walked away from her. This time it
was she who felt dead inside.

Chapter 4

Kane strode through the night, each step pounding home his conviction; there was nothing she could say or do that would convince him to take up his sword again, to kill again. And while he might be willing to die for her people, he certainly wasn't, despite the occasional thought that death might be preferable to living with the memories that haunted him. And death would be exactly what he would be facing, if ever he left the safety of these mountains.

He wondered, mainly because it kept his mind off the woman who refused to leave him in peace, when he had become so convinced of that. Was it simply because Tal had told him, and he'd come to learn Tal was rarely wrong? Even when he refused to tell Kane where the prophecy had come from, from what source he had heard the prediction that if the mythical warrior known to all as Kane ever left his mountain haven he would cease to be, Kane found himself believing. He who never believed in that sort of thing, who thought people's fear of magic and sorcery absurd because such things did not exist, found himself believing in this; such was Tal's power of persuasion.

His power of persuasion and a record of never making a mistake, Kane thought wryly. That was hard to disregard. It was eerie. Uncanny. More even than the

fact that the man apparently communicated directly
with that silly raven of his.

Yes, if ever there was a man he could believe a
wizard or worse, it would be Tal. And he liked him
in spite of it. How could he not? Tal was the only
man he'd ever known who didn't look at him as either
a myth come to life, or a thing with which to terrify
small children into behaving.

Or a tool to be used.

Kane stopped dead. *No,* he protested silently, *not
now. I cannot deal with this now.*

But it was to no avail; the memories, so long held
at bay, rose up in a wave, threatening to engulf him.
Memories of another man, who had looked at him
and seen only a tool to be used. A deadly, merciless,
very effective tool.

He fought the memories down. Or tried to; it had
been so long he'd almost thought himself free of them,
and had lost the knack. He was losing now. The
bloody images were growing stronger, the dying
screams were growing louder, and the thread that held
them all together was the remembrance of how easily
he'd done it, stepping over and on the bodies of those
he'd killed or had killed, never taking his eyes off the
goal, just as he'd been taught.

Until the day he'd looked down to find himself staring into the face of a child, a sweet-faced little girl,
huddled protectively over the shape of a smaller boy.
A child who reminded him of his own dead sister as
she had so often tried to protect him. A child who
had stared up at him with the eyes of an ancient, and
begged him not to kill her brother.

Until the day he'd looked down at that child and
realized he was ankle deep in blood and carnage. Until
the day he'd looked down at that perfect, angelic
child, and she had bent her head as if offering her
slender neck to his blade in payment for the safety of

the boy she sheltered. As his sister had offered her battered face to their father's vicious backhand, so that he wouldn't turn on the younger, smaller Kane . . .

He was running. He hadn't even realized it until now, until he had to work harder to draw air into his aching lungs, until the hammering of his heart echoed in his ears.

He didn't stop. He knew he couldn't outrun the evil visions, but he had to try. For if they caught up with him again he would be lost. Utterly, truly lost. Whatever tiny bit of his soul he'd managed to rediscover and hold on to here on the mountain would be lost, washed away by the flow of bloody memories. He knew it, without knowing how or why he knew.

He ran. Heedless of his direction, or the noise he made with his passage, he who usually moved with the stealth of the lion whose pelt he wore, instead crashed through the underbrush, recklessly, loudly.

In the darkness, a root caught his toe and sent him tumbling forward. He somersaulted, came to his feet in the same motion. He ran on. He hit a patch of loose shale and nearly lost his footing; he skidded downward until he reached solid ground again. He ran on.

It was the stream that was finally his undoing. He misjudged the depth and stumbled, at last falling to his knees near the far bank. The water was icy as it ran down from the snowfields above. He sat on his haunches, welcoming the cold, the numbness it promised. He would do it, he thought. He would end it, once and for all. He had to.

"Kane."

It seemed faint, far away, but he was vaguely aware of someone or something close by. That it spoke his name told him it was human rather than predator, but who knew better than he that the most vicious predator of all was man?

"Kane."

It came again, and he tried to lift his head. He saw a lean, wiry figure, clad in simple leggings and tunic and boots. He saw the raven's head carved on the hilt of the dagger.

Tal.

Slowly he raised his head.

Tal took one look at his face and swore, low, harsh, and heartfelt. Kane felt, as much as he was capable of feeling anything at the moment, Tal's hands strongly gripping his shoulders.

"Look at me."

Kane blinked. Tal's hands tightened.

"Look at me!"

Tal, Kane thought with an odd sense of detachment, could have commanded a battle force with that voice. He'd never heard it from him before.

"Damnation, Kane, look at me! Now!"

He blinked. Focused.

Tal's eyes were glinting gold, reflecting far more light than should be available here in the darkness. Kane stared at the odd glow as if transfixed.

"Let it pass, Kane."

Tal's voice had changed, become soft, coaxing. Kane listened, then felt an odd sensation, as if he'd found some new source of energy.

"Release it," Tal urged, never looking away, the golden gleam growing stronger, his grip on Kane's shoulders never wavering. And slowly, bit by bit, Kane felt the pressure inside him began to ease. He heard Tal suck in a quick, sharp breath, as if he'd taken a blow. But when he spoke, his voice was as gentle as before.

"Give up the past, Kane."

Kane took a breath. The string of grim, vicious images slowed. He took another breath. Tal kept looking at him steadily. Kane knew that the infusion of strength, and the lessening of pain, was somehow coming from Tal. He didn't know how, couldn't care; he could only take the gift.

" 'Tis all right, my friend."

Kane felt a shudder ripple through him as the images finally faded away. "I . . ." He shook his head. Blinked.

"Kane?"

He shuddered again, but this time it was from the cold of the stream he was kneeling in. "I . . . I'm all right."

"You're certain?"

"Yes."

Tal moved then, releasing Kane's shoulders. For a moment he seemed to reel slightly, but Kane thought it must be just his own unsteadiness. Although Tal did look rather pale; his skin had taken on the ashen color of blood loss Kane had seen far too often.

"Tal?"

Kane thought he saw him shudder in turn. Then Tal lowered his head slightly, his hair fell forward, shielding his face from Kane's view, and Kane decided he was probably mistaken; there wasn't enough light to really tell. Of course, there wasn't enough light to account for that golden gleam in Tal's eyes, either.

Then Tal lifted his head, pushed his hair back out of his eyes, looking as he always did, and Kane was sure he'd been wrong.

"I think," Tal said in his usual, mocking voice, "getting out of this water would be wise."

Questions rose in Kane, but one look at Tal's face told him he would be getting no answers. Whatever had just happened here would stay unexplained.

Kane staggered slightly as they made their way up

the bank. And shivered as the breeze chilled his wet clothing even more than the water itself had.

"Come, sit by the fire," Tal said.

"What fire?"

Tal gestured ahead of them. "That fire, of course."

Kane raised his head. A blaze just short of a bonfire danced merrily just a few yards away.

"That . . . wasn't there before."

"You were probably too . . . distracted to notice."

Kane opened his mouth to say he would have to be dead not to have seen this roaring fire. And closed it again; he'd been close enough to dead, inside at least, that Tal could very well be right. And he wasn't sure he wanted to push Tal for an answer; while he wasn't the kind who felt those thought to have . . . unusual talents should be executed—how could he, when he did not even believe in such things?—he didn't want to hear Tal lay claim to such skills. Tal was his friend, in truth his only friend; he did not wish to risk that.

"Convenient," Kane muttered as he did as Tal directed and sat by the fire, welcoming the heat, "that you chose to camp here."

"Not really," Tal muttered. "Here, use this blanket."

Kane blinked as Tal held out the heavy cloth he seemed to have produced out of nowhere. "Where did that come— Never mind." He took it, then eyed Tal up and down. "You were nearly as wet as I."

"I'm fine. I wasn't in so deep as you, and these"— he gestured at his leggings—"repel water nicely. Rest, my friend. Just rest. You need it."

Kane pulled the blanket around him, thinking it surprisingly warming, even as heavy as it was.

"Sleep for a while," Tal urged.

Kane shook his head. "I . . . cannot."

"The dreams will not bother you," Tal promised.

It was as close as he'd come to talking about what

had just happened. And Kane knew it was as close as he would come. He also knew Tal did not make promises lightly. Still, he hesitated; he had no wish to confront the nightmares yet again. Asleep or awake, they were no less ugly, no less barbarous, and the self-condemnation he felt no easier to bear.

"Sleep, Kane," Tal put his hand on Kane's shoulder. "Take what peace slumber can give you."

Perhaps he could sleep, Kane thought. Just for a while. Lightly. Lightly enough that he could wake himself if the dreams threatened. Just for a while.

She had failed. She had come all this way, only to fail at her sacred duty as the Hawk. There was only one man who could help them, and she had at last reached him, only to be turned away without hesitation. She hadn't made the least impression on him, hadn't been able to even begin to convince him. So the Hawk clan would end, because of her failure. They would die, all of them, because of their foolishness in entrusting her with their future.

The only thing left for her to do was to go back and die with them.

Why had they thought she could do this? When she'd told them what she was going to do, that she would bring back the mythical warrior Kane to lead them, they had cheered, certain in their desperation that she had found the answer. She had tried to credit the storyteller, but the old man had demurred, insisting it would be she who carried out the task.

"Your faith was sadly misplaced," she said to the old man, as if he were there to hear.

"No, Jenna. It was not."

She whirled, staring into the darkness. She saw nothing. She noted vaguely that her ankle was much improved, although it mattered little to her anymore; if she died on her trek home, at least she would be spared the humiliation and agony of telling her people she had failed. She held her breath, her certainty of what she'd heard fading as the moments silently passed, broken only by the distant sound of some night creature moving, and the slight rustle of leaves in the shifting air.

She sank back onto her log seat, stirred the fire, and added a log. She tugged the blanket closer around her. After a few minutes, she felt oddly drowsy. She slipped down to sit on the ground, using the log as a rest for her back.

Her eyelids drooped.

"You must give him time, Jenna."

Her head snapped up. She was dreaming. She must be, she told herself, although it was uncommonly vivid. But a dream it had to be, for here beside her sat the storyteller, his eyes glinting gold, his hair glinting silver in the firelight.

"He keeps his heart well veiled, well protected. He is hiding, child."

She would speak to him, Jenna thought. That would prove that this was a dream; dreams were never sensible.

"Hiding from what?"

"Himself."

She blinked. He'd answered her. As if he were real, as if this were not a dream at all. She tried again.

"But why?"

"He has much to regret. Much to hate himself for. So he hides from the pain." The storyteller looked inexpressibly sad for a moment. "But this means he must hide from the joy, as well. From everything."

She forgot for the moment that this was a dream, and spoke from her heart. "You speak truly. I have seen Kane's eyes."

The storyteller nodded. "Then you know he is a man tortured by memories."

She studied the man for a silent moment. "If he is so tortured, why did you send me to him?"

"You are the only one who can help him."

Jenna was suddenly reminded this was a dream. "Ah. There is the nonsensical turn I've been expecting. You have it backward, do you not? 'Tis Kane's help I came seeking."

"Yes. But he needs yours as badly."

"Mine?" She stared. "What in the name of the heavens could I do to help such a man as Kane?"

"You can give him salvation."

"I? How?"

"He believes himself beyond redemption. You can show him it is not so. But you must be gentle with him."

"Gentle?" An image of Kane, tall, broad, powerful, rose in her mind. The idea of having to be gentle with him seemed ludicrous. But then, sitting here talking to an illusion was ludicrous. Yet it seemed so very real. . . .

"He has so little faith left, in anything, but most particularly himself. 'Tis like a candle on a windy night, a very fragile light."

Jenna was becoming confused. And the tiniest bit suspicious. "You guided me here to help my people. Now you speak only of helping Kane."

"The one will result in the other."

"Make sense," she said sharply. "Thus far I have seen no sign that either is about to happen."

"Did you ever wonder why a warrior like Kane would abandon all and retreat to these mountains?"

"No. I know only that Kane wishes me gone, and has unreservedly refused to help us."

"He has too many ghosts haunting him, Jenna. He has caused the deaths of many, and they plague him ceaselessly. He has no wish to cause more. He will not fight again."

"But I want him to *save* lives!"

"And how is he to do that, except by taking other lives?"

"I—" She broke off, unable to counter that unerring logic. "I didn't think of it that way."

Perhaps it wasn't a dream; how could a dream made up of her own imaginings have produced something she had never thought of? She shook her head as the storyteller spoke again.

"You thought only of the needs of you and yours, nothing of what it would cost Kane."

"But you told me he would help."

"Do not mistake me, child. I said he was the only one who *could*."

He had always been annoyingly precise, Jenna thought. Except when he was being so mysterious nothing he said made sense. But he was right. She had only thought of the needs of her people, and nothing of what it would cost Kane. She hadn't even thought of him as quite real, hadn't thought of him as a man with any kind of feelings.

Slowly, feeling a bit abashed, she asked, "What am I to do, then? You know that I will do anything, whatever I must. But what? If he is the only one who can help us, but he will not fight . . ."

"He will not, because it would cost him what little remains of his soul."

Jenna sighed. "That is too much to ask of any man."

The storyteller looked oddly pleased. Then, almost briskly, he said, "Because he will not fight does not mean he has forgotten how."

Her brows furrowed. "You are being obscure again."

The storyteller smiled. "You are a very clever girl, Jenna. You will reason it out."

Her mouth twisted doubtfully. The fire flared up suddenly, and she looked that way. For a moment she gazed at it as if the answer were hidden somewhere in the dancing flames.

When she looked up again, the storyteller was gone. She had no sense of rousing from a dream, no sudden start of awakening. The fire had returned to normal and he was simply gone. And she was not sure she was any better off than she had been before.

It took her until morning to work out what the storyteller had meant.

Kane blinked, squinting against the morning sun as he looked at Tal.

"Aren't you . . . grayer than you were yesterday?"

Tal looked up quickly. "Grayer?"

"Your hair. 'Tis distinctly grayer."

Tal's eyes rolled upward as if he could see his tousled locks. He grasped a strand of hair and pulled it in front of his eyes, fruitlessly since it happened to be a dark strand. At last he reached for the dagger sheathed at his narrow waist, and peered at himself in the polished blade.

"Damnation," he muttered. "I never could get that right."

He ran a hand over his hair, brow furrowed as if in great concentration. He repeated the motion. And peered into the blade again. And sighed.

"It will never be as it was again. I should have paid more attention to that lesson."

Kane stared at his friend, who seemed to suddenly be reminded of his presence. He gave Kane a wary look. His hair, Kane noticed, was back to normal, at least the normal he was used to seeing; raven dark shot with moonlight silver. He said nothing, only looked.

" 'Twas merely the light," Tal said.

"Of course," Kane said.

Tal looked surprised at having his own common

phrase turned back on him. After a moment he grinned widely. Despite himself, Kane smiled back. He'd had a more restful night than he would have believed possible; most times when the visions came, it took days for the effect to wear off.

But they'd never hit him when Tal was around before.

"So," Tal said cheerfully, "do you believe your flame-haired visitor has given up by now?"

"I can but hope," Kane said wryly.

"She seemed . . . quite determined."

"She is."

"What will you do if she is still there when you return?"

Kane sighed. "I don't know."

Tal looked thoughtful. "Perhaps you could simply frighten her away. You're intimidating enough."

"I don't intimidate you," Kane pointed out.

"That's different. I know you won't damage me."

"You do, do you?" Kane said mildly.

"I do." That certainty again.

"Has anyone ever told you that habit of yours is quite . . . irksome?"

Tal laughed. "Many."

Kane's mouth twisted. "And it had little effect, I see." Tal shrugged. Kane sighed again. "She may be young, but she is no shorter on courage than you, my friend. I doubt she'll give up easily. Unless I can determine what would frighten her, I fear myself doomed to endless importunings."

"I leave that to you. I must find Maud. That silly bird has flitted off somewhere, no doubt to wreak havoc on some unsuspecting innocent."

Kane watched as Tal gathered his few belongings, rolled them up in the blanket Kane had slept in, fastened them with a strap he then slung over his shoulder, and turned to go.

"Tal?"

He looked back.

"Thank you."

Tal smiled, a gentle smile quite unlike his usual mocking grin. "Good luck, my friend. Whatever you decide to do."

He vanished into the woods as if they had welcomed him with open arms and the trees had folded around him protectively.

Whatever he decided to do.

What could he do? He could not help her. No matter how she might pester, no matter how tenacious she might be, last night had proven beyond a doubt that he could not take up weapons again. Yet she refused to accept his answer.

So he must find some other way of ridding himself of her.

'Twas too bad; she really was quite lovely.

But she had to go. And he would do whatever it took to see that she did.

Chapter 5

"A bloodsucking gnat could take lessons from you," Kane muttered wearily. "I have never encountered a more persistent creature. Can you not see my answer is final? Will you not give up?"

"I cannot give up," Jenna said simply, staring into the fire.

He knew that her persistence was driven by desperation and fed by her love for her people, but he told himself firmly it mattered not to him.

" 'Tis pointless."

"Even so," she said.

He tossed the bone he'd cleaned of meat into the fire. He had returned late this afternoon, knowing he looked like a man who had passed a night in hell. He *had* passed a night in hell, a personal hell of his own making. Jenna had given him a look tinged with an unexpected compassion, a look that made him very wary because of his own equally unexpected response to it. And because he had no idea why she would have the slightest bit of kind feeling for him.

Without speaking, she'd set about preparing a meal of the remaining rabbit. He'd not commented upon her industry, had merely sat and eaten in silence.

She, on the other hand, had used his silence to her

advantage, trying once more to persuade him to help her save her people.

"They cannot hide in the village, relying on the glade's protection forever. Many of our fields are outside the protection. We must plant crops soon, or there will be starvation this winter."

"Does not your magical forest take care of all your needs?" he asked, a tinge of derision in his tone.

"It helps those who help themselves," she retorted. "It does not do the work, it merely provides a greater yield from a smaller amount of land."

"Can they not simply hunt in bands, for protection?"

"We do not hunt. Not with weapons. We have none. We build traps, snares, for the game we need. There was never a need to store more than a winter's worth. There was always more."

Kane shook his head. "Helpless flock. No wonder some warlord saw them as easy prey."

"Only because they have never needed to deal with such things."

He shrugged. "Leave. Flee to safety."

"We cannot leave our home place."

He grimaced. "Life is precious and short. The land is eternal, and cares not that men die for it."

"But Hawk Glade is a sacred place, the history and very heart of our people resides there." She saw in his expression what he thought of such foolishness, but she went on doggedly. "But soon they will have to venture out past the safety of Hawk Glade. And when they do they will be slaughtered."

"I will not fight again. For you, or anyone else."

She looked at him for a silent moment before she asked, "Even for yourself?"

"Especially for myself."

She shivered, as if something in his voice had made

her feel the coldness he carried with him every day of his life. She turned away from the fire to look at him.

"I'm sorry," she said quietly. "But I cannot give up. The lives of my people depend on me—"

"That is your problem."

"Yes. And my responsibility. Don't you see, that is why I must convince you—"

"You will not." He looked at her. She met his gaze steadily, determinedly. After a moment he shook his head wonderingly. "I will confess, although you are tormenting me to distraction, I admire your tenacity. That you are even here in this place speaks well of you. 'Tis not an easy place to find or reach."

"I know," she said ruefully. Then, sliding him a sideways glance, she added, "And I must thank you for your care of me. Feeling as you do, it was most . . . generous."

It was not hard to follow her thoughts. He could almost see her thinking that surely a man who could be generous about such a thing was not yet lost to humane feeling. Thinking that she could yet convince him to help her.

" 'Twas necessity," he said shortly. "The sooner you are healed, the sooner you can leave."

Jenna sighed.

"If you had thought because I tended your wounds I was . . . amenable, you were wrong. I wish you gone from here. You have invaded my domain and disrupted my peace."

She flushed slightly, as if chagrined at how easily he seemed to have read her. When she spoke, it was with an edge in her voice, "True peace comes from within, not simply from ignoring chaos."

Kane laughed coldly. "And what would you know of it? You're barely more than a child."

He wasn't sure who he was trying to convince of that; he certainly knew it wasn't true. As did his body, which responded to the memory of her nudity before he was even aware the image had crept into his mind yet again.

At his words Jenna drew herself up. "I am a woman grown, old enough to hold the sacred Hawk. And I know that you will never find the healing you seek like this."

Kane's eyes darkened. "You know nothing of what I seek. An innocent like you could never know."

"I may be innocent," Jenna said, "but I am not a fool. Do not mistake the one for the other."

No, she was not a fool. Despite the foolishness of her errand, he would never have accused her of that. He stared down at his boots; they'd not been new for a long time, but they looked even worse now, after his breakneck race down the mountain last night.

His jaw tightened. He hated that he couldn't remember what he'd done, that he remembered nothing except the horror that had threatened to suffocate him until the moment he'd come back to himself, sitting in icy water, Tal's hands on his shoulders. He didn't know what would have happened if Tal hadn't been there. Or rather, he knew what would have happened. And he wasn't sure if he should be glad it hadn't.

"You will not fight."

It wasn't a question, and Kane looked up at Jenna, wondering if at last she had realized he meant what he said.

"I will not fight," he confirmed.

She took a deep breath, steadied herself. "Then you must teach me how."

Kane blinked. "What?"

"You must teach me how to fight. And how to teach my people to fight. It is our only hope."

"Teach you?"

"Yes," she said her tone brisk, as if that alone would convince him. "You will not fight for us, so I must learn, so I can in turn show my people. And there is no one else to teach me."

"Teach you," he repeated, still a little stunned at the turn this had taken.

"You must," she repeated.

"That is impossible."

"It is essential," she insisted. "Of our people, only the storyteller knows anything of war—"

"Then let him teach you."

"He cannot. He can but tell tales of battles." A trace of a smile flickered over her lips and was gone. "Very good tales, yes, but only tales. He knows of weapons, and warfare, but only as a watcher. Besides, even though he moves like a youth, he is an old man, his hair as silvered as moonlight. 'Twould be asking too much, even had he firsthand knowledge."

"It is too much to ask of me, as well," he said sourly.

"But I am not asking you to fight. Merely to teach."

He didn't know whether to laugh or to shake her. He doubted the latter would stir any sense in her, so he settled for the former.

"Certainly," he said grandly. "My sword is merely half your weight, you should be able to wield it with little trouble. And my armor should only drag on the ground, if it does not crush you first."

"I am not a fool," she snapped. "Do you think I do not know that? Besides, there is no time for my people to become expert in swordplay. But I find it hard to believe Kane the Warrior cut such a wide swath with only a sword. Was your training so poor then, that you learned only one weapon?"

Kane's brows rose. She was glaring at him, her vivid blue eyes flashing as if infused with the fire of her hair. He'd told Tal she was not lacking in courage, and she was proving that anew, facing him down as few men would dare. She had wit, too, and it was seemingly sparked easily by anger. No, she was not a fool. The innocent she'd admitted to being, perhaps, but never a fool.

And beautiful. He could no longer deny that; now that she was recovering and no longer an invalid, he could no longer deny she was, as Tal had said, quite striking in appearance. Not a quiet, meek woman as he generally preferred, but a woman any man would have to beware of taking for granted.

"What . . . weapons did you have in mind?"

"Whatever there is that can be learned quickly and made easily. Bows. I've heard of men who can shoot arrows a great distance. And of bows of a different kind, that fire bolts instead of arrows, but with much more force. And are there not hammers, that can be thrown with great power—"

"For a peaceful clan, you have an unexpected knowledge of the weapons of war."

"The storyteller," she said. "He knows of many things. 'Tis he who sent me here."

Kane's brow furrowed; this seemed impossible. "Your storyteller sent you to me?"

"He told me you were not simply a myth, and that you were real, that you were a warrior worthy of the name, and the only one who could help us."

"So you set off on this journey on the basis of that? An old man's tales? Does your clan run to such craziness as your storyteller?"

"He is not crazy! He simply . . . sees patterns that others miss."

Something about her words distracted him for an instant, but he was too intent on something else to let it divert him completely. He wanted an answer to this; he'd let it slide while she was in a weakened state, but she was clearly well enough now. Well enough to stand up to him.

"How," he said quietly, "did you find me?"

She blinked. "I told you. The storyteller sent me."

"That is the why. I want the how."

She looked puzzled. "They are one and the same."

Kane went still. "This storyteller of yours told you where to find me?"

"Of course. How else would I have known? As it was, I nearly took many wrong turnings. As you said, 'tis not an easy place to find."

"No," Kane muttered, "it is not."

And no one knew where it was. Some had stumbled upon it by accident, but no one seeking him had ever found it by intent. In the beginning there had been some near moments, when he'd thought he would surely be discovered, but he'd managed to avoid any contact with those from below. And after a few years, his reputation had made the turn into legend, then into myth, until most were convinced he'd been an invention all along. The only ones who searched for him now had blood on their minds. And their hands.

And yet this slip of a woman had found him.

And this storyteller of hers had apparently told her how.

"So, when do we begin?"

He ignored her question, still focused on his own. "Tell me of this storyteller."

She shrugged, then obliged. "He came to us shortly after the attacks started. In fact, he was the first to warn us that the warlord had set his eyes on our forest, as the easiest route to the north, where he planned to expand his territory."

Again something tugged at his mind, but he had to have the answer to this first.

"He came to you from where?"

"He came out of the forest, but where before that no one knows for certain, except that he passed through lands already bloodied and conquered."

"His name?"

She looked almost sheepish for a moment. "I . . . we do not know. He is simply the storyteller."

Kane stared at her. "You are under siege but you have taken him among you, and you do not even know his name?"

"It sounds strange, I know. But there is something about him that makes it seem . . . unnecessary. When you are with him, it does not even occur to you." Jenna shrugged. "Besides, names are what you make of them."

Kane felt a shiver arc through him.

"Yes," he said flatly. "They are."

"So, when do we begin?" she asked again.

"We do not."

"But we must. This will not cost you, Kane. You must only teach. Then I shall leave, and you can go back to living as you did before."

"I can do that much sooner if you leave now."

"I cannot. I will not."

He believed her. It was there, the determination, in her refusal to avoid his eyes, in every quivering line of her body as she faced him. She would not leave. She would not give up. She would badger him until he gave in.

"Then perhaps I shall have to simply kill you," he said.

She held his gaze, never flinching. "Then it will be done," she said simply. "But I do not think you will. Not if you meant what you said, that you will never fight again."

"You would not give me much of a fight," he said wryly, but it was without heat; she was right, he would not kill her. The old Kane might have; he could not.

He could, he supposed, cart her down the mountain himself. Except that she would no doubt find her way back. He could blindfold her and abandon her someplace else on the mountain, he thought. And his reaction to his own idea startled him; the thought of her certain death should he do so bothered him a great deal. She was brave and far more noble than he had ever been, and deserved better than such a fate.

If there was only some way he could confuse her, disorient her somehow, so she would not be able to find her way back. If he could do that, then he could leave her on the road back to her home, and she would have no choice but to take it.

His mouth twisted. Perhaps he should ask Tal for help with that. Kane knew he wouldn't be the least bit surprised if the man could do it, could cloud her mind somehow. That he had just thought of asking his only friend to cast a spell for him didn't bother him nearly as much as it should have. What had happened to his certainty that such things as magic and sorcery did not exist? Had it vanished as his nightmare had vanished under Tal's hands?

He shook his head sharply. Even if it worked, and she went home, what then?

He turned away from the thoughts of what would happen then, of the certainty that if her people died, Jenna would die with them. She would have it no other way.

They deserved no better, he told himself. If they were foolish enough to believe that peace was a gift given instead of a right fought for, they deserved to lose it.

And Jenna? Did she deserve to die for it?

"I will not leave," she repeated, and he wondered how often she'd said it before he heard it this time, so lost in his contemplation had he been.

"I will not teach you," he retorted.

"You must. You are the only hope for my people. We are innocent of the ways of war, of killing. But we can learn. We must learn."

Innocent. That word again. It kept recurring.

I may be innocent . . .

. . . to wreak havoc on some unsuspecting innocent.

Tal's words came back to him. Although he'd been speaking again of that uncanny bird of his, the phrase sparked a half-formed idea in Kane's mind.

. . . she had to go. And he would do whatever it took to see that she did.

His own remembered thoughts put the seal to it. Although she was clearly, as she had said, a woman grown—most delectably grown—she was an innocent. And she was proud. Rightfully so, he would grant her; he'd already admitted it would take an amazing woman to make the journey she'd made.

And there was one sure way he could send a proud innocent running.

He looked at her, his eyes narrowing intently. He let his gaze move slowly over her, from tiny bare feet upward to the glorious waves of red gold hair. The tunic she wore over slim, travel-worn leggings was loose, shapeless, but his mind too well remembered the shape of the body beneath; that image of her as he'd stripped her naked, before he'd covered the tempting vision with his own shirt, had never left him. 'Twould not be hard to feign the mood he needed to take on now.

'Twould be harder to convince himself he was only feigning.

"Such lessons do not come cheaply," he said, beginning slowly.

"I did not expect them to. We had intended to pay you for your help. Not in money, we need and have little, but in the riches of the forest."

"I have the same here."

"Then whatever we have that you wish is yours."

"You cannot afford my lessons, Jenna," he warned.

"You are our last hope. I will pay what I must." She took a deep breath. "Even the greatest of prices."

Kane drew back, surprised she had brought it up before he had. Had he betrayed something in those moments just now when he had looked over her body? Or had he somehow betrayed himself when those memories of her naked body had intruded upon him? Was his plan about to miscarry?

"Even that?" he asked softly.

She shivered slightly, grimaced in apparent self-disgust, then lifted her chin as if in denial of her own weakness. He understood her repulsion—his scarred face was hardly the kind of countenance women swooned over—at the same time he admired her courage. Even this, it seemed, she would do for her people.

"The golden Hawk is worth a great deal, no matter where you might take it. 'Twill more than compensate you for what time you will spend."

Kane drew back again, staring. "The golden Hawk?"

She bit her lip. " 'Tis literally that. Gold." She held out her hands to measure an astonishing size for what she spoke of. " 'Tis that large. And it is also the heart of my people." Her chin came up, jutting out with renewed determination. "But better to lose it than to see them all dead, to see the end of a people who have managed to live in peace for generations."

"The golden Hawk," he said again, this time stifling a chuckle; his plan was intact, and he would soon be alone again. As he wished to be. "You are an innocent, aren't you?"

"What do you mean?"

"I have no wish nor need for your precious golden Hawk. I do not covet such things, and the wealth it might bring would be meaningless here."

Jenna stared at him. "But I . . . we thought all outside our village treasured such things."

"Not all. Most, but not all."

Distress darkened the blue of her eyes. "But then

what will you take? All we have is the glade, and what is the difference between giving it up to you and losing it to the warlord?"

"I do not want your land, either."

He said it evenly enough, although there was a time when the accumulation of land had been his only goal, when fulfilling the wishes of one who coveted land above all else had been his sole aim in life.

"But then . . . what can we offer?"

"I care for nothing from your precious people, Jenna of the clan Hawk." He rose then, and went to her. He crooked a finger beneath her chin and lifted her head. "But you . . . you can offer me something I want."

"I?" She looked utterly bewildered.

Innocent . . .

He smothered the qualm and went on; despite his body's urges to the contrary, he had no intention of despoiling this innocent, only of finally and forever frightening her away. And he would ignore the sudden burst of heat that had shot through him at the thought of teaching this particular innocent much more than the ways of war.

"Exactly."

"I don't understand."

"I've been a long time without a woman," Kane said, his voice suddenly husky in a way he couldn't seem to control. "So long that, although I'd prefer one with experience in pleasing a man, I will settle for one who knows nothing."

Jenna's eyes widened as his meaning reached her.

"Me?"

"You, Jenna."

"You want me . . . as a man wants a woman?"

A flick of irritation nudged him; were the men of her blessed Hawk Glade eunuchs, that this was so astonishing to her? She was looking at him as if he were the first man ever to look at her with desire. He could not believe that was true.

He did not want to believe his own reaction was true. And he tried hastily to tamp it down, bury it beneath cruel words.

"What other use could I possibly have for you?"

Chapter 6

"I . . ."

She lowered her eyes. Two spots of high color stained her cheeks. He had her now, Kane thought. A few more good thrusts and she'd be out of his way.

He could wish, he thought wryly as heat jammed through him again in a rush, that he'd used a different word. Still, he pressed on.

" 'Twill be annoying, virgins are far more trouble than they're worth. In fact," he said thoughtfully, "perhaps I'd best be sure you are worth it first. If you'd remove your clothing, so I may inspect you?"

He said it in the polite tone of an order masked as a request. Her head came up, and he knew she'd heard the steel in the words. He had expected her to be cowed, as armed and armored men had been by that voice of command, but he quickly saw he was mistaken.

"You had more than enough chance to *inspect* me when I was lying senseless in your bed."

It was all he could do not to laugh with pleasure at her spirited retort. Had it not been for the vivid image her words called up, he might have done it. But he found himself instead having to concentrate on controlling his body's fierce response to the remembered shape and feel and look of her.

He had indeed been without a woman too long.

"Perhaps you are right," he managed after a moment. "I suppose I've seen enough to know the process would not be intolerable."

"The process?"

"Of removing your innocence."

Her cheeks were still flushed, but to her credit she didn't look away. She held his gaze evenly, with that courage he'd had to admit never seemed to fail her.

"This is your price?"

Enough of this, Kane thought sharply, angered at her refusal to be intimidated, angered at his own body's unruliness. He would have done with this, and now.

"It is."

She took a deep breath, and spoke again. "You will teach—"

He cut across her words sharply, speaking what he must before he could get to the words that would surely drive her away. "I will teach you how to train your people to fight, with what weapons you can make yourselves. I will teach you tactics, planning, and how to withstand a larger force."

Relief glowed in her eyes. And that angered him as well, as much for the way his blood was heating as for her silly innocence.

"And in return," he said, his voice sounding as harsh as a raven's cry, "you will become my woman. You will allow me the freedom of your body in whatever way I wish, whenever I wish, without complaint."

Her color deepened. "I . . . know nothing of such things."

"That is obvious."

He said it tightly, hating the way his blood was pooling low and deep inside, until soon no amount of innocence could prevent her from realizing his own body was out of his control. He knew too well it was never good to let your enemy know they affected you in any way, yet his body continued to betray him, and he did not understand why. Yes, she was a strikingly beautiful woman, but he'd had those before. And never had he been so unable to conquer his own responses. This was a dismal side of his clever plan he hadn't expected.

"Then . . . please . . . you must explain . . . exactly what you expect of me."

By the heavens, what did she want from him? A crude, detailed description of every urge that had just swept him, urges that startled even he himself, and would no doubt shock her virtuous ears? Did she want a description of the images that had gripped him, of her naked beneath him, her legs wrapped around his waist, of her astride him, her hair streaming over them both?

He opened his mouth to give her just that, certain this at last would drive her away. Then he stopped, shamed by the sudden realization that he was so aroused that were he to voice those desires, were he to describe in intimate detail exactly what he expected of her, he would no doubt humiliate himself where he stood, without ever having touched her, or her having touched him. So instead, he gave her cold, ruthless demands. Surely they would serve as well to send her running from his mountain, glad of her narrow escape.

"You will stay here as my woman," he said harshly. "And service me at my will. At least until the next full moon."

She went pale, and Kane knew he'd succeeded. She was frightened now. And well she should be; if she knew how fiercely he wanted her at this moment, she would already be taking to her heels. And he would be left to deal with his aching body alone.

"The next full moon?" she whispered.

Of all he'd said, *that* was what she fixed upon? Kane stared at her.

"My people could be . . . beyond saving by then."

Her people. Did this woman think of nothing else? Did she not think of her own welfare, to find only this to be concerned about in the words of a man ready to degrade her in this way? He was not, of course, but she did not know that.

"There are fewer than a hundred of us now," she said in a pleading tone he heard from her only when she spoke of her clan. "And they are hunted like rabbits—"

" 'Tis not long enough to even begin to train a novice in warfare," he said, finding his voice at last. He eyed her once more with the most evil leer he could manage. "Let alone a virgin in other arts."

"No, I—"

"You would not be able to save them anyway," he said with a shrug. He'd known she would say no, and should have realized she would face him to do it, not run. He did not think this woman had run from anything in her life. "I could train you in all I spoke of and it would still be useless. There is nothing I could teach you in such a short period of time that could help you defeat a determined warlord."

That he knew too well; he'd worked for the most determined, brutal, and ferocious of them all. He'd been his right arm, had done his bidding without question. And even the rest of his life was not enough to atone for that. All he could hope for was a higher rung in Hades.

"I know we cannot defeat him. All we wish is to make him think there is perhaps another, easier way to gain his path to the north."

It was a pragmatic view he hadn't expected from her. He'd thought her idealism and anger would have demanded they defeat the enemy who had taken so

much from them. That she was able to temper her
need for revenge for the murder of her family with
such prudence spoke of a wisdom beyond even what
he'd guessed at. He decided to test it even further.

"And what of the people who stand in his way to
the north?"

She shivered. "I cannot think about that. We will
try to warn them, but they must see to themselves.
The Hawk clan must be saved before I can worry
about anyone else."

The implication that she had not rejected his obscene bargain out of hand staggered him. He'd been
so certain this would work, that she would take to her
heels at the very idea. He frowned; he rarely made
tactical mistakes. Could he truly be so rusty? Or had
he simply misjudged the determination of this woman?

*The Hawk clan must be saved before I can worry
about anyone else.*

Perhaps he'd underestimated the value she placed
on her dwindling clan. Perhaps he'd let her youth, her
gender, her beauty blind him to the fact that none of
that made her any less a devoted leader. He'd encountered leaders willing to die for those they led before,
just never one in such a distracting guise.

He'd heard all his life women were weaker, worth
a man's time for only one thing. Could he have forgotten how his sister had shown him otherwise, and had
driven the lesson home with her life?

His breath caught in his throat as his mind shied
violently away from the too-vivid memory; he could
not let it happen again, not here, not in front of this
woman could he be swamped anew by the ugly
visions—

"I wish to completely understand," Jenna said,
doing what his mind could not, pulling him back from
the edge of the morass of seething, malevolent memories. "You will teach me how to train my clan to fight

if I stay with you, and play your whore until the next new moon? And when that time comes, you will let me go, freely?"

He didn't care for her phrasing, although why it bothered him he wasn't quite sure. But he nodded, still hoping she would run.

"You will give me your word?"

His mouth twisted. "My word for your body?"

"The storyteller said above all else, you were a man of your word."

Irritation sparked through him; this storyteller, who-ever he was, presumed far too much. "Did he also tell you most times the word I kept was to destroy?"

"Yes." She seemed unfazed. "Will you give it?"

Some small part of his tactical mind warned him to examine this more closely, but he couldn't quite be-lieve this lovely creature could truly outwit him.

"If you wish. Yes, I give you my word."

Jenna drew in a very deep breath, held it for a moment.

"Perhaps I should ask in turn if you are a woman of your word, Jenna of the clan Hawk."

When she looked at him then, Kane suddenly thought all his assumptions about her youth and na-iveté a lie; these were ancient, weary, knowing eyes. Eyes that had seen death and destruction, eyes that had seen the burial of all close to her, the loss of all that mattered.

He knew that look. He knew it because he'd seen it in his own eyes every time he saw himself reflected in a pool of still water, or in the polished piece of brass he used as a mirror for shaving. He knew it because he *felt* it, felt it deep inside, emanating from the dark, shivery place where those haunting visions lived.

"I am," she said quietly.

He studied her, suddenly aware that he had underestimated this woman. She would do what she had to do. And in the next moment she made his thought fact.

"I will do what I must, for my people. You shall have what you wish, although I doubt it will be what you want."

He lifted a brow. "An odd thing to say, under the circumstances."

"It doesn't matter. Do we have a bargain?"

She truly was going to do it. She was going to agree to become his leman.

Heat blasted through him, so swiftly he didn't have time to protest that he didn't really want this, that her actually accepting his debauched offer had never been part of the plan, that all he'd ever wanted was to be rid of her.

She was looking at him, the blue eyes that only moments ago had been so discernible, so rife with that ancient knowledge she seemed too young to possess, masked and unreadable now. Looking at him as if she cared nothing about the bargain she was about to make.

Cared nothing about the price she was about to pay.

"You don't truly want this," he said, his voice sounding oddly thick even to himself.

"What I want," she said in a tone so flat it sounded as dead as he'd felt last night, "is nothing against the survival of my people."

His mouth twisted. "And your people will let you make this . . . sacrifice?"

"They need only know that they will have what they need. What I . . . pay to get it is my concern."

The hesitation was barely noticeable, but it told Kane the words were not quite as effortless as she tried to make them sound.

"Do you value yourself so little?"

"I value my people more. Do we have a bargain?" she repeated.

Kane wondered what had happened to the cool, analytical man who had gone into armed combat without a second thought. He'd come here to bury that man, but he'd thought he would never succeed. Until now, when he could use some of that ruthless decisiveness and couldn't find it in him.

"Will you renege now on this . . . trade you offered?" she asked, looking at him as if he were a merchant quibbling over the price of a loaf.

He had, it seemed, seriously miscalculated. She truly would do it. She would sacrifice herself for her people. Nobility ran deep in her. And nobility, Kane thought, was a fool's game. He had a sudden flash of insight, that if it was her life that was demanded, she would give that, too.

Which could easily happen if she went back, whether it was now or at the next full moon.

Unless he refused to let her go. Unless he kept her here, until the inevitable destruction of her home was over. The idea held a certain appeal that he could not deny. And that it did made him very nervous. But the thought of sending her, with her bright, extraordinary courage, back to die a useless death made him feel ill.

"Well, Kane the Warrior?" she prompted, clearly too caught in her own crisis of decision to notice his.

"You will regret this."

"I should regret the death of my people more. Do we have a bargain?" she asked a third time.

Kane was amazed at the resolve it took to voice what should have been a simple answer, an answer that gained him what his body was aching for and would cost him little. She deserved better than to be dishonored by the likes of him. The kind of blood that was on his hands should be kept far away from one so unsullied.

He'd once been the kind of man who would have scoffed at such reservations, and at paying in any way for what he wanted and could simply take by sheer force. He wasn't sure that the change was an improvement. If he'd become the man he wanted to be, he would have sent her away untouched.

If he'd become the man he wanted to be, he would have left his mountain, fought her battle for her, and if he died as the prophecy foretold, then so be it. He would be at peace at last. At least, as much peace as he would likely find in the fires of Hades.

But he was not that man. He was not even man enough to say no to this.

"We have a bargain," he said roughly.

Jenna let out a long, sighing breath. "Thank you."

"You won't thank me, before we're done."

She lowered her eyes. "Nor will you. You've made a sorry pact. But when you are dissatisfied, I will hold you to it still."

"Dissatisfied?"

" 'Twill happen," she said with a shrug. "You wish a female for the indulgence of carnal passions. Instead you have one without any passion at all."

Kane blinked. Without passion? This woman who had found the place where he'd been hiding, when no other ever had? This woman who faced down a man she should by rights have been terrified of? This woman who felt so strongly about her clan she would die for them? She, passionless?

He couldn't help himself; he laughed aloud. She gave him a startled look, color flaring anew in her face. Then she turned away, and for the first time, fled from him. He watched her go, watched the barely noticeable limp caused by her still tender ankle, watched the gentle sway of her body, the movement of the waist-length fall of her hair.

Passionless?

He was beyond rusty, he was half-witted if he'd misjudged *that*.

Jenna wondered if it was part of the torture. If, in addition to the exhausting, bruising, muscle-burning work he'd been putting her through, he intended the other as some kind of exquisite mental torment.

She'd expected, after the way he'd spoken, to be summoned to his bed that first night. Instead, the opposite had happened; he had ordered her out of his bed, telling her if she wanted to train like a warrior, she would do it completely, and that included making do with a blanket on the ground. She'd managed not to question his bed of soft furs, but he'd answered her as if she'd spoken.

"I'm no longer a warrior." And then, as if reminding her yet again, he added, "Nor will I ever be again."

She was relieved enough at apparently being spared paying her part of their bargain for the moment that she retreated without a word.

And every night since then, she'd been too tired to do anything but roll up in the heavy blanket he'd used himself and fall into exhausted, happily dreamless sleep, heedless of the hard ground beneath her. Twice she'd fallen asleep in the middle of his lesson on tracking, but to her surprise he didn't berate her, merely started anew when she awoke.

She'd never expected this. Her body had never betrayed her in any significant way, and she'd never thought herself weak, but Kane was making her feel that way. He drove her mercilessly, ordering her to do things she never would have thought part of their deal. He made her run endlessly through the trees, down his precious mountain, then, when she was winded, turn around and run back. Uphill.

He made her do exercises lifting heavy logs and

rocks that she saw no point to until he handed her a
bow and told her to pull back the bowstring. She managed a bare inch of movement. Silently, Kane took it
from her, fitted an arrow to the nocking point, and
drew it back, all in one smooth movement. Drew it
back so far, and with such ease, Jenna's eyes widened
in amazement. He sent the arrow flying, fast and
straight, and so far that it disappeared far into the
trees before, seconds later, she finally heard the
thwack as it struck a distant tree.

She went back to the rocks and logs without
complaint.

And that was only the beginning. No sooner had she
begun to feel not quite so exhausted while running, he
loaded a pack with some of the rocks and made her
carry them. And still he made her lift them repeatedly
when they returned. And not once, other than when
he'd used the bow to quiet her questions, had she
been within arm's length of any kind of weapon.

And not once had he called upon her to fulfill the
carnal side of their bargain. While she was too weary
to linger upon it as she lay alone in her blanket by
the night fire—after being lectured sternly by Kane
never to stare into the flames, for it ruined your night
vision—it never ceased to nag at her while she was
awake. The only thing powerful enough to supplant it
was the knowledge that every day she spent here was
another day away from the people who were de-
pending on her. Still, she was ever conscious of Kane's
eyes following her every move, and helplessly wondered what he was thinking. Wondered if this would
be the night he would summon her.

And being poignantly thankful that there was no
one left of her family who might feel bound to defend
the honor she was handing over to Kane the Warrior.
If he ever took it, that is.

She knew men found her attractive enough; many

in the clan had approached her mother asking to pay court to her. Thankfully her mother had always said such things were her daughter's choice, and Jenna had made that choice easily; she had no interest in such things. It was not that she did not like the boys of her acquaintance, some of them were her dear friends, it was only that she would much rather walk for hours through her beloved forest, go fishing in the stream, and in the evenings listen to the storyteller weave his magical spell with story and song.

As a girl, after overhearing an older boy suggesting her fiery hair must indicate equally fiery passions, she'd once asked her mother why she never felt the way her friends seemed to, why she'd never looked at a man with longing as Cara and the others did. Her mother had smiled and said something about the greatest of passions requiring the greatest of sparks, which made no sense to Jenna. Her mother had laughed then, and told her to stop worrying; she was fine as she was, and the women of her family were often late to bloom.

And some, Jenna had decided when she reached her twentieth summer, never bloomed at all. Kane had made a poor bargain indeed, if he expected her passion to match her appearance; she just did not have it in her. As fascinating as she found him, as much as she found herself watching him simply to see him move in that powerful, gliding way, she knew she did not have it in her. She never had.

Perhaps, Jenna thought as she clambered as quickly as she could up the particularly steep trail he'd sent her on today, he'd realized that she'd spoken the truth, and that was why he had not claimed her although they were fully a week into their agreement.

She came to an abrupt halt in a small clearing as she came out of the trees to face a steep wall of rock, smooth in some spots, seamed with cracks in others.

Still puffing a bit from the uphill run, she looked around curiously, but the trail seemed to end here. She waited, knowing Kane was close by; he always was. That he duplicated what she was doing with such ease was yet another goad that prodded her to keep going when she felt only like dropping to her knees and pleading for mercy.

"Well?"

His voice came out of the trees to her left.

"What now?" she asked. "The trail ends."

"Does it?"

He stepped out of the trees, as usual showing no sign of effort, not even quickened breathing. She wanted to take one of the stones from the detested pack and throw it at him. Except that he would probably just catch it and toss it back at her without a word, giving her only that annoyingly amused look that was still another goad that kept her going when she wanted to collapse.

He stood beside her, looking up at the stone face of the cliff. Well, maybe not a cliff, it wasn't quite that straight up and down, Jenna thought, but it was near enough.

She risked a glance at him, wondering just what it would take to get this man to show the slightest sign of exertion. She wouldn't ask for much, just a couple of deep breaths, a tiny drop of sweat, something. Anything. Anything that would move him from this seemingly impervious calm.

Even passion?

The thought hit her unexpectedly, and she nearly gasped. How could she so dread the call she feared would come every day, the call to join him in his bed, and yet spend so much time simply looking at him? And taking pleasure in it?

Perhaps it was just that he was quite the most impressive man she'd ever seen. If ever one deserved to become a legend, it was this one. But the tales had omitted the beauty of him, of his stance, his way of moving, his eyes. . . .

Her gaze flicked up to his face, unerringly drawn to the scar that marked his face, the thin, oddly neat white line that ran from his temple to his jaw. Knife? Sword?

He turned then, catching her staring at him. At the scar. His eyes turned frosty, although he said nothing. Jenna started to utter a stumbling apology, then decided it would only make things worse.

"If the trail continues," she said instead, "I cannot see where."

"Can you not?" he said, his voice deadly quiet.

"No, I—" She broke off suddenly, remembering how he had been staring up at the rock face. "Surely you don't mean"—she gestured a little wildly at the crag—"*that*?"

"It appears the only way."

"But that is impossible! I am no bird, to fly up such a cliff."

" 'Tis hardly a cliff," he said mildly. "And you may take off your pack."

"Thank you," she said, her voice laden with mockery. "I suppose you have climbed it countless times, carrying your blessed sword?"

"Countless," he agreed, his tone unchanged.

"Kane, I cannot."

It was the first time she'd ever refused anything he'd asked of her, but this, this was too much.

He studied her a moment. "Have you a fear of heights?"

"From a distance, no."

She thought she saw his mouth quirk. "It is not so hard. There are hand and toeholds aplenty. I will help you from here. And you will find the fear of falling a great motivator for improved balance."

"My balance is good enough."

"Good enough to fire a crossbow while running along a narrow stone wall? Good enough to shoot an arrow while leaping away from one shot at you? Good enough to move through the treetops like a wild thing, leaving no trail on the ground for your enemy to follow?"

She sighed. He always had such reasons for everything he asked her to do, even the things that she could not see the purpose of. So many things to learn, and brutal, ugly reasons to learn them. And he had lived his life like this, with his mind taken up in such ways, how to kill and avoid being killed. She could not imagine such a life.

But she could easily imagine it putting that dead look in a man's eyes.

She turned to face the steep wall of rock.

"What must I do?"

It was a moment before he answered, and when she glanced back over her shoulder, she caught a glimpse of pure admiration on his face that startled her. And then it was gone, and his usually expressionless mask had replaced it.

"Climb," he said simply.

Chapter 7

"You're pushing her very hard."

Kane didn't jump this time; he'd seen the raven circling overhead, far above even the woman who had nearly reached the crest of the rocky bluff, so he knew Tal was nearby. For the first time since she'd begun her slow, torturous climb he took his eyes off Jenna's slender figure. Tal was watching, not the woman clinging precariously to the stone wall, but the man who had set her to the task.

"If I push her hard enough," he muttered, "she just might survive a day or two when she goes back."

Tal didn't ask why she was even still here, and Kane didn't explain. He'd grown, if not accepting, at least used to the fact that there was little that went on that Tal did not know about. He only hoped he didn't know the details of the bargain he and Jenna had struck; he wasn't sure he cared to have his friend learn just how mercenary he could be.

Tal looked thoughtful. "You almost sound as if you care if she does or not."

Kane shrugged. "I admire courage. I hate to see it wasted in a hopeless battle."

"Is it? Hopeless?"

"A clan of farmers who have never held even a bow against a warlord's fully armed force? How could it be otherwise?" He turned the subject before Tal could make him look at it too closely "Where have you been?"

Tal waved vaguely toward the woods. "Rambling."

"You and your . . . companion have been scarce of late."

Tal grinned then, a flashing, brilliant grin that was infectious. "I saw you had decided to teach her. It seemed you had your hands full."

"Oh?" Kane drawled. "I thought perhaps you were afraid of my . . . student."

Tal's grin widened. "Wary, perhaps. A man would do well to be wary around a woman as clever and determined—and as beautiful—as she."

"I thought you were free of such things."

Something flickered in Tal's eyes, something shadowed and dark, and Kane wished he hadn't said it. But it vanished as quickly as it had appeared, and Tal spoke easily enough.

"I am. But because such things have no effect on me does not mean I don't see them. I am not blind, my friend."

"Far from it," Kane said wryly. "You see things no normal man could."

He didn't deny it. For a long moment Tal just looked at him. "This . . . bothers you?"

Kane glanced up at Jenna, who was nearing the top, both to check her progress and to gain a moment of time. Tal did not prod, did not persist. But the question he'd asked hung there between them, unanswered and disturbing.

At last Kane faced his friend squarely. "I do not know how to explain some of the things you know and do, without resorting to things I do not believe in. So yes, in that way, I am bothered."

"Yet you . . . remain my friend."

Kane's mouth quirked. " 'Tis worth the bother."

Tal smiled at his mocking tone, nodded in acceptance of the tribute, but his eyes remained serous. "Thank you. Some would not have your . . . tolerance."

It was as close as Tal had ever come to admitting there was something different about his unique gifts, something that would inspire intolerance in some.

"I have known you nearly since I came here," Kane said. "And while my judgment is . . . impaired in some areas, I do not doubt my first assessment of you. There is no evil in you, Tal. Only good. And that is rare enough in any man to be worth more than the dilemma I find myself in."

"Dilemma?"

Kane grimaced. "Having a wizard as a friend, when I don't believe in them."

It was Tal's mouth that quirked upward this time. "Wizards, or friends?"

Kane smiled wryly. "There was a time when my answer would have been 'Both.' "

"And now?"

"You are my friend."

"And that is as hard for you to believe in as any wizardly doings, isn't it?" Tal asked softly.

Kane didn't deny it. He couldn't think of anything to say, and Tal already knew it was true. He glanced once more at Jenna. She had reached, at last, the top of the rocky face. It had taken her a very long time, but never once had she given up. She followed his called-out directions carefully, had sometimes been forced to stop and rest, but she had done it.

She freed one arm from her last handhold, looked down and waved at him, triumph evident in every movement. She was, as Tal had said, beautiful. And never more than at this moment. He glanced back toward Tal, wondering if his friend were truly so dead to such things that he failed to respond to the lovely vision of Jenna in her victory, her slender body atop the precipice she had conquered, her red gold hair streaming in the breeze.

Tal was gone.

Wait there.

Kane's words echoed in her head as she sat looking out from her steep perch. Wait for what? Not that she hadn't earned a rest, a nice long one. Her hands and toes ached from the impossible climb, she had too many scrapes in various places to ignore easily, and the thrill of success was at last beginning to fade, leaving her with the daunting prospect of having to go back the way she had come.

She flexed her sore fingers, groaning at the thought of putting them through that again, clinging to holds that were little wider than a fingertip. If the promontory had been any steeper, she doubted she could have done it. And if she were to be honest, now that it was safely done, it wasn't *that* steep, merely a bit dizzying to one unused to climbing in such a way.

And she *did* feel wonderful at having done it. And she had, as he had said she would, learned a great deal about balancing and controlling her body. Perhaps she wasn't quite as angry at Kane as she'd thought—

Her musing halted and her jaw dropped as he strolled out of the trees that ringed the top of the rocky bluff she had finally reached. She leapt to her feet. He looked so unruffled, strolling toward her with all appearance of ease.

"Ready to go back?" He could have been asking her to take a Sunday promenade with him. " 'Tis a pleasant walk, this way." He gestured toward the trees he'd emerged from.

"Are you telling me you . . . walked up here by some hidden, *gentle* path through the trees? While you made me scale that cliff like some mountain goat?"

Her fury only seemed to amuse him. "I wouldn't call you a goat, exactly, although you could use a bath."

"You . . . you . . ." she sputtered. She knew it was futile but she hit at him with her fist anyway. It was like hitting a tree trunk. And he laughed.

"You're the one who wanted the training," he pointed out.

She grimaced. She lowered her fist. She stared at him for a long moment. And then she sighed. "I'm sorry. You're right." She grimaced again. "And probably about the bath, too."

Kane chuckled. A little shiver went through her, as it did every time he laughed. He seemed so bemused by the sound, as if it had been a very long time since he had laughed. She wondered just how long it truly had been.

She lagged a few steps behind him as he led the way down the path she'd not known was there. She'd spent much of the last week hating him, the rest being unwillingly fascinated. Even now she caught herself staring at him again, at the smooth power of his stride, the taut alertness of his body, as if he expected attack even in this place he called haven. His dark hair fell past his shoulders, gleaming whenever he reached a spot where sunlight worked its way through the trees. In her mind's eye she could clearly see his face, intense, with planes more hewn than carved, that long, thin scar serving as warning as much as reminder. He was nothing like the men she knew. The faces she remembered were different in some fundamental way, not so much on the outside as in their expression.

The faces she remembered, before the trouble began, were clear and untroubled. Soft even, she supposed. Kane's jaw could have been chipped out of granite, and his expression spoke of trial, tribulation, and pain, and she wondered what dreadful sights he had looked upon in his years as a warrior.

Were it not for the storyteller's words, she would have thought him hardened beyond redemption. He'd certainly been unmoved by her pleas. Yet did it not speak of a soul not truly lost that he had come here at all, that he had turned away from his warrior's life and come here seeking only to fight no more?

A small twinge in her shoulder made her grimace, but it felt no worse when she moved it and she knew it was merely strain. She nearly laughed at herself then, for thinking there was any softness in this man. He'd pushed her, prodded her, yelled at her, and then seemingly gone out of his way to dream up even more absurd things for her to tackle. Everything, it seemed, except what she needed to learn.

She wondered if he was testing her somehow, testing her resolve before he moved on to the weapons she needed to learn. She hadn't failed yet, but if he kept pushing—

Her thoughts halted abruptly. She hadn't failed yet. She thought back over the past few days. He'd made her exert herself in ways she never had before. He'd made her do things she never would have thought herself able to do. But she hadn't failed yet.

And until today, when her shoulder was virtually well again, he had asked nothing of her that would have put undue strain on it. And however hard he had pushed her, however impossible she thought the task he set her to, she had somehow always found the strength to do it. Even when she would have sworn she couldn't, she found that last ounce of determination. . . .

Could it be? Had he judged her so well, that he had pushed her to her limit, but never beyond? Had he truly been that exquisitely careful, demanding everything, but never more than she had?

She pondered this until they came out of the woods by the cave, much sooner than she had expected. He looked back at her and clearly read her expression of surprise.

"You must be always aware of where you are, and where that point is in relation to everything else. There may be times when your normal path is cut off, and you must find a new way to reach your goal."

She thought of the morning when he had led her on a long trek through forest and clearing, uphill and down, sometimes seeming to double back on their own tracks. At last he had stopped, turned to her, and told her to lead them back. She'd stared at him in shock, having no idea which way to go in this strange place. She would not soon forget the lecture she'd gotten on watching her back trail in case she had to retreat through unfamiliar territory.

"Retreat?" she'd said, embarrassed. "I would think that word unknown to the great Kane."

"Knowing when to fall back is as important as knowing when to stand and fight. Those who are too proud to retreat die early."

This time she knew better than to dispute his words; she merely nodded in acceptance.

"Good," he said. "When you are on your own ground, you will know where you are, but there may come a time when you must take the battle to the enemy, in his domain. You must always have your escape planned, and more than one route. Make sure all your people know them, and know what to do should they get separated from the group."

She nodded again. This, at least, was what she had come for. Perhaps he had not let her even handle a weapon yet, but he had begun these lessons immediately. She wasn't sure what use she would put them to, but she told herself not to question the teacher she'd come so far to find.

She watched as he walked over to the cave entrance. He bent to pick something up, and when he came back toward her she saw he held a plump pheasant.

"And you think our forest magical?" she said; she knew the bird had not been there when they had left this afternoon.

"This," he said, "is not courtesy of the forest."

"What, then?"

"Who."

Her forehead creased. "What is it, some kind of offering?"

"In a way." He gave her a speculative look before he added, " 'Tis courtesy of the local wizard."

Jenna blinked again. She sensed she was being tested in some way again, but she did not know what result he wished.

"You have . . . a wizard?"

Kane shook his head sharply, not in negation it seemed, but more at his own folly. "No," he said, denying his own declaration in a very wry tone. "Just a friend who is far too clever."

He did not look convinced, and Jenna wondered just who this friend was. She would, she admitted, wonder about anyone with the temerity to befriend the mythical Kane.

"Clean up from your climb," he said abruptly. "I will prepare this."

When she was clean again, the shadows had begun to lengthen. She took a seat by the fire and watched as Kane turned the spitted bird over the flames. He did not even glance her way, but she'd become used to that. When he wasn't pushing her up and down his precious mountain, or making her climb cliffs only the raven she'd seen this afternoon could easily reach the top of, he barely looked at her.

Which, she thought as she stole a quick look at him, probably explained why he hadn't collected on her side of their agreement. She rubbed at the shoulder that had begun to ache again. Perhaps he'd changed his mind and decided he'd made a bad bargain. Perhaps he'd realized she'd spoken the truth, that she, of all the women of her line, was the one who had been born without that kind of desire. She cared passionately about her people, she had loved her family with the same intensity, but there was nothing for anyone else. No passion of the kind it would take to please a man like Kane.

Not that she knew the first thing about what it would take to please a man like Kane.

"We will start your new lessons now."

Jenna gave a little start as he spoke the words she'd been expecting he would say every night since they'd struck their bargain. She shouldn't have been surprised, she thought, but still she was caught too off guard to prevent the rush of color that flooded her face. At first she hoped he could not tell in the rapidly darkening dusk, but then remembered he had proven more than once he had vision to equal a panther's at night.

She knew he had seen, when his brows lowered as he looked at her. Then, slowly, his expression shifted to his usual unreadable mask.

"We will begin shooting in the morning."

Rarely in her life had she felt such a fool. The only thing that prevented her complete humiliation was that she had not spoken her thoughts.

"With the bow?" she managed to get out. "But I cannot even draw the bowstring."

"A crossbow, I think. 'Twill give you more power. We will make a smaller one. You will need to learn that skill well."

She nodded.

"You understand your only hope is defense?"

"I understand. We only wish for them to chose another route."

"Then you must make the route they wish to take
more trouble than it is worth."

Jenna sat up straight, ignoring the many aches in
her weary body; she sensed he was at last going to
tell her something of real use to her. "How?"

"Your chosen defenders will have to leave the con-
cealment of your glade," he warned.

I . . . know, Jenna thought. She would do as much
as she could herself, but she knew she could not do
it all herself. She hoped there would be some left willing to risk themselves when she returned.

She hoped there would be some left, at all.

"How?" she asked again.

He pulled the bird off the spit and divided it.
Evenly, as he always did. And as she always did, she
gave him part of hers back. He'd refused it the first
time, but she'd insisted, saying the difference in their
sizes was a fact, and she did not need as much food
as he. It had become a small custom. To her it was
merely logical, but she had the feeling that to him it
was something more. She did not ask; she doubted
she would like the answer.

"Small raids," he said as they began to eat. "Keep
them secret, if you can. Steal their food. Small things,
daggers, boots, cooking pots."

Jenna drew back, startled. "Boots and cooking
pots?"

"Anything small enough to be stolen without the
stealer being caught. And not always weapons so they
suspect an enemy arming themselves with their own
weapons."

"Oh."

She resumed chewing thoughtfully. Kane tore off a
strip of meat and ate it more quickly, then spoke
again.

"Harass them. Have they horses?" She nodded. "Send your most silent mover in to loose them. Do not steal them, their tracks will only lead the enemy to your glade."

"We know little of horses."

"Just loose them, and use a switch to send them running. 'Twill be enough." He paused for another bite. "You have a healer?"

"Yes. Evelin. She is very learned."

"I presume she can concoct potions to cause illness as well as curatives?"

Jenna blinked. "I . . . suppose."

He lifted the battered metal cup from which he drank.

"Taint their water," he said, gesturing with the cup. "Their ale, if their water supply is not separate from your own."

Something about this puzzled her. "You do not suggest we simply poison them?"

Kane's mouth twisted downward at one corner; the scar flexed in the firelight. "Have you become bloodthirsty simply by association, then?"

It took her a moment to realize he meant by association with him. It was very odd, she thought, that he seemed . . . disturbed by the idea. And odder still that although she knew who he was, knew his fierce reputation for ruthlessness, she could not picture him as a cruel, callous killer. She told herself she was a fool to think him anything other than how the legends painted him, and chose an answer she hoped would not disturb him further.

"No," she said, "I simply wondered why a warrior trained to kill would say not to."

After a moment he seemed to accept her explanation. "Any warlord who hopes to keep his men with him must avenge the death of any of them. But illness is something else again. A nuisance, with nothing to blame for it. If your healer is as clever as you say, she should be able to have them thinking the place is cursed before long."

Jenna's eyes widened. "This is how you would have us fight?"

"This," Kane said coldly, "is the only way you will be able to fight. Even if I had the powers of the Kane of myth, I could not teach you enough battle skills in such a short time to enable you to give any experienced warlord a real fight."

The bitter truth of his words turned Jenna's voice sour. "Then why bother to teach me of the bow or any other weapons at all?"

"So your people can at least have some chance to save themselves if they are caught outside your . . . magical glade."

She heard the scoffing tone of his voice, wondered at it, but was too caught up in what he'd been saying to pursue it. She'd never thought to hear that retreat, diversion, stalling, and minor harrying were as valid as weapons as were frontal attacks. Yet she could not deny that what he told her made sense; they were a small, untrained group, they could not hope to take on Druas's force in normal ways.

She finished the last of the pheasant and tossed the bones into the fire. Kane had finished before her, as usual. He seemed to be through talking for the moment, so she merely sat in silence.

Absently she rubbed at her shoulder, wondering what Evelin would say when asked to concoct a potion to cause illness rather than cure it. Then she remembered the woman's expression when they had buried her mate of decades, one of the first casualties, killed before they were even aware they were under siege, taken by an arrow in the back while gathering beans from the vines. Evelin was, perhaps above all of them, a peacemaker. But she would do this. For Buren, she would do this.

Kane had gotten to his feet, and Jenna had thought him ready for another of the long walks he took at night, often not returning until after she had fallen asleep. But instead he did something that nearly stopped her heart; he walked around and knelt behind her.

"You are sore," he said quietly. So quietly her skin tingled as she wondered at the sound of it.

"Yes," she managed to get out; she could hardly deny it when she knew it was obvious.

"You did well today."

It was the first time he'd said such a thing, and she was astonished at the gratification she felt. "I . . . thank you."

"Do not thank me. 'Tis simply the truth."

"Then I thank you for saying so. I—"

Her words cut off abruptly as his hands came down on her shoulders. For a moment they were still, and in that instant all she could think of was the incredible heat of this man; the warmth of him spread through her like Evelin's best balm.

She held her breath. So it was to begin at last. She supposed she should be grateful for the week's reprieve he'd given her. Indeed, she was surprised he had the grace to have given her any time at all to get used to the idea of what was to come.

"Do not tense," he said in that same quiet voice. "You will only make it worse."

As if she could relax, she thought. He would take her now, and she would keep to her word, and allow him the freedom of her body without complaint. He would have his man's pleasure, and she would endure. Her body tightened oddly, as if it knew of the coming violation. It was a strange sensation, an ache that was

not quite pain and curiously hollow, a sensation she'd
never felt before.

And then his hands began to move, slowly, rubbing
her aching muscles with a firm but gentle touch, his
fingers flexing with just enough pressure, working out
the soreness and stopping before it became pain.

"Let it ease," he murmured, letting his thumbs mas-
sage between her shoulder blades. "Drop your head
forward."

She was not sure what this had to do with mating,
but she did as he asked; she had given her word. He
paused in his actions for a moment, and she felt him
gather the thick fall of her hair to move it out of the
way. He seemed to hesitate for a moment, and she
thought she felt a slight tension on the long strands
of hair, as if he were running his hands through it.

She heard a sound oddly like a sigh, and then his
hands came back to her shoulders, rubbing, kneading.
It felt so very strange, this gentleness from such a
powerful man, a man most would suspect incapable of
it. It felt stranger still, the spreading, relaxing warmth
that seemed generated by his fingers.

It felt *good*.

The thought startled her, and she would have stiffened anew had it not been for the lulling, soothing
motion of his hands seeming to steal her very strength
from her. All she wanted was for him never to stop.
That thought disturbed her in turn, and she struggled
to rise from the languorous mist she seemed to be
sinking into. While it might be more pleasant to be in
this floating, golden haze when he took her, her mind
rebelled at the idea.

"I will . . . keep my word. You do not have to
do this."

His hands went still. "What is it you think I'm
doing?"

"Whatever you do . . . to bend women to your will."

His laugh was short, sharp, and utterly without humor. And his fingers tightened convulsively on her shoulders.

"What makes you think I care about bending a woman I can simply take?"

"I . . . don't know. I just know that . . . I've not felt anything like this before. This . . . heat, this lassitude."

She heard him suck in a quick, harsh breath. "Damnation," he muttered.

Then he got to his feet and strode off into the dark trees. She lifted her head with an effort, startled out of her languor by the abruptness of his action. The warmth faded, turned to chill as she stared after him.

And wondered why she felt so oddly bereft.

Chapter 8

He would not survive this.

He had survived the bloodiest battles ever seen on this earth, had survived the most brutal father conceivable, but he would buckle if he had to spend one more day in the company of this woman.

He walked along the familiar path beside the stream, staring at the rushing water, hearing the cheerful sound of it, yet thinking of only one thing, the one thing that had occupied his mind so completely for days now.

That his current state was his own fault only made it more impossible to bear.

I will . . . keep my word.

She'd said it, even as her body had gone soft and warm beneath his hands.

Whatever you do . . . to bend women to your will.

Innocent, he thought with a groan, was not the word for it. She truly did not know what she was feeling, thought he was casting some sort of spell over her. Was there no one in the world save he who did not believe in such nonsense? Or was it of comfort to her to believe this, when indeed it was her own untutored body betraying her, when it was her own response to his touch that had caused the heat and lassitude she spoke of?

Why this was suddenly more arousing to him than any skilled whore's tricks, he did not know. He only knew that he regretted every second of every hour of every day since he'd agreed to this fool's bargain with her.

So, he told himself, make her keep her part of it. Simple enough. Order her to lay down for you and take her. Forget your silly idea of forgoing the benefit this fool's deal gives you, and hold her to her word. Better than walking half the night, most of the time like a hunchback because your rod is too damned hard to let you stand up straight.

It must be simply that he'd been so long without a woman. He'd ignored the urges with the same strength of will it had taken to walk away from his entire world. Eventually they had faded, until only occasionally did the old sensations rise within him, and even then they seemed a faint shadow of old needs. But now they were back, with a fierceness beyond anything he had ever felt, or even imagined, burning him alive and making his idea of simply teaching her what he could and letting her return to her precious people as untouched as when she'd left seem as impossible as storming a well-fortified fortress with his bare hands.

He did not understand it, did not understand his own body's betrayal. He told himself it was simply that it had been so long, it was only natural that he react strongly to the first woman he'd been close to, the first he'd even seen in a very long time. That she was so lovely only made the reawakened need more intense.

He didn't know why he hadn't held her to her word yet anyway. While it was true that even at his worst, he'd never taken to raping virgins as the spoils of war, this would hardly be rape. She'd agreed to his terms, and she'd made it clear more than once she expected to have to fulfill them.

Maybe that was it, he thought wearily as he reached the sharp bend in the stream where the water pooled dark and deep. Maybe it was the way she kept looking at him, the question in her eyes, so clearly wondering if he would take her now. Maybe it was the irony of it, that in his mind her sacrifice of her body only proved her nobility; she would surrender her virtue yet remain virtuous, a pretty trick.

He climbed in two long strides to the top of the boulder that hung out over the pool. For days now, he'd been torn like a man on a rack, fighting a battle within himself, aroused beyond anything he'd ever imagined by her courage, determination, spirit, and beauty, yet finding himself reluctant to enforce his claim for those very reasons. Watching her as she accepted every challenge he threw at her, as she conquered every task, filled him with both admiration and desire, a combination he'd never felt before.

And somewhere, deep in his mind, was a voice telling him that the very things he admired were the things that made her far too worthy for such as he.

In sudden haste he pulled off his tunic. The heat he'd finally managed to walk off had begun to pool low and deep in him once more. The images were assailing him as no armed enemy ever had; Jenna, delicate jaw set with determination, hair flying like a wind-whipped flame, eyes sparking with that spirit he'd begun to think indomitable. And with each successive vision his body responded, fiercely, until he groaned aloud at the hot, pulsing ache.

He stripped off his leggings, freeing flesh that had hardened anew with a speed that made him wonder that there was any blood left anywhere else in his body. The chill night air was nothing to the heat building within him. Briefly he thought of using his own hands to ease his need, but the poorness of the substitute held little appeal.

Instead he did as he'd been doing every night; he dove into the icy mountain water. The shock of it was expected but no less jarring. It accomplished in seconds what he came here for; the heat faded as his body sent blood pumping elsewhere to ward off the sudden cold.

He stood there, water to his shoulders, until he was shivering, swimming only when his teeth began to chatter. The internal heat gone, he began to wonder if he was losing his mind. He'd never had an interest in a woman beyond the easing of his immediate needs. The only passions that had ever possessed him were those of a warrior; weapons, tactics, the battles themselves. Even the goals he had fought for, had risked his life for countless times, had been someone else's. He'd never—

"You're risking a fierce fever with these midnight swims, my friend."

Kane slicked his wet hair out of his eyes as he jerked around in the water to look up at the man and the bird who had appeared noiselessly to sit upon the boulder he'd jumped from.

"I'm risking worse without them," Kane muttered.

"The heat is truly so intense?"

"Easy to doubt for one who is not subject to such things," Kane said, his tone sharper than he'd meant it to be.

Tal's eyes went as cold as the water Kane stood in. Colder, indeed, they looked as icy as the snow from which the water came. "I once knew a heat that would put any other to shame," he said in a tone to match his eyes. "I have not forgotten."

Kane stared at his friend. Never had he heard such a tone from him, nor had he ever seen such a look in his eyes. And never had he heard Tal refer to his own past so specifically.

"Tal, I—"

"No." Tal shook his head sharply. And as quickly as that the ice was gone. "It is not important."

"I did not know. I thought you had . . . always been as you are now."

Tal's mouth twisted wryly. "By most measures of time, I have." He gave another shake of his head. "It no longer matters. It was a very long time ago, in another lifetime. An old memory that should be forgotten."

But Tal had not forgotten, Kane thought. No matter how long ago it had been.

"So tell me of your guest. How does the training progress?"

"If you are so curious, you shouldn't have disappeared like an accursed phantom this afternoon."

Tal laughed. He reached out and stroked a hand over the raven's gleaming feathers. "Maud was on the hunt," he said, "and she had no wish to tarry."

"That bird," Kane said, moving at last toward the edge of the pool, "is more hawk than raven."

For the first time since he'd known him, Tal looked genuinely startled. He stared at Kane as if trying to divine some hidden meaning in the observation Kane had meant merely as a joke.

"Can you deny it?" he asked. "She flies and hunts with a hawk's ferocity and silent skill, not a raven's trickery and noise."

"Yes," Tal said softly. "Yes, she does."

Kane wondered at his odd tone, but abandoned the thought as he came out of the water and the night breeze struck his already chilled body. What had seemed essential before seemed overmuch now, and he fought down the shivering.

"Here."

Tal held out something that Kane at first thought was his clothing, but now saw was a rough-textured cloth. Kane looked at him curiously.

"Dry off. Unless you're fond of the battle of getting wet skin into leather leggings."

Kane chuckled and took the cloth. He dried himself, making no effort to hide his scarred, battered body from Tal. The man had seen most of the marks he carried already and had wormed the grim stories behind them out of Kane, for what purpose Kane couldn't guess; Tal had no fondness for warfare, yet he seemed intrigued by the tales. And he had to admit he'd felt oddly lightened himself by the telling.

"Is it truly the woman who has you seeking out icy baths in the middle of the night?"

" 'Tis myself," Kane said as he yanked his clothes back on. "I've become a raving idiot, nothing less."

"Hmm," Tal said thoughtfully. "I hadn't noticed."

Kane grimaced with wry humor despite his inner turmoil.

"What has you so tormented?"

Kane hesitated. He did not wish Tal to know of the cold bargain he'd struck with Jenna. He'd tried to tell himself she'd forced it upon him with her refusal to give up, that she'd backed him into a corner by refusing to take off running as she should have at the very idea of letting herself be used by a man like him, but all his fine arguments came back to the simple fact that he hadn't been able to withstand the pleas of one small woman, and had gotten himself into this muddle through his own weakness.

"What is it, Kane? She . . . refuses you?"

Kane made a choking sound that was half laugh, half groan. The words burst from him before he could stop them. "No. She simply waits, watching me like a frightened deer, waiting for me to take her as we agreed."

Tal went very still. "Agreed?"

"Why else would I be so torn? The solution to my problem is within my grasp, yet I hesitate to take it."

"The solution?"

"Jenna."

"I . . . see."

Tal sounded odd, disturbed. Kane finished tying the lacing of his tunic with sharp movements, not able to meet Tal's eyes.

"I told you I was a bastard," he said gruffly, reaching for his belt. "Now you know 'tis true in all senses of the word."

"Yes, you told me."

"I am Kane, the most ruthless warrior of them all, the coldest, most unfeeling bastard alive, just as the legends say. Was it not you who said most legends are built upon truth?"

He put the belt around his waist and jerked it tight, fastening it as if speed were imperative as he went on mercilessly.

"Well, that is the truth of Kane, Tal. He is as bad as the legends paint him, and he will never change. He is the kind of man who would lay waste to an entire land, wreak havoc on people who have done no more than get in his way, and leave the dead behind him to rot." He settled his dagger in its sheath with a short, sharp, angry motion.

"Are you through scourging yourself yet?" Tal asked, his tone strangely mild.

"Not nearly." Kane made himself face his friend now, thinking it quite likely it would be for the last time; Tal was not the kind of man who would approve of what he'd done. But perhaps it was time Tal knew just what kind of man he was dealing with. Tal was looking at him with that intensity that was so unnerving, nothing of his thoughts showing in his eyes.

"Kane is the kind of man who would demand of an innocent the one payment that should never be forced, who would trade lessons in war for the purity of her body, because he was too feeble-willed to simply send her away as he should, and too feebleminded to realize she would call his bluff."

Something changed in Tal's eyes at those last words, and Kane could have sworn he saw a glint of that odd golden glow he'd seen the night Tal had found him in the stream.

"So that's how it happened," Tal murmured.

Kane answered only with a grunt of disgust as he bent to tug on his boots.

"It was a ruse, wasn't it?" Tal said softly. "You offered her a trade—your lessons for . . . herself—that you believed she would refuse."

"She should have," Kane muttered. "She should have fled like a rabbit scenting a wolf."

"But she did not."

"No."

"Why?"

Kane slammed his heel down into his right boot. "Because she is a fool. Because she is blind. Because she is too witless to take care of herself."

"Because she loves others above herself? Because she sees too clearly what will happen to them? Because she is so desperate she cannot think of her own welfare?"

Tal countered his accusations one by one, in a voice barely above a whisper.

Kane straightened slowly, staring. "You speak as if you know her."

"I do. As well as I once knew another, so like her . . ."

With a short, jerky motion unlike any Kane had ever seen him make before, Tal turned away. And Tal, who was always in such perfect control of his body, who never made a false move, was never in anything but perfect balance, nearly slipped as he jumped down from the rock.

He steadied himself, still looking away, but Kane

sensed somehow that if he could see his friend's eyes, he would see that same shadowed look he had seen before, the look of a deeply buried memory that brought great pain. 'Twas that Tal was thinking of, Kane thought, not Jenna herself. If the two had truly met, Tal would hardly be avoiding her now.

Maud, as if sensing something wrong, gave a quick flap of her wings and alighted on Tal's left shoulder, something Kane had also never seen before. The bird pecked at Tal's ear, so gently it was more of a nudge.

Tal took a deep breath, then whispered something to the raven Kane could not hear. The bird's head bobbed, but she did not leave his shoulder.

"I'm sorry," Kane said.

Tal's head came up. Any trace of tension had vanished, replaced by his usual mocking grin. "The mighty Kane is sorry? That's enough to worry a man, imagining what that would take."

For once, Kane refused to let himself be diverted. He wasn't certain why. It was not a warrior's habit to make friends. The cost ran far too high. And there were few men he'd met he would care to call friend anyway. Especially the kind of friend privy to the sort of emotional strain Kane hated to even admit to.

But Tal was . . . different. He'd always been different. And although he didn't want to admit this any more than the other, he couldn't deny that Tal had a habit of turning up at the times when that strain he didn't care to acknowledge was at its worst. He wasn't sure exactly what had happened the other night, wasn't sure he wanted to know, he did know he owed Tal for it. And he'd never thought to have a chance to repay him. Other than the occasional flicker of darkness in his eyes, Tal had seemed unaffected by such things. Until now.

"I'm sorry," he said again, "for whatever you were thinking of just now."

For a long, quiet moment Tal just looked at him. There was nothing of mockery in his face, nothing of that mysterious glint in his eyes, nothing of the mask in his expression. And in that moment, for the first time, Kane thought he was seeing the real man Tal was. Or had been, once.

"Who are you, Tal?" he asked.

"You know who I am. Better than anyone."

Kane looked at him steadily. "Then who *were* you?"

"That," Tal said, "no longer matters. That man doesn't exist anymore. He hasn't for a very long time."

Kane went very still. After a moment, he said slowly, "That's why you understand, isn't it? You've . . . left yourself behind just as I have. Or have tried to."

Tal's dark brows rose. "You've come a long way."

Kane grimaced. "Not far enough."

"Tell me, were you this critical of the men you led, or only of yourself?"

"A leader is supposed to be harder on himself than anyone."

"But you lead no one now, why continue?"

Kane lifted a brow. "If you think I judge myself too harshly, you are misguided, my friend."

Tal shrugged. " 'Twould not be the first time."

Kane drew back a little, surprised. Tal usually accused him of doing just that, being too merciless with himself. He hadn't realized until just now how much he'd come to count on Tal's quiet assurances that he wasn't the devil most believed him to be. That he wasn't the devil he thought himself to be most of the time.

The answer came to him quickly; it was what he'd done to Jenna, no doubt, that had changed Tal's mind. Just as he'd feared, their friendship could not withstand such a thing. Tal was clever, quick, strong, and possessed of those unique gifts that made Kane uneasy, but above all, he was a gentle man, and he would not care for the mistreatment of innocents.

"I warned you," Kane said flatly, turning away, knowing that once more what he was had cost him something he valued.

"We have both paid a heavy price for what we once were, my friend. It makes for a bond not easily broken."

Kane whirled back around at the unerring accuracy of Tal's words and found himself facing the same smiling, faintly amused Tal he had always known.

"And you swear you are not a mind reader?"

"Is it so strange, that two men who have had such common things in their lives, should think in similar ways?"

He had no answer for that, so he stayed silent. The raven made a sharp noise, then left Tal's shoulder to vanish into the night with a minimum of fuss, and Kane knew Tal was back to normal. And that he would soon disappear with little more fuss than the bird.

"I wish you luck in your current predicament, Kane, my friend. You will need it, I believe."

Kane watched him go, and stood for a long time after, pondering the mystery of his friend, and the wonder that he still, apparently, was a friend.

And the fact that he had little doubt Tal's last words were absolutely true.

It was the first time she'd been out on the mountain alone, and Jenna was savoring it even as the apprehension played counterpoint to the thrill. She'd never hunted for food in her life; what if she failed? She'd only been shooting the small, lightweight crossbow Kane had helped her make for four days now, although the constant minor ache in her arms and shoulders made it seem much longer.

True, she had made progress, she had moved from stationary targets to ones Kane tossed rather quickly, and he himself had said she had a good eye, but firing at a living, moving animal was quite a different prospect. Not to mention her apprehension at killing another creature so . . . directly.

She smiled ruefully at the irony of worrying about slaying a rabbit when her heart was crying out for her to slaughter those who had slaughtered her family and friends. It still cried out, despite knowing that Kane was right, that they could have no hope of vengeance; saving what was left was the best they could hope for.

She shivered, but knew it had little to do with chill, or even her own bloody thoughts, and everything to do with Kane. Still he had not called upon her to honor their agreement, and the waiting was making her more nervous than she had ever been in her life. And she knew as well that a great deal of her uneasy state was because of the new tack Kane seemed to be taking; every night, as he had the day she'd climbed the cliff, he knelt behind her to ease the stiffness out of her weary muscles with his strong yet gentle hands.

And every night, she fell under the warm, languorous spell he seemed to weave over her, until she felt as good as boneless in his grasp.

Boneless, but not nerveless. In fact, when Kane touched her in that slow, stroking way, she discovered nerves she'd never known she had, nerves that first tingled, then sparked, then burned, filling her with sensations she'd never felt, never known it was possible to feel.

A shiver rippled through her as she remembered last night, when she'd felt a new kind of creeping warmth, and a tension utterly unlike that of her weary body, as he'd massaged her into that limp, slack state of relaxation, then slid his hands forward to gently cup her breasts. She'd been so softened by his touch it had taken her a moment to realize an entirely new kind of heat had begun to pulse beneath his hands, and before she realized it, a low moan had escaped her. In that same moment, before she had instinctively stiffened and pulled away, he had rubbed his fingertips gently over her nipples, sending little darts of fire shooting through her, making her suck in a shocked little breath.

By the time her body had gone rigid with that shock, he had released her.

"Are there no men in your clan," he muttered, his voice low and rough, "that you remain untouched?"

Before she could gather her oddly scattered thoughts to answer that the problem was she herself, not the men of Hawk Glade, he had gone, off on another of his nighttime excursions. This morning he had not mentioned anything, merely sent her down the mountain with the small crossbow, saying they would eat the results of her hunt, or not at all. Jenna wished he would just take her and get it over with, before the anticipation drove her mad.

And found herself wondering if it would truly be so bad, as long as his touch remained as gentle as it had been.

A sudden commotion and the sound of wings beating the air stopped her in her tracks. Quickly, she notched an arrow, her eyes searching the trees to her right, from where the sound had come. A flock, at the least, she thought; from the noise—

And there they were, pheasant, several of them with their distinctive long tails and their odd, coughlike cries, the males bright against the backdrop of trees, the females a muted contrast. Jenna wondered what had flushed them from their hiding place, and breathed a small prayer of thanks as she drew back the bowstring, that it hadn't been quail; she had little faith in her ability to bring down one of the smaller birds.

She never fired.

A shout, a man's shout, from close by, startled her into nearly letting the arrow fly wildly.

What had flushed them from their hiding place?

Her own thoughts came back to her, along with Kane's stern admonitions to always be aware of what was around her, and to never concentrate so much on one thing that she lost sight of all else.

She crouched down behind a large, low bush, her heart pounding; she had done exactly that, been concentrating so intently that she'd overlooked the possible danger even when it had crossed her mind. She wondered if perhaps Kane had followed her, keeping out of sight among the trees. She even began to hope it was him.

She heard another shout, of a man's name, William, she thought. Then an answering bellow. Both voices were male, neither Kane's. And then, in the first voice came a chilling command.

"Kill him!"

There was a moment of unearthly silence, then it was broken by the harsh cry of a raven. A cry that was almost human in its rage. A cry Jenna could almost swear was tinged with fear.

Chapter 9

Jenna resisted the urge to run; she could no longer afford the luxury of self-preservation, and she might as well accept the fact now. Should it be true that Kane had followed her, it could well be him in trouble just beyond those trees, as impossible as that seemed.

Keeping her small crossbow at the ready, she began to move toward the sounds, keeping low and moving with as little noise as she could manage, as Kane had taught her. She heard the raven again, closer now, and crouched even lower.

"Watch him! He'll try some sorcerer's trick!" The first man again, she thought.

"Then *you* kill him," the second voice said, somewhat fearfully.

"What's wrong with you?" the first man sneered. "Are you afraid of him? Look at him, he has only a dagger, and no armor at all!"

"If he's a sorcerer, what need has he for armor?"

The image flashed through her mind, Kane holding a plump pheasant like those she had just seen.

. . . courtesy of the local wizard.

The rest of their exchange echoed as clearly.

You have . . . a wizard?

No. Just a friend who is far too clever.

Could it be Kane's friend in danger here? She crept forward a little more.

"If I am truly a sorcerer, all the armor you wear will not help you."

Jenna stopped suddenly, hunkering down behind the branches of a spreading plant, wary of what looked like thistles. That voice, she thought. It sounded familiar. Not just the voice itself, but that faintly amused tone, that of a man entertained by something only he could see. She dared a prickly seed head and peeked through the bushes.

Two men, big, bulky, draped in some kind of metal fabric that appeared dull with age and wear, and armed with rather unclean swords they had drawn and held at the ready, had a third man backed up against a tree.

"And if I am not," the trapped man said easily, "you have no reason to kill me."

He did not look, Jenna thought, like a man whose life was in danger. Smaller than his hulking adversaries, he nevertheless looked wiry and strong in simple leather tunic and leggings much like those Kane wore, and she thought his size might prove to be deceptive. He leaned against the tree as if casually passing the time, one booted foot drawn up and resting flat against the trunk. He wore no armor, and no weapon that she could see except for a small dagger with a carved hilt at his narrow waist. His hair, brushing his shoulders, was dark, shot with silver at the temples. And his mouth was curved upward at the corners in the barest hint of a smile.

"Who but a wizard would have such a creature at his beck and call?"

The second man she'd heard speak gestured with his blade, and only then did Jenna see the black bird perched on a branch just above the third man's shoulders.

"And the damned thing clawed at my eyes!" exclaimed the first man.

"Aye, I saw it," the other agreed. "He is evil, in league with the devil."

"I swear he set that bird on me!"

"She does as she chooses," the man leaning against the tree said.

What *was* it about his voice? Jenna crept forward to get a better view. In the moment she did the man against the tree went very still. Slowly, as if to avoid drawing the armed men's attention, he glanced her way. And stared as if he could see right through to her hiding place, as if he knew exactly where she was.

Jenna's breath caught. Those eyes. She knew those eyes, knew that fierce intensity. But pinned by it, she could not think, could not remember.

He looked away at last, and she let out a breath she hadn't been aware of holding. She felt a little dizzy; she didn't know this man, she knew she did not, but for a moment . . .

" 'Tis time for this to be done," he said in a tone that belied his position against the two bigger, armed and armored men.

"You have the right of that. The devil's minions must be destroyed," the first man, the bigger of the two snarled. He lifted his sword. "William!"

The other man closed in, his sword held at a lower level. Even she could see their plan, and guessed they had worked it together before; the smaller of the two in close to keep their victim from moving, possibly reaching for the one weapon he had, the larger wielding his vicious blade in an arcing blow that would cleave the man in two.

She didn't hesitate. She hated bullies and doubted Kane had so many friends he could spare this one. She stood, forgoing the protection of her hidden position. She lifted her small weapon and took careful aim.

In the instant she let the short arrow fly, the scene erupted into chaos. The black bird gave a murderous cry and dived at the smaller man. He careened back. The bigger man, whose sword had begun to descend, shouted as if in pain, whirling in her direction. The bird's flitting, clawing, noisy attack on his companion drew her attention, and as the man reeled toward her she quickly notched another arrow.

She didn't need it. Something very odd happened. There was a sound, a sharp, piercing whistle. The raven answered, withdrawing from the fray to circle above with a flap of glistening black wings. Both of the armed men were staring at the bird as if they were seeing something far more terrifying than a relatively small but admittedly defiant and wrathful raven.

Only then did she see her arrow had struck the bigger man in the forearm, the arm that wielded his heavy sword.

"Go. Now."

It was their intended victim, the man she had feared to see bleeding his life's blood into the ground, giving an order as if he were holding the swords, as if he wore the armor. It was a voice that held the ring of a steel stronger than that of their blades, and both men seemed to know it. Although he still stood there, armed with only a small dagger he had never drawn, the men went pale.

And ran. As if the hounds of Hades were at their heels.

There was another whistle, an odd up-and-down tremolo; she saw him do it this time. The raven remained silent but flew off in the direction the fleeing men had taken.

Then he turned to look at her.

Slowly, as he walked toward her, his eyes went over her with an interest and intensity that was obvious. Yet she felt nothing of male heat in it, only curiosity, the curiosity of a man seeing something long heard of but only now seen up close. When he stopped in front of her, his gaze lingered for an instant on her hair, her eyes, and at last on the small crossbow she carried.

" 'Tis a small weapon, to take on two such as they," he said mildly.

"I could say the same," she said, nodding toward the dagger. "Although your friend is a formidable opponent."

"My friend?" He looked puzzled for a moment. "Kane is with you, then?" He glanced about as if he couldn't believe he hadn't seen the big warrior.

Her mouth quirked. "I meant the feathered one."

His gaze shot back to her face. And then, suddenly, he grinned. It was a sparkling, infectious expression, and she found herself smiling back. He was a very comely man, and he moved with a grace she'd rarely seen. Was it something about these mountains that bred exceptionally fine-looking men? she wondered. Those two who had fled not withstanding, of course.

"Ah," he said. "Maud. She is a valiant creature, is she not? And loyal. As are you, Jenna of the clan Hawk."

The fact that he knew who she was confirmed her guess that this was Kane's friend. She shrugged.

"I am not. I merely have had quite enough of late of big, blustering men who trample those weaker or smaller or less well armed."

He nodded thoughtfully. "Still, they could have turned on you, hurt, or even killed you. 'Twas courageous of you to risk yourself so. And for a stranger. I thank you for your fine shooting."

She hadn't thought it courageous, she'd only done it. Without thinking. "No thanks are necessary." Her mouth quirked. "Besides, I was aiming for his knee, in hopes of making him fall."

He chuckled, an odd light coming into his eyes.

Those eyes that seemed so familiar to her. "Whatever your aim, you achieved the goal. And I do thank you."

"You are Kane's friend, are you not?" she asked.

"Who has lost his manners," he said suddenly. "My apologies."

With a sweeping, grand gesture he bowed at the waist. "I am Talysn ap Bendigeidfran, at your service."

Jenna blinked. "Tal—uh . . ." she began, her brows furrowed.

"Talysn ap Bendigeidfran," he repeated, grinning now.

She shook her head. "Are you . . . named for someone?"

"The last part is for my feathered friend, as you put it. It means blessed raven. The first, for some*thing*, more accurately. But it doesn't exist yet, so there's no need for you to learn it."

"Oh." She was feeling a bit lost; he wasn't making much sense.

"Just do as Kane does," he suggested. "Call me Tal."

His humor was irresistible, and she smiled at him. He *was* charming, if a little nonsensical. "All right. Tal."

"And I do thank you. 'Tis not often I find someone willing to take such a chance for someone they do not know."

As the memory of what had happened after she'd fired came back to her, she eyed him a little warily. "I'm not at all certain you needed my help. Or anyone's."

"That," he said, waving a hand in negation, "doesn't matter. What does is that you were willing to risk your life to give it. I shall have to think of a proper way to repay you."

"That is not necessary—"

"But it is," he insisted. "To me. 'Tis worth more than you know to an old man like me to find one of such bravery and generous spirit."

"Old?" Jenna stared at him; he was hardly that, despite the gray that graced his temples.

Tal blinked, looking for the moment like nothing more than a small, muddy boy caught by his mother.

"Do not mind that," he said, rather hastily. " 'Tis you I'm speaking of. A rarity such as you, in this world, should be treasured, fostered. This kind of courage should be honored and revered, acknowledged in some appropriate manner."

He looked thoughtful, while Jenna blushed at his flowery praise. The man had a tongue sweet enough to match his looks, she thought. "Please, you must stop."

"Modesty as well," he said. "It suits you. There will come a time when such a mixture will be rare indeed. And the world will be a sadder, sorrier place because of it. 'Twould be a pity if this particular pedigree for courage were to die out . . ."

He looked suddenly thoughtful, and Jenna wondered if Kane's friend was . . . quite right in the head.

He laughed. Loud and joyously, like a man who has just made a wondrous discovery.

"That is it!" he exclaimed.

Jenna resisted the urge to back up a step; she knew somehow this man was no danger to her, yet he was making her exceedingly nervous.

"What is it?" she asked warily.

"The perfect recompense for your bravery in coming to my aid."

"I have told you, I don't wish—"

"Of course. If you sought it, I would not give it."

"Give . . . what?"

"A gift that will extend down into time eternal."

Jenna drew back slightly. "Are you sure you were not injured?"

He laughed again. "I'm worrying you, aren't I? I am sorry, Jenna. But you will see that you need not be concerned. It is a most befitting gift, I think."

She wondered if there was any point in repeating her assurances that she neither wanted nor expected anything from him. Before she could decide, he startled her with a quiet question.

"What is most important to you, Jenna of the clan Hawk?"

She did not have to think to answer that. "My people. They are dying, being slaughtered. That is why I am here, with Kane."

"And would it ease your pain to know that they will never die? That no matter what happens now, or in the future, there will *always* be a descendent of the Hawks walking this earth?"

"I . . . of course it would. But no one can promise that." The ever-present ache settled onto her heart anew. "No one can even promise they will be alive when I get back."

"That is true," Tal said softly. "But you, Jenna, your line, your blood . . . that I can promise."

She lifted her gaze to his eyes. Something glinted in the depths, something golden and glowing and infinitely mysterious. Changeable eyes, she thought vaguely, caught and held by them as surely as if she'd been gripped by one of Latham's snares. And in that moment, if he told her man could fly, she would believe him.

"I would trade it," she said in hushed tones, "for the lives of my people."

"I know that you would." His voice was so incredibly gentle her heart ached. "But I cannot. I haven't the power to save so many. But this one thing I can give you, Jenna. Your line will continue. You will be the beginning, and your heart, your soul, your courage, your blood will continue in an unbroken line, forever. Should fate step in and reduce your line to but one, it shall still go on. I promise you this."

Jenna caught her breath, startled despite the hypnotic effect of his eyes and voice. "You know? That I am . . . the last?"

"I know."

"How can you promise such a thing?"

"That does not matter. Just believe that I can."

Perhaps he *was* a wizard, she thought, her brain feeling oddly foggy. Or perhaps just a lunatic Kane had befriended.

"I . . . how?"

"You don't understand, yet." His dark brows furrowed. "Nor will those who come after you. So there must be a way," he said, as if musing aloud, "for those who are the last of the line to know, to understand what they must do to assure it continues. Something to guide them along the right path . . ."

Lunatic, she decided, now that he was no longer looking at her and she wasn't held captive by that incredible gaze. A lunatic talking nonsense.

He nodded sharply, suddenly. "I will make it so."

She drew back slightly. He looked at her again, and Jenna braced to look away; she didn't like the fogginess that had come over her when he'd been staring at her before. But the golden glint that had held her so rapt was gone now; he looked like any other man. Any other charming, handsome man with a devilish grin, she amended silently. She could but hope that grin only appeared devilish.

"Do not fear, Jenna. I promise you there is no evil involved here. Only my thanks, for your courage."

Startled by his perception, she looked at him doubtfully. He smiled.

"I see you are ill at ease. I will say no more, except that when the time comes, you will know. You will understand."

He cocked his head to one side suddenly, then smiled. A moment later, the raven appeared, wings flared as she slowed to land with a small flourish of feathers on Tal's shoulder.

"They are long gone," he assured Jenna.

She eyed first the bird, then the man, with equal amounts of wariness.

"She would not have come back," Tal explained, "had they not been well away."

That seemed a simple-enough explanation, and she supposed a bird as clever as the raven could be taught such things.

"Come," he said. "I will walk back with you. Oh," he added, bending and reaching behind him, "you might as well take these."

He held out a pair of the rabbits she had never even thought of trying to hunt; their darting quickness was far beyond her fledgling skill with the crossbow. She eyed him curiously for a moment; she hadn't seen the animals until this moment, yet he'd obviously had them close by.

" 'Tis only fair," he said. "You would have had one of those pheasants had you not stopped to save my life."

She flushed, entirely uncertain that she'd done what he said. Or that she would have had one of the pheasants, either.

He glanced at the bow she'd slung over her shoulder as they began to walk. "A nice bit of work."

"I . . . yes," she agreed, thankful for the less unsettling topic. "Kane is . . . well versed in such things."

"Yes."

"You progress quickly, to be handling weapons so soon."

" 'Tis not quickly enough," she said. The nightmare of what was happening in Hawk Glade rarely left her, it remained hovering at every moment. Except the moments when Kane's hands were on her. She could think of nothing but his touch, then, and for that alone she welcomed the contact. And the fact that her heart sped up at simply the thought of him touching her meant nothing other than that she was on a razor's edge, waiting—

"And do you progress elsewhere as quickly?"

She smothered a gasp and gaped at the man beside her. Had he read her thoughts? Was he in truth the wizard Kane had jokingly called him, or the sorcerer those men had judged him in their fear?

"I mean," he said calmly, "in the lessons of tactics, of course."

"Oh."

She felt herself flush, and averted her face. But even looking away, she could still clearly see that moment when something of realization had flickered in those changeable eyes, as if he'd not only known of her bargain with Kane, but had guessed it had not been fulfilled, and she had somehow confirmed it for him. But he could not know. Unless . . .

She stole a sideways glance at him. "Those men . . . they called you sorcerer."

"Yes." He shrugged. " 'Tis a common habit among the fearful when confronting anything they do not understand."

"Kane called you the local wizard."

Tal's brows rose. "Did he?"

"In jest," she hastened to add.

"You're certain of that?"

Her forehead creased. "That it was in jest? Yes, I believe so. He very quickly denied it, saying you were but a friend who is far too clever."

Tal nodded, as if he'd expected that. "Kane . . . finds it hard to have faith in anything he cannot see or touch."

He has so little faith left, in anything, but most partic-

ularly himself. 'Tis like a candle on a windy night, a very fragile light.

The storyteller's words rang in her mind, and it suddenly came to her, what had been nagging at her since she'd first seen this man. He reminded her of the silver-haired man who had so often held her rapt, who had given her a quiet support that gave her a strength that amazed her, who had appeared to her in that oddly vivid dream like no dream she'd ever had. . . .

It was the eyes, she thought. He had the storyteller's changeable eyes, the misty green of the forest one moment, then glinting oddly golden the next. And the storyteller had his way of moving, with a tightly knit grace and balance that belied his age.

"Jenna?"

She'd been staring at him, she realized. "I'm sorry. It's just that . . . you remind me of someone."

Something flashed across his face that looked oddly like wariness. And the raven shifted upon his shoulder, as if she'd felt it in him. "Oh?"

"Your father . . . does he still live?"

The wariness vanished, and she saw a split second of pain in his expression before he shook his head. "He died a very long time ago."

The pain was gone, his expression neutral now, but she did not doubt that she had seen it, and she regretted having caused it. "I'm sorry," she said. "It was foolish. The storyteller never mentioned a son, but I thought perhaps . . ."

She let her voice trail off, feeling worse than foolish. They walked in silence for a while, until the raven made a harsh cry and stretched out her wings. Tal looked at the bird, then shrugged.

"Go," he said.

The bird lifted off his shoulder with a strong flap of her wings and was gone. Jenna looked at him questioningly.

" 'Tis not wise to approach the camp of a warrior like Kane unannounced. His reactions are . . . swift."

"I've noticed," Jenna said wryly. She glanced in the direction the bird had flown. "The bird is your . . . messenger?"

He glanced at her, that faintly amused expression back on his face. "Thinking I'm that sorcerer they called me?"

"Are you?" she asked simply.

He studied her for a moment. "The thought does not seem to bother you overmuch."

"I live in a place where we are given gifts daily that have no explanation most can accept. We have learned to accept what some would fear, because with it comes a peace that has been unbroken for generations."

"Until now."

"Until now," she agreed. "But it will come again. I will see to it. Or I will die in the effort."

"You will not die, Jenna," he said softly. "You will live, and your children after you, and their children, and their children's children. It will go on, Jenna. Forever."

He said it with such certainty, with such conviction, that for an instant she saw it as he said, an unbroken line, descending down over the ages, into a future shrouded with the mist of the unknown, yet in this moment as clear as any sunny day in Hawk Glade.

It will go on, Jenna. Forever.

It was a tempting vision, and she felt a powerful urge to believe.

But she knew that all the believing in mystical promises in the world wouldn't save her people. Only she could do that.

They walked out of the trees into the small clearing near the cave. Kane was there, tossing a scrap of something to the raven, who snatched it eagerly.

"She's a bit fierce today," Kane said, his eyes still

on the bird as he rose. "What has her stirred up so? Did you—"

He stopped as he at last looked their way. Jenna saw the surprise in his face and guessed that he had expected Tal alone. He looked at them assessingly, and something else showed in his gaze for a moment, something she couldn't recognize. She glanced at Tal, who again wore that faintly amused expression as he looked at his friend.

"You look a bit fierce yourself, my friend," Tal said to Kane. "And you have no reason. You should know that better than anyone."

Jenna had no idea what Tal meant, but Kane clearly did; to her amazement he flushed. He looked away, then back at them uncomfortably. At last his gaze flicked to the rabbits she held.

"I thought you were going after pheasant," he said.

"I was. These are not from my hunt," she said honestly.

Kane looked at Tal and frowned. "Doing it for her will not teach her what she needs to learn."

"She saved my life," Tal said smoothly. "It seemed the fair thing to do."

Kane blinked. "She what?"

His gaze shifted to Jenna, and she blushed. " 'Twas nothing, really, I—"

"I beg to differ," Tal said with some humor. "My life may not be worth much in the grand scheme of things, and there are times when I'd as soon it be done, but this was not one of them."

Jenna's blush became a flush of embarrassment. "I did not mean that, I only—"

"I know," Tal said.

"You're serious," Kane said, staring at them both. "What happened?"

"I will tell you the tale," Tal said, "for if I leave it

to the lady, she will belittle her part in it out of existence."

Jenna knew she couldn't listen, Tal was so overly grateful she would be self-conscious beyond bearing. She muttered something about cleaning the rabbits and retreated.

"You can quit looking so stormy, my friend," she heard Tal say as she walked away. "Were I to ever be affected by a woman again, I would hope it would be someone like Jenna, but 'tis not likely, so you have no reason to be jealous."

Jenna nearly stumbled as Kane muttered something in reply that she couldn't hear. She recovered and hastened out of sight, and more importantly, out of hearing.

Jealous? Kane? Over her? And his own friend?

It was impossible, she told herself. Tal was mistaken. Kane had not even made a move to collect on their bargain. He did not even want her in that way enough to take what she had promised, so he could hardly care enough to be jealous. She doubted he would ever care about a woman in that way, enough to be jealous.

Except, she thought, as a man might perhaps care about any possession he held as his. And she had agreed to be just that, his, for the duration of her time here. Could that be it, that regardless of whether he asserted his own claim, he looked upon her as his exclusive possession? To the point of expressing his displeasure to the only friend Jenna had ever seen or heard him mention?

Besides, as well favored as he was, the beguiling Tal did not have the effect on her that Kane did; he was beautiful, but he did not make her stomach knot or her heart race. She was not sure what that meant, only that it was Kane alone who made her feel so.

Perhaps she was not as free of that kind of passion as she had thought.

The thoughts tumbled around in her head in a seemingly endless circle as she prepared the rabbits, only vaguely wondering what Tal hunted with, since there was no sign of a wound on either animal.

When she was done, and she thought she could at last face them with no sign of her foolish thoughts showing, she walked back around the side of the rocky bluff that held the cave.

Kane was alone.

Jenna glanced around, but there was no sign of the rather mysterious Talysn ap Bendigeidfran.

"Tal . . . he will not be joining us?"

"He will not." Kane sounded very odd, and he would not look at her.

"I thought . . . he would stay. They are his rabbits, after all."

His head came up. "You risked your life for him. You did not even know him. Why?"

"It is as I told him. I have had more than my fill of bullies of late."

"Is that all?"

She looked at him for a long moment, wondering what he expected her to say. His expression was unreadable, but his eyes were shadowed to the color of a stormy day, as if some demon were riding him hard. At last, she gave him the simple truth.

"I guessed he was the friend you spoke of."

"You expect me to believe you risked your life . . . because he is my friend?"

Something in his tone stung, and she drew herself up straight. "I don't see a wealth of them gathered around you," she said rather sharply. "I thought perhaps you might be loath to lose this one."

He closed his eyes for a moment, and she almost regretted her tone. Then an oddly regretful expression crept over his face. He opened his eyes and looked at her.

"He is my only friend. If the truth be known, probably the only true friend I have ever had. I thank you."

Taken aback by his gentle tone, and aching at the sadness his words caused in her, Jenna spoke quietly.

"You are welcome. Although I'm not convinced he truly needed what little help I rendered."

"Tal is . . . uniquely talented," Kane admitted. He eyed her speculatively. "He said . . . you did well."

"I hit my target," she said, then added honestly, "although not the exact part of it I was aiming for."

"Sometimes that is enough."

"I thought you would disapprove of my failure," she said, genuinely surprised.

"Your courage did not fail you. That is something that cannot be taught."

"I . . . thank you."

"You are . . . enough woman to do what you must," he said, an undertone in his voice she could not name. But when she looked into his eyes, when she saw the heat there, she knew what it meant. "Tonight," he said, his voice thick, rough.

She lowered her eyes, and a shiver ran through her as she realized the waiting was at an end.

Chapter 10

She was looking at him, Kane thought wryly, as if she expected to be jumped at any moment. Every time he moved, she tensed; when she nearly gasped as he reached for his cup of water, which sat near her right elbow, he wondered if he should reconsider.

As if, he thought in sour self-realization, he could. As if he hadn't already spent days on end fighting a raging need to take her without further delay. As if he didn't know perfectly well he could not beat his inflamed body into submission one more time. It had taken every bit of his will, more than it had ever taken him to fight any battle on the field, to win the battle this woman caused in him every time he heard her soft, melodic voice, every time he watched her move, every time he looked into blue eyes more vivid than the polished stones he'd once seen, reputedly from some faraway potentate's treasury.

He'd never been a man to value possessions. He'd had a horse or two he'd held a certain fondness for, and the sword that old man in the northern lands had made for him was of such perfect balance he had guarded it with care before he had buried it along with all the trappings of his old life, but for the kind of trinkets other men seemed to prize, he cared nothing.

And never, ever, had he felt possessive of a woman.

Until today.

Until Jenna had walked out of the trees with Tal close by her side, and he'd been seized with a possessiveness unlike anything he'd ever known. So strong was it that, for that moment, he had felt anger toward the one man he called friend. So strong was it, that that man had seen it clearly, and felt compelled to remind him he had no interest in such things.

He would have been ashamed, had he not been so astonished at the feeling.

It was then that he knew the game he played was over. He would wait no longer. He could wait no longer. And if his soul was damned to eternal flames for it, so be it. He was no doubt headed that way already; what was one more eon in Hades against all he already had in store?

And the moment he'd decided, his body had raged to life with a fierceness and speed that had left him breathless. He craved this spirited woman as he'd never craved anything in his life except the peace he'd retreated to this mountain to find. And at this moment, watching the glow of the flames dancing on her hair, seeing the courageous tilt of her chin, the soft fullness of her mouth, the fearlessness that shone in her eyes despite her obvious nervousness, he wasn't sure he wouldn't throw away the one to have the other.

He tossed the remnants of his meal into the fire. Jenna jumped yet again.

"Must you do that?" he snapped.

"Do . . . what?"

"Jump every time I move."

"I . . ." She looked down at her hands, folded tightly in her lap. "I'm sorry."

Exasperation filled him. "Is the thought of fulfilling your part of the bargain so horrible?"

She looked up at him then. "No. In truth, I am . . . glad."

Kane blinked. This, he had not expected. He had to swallow before he could speak. "Glad?"

"The waiting . . . has been difficult."

"You are telling *me* this?" he muttered.

"I would rather . . . have it over, than to have it shadowing my every step."

He wasn't sure he liked the way she'd put that. "I know I'm hardly every maiden's dream." He just stopped himself from raising a hand to his scarred cheek. "A sword slash took care of what little I had of pleasing looks—"

"No!" Her interruption was quick enough, and full enough of astonishment as to be oddly warming. "The scar, it does not mar you, 'tis only a minor thing."

"It is but one of many," he said warningly, with an effort keeping his pleasure at her words from showing in his voice. "And the sum of them all is not a pretty sight."

"You are a great warrior," she said simply. "What is more natural than that you bear the marks of one?"

Right now he did not feel like a great anything, except perhaps a fool. He stared, as he never did, into the fire.

"Tal seems . . . an honorable man," she said tentatively.

"He is," Kane said, wondering with some irritation why she'd felt compelled to bring him up now.

"He would never . . . tamper with what is yours."

His head came up swiftly. His eyes searched her face, looking for some clue to her meaning. He found none, only a woman with soft lips and vivid eyes watching, waiting.

"Are you?" he finally asked, though he tried not to.

"Some men feel women have no honor. They are wrong. I gave you a promise. I will honor it."

She looked up at him, her expression calm. He'd seen that look before, on the face of a man facing execution for refusing to tell the warlord Kane served the hiding place of his fellow villagers. He scrambled to his feet, startled and irritated simultaneously by the anger that shot through him.

"Do they train you in self-sacrifice, these cherished people of yours?"

She didn't quail at his anger or his swift movement, merely held his gaze steadily.

"No. But they teach the sacredness of a promise made, that it must be kept. That your word once given is the measure of who you are."

She'd told him many such things, the teachings of a wise, gentle people, people who had lived across the years in a way he would never have thought possible for men, in peace, in mutual respect and honor. At first he'd thought her lying, trying to win his favor. But he'd soon seen that lying was something she'd not learned to do; any time she tried she gave herself away with lowered eyes and the color in her cheeks. Then he'd thought her words merely tales, perhaps invented by her storyteller, but he'd come to realize these were not fantastic tales of some fanciful, perfect community, but merely the things she was used to, had grown up with.

As if something in the way he was looking at her pulled at her, she rose slowly to her feet. Her eyes never left his face, her composure never wavered. It was as if what she'd said were in fact true; she would rather he take her now, rather have it over, than to have it hovering.

The fire that shot through him at the thought of easing his body's needs right now nearly wiped any misgivings away. He could not expect her to feel any differently, to look at this as anything other than a sacrifice she must make, an unpleasant price she must pay for his help. Yet he wanted more from her. He wanted her . . . not to want this, that was too much to ask, but at least give some sign it would not be a horror for her, despite his scarred face and body.

And the fact that he wanted this at all shook him to the core. He was Kane, ruthless, cruel, savage, what cared he if a woman he wanted did not want him in return? He took what he wanted, and it was her place to submit. He was paying Jenna as he paid any woman he took, 'twas only the coin that differed. And paying at all was more than most of his position would do. She should be grateful.

She should be grateful. He reached out to pull her to him, to prove it. That he was not sure who he was wishful of proving it to was something he did not care to dwell upon.

He'd meant to brand her with a kiss of possession, for he did own her. For this time, he owned her; she had surrendered to him any rights he wished. But the moment his hand slipped to the back of her head, his fingers threading through the silken fire of her hair, to tilt her head back for his mouth, what he'd meant to be an unrestrained declaration of ownership somehow became a soothing, gentling touch, a coaxing he'd not thought himself capable of. And when he kissed her, it was not the primitive claiming he'd intended it to be; that thought was lost the moment his lips came down on hers.

For a moment she was still, almost stiff in his arms. This was not what he wanted, he thought. He wanted her as she was when he massaged her aching muscles at night, soft and pliant beneath his hands, succumbing to sensations he knew she, in her innocence, did not even recognize. That she felt them anyway, at his touch, had brought him a pleasure he'd never known before; he was not used to such an honest response from a woman. He doubted he'd ever received such a gift in his life.

He did not deserve such a gift, yet she had given it to him. And rather than being satisfied with it, he had found he only wanted more. He wanted all she had to give, things he'd never cared about or asked for from a woman before.

He moved his mouth slowly on hers, urging her lips to ease, to soften. He held her gently, his fingers flexing through the thick mass of her hair as they did when he rubbed her shoulders. He felt her begin to relax, felt her tense muscles begin to slacken slightly, and he pulled her closer, letting the heat of his body continue the cajoling his hands and mouth had begun.

He flicked his tongue over her lips, tasting her, savoring a soft warmth that seemed hardly possible. She made a startled little sound, and he spoke to soothe her.

"Just a kiss, Jenna," he murmured, surprised at the husky sound of his voice. "Open for me. You are indeed the sweetest thing I ever tasted."

He felt the moment of hesitation, and probed with exquisite gentleness at her lips with his tongue. With a tiny sigh she parted them, and with delicate care he slipped inside, his own breath catching at the blast of sensation that swept him.

He shuddered, helplessly, at the onslaught of rioting pleasure that rippled through him as Jenna yielded completely to his kiss, as she lifted her hands to cling to his shoulders, her fingers digging into his flesh even as she sagged against him. His body surged to full attention, rapacious, demanding, ordering him to take what was within his grasp now, right now, warning him it would brook no denial this time.

Some small, still-functioning part of his mind knew that he was dangerously out of control, and with one of the greatest efforts of his life, he pulled back.

Jenna made a soft, quiet sound in the back of her

throat, a sound of protest, of loss. It was that involuntary sound that undid him; he'd never thought to hear such a thing from a woman, such an expression of genuine need, of regret that he'd abandoned her. And that quickly his need shifted, changed, becoming no less powerful but somehow different. He didn't just want release, he didn't just want to drive himself mindlessly into her body, seeking that momentary easing of tension, he wanted . . . more. He wasn't even sure what it was, wasn't sure it even existed. But that tiny sound Jenna had made had made him wonder if it did, for the first time in his life.

He stared down at her, suddenly realizing that the proof of all her stories of her people stood before him. What could have produced a woman like her, except a society such as she described? What, short of a people who deserved such a sacrifice, could drive such a proud, brave woman to making it?

He felt a sudden, relentless chill, as if he'd looked into the dark, seething well of his soul and seen the devil he'd so often been called.

"Jenna," he said, not realizing he'd been going to say her name, and barely aware that his voice held everything of what he'd just felt.

She stared up at him, her eyes wide and soft with the remnants of arousal, her lips soft and slightly swollen from his attentions. Something flickered across her face, some combination of pain and empathy and compassion that made him want to protest that he neither needed nor wanted any soft feelings from her. But he didn't. He couldn't.

Slowly, she lifted one hand from his shoulder, and raised it to his face. With one slender finger she traced his mouth, sending tiny bursts of heat surging through him. His lips parted as his breathing became as labored as if he'd run the length of a field of battle in full armor. Then she moved again, cupping his cheek—his ugly, scarred cheek—with her palm.

It was too much. He could not do this, could not accept this, whatever it was she was offering. She should hate him for forcing her to this with his devil's bargain. Yet she touched him as no woman ever had, gently, caressingly, with a sincerity he could not doubt. And she responded to his touch in turn as if she felt the same rising, crazy need he felt, although he knew it impossible for any woman to feel such for the likes of him.

Confusion careened around inside him, and he pulled away from her. And for the first time in his life, the man who had fought against odds beyond imagining, who had faced death countless times, who had found within him the courage to leave everything he'd ever known behind, ran. He turned and ran, fleeing one small woman as if she had the power to destroy him.

He was not entirely certain she did not.

He wished Tal would show up, in that mysterious way he had, always seeming to know when Kane was wrestling with a demon or two. He could use some of his friend's quiet wisdom about now, even though this demon was a new one.

But perhaps even Tal could be of no help with this; he'd said more than once that for all his cleverness, matters between men and women were beyond him. As, Kane thought wearily, was being in two places at once; Tal had said he was going down below again, despite the bloody turmoil they both knew was rampant. And all of Kane's efforts to convince him not to risk it had been fruitless; Tal did not make capricious decisions, but once his mind was made up, there was no changing it.

He'd been worried that Tal's decision might have something to do with his preposterous reaction when he'd seen him with Jenna, but Tal had assured him it did not. He hadn't even laughed at Kane's discomfiture, something Kane had been surprised at even as he was relieved.

Maybe even Tal could not help with this, Kane thought as he perched on the boulder and stared down into the chilly waters. Maybe there was no help for this kind of insanity. How was it possible for a man who had once been so lucid, so single-mindedly clear of thought, to have reached such a pass? How could it be that he was now torn in so many directions he barely knew who he was anymore? Perhaps it was hopeless.

Nothing is ever hopeless, my friend. It is simply more difficult at times to find where hope resides.

Tal's quiet words came back to him now, as vividly and strongly as if the man stood beside him. So vividly Kane caught himself looking around, half expecting to see his friend, or at the least that extraordinary bird of his. He saw nothing but the familiar shapes of the trees, the faint reflection of the half-moon in the water of the stream. He listened, and heard only the quiet sounds of the forest at night. His mouth twisted ruefully at his own fancifulness.

Nothing is ever hopeless, my friend.

"I wish I could believe that," Kane muttered under his breath. If he could believe that, perhaps he could believe there was a way out of this quandary he found himself in.

An image of Jenna formed in his mind, clear and vivid. Jenna, looking up at him as she had, a world of benevolent emotions in her eyes. Touching him, with a touch more tender than any he'd ever known. It was a kind of gentleness that had died in his life when his father had struck his sister down for that last, lethal time.

He shook his head and stared at the stream once more, eyes fastened on the rock that tried to divert it but failed; the water simply divided and rejoined, becoming again as it had been before.

Unchanged.

He knew then what he had to do. What he must do. If he did not, his time here would truly have been for nothing, and he was truly the same cold, brutal man he had been before.

He would send her home.

Unchanged.

Untouched.

He got to his feet and headed back to the austere, stark cave that was the only real home he'd ever had. His steps slowed the nearer he came, until he was fighting for every stride. When he reached the clearing, he knew it was going to take every bit of his resolve to do this.

He crept silently past the outside fire, not even looking at the tangle of blankets, checking only to see if the fire would keep for her until morning. If she was asleep he would not wake her; time enough in the morning to tell her that their pact had been severed. He would teach her what he could, but he would not hold her to her part.

He pulled aside the hanging cloth and stepped into the cave. Weary as much from the mental battle as from anything, he yawned as he removed his belt from his waist and the lion's skin from his shoulders.

Perhaps he would even tell her that he'd never meant it to be that way in the first place, that he'd thought to scare her away. That he'd underestimated her nerve, her courage, her determination. She'd earned that much and more, he thought, and she seemed to treasure what small bits of praise he gave her.

Yawning again, he pondered the chill, added one more log to the small fire that heated the stones. She'd more than proven she was tough enough to take whatever he threw at her; he would have her begin to sleep in here, before this fire; 'twas much warmer. And if it cost him some sleepless nights, so be it.

Sleepily he walked over to the furs piled over soft branches. Rubbing at gritty eyes, he stripped off his tunic and leggings and laid them to one side. Naked, he knelt to climb into bed.

The removal of his own shadow, which had fallen over the bed, revealed what had been hidden; Jenna, her hair a red-gold splash of color against the dark fur, lay there. In his bed. Curled up with one hand, the hand that had stroked his cheek, curled beneath her own. As if she'd come there to await him, and fallen asleep.

Kane knelt there, shivering suddenly as if the relatively warm cave had turned to ice. He felt his grip on his intentions slipping; just looking at her was sending all rational thought flying away swifter than Tal's damned raven.

And then she moved, just slightly, beneath the single fur that covered her. The motion neatly outlined the slender lines of her body, and shifted the fur just enough to bare her shoulder and part of her back. And Kane was hit with the stunning, gut-plowing realization that beneath the fur she was as naked as he was.

It was more than he could bear. If it damned him to eternal fire, he could not walk away. He doubted if the fact that he had tried would earn him much when the time came to face his own accounts, but it didn't matter now. Nothing did. Nothing on earth could stop him from claiming her now.

Not even the sudden certainty he felt that he was about to put an end to more than just her innocence.

Chapter 11

Jenna came awake the moment she felt the tug on the fur that covered her. For a moment she lay still, puzzled by the faint light and the softness beneath her; she'd become used to the hard ground and the surrounding darkness. And then it came back to her in a rush, and she sucked in a quick, apprehensive breath.

She was in the cave, the light was reflecting off the walls.

She was in Kane's bed.

Kane was here.

She fought her panic; she'd decided this, of her own will, to wait for him here, to show him she understood she was to be held to her part of their bargain tonight, as he'd told her. She would not renounce her choice now, simply because she was now faced with the reality.

Even though it was a reality beyond anything she'd ever imagined. She'd always known Kane was big, powerful, but somehow he seemed more so now. Even naked he seemed massive, and she had the quick, idle thought that in armor he must have seemed invincible.

In the faint light she saw the twisted whiteness of a scar here, the thin, curving line of another there. As he'd said and as she'd expected, he bore the marks of a warrior's life.

"If you wish to change your mind, it's far too late."

His voice was low, harsh, and gruff, and startled Jenna out of the odd sense of detachment she'd been lost in. And made her realize what her mind had been carefully skirting; this warrior, this big, powerful man, was aroused far beyond anything her limited knowledge of such things could have prepared her for.

He saw where her glance had fallen, and sat back on his haunches slightly, as if to give her a clearer view. The idea flooded her with heat and embarrassment, and she closed her eyes.

"Look!" he snapped.

Her eyes came open.

"I have fought this from the day you fell at my feet," he ground out, his tone telling her it was not pride in his maleness or the evidence of it that had made him do it, but rather torment at the loss of whatever internal battle had kept him from taking her the moment she had agreed on the price for his tutelage.

"You . . . needn't have fought," she said, wondering why she felt the need to point out what he already well knew.

"I didn't . . . I wanted . . ."

He broke off, letting out a harsh, compressed breath, and Jenna wondered if he ever in his life had stammered so, had been so torn by whatever it was that raged inside him.

"It doesn't matter," she said, moved by an urge she didn't quite understand to comfort him. As if a man like Kane would want, need, or take her small comfort.

"No, it does not," he agreed, his voice little more than a growl. "I will take what you will give, and if it is not enough, 'tis my own foolish fault."

Jenna went still, "I . . . warned you. I told you I had not the kind of passion in me a woman holds for a man."

He laughed, short, sharp, and wondering. He shook his head. "No passion? You, who practically melt beneath my hands, you, who nearly sears us both with merely a kiss?"

Her brows furrowed. "But that is . . . surely not passion? I thought passion was a flying thing, not . . ."

"Not what?" he asked, his voice suddenly soft.

"Fire," she whispered.

"Fire is exactly what it is," he said huskily. "The flying comes after the flames."

He moved then, lifting the fur and sliding in beside her. She gasped at the shock of it, of his naked body against hers. She'd given him back his cloth shirt, and hadn't been able to find it to borrow this night. Awaiting him fully dressed had seemed wrong somehow, as if she were denying his right to the freedom of her body their agreement had given him. But now she wished she had; his heat was about to consume her.

She'd known that he generated a heat that amazed her .. but this, this was beyond imagining. Everywhere his skin touched hers she burned. And when he reached for her, she cried out at the touch of his hand, not because it hurt, he was far too careful for that, but because his merest touch set her afire all over again, yet made her shiver as if she were chilled.

He stopped at the sound of her cry. "You did not seem to mind my touch outside by the fire," he said, his voice low and harsh.

"I . . . do not. Truly. But it feels . . . so strange. Fire. And ice. Together."

His hands tightened on her arms, and she felt a movement ripple through him as if he'd felt the same sensation she had moments before.

"I know little enough of a woman's pleasure," he said tightly. " 'Twas never my concern."

She supposed it was a warning to her, that she was not to expect anything of pleasure from this joining.

"There was no mention of such in our agreement," she said, trying to control the heat that threatened to flood her face; she had already felt more pleasure from his gentle touches in the evenings by the fire than she had ever dared expect from this cold, powerful man.

"Nor have I ever . . . dealt with a virgin."

Trepidation rose in her, but she fought it down. It was the price he had demanded, and she would pay it. She would have laid down her life if it would help her people; next to that her body seemed a small-enough sacrifice.

"That is not your concern, either."

"Once," he muttered, his voice oddly strained, "You would have been right on both counts."

She shifted, trying to see his face. At her movement, Kane groaned. His hands tightened yet again on her arms.

"I can fight this no longer." His voice was little more than a growl.

And then he pulled her hard against him, his mouth coming down on hers. This was not the gentle, coaxing kiss he'd given her earlier, this was demand, declaration, and warning all in one. He was claiming his prize, declaring his possession, and making it clear there was to be no turning back this time.

'Twas only what she'd said before, Jenna thought dazedly, 'twas only that it was a relief to have the waiting over. That was what had turned her to soft wax in his arms, nothing else. It was not the feel of his lips on hers, not the shocking invasion of his tongue into her mouth, not the fierce heat and exciting feel of his naked body next to hers.

And then his hands began to move, to stroke and cup and mold, seeking out each curve, lingering in each hollow. Her body twisted in his grasp, to get away, she assured herself, although it seemed to her that she was arching toward his touch more than away.

She was afraid, that was why she trembled, she told herself, wondering why it was so hard to think, wondering what this odd haze enveloping her was. But fear had always turned her cold before, not swamped her with heat, not sent arrows of flame racing through her, not made her cry out not in a plea for it to cease but in a plea for it to go on and on.

Kane deepened the kiss, his tongue probing into the depths of her mouth. Driven by an instinct she didn't understand but couldn't resist, she tentatively, briefly, met his probing caress with a flick of her own tongue.

Kane went rigid, as if she'd flicked him with a whip. A low, rough sound rumbled up from his chest, and he rolled her onto her back, covering her with only one side of his body, as if afraid his full weight would crush her. She wondered if it would. If she would survive it if he took her as roughly as he could. She knew only of love between a man and a woman, she knew little of this, but she knew enough to know that it was generally the woman who was most vulnerable, simply because of the superior strength of the man. And Kane was a very strong man.

And then his hands were at her bare breasts, and she knew nothing, nothing except the shock of sensation that jolted through her. He cupped and lifted the soft flesh, and rather than feeling embarrassment, an unexpected and utterly new excitement pounded through her. She felt her nipples draw up tight, tingling in a way she'd never known.

Kane lifted his head, freeing her mouth at last, and she drew in a breath she hadn't known she needed so badly. Perhaps that was why she felt so odd, she hadn't been able to breathe, hadn't—

She saw where Kane's gaze had gone, that he was staring at her breasts, at the achingly taut crests, and the embarrassment struck at last. It had to be embarrassment; what else could explain the rush of heat that flooded her?

And then Kane, that low, growling sound rumbling out of him again, lowered his head—and his mouth— to one breast. Jenna gasped as his lips closed over her nipple, but the alarm at what he'd done vanished in an instant amid the burst of sensation that erupted in her from beneath his suckling caress.

She couldn't help herself, her body arched violently upward and a cry escaped her. It rang in the silence, echoing off the walls, taunting her with the undertone of shocked pleasure that she could not deny.

She was not afraid, it was not relief. It was Kane, and what he was doing, it was the feel of him, his body, his hands, his mouth on her that was causing this firestorm within her. She had heard that what passed between a man and woman was good, when there was love. She had been warned by her mother that outside Hawk Glade there were hard, cold men who could make it an ugly, painful thing, and she had feared Kane would be one of those. But now, whatever it was he was doing to her was neither cold nor painful, and even though there was no love in it, it was beyond anything she'd ever imagined.

The realization made her tremble anew. Kane lifted his head, and she nearly cried out again at the cessation of the hot, sweet suckling.

"Did I . . . hurt you?" His voice was thick, husky, and she had a fleeting impression of a raging need held back.

"No," she said. It came out as a tight little whisper, but she couldn't help it. "No," she repeated.

It was all she could say. How could she tell him he'd far from hurt her, that it was the fierceness of her own response that frightened her? The men in her world were nothing like him, they were calm, quiet, restrained men who led their lives in peace. There had been a few, over the generations, who had had a wilder streak, but they rarely stayed in Hawk Glade once they were old enough to strike out in search of the adventure they craved.

Jenna had never understood that drive. Until now. She'd never encountered anyone like this warrior. She had never expected to. But suddenly she understood why some thought Hawk Glade too calm, too quiet, too peaceful. Whatever they sought outside that tranquil place was here in this man, in the wildness of his spirit. He was untamed, and ever would be.

She had never known there was a part of her that craved that kind of wildness. Until now.

"Jenna," he said, low and rough.

He was looking at her as if her thoughts were written in her face. As perhaps they were, she thought; how could such a discovery not show? She stared up at him, knowing her wonder was showing in her eyes. And after a moment, a no less wondering look spread across his face.

"You look at me as if . . ." He stopped, shook his head sharply. He muttered something under his breath, something she thought sounded like "Don't be a fool."

She didn't know what to say. She had no words to explain, she did not understand herself what was happening to her. She only knew that, in making this bargain she had thought of as the only way to save her people, she had learned something she had never known of herself.

"I did not know," was all she managed to finally get out.

She knew she was still staring at him, but she could not help that, either. She took in the powerful width of his jaw, the dark slashes of his brows, the strong line of his nose, the unexpected softening of his mouth. The thick fall of his hair shadowed his face, threw the sharp angles and planes into stark relief, made the scar on his cheek almost invisible. And his eyes, those eyes that had seen so much, and that sometimes betrayed so much of bleakness and remembered pain . . .

She reached up slowly, with one hand, to cup his scarred cheek as she had done before. Gently, as if she could somehow ease that long-ago pain. She heard an odd sound, as if his breath had caught deep in his chest.

"Kane . . ."

He shifted his body over her, nudging her legs apart so he could slip between them. Jenna tensed, the amazement of her discovery fading in the fear of what was to come. She could feel the heat and size and hardness of him against her belly, and the image of him as he'd been when he'd knelt before her, open to her gaze, seared through her mind. It seemed impossible, it could not work. Yet it did, it had, for centuries.

As if he'd read her fear—and perhaps he had; she'd conveyed it clearly enough with her sudden tension—Kane bent to kiss her again, this time with a soft persuasion that was beguiling in its gentleness.

"I will try not to hurt you," he said against her lips. "But I've been a long time without a woman, and I am . . ."

His words trailed away, but his hips shifted slightly, reminding her of just what he was. She should feel grateful he thought even that much of her; it was not part of their bargain that he be careful with her, only that she not complain, no matter what he asked of her.

What she should feel about the unexpected sensations his touch roused in her, she did not know.

She had thought he would simply take her now; there could certainly be no doubt about his readiness to do just that. So when his hand slipped between them, and she felt the probing touch of his fingers she was startled. But even more startling was the realization that his fingers were sliding easily over her most private flesh, that she was slick and, shockingly wet. And then he reached a spot that sent a shower of heat sparkling through her, and she cried out in surprise at yet another discovery.

"I cannot wait," he growled.

She felt it then, his fingers replaced by blunter flesh as he guided himself. And it struck her then, the meaning of that shocking, wet slickness; her body had been preparing for this, as if it knew she would not take a man of Kane's size easily.

And she did not, even then; she thought he would tear her apart as he probed her. Instinctively her body tightened against the invasion.

Kane stopped. She felt a drop of moisture, and realized sweat had beaded on his brow. She looked up at him, and her breath caught at the mixture of pain and need on his face.

"I . . . have no wish to hurt you, but the heavens help me, I cannot stop now. I cannot."

It took her a moment to understand. She drew in the breath that seemed to have lodged in her throat. She hadn't meant to fight him, had no right to fight him, yet her body had done so instinctively. She took another breath and made herself relax.

"I cannot make it . . . painless for you," he said roughly. "But I will try to make it . . . quick."

He pushed forward a bit more, she felt the incredible stretching of her body, and had to fight not to tense again. Kane muttered something low and guttural, and she realized he was fighting as hard as she, fighting to move in haste. Fighting not to hurt her.

That he would do so, when it was not required of him, warmed her; she supposed she was foolish to find any small comfort in this cold, ruthless man's actions, but she did.

The pressure built, but still he pushed further. Slowly, until she was sure she could take no more. And in the moment she almost told him, he moved quickly, thrusting forward sharply. She felt the tearing deep inside, and bit back a cry of pain.

Kane gathered her close, holding her, nuzzling her hair with a tenderness she never would have expected from him.

" 'Tis the worst of it," he said.

The pain was already ebbing. In its place came a flood of realizations that came so quickly Jenna could hardly keep pace. Kane was inside her, fully inside her, his body buried to the hilt, his hips pressed hard against hers. He was holding himself stock-still, yet shudders seemed to rack him, and his breathing was coming in rapid pants. And to her surprise she took his weight easily. Most startling of all, it felt . . . right somehow, that she was cradling him this way.

The foreign presence intimately within her was shocking, but at the same time it filled a hollow place she'd always had yet had never known the answer for. She'd thought it was some lack in her that had made her feel that way, part of that lack of passion she'd always felt. She'd never thought that perhaps it was simply something that she was missing, something someone else could give her.

Kane began to move then, and the friction of his male flesh stroking her from within set up a burgeoning sensation she neither recognized nor knew how to cope with. She could only respond. And her body did, moving in time with his movements in a way she could not control, could only let happen. It was as if her body was controlled by his, as if each of his thrusts demanded she lift herself to meet him. And she did, her hips moving in a way she'd never known, yet seemed to have known forever.

And within her the tensions built, the fire flared,

and she wondered what it meant that she could feel this, and that she could feel it with a man such as Kane, and what did it mean for their bargain, this had not been part of it, that she should feel such fierce, searing pleasure, that she should be driven even higher with every move of his body, that she become certain with every passing second that there was something, something just out of reach, something more powerful than she had ever imagined, something that would answer every question she'd ever had—

The flying comes after the flames . . .

For an instant she thought Kane had spoken the words again, but no, he had only cried out her name, in a voice full of triumph unlike anything she'd ever heard. His body arched as hers had, driving him into her fully. She looked up at him, and the raw, pure exhilaration she saw drawing his face taut was the spark to her own passion.

The greatest of passions require the greatest of sparks . . .

Her mother's words came back to her in that moment when her body gathered itself, and that which she had not understood as a child became perfectly clear to her now.

And she learned then that the flying truly did come after the flames.

"Drive up with the blade, the instant you unsheath it. If you wait to raise it and strike downward, you will be cut in half before you draw blood."

"If he is that close," Jenna said glumly, "I will most likely die anyway."

"True," Kane observed mildly. His tone was at odds with the feeling that had spurted through him at her all-too accurate comment.

It had struck him hard the morning after they had consummated their agreement. He had awakened feeling pleased, lazy, and utterly sated; twice more he had turned to her in the night, each time astonished by her welcome and the swiftness of her response. And the pattern had continued as begun in the nights since, making them a haven of warmth and passion he would have doubted could exist, especially for himself.

He knew her swift passion had to be unusual for an untried woman—in fact, he suspected, for any woman—yet he could not deny the truth of it; he felt the proof each time he was buried to the hit within her and he felt the pulsing clasp of her climax around his swollen flesh. Likening what he'd known before to this was like comparing a snowflake with the glaciers of Snowcap: one was small and fleeting, the other vast and eternal. The idea would have frightened him, had the pleasure not been so great as to wipe any such concerns out of his mind.

He stifled a shudder of need; only the knowledge that her body was no doubt sore had prevented him from reaching for her more often that first night. He'd never expected this, he'd thought once he had slaked his need, a need he thought only natural after so long a time of celibacy, that the urge that was nigh unto driving him mad would ease, that once he had her, the need to take her would pass.

It had not.

"Show me again," she said.

Kane let out a breath, reminding himself that she meant the dagger she held, not the dagger he wielded in their nights together. After her body had grown used to his presence, he turned to her often in the darkness. And always she welcomed him, seemed eager, even.

And he told himself to ignore the tiny voice that reminded him that she had no other choice.

She did *not*, he argued endlessly with himself, have to appear eager. Nor did she have to pour such plea-

sure into her tiny cries, or caress him so sweetly in
return. Never had he asked her to pretend she *wanted*
this, only that she submit.

He had less success trying to ignore that part of him
that wanted her to want it, that wanted every cry he
wrung from her to be true and real, wanted every
convulsive movement of her body to result from her
passionate response to his touch.

He refused altogether to acknowledge that some
even more deeply buried part of him wanted it to be
only his touch that she rose to.

"Like this?" she asked.

The sun caught the blade, flaring silver light in all
directions. And he thought again of that first morning,
when he'd awakened so content, still half asleep as he
pulled Jenna close, threaded the fingers of one hand
through the silken length of her hair, remembering
the feel of it as it had brushed over his body, letting
his other hand rest gently on her hip, his shaft already
rousing to the memories of being clasped so tightly by
her feminine flesh.

And then it had struck him, like the worst of blows
to the gut, stealing his breath, his hearing, and nearly
his sight. She would leave here in a few days. And
when she did, she would probably die.

"The blade is at your waist," he answered by rote,
relying on the old lessons he had once learned, then
taught. "Do not spend time bringing it upward to
strike downward. The moment you have it clear, drive
up and in."

"Beneath the ribs." She repeated what he'd told her
when, after walking to this small but level clearing
near the stream they'd begun the lesson this morning. "Why?"

"The ribs are there to protect what is most
vulnerable . . . and vital. That is where you will do
the most damage."

She nodded, practicing the motion he'd shown her with the same intensity she had turned on his instructions with the bow, the crossbow . . . and in bed.

The stab of desire he felt now nearly doubled him over. He wanted nothing more than to throw away that silly little dagger that would never save her, lay her down on the soft mountain grass, and take her right now. He wanted to see the sun turn her hair to fire as it lay spread over the green grass, wanted to look up at the sun through it as he taught her to ride him. He wanted to measure the length of his already swollen male flesh against her, then plunge it into her, remembering in his mind's eye so he would know just how deeply inside her he was.

He wanted to be so deep inside her that there would always be some part of her no one else would ever touch.

He wanted to hold her here, keep her here, safe, not send her off to what would surely be her death. And as if holding her body could somehow accomplish it, the need to do just that became unbearable.

"Kane?"

She was staring at him, wide-eyed, and he could only guess what he must look like. He had to stop this, had to control these urges that came upon him so quickly, unlike anything he'd ever known before. He had to control this.

Why?

The question rang in his mind, and on its heels came the memory of his own words, the words of their bargain.

You will become my woman. You will allow me the freedom of your body in whatever way I wish, whenever I wish, without complaint.

He reached suddenly for the dagger she held. Wresting it free of her grip, he flicked it aside heedlessly.

"Undress," he growled.

Jenna drew back slightly. "What?"

He yanked at the laces of his own shirt, and drew it over his head with a haste that betrayed his urgency. He did not even care that every mark that marred him, every scar that twisted his flesh would be lit by the glaring light of the midday sun. Jenna seemed remarkably unsickened by them when she touched them in the dark; surely that was worse than looking at them. Perhaps it was easier for her, knowing it was only for a brief time.

Jenna was staring at him, and for an instant he thought he saw a certain pleasure in her eyes as she gazed at his naked chest. It was enough to fire him to even greater urgency.

"Now," he said, his voice a tight, throttled sound.

Jenna blushed as understanding clearly struck her. Her eyes flicked downward, to the rapidly expanding evidence of the need that had seized him. Mere days ago she wouldn't have had the knowledge to look; she'd learned much in their time together, not the least of which was how to arouse him beyond bearing with simply a glance.

He toyed with the idea of having her unlace his leggings, but doubted he could stand it and did it himself, a near gasp of relief escaping him as swollen male flesh sprang free as he pulled them off. And when she slowly, as if in a trance, moved to undo her own clothing, he doubted he would stand that sight without humiliating himself, either.

But he watched. He watched as she undressed for him, her movements awkward for a woman of such grace. He watched as she straightened, standing naked before him, her body slender yet ripely curved in all the places that made her woman, her hips tempting, her breasts full and beckoning, her nipples already drawing up tightly, as if in invitation. Aware of his own fierce arousal, he watched as, at his command, she loosed her hair and let it tumble down, a living flame against pale, perfect skin.

And when he moved toward her, he would have sworn she did not quail. Would have sworn she looked at his body with at least a touch of the same hunger that drove him when he looked at hers. Would have sworn that there was some small bit of eagerness in the way she lifted her arms to him.

He would have sworn to all of it, had it not been for the simple fact that he knew he was worse than useless when it came to judging a woman's true feelings. They had never mattered to him, so he had never tried to discern them. And he was a fool for letting them matter now.

Especially with a woman who would die when she left here as surely as he would.

And later, as they lay under the brilliant sun, as he cried out with the force of the incredible pleasure that swept him, he wondered for the first time if perhaps there weren't more things worth dying for than he'd been taught.

Chapter 12

"Who is Meg?"

Jenna felt Kane go very still.

"Where did you hear that name?"

"You spoke it, in your sleep."

After a moment, she heard him let out a long breath at the same time his body relaxed against her. She waited, but he said no more.

She rarely dared to speak herself—he was still Kane, after all—in those quiet moments, the moments after the explosive encounters, the moments when they awoke in the morning and she found herself tucked into the strong curve of his body, their legs entwined, Kane's arms tight around her. This had surprised her; she had not thought he would want her to stay with him, had thought he would gain his release and then send her away until the need was upon him again.

But then, she had not expected to feel such astonishing things herself, any more than she had expected the pleasure she took in these quiet moments in his arms. It was his strength, she supposed. Here in his arms, feeling the size and heat and power of him so intimately, she could easily believe the legends they told of him. She could easily believe he had been the right hand of the most powerful of warlords. She could easily believe he was as much myth as man, although it was the man who shouted his exultation as he convulsed in her body.

And it was the man who, asleep, had moaned a woman's name in tones of such anguish she had steeled her nerve to speak of it.

"Meg was my sister."

Jenna went very still in turn. She who had been through so much loss of her own knew all too well which word was crucial in that short, blunt admission that seemed to have been torn from him against his will.

"Was?" she said softly.

"She is dead," he said, confirming what she had already guessed. "She died at my father's hand, after trying to protect me from a beating she feared would kill me." He took in a shuddering breath as Jenna held hers. "She was but twelve. And she had spent nearly half her short life trying to protect me from him, because I was three years younger than she."

"Your own father . . . killed her?"

"She stood in the way of the punishment he wished to give me."

Jenna tried to keep her horror from showing; she'd learned any show of sympathy made Kane shut down, as if he were not equipped to deal with such soft emotions.

"What . . . had you done?"

"I refused to kill her dog."

Jenna drew back sharply. "What?"

"She treasured it, that small, furry, spotted thing. Still a puppy. I could not do it."

"But why did he . . . want it killed?"

"Because she loved it." He shrugged, a motion she felt more than saw in the dim light of the cave in this hour before dawn. "But more important to him, he wished me to kill it."

Jenna suppressed a shiver; she could not comprehend this kind of treatment, she who had known only love from her own parents.

"Why?" she asked after the moment had passed. "You were but a child!"

"To make me follow his orders, no matter what it was he asked."

"What . . . happened?"

"He told me there was a price to disobeying him. He told me again to kill the dog. I refused again. So he did it himself, crushing it beneath his boots."

Jenna winced at the image, and her stomach churned.

"He turned on me then, and I thought he would kill me for disobeying him. But he did not. He killed Meg instead."

Jenna gasped.

"I never again disobeyed him. Until the day I came here."

Through her shock at the cold recital of the grim, harsh story, Jenna felt the sting of moisture in her eyes. She fought it, but it was too much. They traced a path down her cheeks.

"I ache for that little boy, Kane. No child should have to endure such cruelty."

"Ache for my sister, if you wish. She deserves it, not I."

His tone was cold, harsh, and she knew he was rejecting her unwanted compassion. She could never explain to him, she supposed, what he had just revealed to her, what he had made her understand about Kane the Warrior, both the man he had been and the man he had become. Nor could she convince him to accept the feelings welling up inside her.

"I wish . . ." She swallowed and tried again. "I wish my tears were worth something to you."

He went as still as he had when she'd mentioned

his sister's name. For a long, silent moment he didn't move, didn't speak. Then slowly his hand moved, and she felt a soft, stroking touch on her hair.

"They are, Jenna. They are worth far more than I deserve."

He turned to her in the way she'd come to know, pulling her close, stroking her, caressing her. The passion that she'd never thought she possessed, that with Kane never seemed far from the surface, rose to his touch as surely as the sun rose over Hawk Glade.

With a shudder so violent it shocked her, Kane went still.

"I don't deserve this, either," he whispered against her hair. "Not what you give me, here like this. I never expected . . ."

"Neither did I," Jenna said quietly as his words trailed away. "I never thought I could feel such things as I feel when you touch me."

She felt his arms tighten around her at her words, she didn't know if her words had pleased or disturbed him. Then he gently nuzzled her ear, and his tongue crept out to lightly trace the curve of it, so lightly that a shiver ran through her, a shiver that she felt to her toes as her blood began to hum in anticipation.

The heat began to build as she thought of the pleasure to come. "It makes me feel so wicked," she whispered, suppressing another shiver.

Kane lifted his head. "Wicked?"

"My people are dying, I should be thinking of nothing else, but I lie here, wishing—"

She bit back the words, fearing the power they would give him over her; he already had power enough.

Kane rolled atop her, raised up on his elbows, and stared down at her. She could feel the rigid column of aroused flesh pressing against her belly, and could not help the sudden, cramping need that seized her. How had he brought her to this, so quickly? Her mother had not warned her of this, had not told her that when that greatest of sparks came, the blaze it began would consume her.

"Wishing what, Jenna?"

His voice was caress and coercion in one, and she was helpless to deny him the answer.

"Wishing you would be in a hurry, this time."

Something flared in his eyes, darkening them to storm-cloud gray. "You . . . want me?" He shifted his hips, nudging her belly with the proof of his own wants.

"I do," she admitted. "I should not, but I do."

In seconds he was inside her, driving hard, and so fast that she could barely catch her breath, and yet she gloried in it, in the power and heat of him, in the soaring response of her body, and most of all the way, for the first time, he cried out her name as he poured himself into her.

He was losing his mind. There was no other explanation. He'd not even told Tal that woeful tale, yet he had told Jenna. He had told her, and she had wept, not for his sister, who at least deserved her tears, but for him, who deserved none of her soft, tender emotions.

She had cried for him, the man who had from that day followed his father's brutal orders to the letter, until he'd become a thing of legend, a cruel, merciless warrior who took no prisoners and whose name was spoken with more fear than even the warlord he served.

Yet Kane, the fighter renowned for his coldness, his isolation, had turned to a chattering fool in the arms of a woman, telling sorry tales and whispering sweet things he did not mean in her ear.

"Again," he shouted, as Jenna lowered the crossbow he'd handed her at least two hours ago.

She gave him a considering look, then set the bow

down and went to retrieve the bolts she'd fired in the last session of shooting he'd set her to.

He was pushing her hard, harder today than ever before. He'd run her up and down the worst of the mountain paths under full pack, had made her fire a full quiver of arrows with her bow, retrieve all but the two she'd sent past the target far into the trees, had stood like a solid oak while she had tried to apply what he'd told her about balance and leverage and using her smaller size to advantage to take him down, then he'd handed her the crossbow.

He knew what he was teaching her had little to do with saving her clan—in hand-to-hand combat they would have no chance—and everything to do with a vain hope that she would somehow be able to save herself in the end that would inevitably come. And that her survival had become important to him was a fact he did not care to admit to.

"You have little time left to learn, do you wish to waste it?" he'd said coldly at her sideways look when he'd handed her the crossbow.

She said nothing, merely obeyed, with a meekness that somehow made him angry. He suspected it had something to do with that nagging reminder that she had little choice, both in what he set her to doing here, or in the nights they spent together.

And his anger wasn't eased any by the sneaking notion that he was punishing her for his own weakness, that he was pushing her today because he'd betrayed so much to her in the soft warmth of her embrace in the dark.

He watched her as she strained to hold the heavy bow steady. She was a woman of rare determination; more, even, than he had at first thought. And now that he had intimate knowledge of the body that seemed so small to him, he was even more amazed at her perseverance. So small, yet she took him with ease, with every appearance of pleasure . . .

It swept over him again, that heated rush of sensation that had struck him when she had said, so simply, so honestly, *I never thought I could feel such things as I feel when you touch me.*

It made no sense, he'd never cared before if a woman felt anything, although he tried to avoid giving pain. A woman was nothing more to him than a way to ease a passing need. He required nothing of her other than that she be willing, and that willingness was usually easily secured by coin.

Or in Jenna's case, by lessons in arts she should never have had to learn. It was the same, only the payment was different. He stubbornly ignored the voice in his head that persisted in telling him that the price Jenna was paying was far higher than merely that of her body and her innocence, that for a woman like her to give herself over to a man like himself was costing her part of her soul. No, it was merely a variation on the old theme, no different than if he were paying her for the use of her body, he told himself.

And that his stomach knotted at the knowledge of what that meant he had to call her made no sense. None of this made sense to him. He was Kane, and he did not feel. His heart, if ever he'd had one, was long dead.

Your heart isn't dead, my friend, merely in a long sleep, as the bears of the mountains in the winter, and someday it will awaken and be ravenous. Someday, the right lady will lay a fair hand at your door, and you will let her in.

Tal's words came back to him, suddenly seeming as ominous as the warning that if he left these mountains he would cease to be. He had scoffed then, arrogant in his certainty that it would never happen, that his heart was as dead and cold as his soul, and that there wasn't a woman alive who could change that. He'd declare it again, were Tal here to listen.

He saw it in his mind as clearly as if his friend were truly standing here, saw the slight smile, saw him glance at Jenna, heard him say in that annoying tone of amusement, "Of course, my friend."

It was Tal's damn fault, Kane thought in exasperation. He'd been doing just fine alone, isolated as he had always been, even amid a throng, when Tal had arrived in his life and simply refused to go away. For the very first time, Kane had learned what it meant to have a friend. He'd gotten used to it, to having someone to talk to who never judged, just listened. It had turned him soft, and now—

"Again?"

He blinked. Jenna was standing before him, the small bow he'd made for her in one hand, the feathered bolts in the other. He stared; had she really fired them all and he'd been so lost he'd not noticed?

"Kane? Are you all right?"

"I . . . yes."

"Again?" she repeated, gesturing with the bolts.

"No," he said. She wouldn't be learning much if her teacher was lost in foolish wonderings, not paying any mind to what she was doing. "You've done enough for one day."

He thought he saw her let out a short breath. Relieved, no doubt, after the day he'd put her through. Still, she made no attempt to relieve herself of the weight of the crossbow, clearly expecting to carry it herself all the way back to the cave.

Before he thought, he reached out and lifted the burdensome weapon from her. She looked startled, then simply thanked him. He grunted something indistinctly as they began to walk, not happy with his own action. But then she gave him a tentative smile that made him forget his disgruntlement.

"You seemed a long way off while I was shooting," she said. "What were you thinking of?"

He tensed. He could never tell her what he'd been thinking. Yet he couldn't find it in him to simply ignore her gentle question as he once would have.

"Tal," he said, seizing upon the only bit of the truth he could give her.

Jenna's expression changed, and she lowered her eyes. "I'm sorry if . . . I am the reason he has stayed away."

Kane drew back. "You?"

"I thought . . . I know he has not been around since the day I met him. I thought perhaps he . . . took a dislike to me and that is why he—"

"It has nothing to do with you," Kane said, wondering why he was in such haste to reassure her, why he cared at all whether she thought it her fault. "Tal does as he pleases. He comes and goes, for reasons only he—and that blessed bird, no doubt—know."

He looked down at her, wondering what she would say if he told her Tal had ventured down from the mountains, into the chaos below. He could not do it. He could not bear to see the memories come back to haunt her, to darken the vivid blue of her eyes with imaginings of what was happening to her people in her absence. It was enough that she cried out in the night, enough that so frequently the shadows darkened her expression without any prompting from him.

It was too much. For the first time in his life all his strength, all his training, all his knowledge of battle could not help him; he had not the power to fight her fears. And that he wanted to, that he wanted to ease her mind, that he wanted to wipe away that dread that left her eyes dark-circled and her slender body weighted down, made him more uneasy than anything had in his life.

The only time she seemed free of it was when they

were locked together in passion, and in the languid calm afterward. Then, at least for a while, she seemed to think of only the pleasure.

While he seemed to think only of how soon she would leave.

"You have known Tal for a very long time?"

He pulled himself out of the conjecture he neither enjoyed nor had a reasonable answer to.

"Yes." Then he thought about it a moment, and corrected himself. "No."

Jenna gave him a mildly amused look. "Both?"

His mouth twisted. He did not like talking of such things, yet she seemed to make it impossible not to. If he changed the subject, she eventually returned to it, and if he refused to answer at all, she merely gave him a speculative look that made him wonder if she was spinning her own answers to her questions. And somehow that made him even more uneasy than answering did.

"In time, I have known him only since I came here five years ago," he said, not knowing how to put it any clearer.

"But it seems as if you have known him much longer?"

Surprised at her accurate guess, he nodded. "It makes no sense, I know—"

"I understand. 'Tis like the storyteller. I had never seen him before he came to us from out of the forest, but yet I felt as if I had known him forever. My brother . . . said he must remind me of someone dear to me."

Kane did not miss the hesitation, the catch in her voice as she spoke of her dead brother, and he waited to see if it would engulf her now, that pained sadness and anxiety that so often gripped her, until she was beyond his reach, lost in a misery he could do nothing to ease. But she seemed to fight it off, and spoke again.

"Perhaps it is that way with Tal? He reminds you of someone like that?"

"I have never known a man like Tal," Kane answered truthfully, avoiding the even more honest answer that there was no one dear to him, that there had been no such person since his sister had paid the most extreme price for his disobedience. For twenty years he had made certain of that, swearing that never again would he give anyone such a tool to use against him. Soft feelings made you as vulnerable as a snared rabbit, helpless, at another's mercy. He'd learned that lesson early and well. Yet Tal had breached his barriers, and Kane had never been able to figure out exactly how.

"He is . . . rather unique," Jenna said. "You called him the local wizard . . ."

Kane stopped in his tracks to stare at her. "It was but a joke. I told you, he is not. And I will thank you not to be repeating such things. There are those who would not take it lightly."

She looked up at him, the slight breeze that rustled the trees stirring her hair. "I know," she said quietly. "I believe I met two of them."

Chagrin flooded him. She had indeed met two of them, had rescued Tal from their lethal intent. An odd feeling he could not name welling up inside him, and words he'd not said since he was nine rose to his lips.

"I . . . I'm—"

He bit them off. Kane never apologized. He had done far worse than this, and had never asked pardon. He was beyond pardon. Far beyond. 'Twould be a waste of words and breath to say he was sorry.

"You worry about him," Jenna said, her voice soft, as if she'd taken no offense at all.

"I would hate to see him fall prey to the fancies of weak minds. He is merely a very clever man, too clever for his own good at times."

Jenna looked at him for a moment, as if she weren't

nearly as convinced as he was—or as he told himself
he was—that there was nothing more to Tal's unusual
abilities than extreme cleverness.

"So you have asked him, then?"

"Asked him?"

"If he has a sorcerer's powers."

"Of course I have not!"

She lifted a brow at him. "It seems a reasonable
question, between friends."

"There is nothing reasonable about such foolishness."

He increased his pace, heedless of whether she
could keep up with his long strides. She did, with little
appearance of haste.

"Is it that you fear Tal's answer?"

He stopped dead and turned to her. "Have you forgotten who you speak to, that you accuse him of fearing mere words?"

"Oh, no," she said, halting to look at him levelly,
with the steady courage he'd come to expect from her,
the courage that allowed her to face him calmly where
armed men would quail. "I have never forgotten. You
are Kane. You walk alone, and all the evil I have ever
heard of you is true. You have told me often enough."

Her words should have pleased him, but somehow
they did not. "Then you should know better than to
speak as you did."

She shrugged. "It merely seems to me that there is
only one reason not to ask. If his answer is no, there
is nothing—"

"I did not ask how it seems to you," he ground out.

"I understand," she said in a tone clearly meant to
be soothing, but that instead managed to annoy him
further, "for a man so set in his mind on such things,
it would be a difficult choice."

"Choice?" His tone was ominous, but she seemed
to blithely ignore the warning.

"If his answer is yes, you must admit there are indeed things beyond that which you can see and touch in this life. And perhaps you must admit as well that you would turn your back on him were it true."

"I admit nothing of the sort."

Her voice went as soft as his had become harsh. "And that is your choice, Kane. If you cannot admit that, then the other option is that Tal lies. And that you could not forgive."

She had put her finger upon it so neatly, the dilemma that had plagued him ever since he had realized there were depths to his friend perhaps better left unplumbed. He had not thought himself so easily read, yet she seemed to know instinctively things he preferred to keep deeply buried.

He stared down at her, wishing for an instant that she was as others, fearful of him, ready to flee at a mere glance. But she stood her ground, stubbornly, foolishly, refusing to give way. And then he had given way, turning on his heel and striding away, Kane the Warrior vanquished by one small, determined woman.

Jenna stayed in the shelter of the trees, out of sight, watching Kane. The contrast between the dark, powerful man, his expression little short of tormented, and the soft, golden glow of the sunbeam that lit him as if intentionally, tugged at something deep within her. It was as if all he was crystallized in that moment, all the dark grimness of his life battling the light of hope.

She felt it in him, every time he touched her, felt the war going on inside him as if the two sides were tangible. The man he could have been fought the man he had become, and she wondered if he would survive no matter who won. And she felt the pangs of guilt; he'd been content here, until she had come. She had brought him to this, forcing him to revisit old habits, and relive old memories. She had brought that look of anguish to his face, had stirred up whatever demons he now battled.

In that moment, to her astonishment, she was glad he had refused to take up arms again, even for the sake of Hawk Glade. She saw now that if he fought again, it would settle the battle for his soul irrevocably; Kane the Warrior would win, and the boy who had refused to slaughter a puppy as mere demonstration would vanish forever, crushed as surely as the small animal had been crushed. As surely as a young girl had been murdered by her own father, also as mere demonstration.

He lifted his head then, turning his face to the sunlight that poured down over him. His features were painted with stark clarity in the harsh light. His eyes were closed, his mouth twisted with what appeared to be pain barely suppressed, leaving the thick, dark lashes the only softness amid the strong features.

Jenna wished the sunlight were healing as well as warming. She'd never known a man more in need of it.

Were it not for the help she must have to save her people—and, if she were honest, the unexpected, soaring rapture she'd found in the arms of this wild, untamed warrior—she would have wished she had never come here.

She had come to know the man behind the legend, and she had no wish to be the instrument of his destruction.

Chapter 13

He could no longer deny the inevitable.

He stood in the opening of the cave, his naked body still tingling, the sweat of passion still damp on his skin. The night air flowed over him, and he thought he was still so hot from Jenna's embrace that he must be steaming like a lathered warhorse.

He stared upward, at the pale orb that flooded the small clearing with eerie silver light.

His body was sated, lax with a pleasantly heavy languor, but there was a tightness within him that even the near-violent release he'd just found with her could not relieve.

The moon was full.

He knew that Jenna knew it as well as he, yet she had said nothing. At least not in words; tonight she had turned to him before he could reach for her, tonight she had been the aggressor, pouring herself over him like sweet, hot fire in a way that had set him ablaze like never before, in a way that had set him crying out her name in a gasping voice he barely recognized as his own, in a way that had seared away all thought of anything except the need to hold this woman into eternity.

He looked away from the moon, staring now out across the small clearing into the darkness of the forest. This tiny bit of a pleasant eternity, all he would ever know, was over. He would go back now to his solitude, and where he had once desired that above all else, he now found it a cold and empty prospect.

"Kane?"

Her voice came softly, from close behind him, and a moment later her arms slipped around his waist from behind. She was still unclothed, and he could feel her warmth, the soft curves of her body as it pressed against his back. He didn't need to see her, he knew every one of those curves now, knew every plane and hollow and secret place. And in turn she had learned him, with an eager innocence that still stunned him with its power; nothing in his life had ever aroused him as Jenna's simple look of wonder as she looked at him, her sigh of pleasure as she touched him, caressed him, and he responded with the fierce, helpless ardor only she had ever brought him to.

He was responding to it now, his body hardening at the mere feel of her closeness.

"I do not know if it is of worth to you," she said quietly, "but I do not wish to leave."

Kane's eyes closed. How like her, he thought, to bring it so simply into the open, while he had been fighting to ignore the meaning of the full circle of silver light that hung above them. He fought down a shiver, not daring to speak.

"When I came here, I was in search only of Kane the Warrior, the legend, the man who had become myth. I did not expect to find a man who fought within himself as valiantly as he ever fought an enemy. I did not expect to find the man who would turn my blood to fire, and my body to some molten thing I no longer know."

"Jenna," he said hoarsely, not caring that his tone was nothing short of begging; he could not bear this.

"I know you will not come with me," she began.

"I cannot," he said, his voice still thick. "I . . ."

"I know," she repeated. "You have no desire to fight again, and now that I . . . understand, I do not wish you to."

"It is not that," he said, the words torn from him against his will. "I . . . cannot leave here. If I do, I will die."

Jenna went very still behind him. "I do not understand."

He swallowed, wishing he'd never begun this, but it had somehow become imperative that she know it was not heartlessness that made him turn her down. It had not bothered him before, but he found he could not so easily dismiss the woman who had made him wish for things that could never be.

"Tal . . . Tal warned me of this, when I first came here. He told me if I left these mountains . . . I would cease to be."

"And you believe him?"

He shook his head, then let it loll back on his shoulders. "You can say nothing I have not already said. 'Tis folly to believe in such things, and you well know I do not believe in prophecy. But Tal, however he does it, however he knows . . . he is right more often than wrong. Much more often. And when he said this, I . . ."

"You chose to believe," she said softly when he did not go on. "Why?"

"Because I *knew* he was right," Kane said, sounding as hopelessly befuddled as he felt.

She hugged him then, tightly. "That is where it began, isn't it? Your predicament, the battle that still wages within you? You believe Tal's words, deep inside, yet there is no way he could know except by methods you cannot accept."

He felt a shudder go through him, and her arms tightened further, holding him even closer. To his amazement, he took heart from it; he who had always stood alone, who had never required help from anyone, was taking strength from this slender woman's embrace.

"You have been waging this struggle for a very long time," she said softly. "You must be very weary of it."

"Tal is my friend," he said, unable to think of anything else to say.

"Yes," she said. "He is. No matter what else he might be, he is your friend."

She fell silent then, and he knew that the time had come. As painful and unsettling as the subject of his mysterious friend was, he knew it had only been an excuse to avoid a subject he feared would be more painful. He looked up at the moon again, wondering that he had never seen mockery in its uncaring cycle before. He shuddered again; telling himself it was the chill of the air, knowing he was lying.

"It is all right, Kane," she said, as if in response to the rippling of his body. "I know you will not come with me. Our bargain did not include—"

Kane swore softly at the mention of the infernal agreement they'd struck. After a moment Jenna went on as if he hadn't spoken.

"I no longer ask it, in any case. Even if Tal's foretelling is wrong, 'twould be a kind of death for you to take up arms again. I do not wish that. You have taught me much in my time here. It will be enough. It must be."

"Don't."

It ripped from him, a rough, jagged chunk of sound.

"Kane—"

"Don't go back."

She released him then. He turned to look at her. She was staring at him, expression puzzled, eyes wide and glinting in the moonlight. He couldn't believe he'd said it, but would not call it back even had he been able. It was not that he wanted her to stay, it was simply that he did not want her to go. 'Twas a fine line, but a line, nevertheless.

"But . . . I must."

"You can't. You know what will happen."

"I have no choice, Kane," she said. "I must return to Hawk Glade, to my clan. They need me. And what you have taught me."

"You will die. And that is a bigger certainty than any prediction I'm fool enough to believe."

"If I do not, I will be worse than dead."

He stared down at her. She stood there, her slender, naked body, the body that had taught him more than he could begin to have taught her, silvered by that damned moon's light. He read determination in every line of her, raw courage in the set of her delicate jaw, and her passion for her people in her eyes. In that moment she looked like a creature of destiny, forged in the fire of some creator with a vision far beyond his own poor sight.

She looked like an avenging angel come to life, and in that instant he thought she just might achieve her miracle; who would ever gainsay such a spirit?

"Can you not understand, Kane?" she whispered.

He did not know. It had been a very long time since he had cared for anything as she cared for her people.

"If it were Meg, and you had a chance to save her, would you not go, no matter the cost?"

Kane stiffened. Her heartfelt plea for his understanding accomplished her goal of easing her departure in a way he knew she had never intended. She had reminded him, all unmeaning, of the harsh reality of the difference between them. Jenna would give her life for the people she loved; Kane had let the one person he had ever loved die. It was no wonder she was eager to leave; why would a woman of such courage and fine mettle want to have any more to do with him than she had to?

That she had apparently found pleasure in his bed had been as big a surprise to her as to him, but it changed nothing. Who knew that better than he, he who had slaked his needs and gone on with less thought of the woman he left behind than the horse he rode? If he did not like being on the receiving end, 'twas his own fault for letting himself be softened by what they had unexpectedly found together.

This was the end that had been destined from the beginning, and he would not quibble with it. He was still Kane, and Kane was a proud man. Far too proud to beg anyone, let alone a woman he'd never searched out in the first place. Let the fate who had dropped her into his life have his laugh; it was time for him to get his small world back the way it had been.

"Will you leave in the morning?" he asked, pleased at the coolness of his voice.

She seemed startled by the sudden change. "I . . . hadn't thought."

"Our bargain is fulfilled. I have taught you all that I can of fighting in such a short time." He didn't dare look at her, standing there like some living sculpture molded by an artist with an exquisite eye. If he did, surely he would sweep her up and carry her back to his bed. "And you have . . . done as you agreed," he ended, fairly steadily.

"Kane—"

"There is no reason to delay."

She drew in an audible breath. "No. I suppose there is not." She looked at him, seeming a little bewildered by his sudden change. "Kane—"

"You have said you must go. So go. It is not the first time I have watched someone march toward death."

"Has Tal foreseen that, as well?"

He stiffened. "Mock me if you will. I need no seer's

eyes, but only a warrior's to see that you have not a chance."

"I meant no mockery," she said quietly. "I just ask why Tal's foretelling is any different than your own."

Perhaps it was not different, he thought. Perhaps Tal simply had a different way of being certain. His own was based on years of ugly reality, Tal's . . . on he knew not what. He knew only that once Jenna left here, he would never see her again. And no matter how he tired to convince himself that was as he wished it to be, he could not help but think of the emptiness she would leave behind.

And he knew in that moment who had truly been the fool in their fool's bargain.

She did not know what had caused the change in him. More than once she had been convinced he would be more than glad to see the last of her. She had disrupted his life, his peace, and he had told her he didn't like the fact. She had thought, once she had begun to spend the nights in lessons of things much more intimate than war, that perhaps he had softened toward her; surely no one could be by turns so tender and so ardent with someone he hated.

Or perhaps he could; she had heard there were men who took their pleasure and departed, unmoved beyond a sense of physical release. She had overheard her mother speaking of such things with Evelin once, when they had thought her asleep. Such men abounded outside Hawk Glade, they had said, expressing their thanks once more to whatever god had sent the hawk to guide them to this place.

The memory of that quiet time of utter safety spurred the need in her yet again, the need to return, to go home. Yet she found herself as reluctant to go as she had once been to stay, and there was only one reason for her quandary, and his name was Kane.

Something in him reached a place within her she had never known existed. There were no men like him in her calm, peaceful world, yet it was that very wildness that made him different that called to her, that made her wish there was some other way.

She thought of coming back, but deep inside her she knew he was right, and the chances that she would survive what was to come were slight. And she knew as well that hoping she might could hamper her, could make her hesitate when hesitation could lose all. She had no wish to hamper herself with a foolish dream of something that could never be. Even if she did survive, Kane had given no indication he would want her back. Indeed, he had tonight given every indication he would be glad to see her gone.

She had thought he would turn to her when they had returned to his bed. Instead, he had looked at her as if he were considering ordering her back to her blankets by the fire. He did not, but neither did he reach for her, nor even touch her. It was as if he had already cut himself off from her, and the completeness with which he did it chilled her. She herself was aching for him, aching for one last shared moment of glory between them. But he lay with his back to her, heedless of her pain, apparently able to shut off his own need in a way that left her shivering.

This was Kane the Warrior, and she had been a fool to ever forget it.

When the dying glow of the fire was replaced by the faint light of dawn, Jenna rose quietly. For a moment she looked down at Kane, who had barely moved all night, apparently sleeping soundly within his heart's armor. She had no reason to feel this way, she told herself. He had kept to his part of the bargain. And more; their agreement had been only that she would act his woman, not that he would care at all if she took any pleasure in it.

But she had. She shivered at the heated memory as she stood there in the chilly dawn air. Oh, she had. And she could not regret it; if it were true, and she was to die in the effort to hold Hawk Glade, then she would die having known the possibilities between a man and woman. If she survived, it would no doubt become a bittersweet torment, but to die without knowing would surely be worse.

She dressed hurriedly, then gathered up her few things and bundled them carefully in her small pack, making certain she had the small diagram he had drawn out on a piece of hide after she had assured him they had craftsmen whose talent could be turned to the making of crossbows. She added a small parcel of dried meat she had prepared for this day. Kane slept on.

She set the small hand bow atop her pack, images flashing through her mind from the two days they had spent in the process of making it, choosing the perfect hew for the flexible bow, the gut for the bowstring, and discarding her first three attempts as Kane—with a patience that had surprised her—had guided her through the curving and recurving of the slender span of wood. And still he slept.

She added the quiver full of arrows they had made the next day, chanting silently Kane's lessons on length, feathering, and balance, knowing she would have to teach it in turn.

And then came the crossbow, the small one built for her alone, the weapon that had its own deadly beauty. And then the bolts.

At last she was ready. She looked back at the bed of furs over soft branches where he had taught her as much as he ever had outside this cave. Still he lay quietly, lost in the slumber that had evaded her most of the night.

She couldn't help herself. She walked over and knelt beside him.

"Thank you," she whispered

She bent and kissed him, pressing her lips to the scar on his cheek. He never stirred.

Fighting the sudden wetness in her eyes, she backed away from him. She grabbed up her things and ran from the cave, thankful to escape before he woke and saw her tears. And a bit surprised; Kane was not normally such a heavy sleeper, and it was unusual that he had not heard her moving about in the cave, especially when she had added a log to the dying fire so that it would be warmer when at last he did awaken.

Perhaps he truly was that glad to have her gone, she thought, biting her lip. So glad that just the thought of it brought peace to his sleep.

She glanced back over her shoulder, but saw nothing but the cloth that blocked the cave's entrance and the faint wisp of smoke that rose from the natural flue. Her steps faltered for a moment, then she made herself turn back to the narrow trail and continue on. She moved quickly, as if putting more distance between them would lessen the pull. She did not slow until she was well away, and the trees were closing in around her. Then she paused for breath, wondering just how far she had come in her emotion-driven haste.

This was not a place to be stumbling around blindly, she chided herself. Had she so quickly forgotten the difficulty of the journey here, that she went crashing along so heedlessly? She had a very long way to go, she should—

"There's an easier path, you know."

Her breath caught and her gaze shot upward to the source of the sound. She'd recognized the voice in the instant before she found him, perched with one foot drawn up to rest on the strong limb that overhung the

barely discernible path, his other foot swinging free.
The black bird was beside him on the branch, looking
at her steadily, much as her master did.

Tal.

He dropped down beside her as lightly as if the
distance were two feet instead of ten. Jenna looked at
him, puzzled. In the shadowy light, the resemblance
to the storyteller was even more pronounced. It gave
an oddly silver cast to all of his hair, not just the
streaks of gray at his temples. And it made his eyes
look the same misty green as the storyteller's when
he was deep in concentration. At least, she *thought* it
was the light. . . .

"Are you not . . . grayer?" she asked at last.

Tal groaned. "Again?" he muttered. Then he lifted
both hands, pulling his hair back from his face in a
weary gesture. "No," he said. " 'Tis just this light."

He lifted his hands and his hair fell back. He tilted
his head, and she saw that he was right; he looked as
he had before. At least his hair did; his eyes still reminded her uncannily of the silver-haired man she
prayed she would find still alive. But it was only a
resemblance, nothing more, she saw now.

"So," Tal said rather quickly, as if to forestall any
further comments on his appearance, "you are
leaving."

She nodded. "It . . . is time."

"And Kane?"

She wasn't sure what exactly he was asking, so she
took his question literally.

"He is sleeping still."

Tal lifted a brow and glanced at the sky to the east,
where the sun was beginning to streak the dawn sky
with pink; early as it was, it was long past Kane's usual
rising time.

"Is he?" he observed mildly.

"I think perhaps he is so glad to be rid of me he

sleeps like a babe." The words were out before she could halt them, and she was glad they sounded merely wry rather than wounded. What was it about this man that made her blurt out such things?

"Kane has never slept like a babe since he was one," Tal said. He gave her a speculative look. "And his life spent as a warrior is hardly training to sleep so heavily he would not hear you leave."

Nor feel you kiss him, Jenna thought, feeling the blush that rose to her cheeks.

"I . . . thought that myself."

Tal shrugged and said nothing, leaving her to draw the obvious conclusion. Kane had been awake. But he had chosen to feign sleep. Why?

"He is a brave man," Tal said idly, as if apropos of nothing, "but he is in new and unfamiliar territory."

Jenna did not have the slightest idea what he meant, so instead of commenting she said, "He said you told him if he left these mountains he would die."

Tal blinked. "Did he?"

Her mouth quirked wryly. As charming and handsome and delightful as Tal was, he had some annoying habits. "The question is, did you?"

He laughed. "Ah, Jenna, you have grown even more intrepid."

He had little to compare her to, so she ignored the praising effort to avoid answering.

"Did you?"

"And persistent, I see." His mouth twisted up at one corner. "I warned him of what would happen if he left these mountains, yes. But why did he tell you of this?"

"He was . . . explaining why he could not go back with me."

A smile of satisfaction crossed Tal's face. "Was he, now? That is good news."

Jenna stared at him. "Only you, Talysn ap . . ."

"Bendigeidfran," he supplied, grinning.

"Only you," she said, ignoring him, "could find good news in any of this."

"Oh, I shall find much more than good news before this is through, child."

"Child?" she looked him up and down. "You're hardly *that* much older than I."

He rolled his eyes upward for a moment. "If only you knew. And I'm aging by the day."

"Are not we all?"

"Quite true," Tal agreed with a laugh. He gestured down the mountain. "You would prefer to take the easier trail, would you not?"

"I did not think there was such a thing on this mountain," she said wryly. "Certainly Kane never showed me one."

"Of course," Tal said. "He would not want to make it too easy for you. I, on the other hand, have no desire to weary such a fragile creature."

She gave him a sideways look. The sparkle in his eyes and the twitching at the corners of his mouth were irresistible, and she burst out laughing.

"A man would give much to see you laugh, Jenna of the Hawk clan."

But not Kane. Never Kane, she thought sadly. "Where is this easy path of yours?" she asked quickly, before Tal could guess at the pang she felt.

"This way," he said, looking at her as if he had indeed sensed her pain.

She followed him without question, not even wondering why. Nor did she wonder any longer why Kane, who professed to believe nothing of sorcerers or prophecy, had believed Tal when he'd warned him not to leave the mountain. There was something about the man that made you believe. You simply could not look into those eyes and suspect falsehood. Although she guessed he withheld more than he told, she could not doubt that what he told was truth.

And as they started down the wide, clear trail that she couldn't believe she hadn't noticed before, she remembered what else Tal had told her, that promise he had made that her line would descend down into history. And for a moment she felt as Kane must, believing yet not believing, caught between the doubt of such things and the power of the man they had come from. And somehow the fact that he had not promised her a miracle, that he had not told her that the remaining Hawk clan would survive, only her own blood, made her both more able to believe, and more reluctant to do so.

Whoever Talysn ap Bendigeidfran was, wizard or no, she doubted he was a man to take lightly.

Yet he seemed like nothing more than an amiable companion as they walked, telling her things of the forest even Kane had not known. He knew each tree, each bush, and what purpose it could be put to. And he knew each creature they encountered, and Jenna did not miss the way the animals showed no fear of him.

"How long have you lived here in this forest?" she asked after he'd tossed some remnant of food he had to a curious jay.

"Several lifetimes," he said lightly.

Jenna studied him for a moment. "Were it anyone else, I would say that was a jest."

"I knew you were a clever girl."

"Do you find it productive, to answer without ever answering?" Jenna asked mildly.

"Often," Tal said with a laugh. Jenna smiled, as it seemed impossible not to, but for the first time in their brief acquaintance, she had the feeling there was something dark and haunted behind the easy facade. Questions rose to her lips, but she held them back;

she barely knew the man, after all. And for the first time she truly understood Kane's reluctance; she was not at all sure what she would do were Tal to confess to a sorcerer's talents. And if she, who had grown up on tales of the magic of Hawk Glade, could react that way, it must be much more difficult for Kane to deal with such ideas.

When they reached the bottom of the mountain, the journey that had taken her four days in reverse, before the sun had begun to drop toward dusk, she looked at him warily.

"I told you 'twas an easier path."

"Yes, you did." She said no more, just looked at him.

"You will be careful, Jenna? You still have far to go."

"I will."

"I cannot accompany you the rest of the way," he said. "I must see to Kane."

"An odd way to put it."

"He is always at his worst when he is battling himself."

She could hardly argue with that.

"When I first found him," Tal said softly, "I feared he might seek a permanent end to his pain."

"She could not argue with that, either. "I . . . sensed his despair. Sometimes it seems consuming."

"It almost was."

Jenna opened her mouth to respond, then closed it. She did not wish to discuss Kane, not anymore. Not even with Tal. She had to put him out of her mind, or she would never accomplish what she had to do.

"I thank you for coming this far."

For a long moment Tal just looked at her, and she had that odd feeling she'd had with him before, that he was somehow seeing clear through to her soul. "I

knew a woman with a spirit such as yours once," he
said softly.

Pain, a living, twisting thing swirled in his eyes, and
in that instant she saw him as clearly as he saw her.
"You loved her," she said, and it wasn't a question.

"I loved her," he agreed. "But I could not save
her."

The twisting pain she'd seen echoed in his voice.
But then it was gone, and in its place something
golden glinted in his eyes. He leaned forward and
pressed a kiss to her forehead. It was a warm, gentle
gesture, the kiss of a friend, without the heat of Kane's
kiss, but with much more of simple comfort. So much
so that she did not draw back in surprise despite the
unexpectedness of it.

"Go with care, Jenna," he said quietly.

"Thank you," she said simply.

"And do not mind Maud. She is feeling a bit . . .
restless of late. She may follow you for a while."

Jenna glanced at the bird, who looked far from restless as she sat in the morning sun, preening uncon-
cernedly.

"Is there anything you wish me to tell Kane?"

She looked back at him. She thought, but there was
nothing to say in the face of Kane's coldness. If this
was his way of saying good-bye, of making the break
cleanly, then so be it.

"No," she said. "Only . . . thank you."

He nodded, turned to head back up the mountain,
then glanced back at her.

"There is but a spark left in him, Jenna. You have
found it. Don't let it go out."

He vanished as quickly and quietly as he had appeared. Only the whistle he gave, that up-and-down
tremolo she'd heard before, lingered, echoing. The
raven cocked her head, then turned her steady gaze
back to Jenna.

"Is he sending you after me, then?"

The bird said nothing, merely waited.

"I suppose you won't tell me if he is truly a wizard."

Still nothing. Jenna sighed, then turned and started on her way. She should be anxious to get home, anxious to do what she could to save what was left of her clan.

But all she could think about were Tal's last words.

There is but a spark left in him, Jenna. You have found it. Don't let it go out.

Chapter 14

"We made a bargain, Jenna and I."

"Yes."

"It is fulfilled. Over."

"Yes."

"There is nothing more to discuss."

"Did I say that there was?"

Kane glared at Tal's innocent expression, nearly snarled at the bland neutrality of his tone. Tal ignored his glower and gave a tug on his fishing line as if he thought he might have missed some shy little trout testing his bait. He seemed intent on his fishing—an odd method utilizing a thin line of some material Kane had never seen before he'd met the man—but Kane did not miss the sideways glances that were frequently cast in his direction.

"No," Kane ground out as he paced beside the rock where Tal was perched, "you merely sit there watching me, as you have for a week, like some predator awaiting a betrayal of weakness so he can attack, like a panther waiting to rip my throat out."

Tal grimaced eloquently. "Must you always use such gruesome analogies?"

" 'Tis what I know."

Tal sighed. "I thought perhaps Jenna had taught you some gentler ways."

Kane went still. "It was I who was her teacher, remember?"

"Yes," Tal said, his voice blandly innocent again. "And 'twas only the arts of war you taught her, nothing of gentler things, I'm sure."

Kane felt the threat of heat rising to his cheeks as he thought of the other things he had taught Jenna. In a way it was true, there had been little enough gentleness in it, because there was little of it in him; their passion had been a fierce, hungry thing. And its absence had left him starving.

"And I'm sure she taught you nothing in turn," Tal said in that same irritating tone of utter insouciance as he moved his line to a deeper, calmer spot in the stream. "What could anyone teach Kane the Warrior?"

Memories of all that Jenna had taught him, not just in the darkness when she had shown him the true appeal of being wanted in return, but in the sheer crackling power of her presence, the blazing undeniability of her courage and heart, flooded Kane, and put an edge in his voice that was arrow sharp.

"And what do you mean by that?"

"Nothing."

"You never mean nothing," Kane said shortly.

"All right. I mean then that I continue to wonder why you work so hard to fight the very transformation you came here to achieve?"

Kane frowned. "I do not understand what you mean."

"I know. You do not even realize you are doing it, it is so ingrained in your nature. 'Tis you who have always said you don't have a gentle side, my friend. Perhaps I've finally come to believe it's true. At least not one you'll own to."

"There is nothing to own to, and I'll thank you to

keep your conjecture to yourself. She agreed to my terms, there was no misunderstanding involved."

Tal shrugged. "I offered no opinion on your bargain. I'm sure Jenna knew what she was doing. She is a very intelligent woman."

"How would you know? You barely showed your face when she was here."

"She is a very intelligent woman," Tal repeated, as if that answered Kane. "Besides," he said, "given the nature of your pact, I thought perhaps you would not find some privacy amiss. And I had no wish to . . . embarrass her."

Kane stopped his pacing abruptly to stare at his friend. "You seem to care little about embarrassing me," he muttered.

"Have I embarrassed you?" Tal's tone was nothing less than delighted. "Indeed, this is good to hear."

Kane shook his head, bemusement filling him. "I do not understand you, Tal. Why does such a thing please you so?"

"Because I feared there was nothing left to embarrass you about."

"You make no sense."

"You have often told me there is nothing left of softness inside you, Kane. Yet if you can be embarrassed, there is some hope."

"Hope? You are a fool if you equate softness with any kind of hope, unless it is for destruction."

"I have been called worse than a fool before," Tal said.

Kane went very still. Yes, he had been called worse. Sorcerer, wizard, mage . . . Kane had heard of the wizard of the mountain forest long before he'd come here, long before he'd come to suspect Tal was the source of those stories. But he'd been secure in his knowledge that such things were merely the beliefs of the weak-minded. Then.

Is it that you fear Tal's answer?

Jenna's words echoed in his head as he stared at his friend. Tal did not look at him, seemed intent now on staring into the stream's clear waters, as if expecting to see the trout he was after appear at any moment. After a moment, Kane stepped up on the boulder Tal sat upon and dropped down beside him.

"Tal . . ."

He said no more, could not think what to say, did not even know what he wanted to say. But Tal looked up then, studying Kane's face, his eyes, for a long, unwavering moment.

"Are you certain you are ready for this?" Tal asked softly.

"I . . ." His voice trailed away. He did not even know what "this" was.

Tal's intensity became an almost tangible thing, and Kane was suddenly full of the kind of anticipation he'd felt before a battle, that building sensation that was not apprehension, not eagerness, not wariness, but a combination of all three that resulted in the long unfelt but not forgotten humming in his blood. And Kane knew then that this was the moment of no turning back; if he did not walk away now, there would be no changing what would come. No avoiding the question Jenna had so perceptively known was at the crux of his relationship with Tal.

"I have never lied to you, Kane," Tal said, his voice still soft, with that kind of deadly intent that Kane knew marked the most formidable of opponents. "I have not always told you all there was to tell, but I have never lied. And if you ask me a direct question, I will not lie now. 'Tis up to you."

He did not want to ask. To ask would be to admit so many things he did not wish to admit. That what he had thought unalterable truth was not. That what he had always believed was wrong. That what Jenna had said was true, he feared the answer.

Jenna.

And that was what he most of all did not wish to admit. That it was she who drove him to this. That prodding him was the emotion he had carried within himself for this week past, not wanting even to acknowledge, let alone name it. Yet it hovered there, refusing to be ignored or shoved aside, haunting his days and tormenting his nights with imaginings somehow more awful than the horrible realities he had seen, until one day in his exhaustion he had idly wondered if he would feel it when she died.

He could not go on like this. In the worst of his first days here, when he had been tortured by the memories of who he had been and what he had done, he had never felt like this, never felt such hopelessness and despair. He had been filled then with only a dogged determination to either succeed or die, and he hadn't cared overmuch which it was. But this, this was killing him. Slowly, eating away at his vitals like some slow-acting poison, clawing at him until he was certain he was bleeding inside.

And he had finally had to face the fact that his fear for Jenna outweighed his fear of Tal's answer.

He lifted his gaze to his friend's face, the face that held the look of youth, with eyes that held the look of ancient wisdom.

"I have no choice," he said, not caring about the bleak sound of his voice.

Tal looked at him steadily, intently, that unnerving golden glint glowing in his eyes.

"I can see that you do not," Tal said at last, an expression of compassionate understanding coming over his face.

Kane took in a deep breath. "Is it true?"

Tal hesitated. Kane blinked, surprised; Tal's self-

assurance had always seemed limitless, yet he hesitated now. And as Kane looked at him, Tal's mouth
twisted ruefully.

"I find . . . it is I who am not ready," he said.
"Ironic, is it not?"

Kane just looked at him, the sight of an indecisive
Tal so unexpected as to be startling.

"I . . . value our association," Tal said slowly. "You
are . . . like the brother I never had. I would dislike
losing your friendship because of . . . something I cannot help."

Kane felt a twisting inside him, a combination of
shock and gladness and unexpected warmth, followed
closely by a sensation of self-recrimination.

*And perhaps you must admit as well that you would
turn your back on him were it true.*

Jenna had said it, and he had known there was truth
in it, but he had been so intent on her at that moment
he had not dwelt on it. But now, put as simply as Tal
put it, it sounded as cruel and callous as anything he
had ever done as a warrior. That Tal feared the telling
as much as he had feared the asking had never occurred to him. That Tal would fear anything had never
occurred to him. That it would be this stunned him.

And it hit him then that he had, without asking,
received his answer. For Tal would not be concerned
were there nothing to tell.

No one had ever worried about keeping his friendship before. True, he had not given it often, and never
so completely as he had given it to Tal, but no one
had ever cared much one way or the other. Mostly
they were too much in fear of him to think of such a
thing, and he told himself he preferred it that way.

So was Jenna right? Would he turn his back on Tal
if his suspicions were confirmed? Would he forsake
the one man in his life he called friend, the man who
had probably kept him from losing that battle he'd

fought when he'd first come to these mountains years ago? And for what? To go back to being that solitary man who walked alone, to pretend that Tal's quiet humor had never taught him that such friendship was possible?

To pretend that Jenna's courage, determination, and gentle embrace had changed nothing, had truly taught him nothing?

"I think you have already answered," he said.

For a moment Tal's eyes closed. His lips tightened as if he feared Kane's next words. When none came, he opened his eyes again. And when he looked at Kane, his gaze narrowed.

"And I think it is time I asked why you have come to this now? Why is it you wish to delve into things you have always avoided before?"

Kane didn't deny it; Tal's words were true enough. And the haunting he had lived with this past week still churned near the surface, close enough that at Tal's prompting, the nightmare boiled over.

"Because I wish to know . . . I have to know . . . if you have some way of . . . learning about Jenna."

For an instant, Kane thought he saw something bright and joyous flash in Tal's changeable eyes. But it was gone as quickly as it came, and Tal's voice betrayed nothing.

"Learning . . . what?"

"How she fares. Her people, Hawk, Glade . . ."

"You do not ask if she still lives," Tal observed in tones of simple curiosity.

Kane's stomach knotted at the words he had refused to say. "I . . . I cannot—" His fists clenched, his nails digging into his palms until he thought they would bleed.

"She lives, Kane," Tal said.

Kane's gaze shot to Tal's face. Tal met it, held it, not flinching now, no hesitation in his manner.

"She lives. She will arrive home tonight. Safely. But I cannot say how long it will last. Things do not go well with the people of Hawk Glade. The warlord who besieges them knows they are there, and it angers him that he cannot find them."

Kane had expected no less, but something Tal said perplexed him. "Tonight? But she left here but a week ago."

Tal's mouth twisted. "I . . . helped her down to the main road."

"Helped?"

"The flatland journey is treacherous enough. She did not need to weather the trek down your precious mountain. She had already proven she could manage it by getting here alive."

Kane eyed him narrowly. "Just how long did it take her to reach the road?"

Tal hesitated only a moment, then shrugged. "She was on her way the same afternoon she left you."

She left you. Kane winced; had he had to put it like that? Then the fact of what Tal had said struck him. "That is a three-day journey for one who knows the mountain well."

"Yes."

And there it was again, hovering between them. Tal watched Kane as if waiting. As, Kane realized, he was.

And perhaps you must admit as well that you would turn your back on him were it true.

I would dislike losing your friendship because of something I cannot help.

Perhaps it was his fear for Jenna, perhaps it was the softening she had engendered in him, or perhaps it was simply the healing he had come here to seek, but he knew he had changed. Had he been too blind to realize it had been happening all along? Was it as Tal had said, that he had been fighting what he had come here for, only now to let it happen?

He did not know. But he did know something else. This much, at least, he had learned in time.

"I do not fully know what you are," he said, "but I know who you are, Tal. You are my friend. And that is a rare thing for me."

Tal let out a visible breath. "Thank you." He gave Kane a sideways look. "In fact, 'tis as rare for me as you. Not many have the strength of will to accept . . . what I am."

In all his wrestlings with his suspicions about Tal, Kane had never thought of it thus. But he did now. "In your way . . . you have been as alone as I, have you not?"

Tal shrugged. "People fear what they do not understand as much as they fear . . . say, a legendary warrior of incredible strength and ruthlessness."

Kane turned over the new idea in his mind. "Has it . . . always been so for you?"

Tal looked at him for a silent moment. "I have not always been as I am," he said at last.

"You mean . . . a wizard?" Kane asked in surprise.

"If that is what you wish to call it."

"But I thought . . ."

"You thought I was born one? Most do. I was not. I was full grown, settled in my life, when . . . it happened."

"Then how—"

" 'Tis a long story, better left for another time."

Tal got to his feet, pulling in his fishing line, glancing at the bare curved thorn at the end. He shrugged and wound the line into a tidy coil. He glanced upward toward the rapidly sinking sun, as if gauging the time until darkness. Then he looked at Kane.

"You are all right?"

"Yes," Kane lied, looking at him warily. "Why?"

"I merely ask before I leave."

"Leave?"

"Maud is too long gone. I need to find her."

"I noticed she is not tracking your every move. In fact, I don't believe I've seen her since you came back." Kane frowned. "Have you not . . ."

His words trailed off; despite his unwilling acceptance of what Tal had admitted to, he found it difficult to ask something as foolish as whether Tal had not in some magical way communicated with his small black shadow.

"I know she is well," Tal said. "But beyond that . . ."

He ended with a shrug and bent to tuck the coil of line into his small pack. Kane watched him for a moment, at first fighting the urge to ask, and then wondering why, since he'd come from acknowledgment to acceptance that Tal had ways of knowing things he could not understand.

"Tal?"

His friend straightened, slinging the small deerskin pack over his shoulder, and met Kane's gaze.

"If I learn anything of Jenna, I will tell you."

He turned then and walked into the trees, seeming to become one with the forest in the way that had always unsettled Kane. Somewhat to his surprise, it unsettled him still. Acceptance and embracing were, it seemed, two very different things.

For a long time Kane stood there, staring into gathering darkness, wondering, pondering.

If I learn anything of Jenna, I will tell you.

For the first time since he'd come here, he felt like a prisoner on his mountain.

Jenna's legs ached, and the ankle she'd thought healed, throbbed, but she kept on. It was nearly dark, but she was so close to home she could almost smell it, could almost smell the sweet scent of the Jasmine that grew in the clearings, the fresh cleanness of the fir-scented air, the warmth of the sun that shone so brightly there, having not just warmth and light but a feel, a soothing balm that eased a weary mind as well as a weary body. There was nothing that could match Hawk Glade's sunlight. Except perhaps the touch of Kane's hands.

She suppressed a shiver. She had thought it would ease, this ache within her, had thought that as she got further from the warrior and his mountain that the pull would lessen. It had not. And she did not know what it meant. She had sold herself for the sake of the Hawk clan, had traded her body for Kane's knowledge. She knew what that made her in the eyes of many, but she did not care about that. It was only the fact that she had found such pleasure in what he had done to her, what he had asked her to do to him, that gave her pause, that made her doubt the purity of her purpose.

She had thought it would be something she would have to endure, carnality without love. Instead she had found a joy she had never guessed was possible, and somehow it seemed to cast an entirely different light on the bargain she had made. She had been willing to pay to gain his help. That she had somehow become the recipient as well confused her. Over and above the fact that she was dwelling in safety and pleasure while they fought to survive, it did not seem right. She felt as if she had not truly made the sacrifice she had set out to make, and it made her wonder if perhaps it would lessen her chance of succeeding in her mission.

She wished she could stop thinking about it. About Kane. About the secret wonders he had shown her in the night, about the marvels she had learned from hands that had once killed so easily. Yet another paradox her weary mind could not fathom.

She pushed onward, wondering if it was possible to become too weary to think at all.

Of course, having Tal's clever raven dogging her every step was far too vivid a reminder to easily dismiss. If he truly was a wizard, he was obviously a very good one; the bird had never wavered on the long journey. And she had to admit that after a while she had come to welcome the company, even talking to the bird as she walked, especially when her roiling thoughts threatened to overcome her. And Maud, watching her intently and cocking her head whenever Jenna voiced a question, had listened with every evidence of understanding. So much so that Jenna hesitated to dismiss the thought as pure fancy.

She welcomed the canny bird's presence for other reasons as well; it had not taken her long—after all, she was descended from a clan who followed a bird to their new home—to recognize the raven's suggestion that she follow her into the woods. Once she had found a thicket of berry bushes that had been a welcome addition to the dried meat she carried, and once fresh, clear water to refill her waterskin.

And twice the bird had saved her life, leading her off the main track and well into hiding as a troop of armed men passed. Some carried insignia she did not know, but the last time, as she neared Hawk Glade, she had recognized the viperous banner of the evil warlord Druas. She suppressed a shudder, chiding herself for harboring some slim, foolish hope that somehow it would have all gone away, that she would return to find things as they had once been.

She should never have stayed away so long. All the time she had spent with Kane, in the safety of his mountain and his legendary presence, her people had been faced with the reality of this, of armed, predatory invaders. That they were within the forest, so close to Hawk Glade, made her cringe inwardly.

She wondered who had died since she had been gone. Evelin? The storyteller? Latham? She wondered who had screamed out the last moments of their life in agony as she lay in Kane's bed, as she welcomed him into her body and soared in his arms.

A shudder of guilt racked her, and she nearly stumbled. Maud made a sharp, warning noise.

Jenna stopped, staring down at her feet. It had not been emotion that had made her stumble.

Sprawled across the path was the bloody body of a dog. Her throat tightened. Latham's dog. The lop-eared, silly-grinned hound that Latham laughingly said was good for nothing but making the children laugh and warming his feet at night.

The dog who never strayed more than a few yards from Latham's side.

Latham.

Her breath seemed to stop, lodging in her chest like a solid thing that would not be moved. Maud called out again, that imperious sound Jenna had come to recognize. Jenna lifted her head. The raven sat on a small branch of a twisted shrub, her wings flapping noisily. Jenna had learned this signal of discovery quickly. Now she wished she could ignore it.

It took all of her remaining energy to move off the path and make her way through the underbrush to where Maud sat. Once she had seen Jenna start in her direction, the bird had calmed, folded her wings, and waited.

Jenna did not know the source of the certainty she felt. She knew only that she did not wish to take those last few steps. But she steadfastly went on.

She saw his feet first, twisted in an awkward manner that should have been unbearably uncomfortable. She was shaking now, but made herself take that last step.

And knew immediately that Latham would be no longer concerned about comfort or its lack. Or anything else in this life. He had been nearly hacked in half.

Jenna went to her knees, fighting nausea. She had seen such horrors before, yet somehow this seemed worse. Perhaps because of the quiet and peace she'd had on the mountain. The quiet and peace she had had no right to, not while this was what was happening to her people.

Maud fluttered her wings, seeming suddenly anxious. Jenna paid her no attention as grief seized her. Latham. Sweet, good-hearted Latham, who had taken no more joy in anything than in the children of the Hawk clan. Latham and his silly dog. The man who could always be counted on, who had never been heard to raise his voice in anger. Who had built her own cradle, who had carved her countless toys as a child, as he had for every Hawk child.

She vaguely registered the raven's increasing restlessness as she fought to slow her raging thoughts. Why had she left? Why had she not been here, perhaps she could have done something. Perhaps she could have saved him, stopped him from whatever it was he had left the safety of the glade to do. As the Hawk, she could have ordered him to stay. She could have prevented this.

"Hurry."

Jenna blinked. Maud's hoarse cry had sounded so much like the word it startled her out of her anguish for a moment. The bird took flight, darting deeper into the trees, then returning, then darting back in the cue for Jenna to follow.

Jenna knew she could not afford to give in to her grief now. Latham was beyond her help. She could not even take time to bury him properly, and it tore at her. But she had to get home.

She stood up.

Maud cried out, urgently this time. It did not sound like a word this time, but the imperative note could not be denied. Jenna ran quickly toward the bird, who led her into a thicket of trees so dense she had to fight her way through.

It was not until she paused for breath that she heard the ominous sounds. The chink of metal, the thud of heavy horses' hooves. Crouching down, she peered out from the heavy corner of the thicket.

Two abreast, they rode past, armor shining, horses snorting and tossing their heads as if in protest of heavy hands on the reins. An endless double column, pair by pair they came, each wearing the unmistakable insignia of Druas, a coiled viper. She had never seen a force so huge. Nor had she ever seen one so flush with arrogance; their laughter and crude talk echoed through the trees as they bragged of men slain and women raped and children broken and thrown aside to die.

This was what she had left her people to face. She was the hereditary leader of the Hawk Clan, yet she had left them to deal with this, while she . . . while she . . .

Despair seized her. She had been wrong when she'd thought she never should have stayed with Kane.

She never should have gone to him at all.

Chapter 15

" 'Tis not your fault, Jenna."

She registered the words vaguely, still wondering why she could not cry. Not a tear had she shed, even when she had reached the perimeter of Hawk Glade to find Latham was just the latest in the grim parade of death that had gone on inexorably in her absence.

Just as it had been when she had buried her mother, and her brother, she could not cry. It was as if all her grief had somehow frozen inside her, and lay there still, unmoving, a solid lump of pain that would never go away.

"Jenna?"

She shook her head, then focused on the speaker. Cara was no longer the ethereal golden beauty she had once been. She looked gaunt and haggard, watching Jenna with eyes that had seen too much, revealing a soul that had grown old far too quickly. She had been the first to spot Jenna and had run out to meet her, bearing the grim news.

"You can say this?" she asked gently, wonderingly; Cara had lost her uncle and her sister during Jenna's absence, the last of her family left to her was her small brother Lucas, even now clinging to her leg, his eyes wide and stunned-looking.

"What could you have done had you been here?" she said with a fatalistic shrug.

Her tone was so lifeless Jenna was startled. It took her a moment to realize the cause; Cara had given up. She could see it in her eyes, could see that she only waited now until her turn to join her murdered loved ones. She wondered if all had given up.

"Does the glade's protection still hold?"

"It does within the glade itself. It is those who venture out into the forest who have perished. But they know we are here, or at the least that something is. And they are growing angry that they cannot find us. Each day they tighten the noose around us. Soon they will walk into Hawk Glade itself simply because they have searched everywhere else. Then all will be lost."

Jenna conceded that was possible; even the magic could not prevent someone who chose or was ordered to overlook the apparent impenetrability of the glade, or began to hack their way through it, from finding it.

"You did not mention the storyteller," she said. "Does he live?"

Cara shrugged again. "We do not know. He disappeared again, and has not returned yet. We think each time he goes that he will be killed, but he returns. He has done the same so often that we have come to think he will always return."

"When did he go last?"

"A week, perhaps more. He's been especially unpredictable of late. Ever since you left, he's been gone nearly as much as here. We never know when he will go or return." Cara's tone did not change, but she looked at Jenna with a vague semblance of curiosity. "I see you did not find Kane the Warrior. So he is but a myth, after all?"

Jenna took a deep breath. It was time to begin. To do what she could to put what she'd learned to use.

"He is not."

For the first time she saw a spark of life in her friend's eyes. "He is not?"

"He is a man . . . unlike any I've ever known."

"But he would not help us?"

"He could not. Not directly. He cannot leave his mountains and live."

She saw the questions hovering and hastened to divert them; there were things she could not tell, would not tell. Kane had not asked her to keep silent, but she would nevertheless not spread his story to all.

"You must help me gather the clan. We must plan."

"Plan? Plan what?"

"Our strategy."

Cara looked bewildered. "Strategy?"

Kane could not come with me," Jenna said. "But he taught me what we need to know. The only way our small clan can hope to hold what is ours."

"Jenna, I don't know if anyone who survives has the will left to try. You don't know how it's been while you've been gone. Druas has brought in the biggest force of men anyone has ever heard of—"

"I know. I saw them."

"Then you must know we have no hope of defeating them."

"Yes. So we will not try to defeat them. Only to divert them."

Cara looked even more bewildered. "What do you mean?"

"Gather the clan. I will explain to everyone."

There were so few left, Jenna thought, fighting not to let her misery show. So few of the once-populous clan left to battle such a powerful foe. Yet they had taken so eagerly to her plans, plans that now seemed silly to her in the face of the huge force she had seen on the road. Yet when she had told them the ideas for harrying, harassing, and annoying the enemy had come direct from the legendary Kane, they had taken heart and hope and scurried off to do her bidding.

Even Evelin had been willing, had in fact looked pleased at having a part.

"I'll be more than glad to give them a taste of pain and cramps and spewing stomachs they'll not soon forget," she said as she lingered to give Jenna a hug of welcome, more than a trace of fury in her normally placid expression as she spoke. " 'Twill take my mind off worrying about Latham."

Jenna's breath caught. She had, incredibly, forgotten for a moment that they did not know.

"Latham . . ." She could not go on.

"I wish we could call him back, now that you're safely returned to us."

The image of his bloody, torn body stole Jenna's ability to answer for a moment. She could not bear to tell of his gruesome death, not yet. Let them cherish the hope that he would return for a while longer. The knowledge weighed heavy on her heart as she asked what she had been wondering since she had found him.

"Where . . . did he go? And why? It was agreed all should remain in the glade unless there was urgent need."

"He felt it urgent, and we could not stop him. You know he loves you as his own child."

Jenna gasped. "Are you saying he went . . . for me?"

"He hoped to find you on your way back, to help you, guard you now that Druas has called in such a huge force."

She moaned, low and harsh, the image of Latham's sprawled body now a thing she knew would haunt her forever in the most awful of ways.

"Do not take alarm, dear," Evelin said. "He left but this morning, and we made him swear if he did not find you he would not remain out through the night. He will return before midnight, and since you are safely back now, he will not venture out again."

Jenna's stomach knotted fiercely. She brushed off Evelin's concern at her sudden paleness, and bade her get about her task, praying the woman would leave before she betrayed herself completely. The moment the healer was out of sight, Jenna turned away, began to run, then staggered.

A strong arm caught her, steadied her. She looked up, meaning to give a hasty command to be left alone. And stopped before the words could be said.

"Tal?" she whispered.

"Easy, child. You are . . . disturbed."

He tilted his head then, and she saw the sheen of silver as the moonight touched his hair. The storyteller. It had been a trick of light, then, light and those eyes that were so like Tal's.

"You're back," she said, unnecessarily.

"Yes. Come, you must sit."

"I . . . cannot. There is much to do."

"Yes," he agreed, "but you have come a long way. You are tired, and your soul is weary of battling itself. Rest for a short while."

She stared at him, then let him pull her gently toward her own cottage. It had been kept scrupulously clean in her absence; present or gone, she was still the Hawk.

She watched as the old man bustled about, starting a fire and putting water on in preparation for one of Evelin's relaxing teas. He was rather more hunched over, and moved more like the old man he was than she remembered, and she wondered that she ever could have mistaken him for the vigorous, vital Tal. Yet there was a resemblance, and no denying that their eyes were uncannily alike.

"Have you relatives up in the mountains?" she asked suddenly.

He went still, then looked over his shoulder at her. "None that I am aware of."

She'd expected that answer, after what Tal had told her. But she'd felt compelled to ask anyway. "I just thought . . . I met someone there who reminds me strongly of you. So much that I thought he might even be your son."

The storyteller's face became expressionless. "I have no son. Nor will I ever."

There was a bleakness in his voice that went far deeper than the admittedly joyless words he spoke. He said no more, merely poured the water that seemed to have heated very quickly and poured it into an earthen mug over Evelin's leafy mixture. He stirred it, then handed it to her.

He waited until she had taken a sip and lowered the mug before he spoke.

"You did not tell anyone of Latham's death."

She nearly jumped. "You . . . know?"

"I returned along the same path."

"Oh. Of course."

"I buried him. And his dog alongside him, as he would have wanted."

Gratitude flooded her. "Thank you. I wished to—"

"I know, Jenna. You had no chance and no time. 'Tis taken care of."

He gestured her to drink, hushing the thanks she would have continued with a shake of his head.

"I . . . found Kane," she said at last when her cup was empty except for the leaves in the bottom.

"I know."

"You returned in time to hear the plan, then?"

"I know it," he assented. " 'Tis a good one. The best that can be hoped for, as things now stand."

Jenna sighed, wishing she did not feel so utterly

weary. "I had much time to think, on my journey here. Too much, I fear. But I have decided something."

"You do not sound as if you like your decision."

"I do not. Nor will the clan. But I see no other choice." She took a breath, then let it out slowly as she tired not to yawn openly. "If this does not work . . . we must leave Hawk Glade. I cannot see them all die in defense of a place. Kane was right. Life is precious and short, while the land is eternal, and cares not that men die for it."

"You have gained wisdom as well as knowledge on your quest, Jenna."

She did not wish to talk about what she had gained, did not wish to even think of it. "I only hope the clan will see it thus. This has been our home for so long . . ."

"Yet not forever. They came from one place to here. They can do it again, if need be. Your forever is not in a place, Jenna. It is in your heart, your blood, your spirit."

Again she thought of Tal and his wild promise. And then she felt a wave of longing for Kane so powerful it nearly made her moan aloud. She closed her eyes against it and felt an odd spinning. She felt herself being eased down to lie on something soft.

"Rest, Jenna," the storyteller said quietly. "Rest."

She was asleep before she could protest that she had no time for rest.

Kane's own cry woke him from the throes of the nightmare, and he sat bolt upright in a cold sweat. Again it had come to him, that bloody, vicious dream in which Jenna, dying, cried out to him for help.

It mattered not that he knew she would die before she would voice such a supplicating plea for herself; she would beg on her knees for her people, and well he knew it. Better than anyone, he knew it, he thought grimly as he shoved his hair back out of his eyes.

It seemed like forever since he'd awakened in the night to feel her soft warmth beside him. Since he'd awakened so full of a consuming ache that he could not stop himself from reaching for her. He'd convinced himself then that it was merely a man's need, too long denied, nothing more. But since she'd gone, since he'd returned to his solitary bed, he had no longer been able to dismiss it as merely carnal compulsion. Not when he ached to simply hold her against him, to feel her slender body pressed to his as she slept safely in his arms.

This was bad enough, but somehow the days were worse, when he would walk a familiar path only to think of Jenna as she had once walked it with him, as he would pass the tree they'd used as a target and he thought of her determination, as he passed the cliff she had climbed and he thought of her fire.

And he fought against admitting that it was not her presence in his bed that he missed, a relatively safe admission for a man so long alone, but that he missed her presence in his life.

And then the horrors had begun to haunt his nights.

"Only a dream," he muttered to himself as he had so many times before. But this time it would not let go, and he had an odd feeling of being connected to the bloody scene he'd just dreamed. "A dream," he repeated, almost fiercely.

Not for long.

The words rang in the air with the strength of his own conscience, which had been plaguing him to near insanity in the past few days since Jenna had gone. He tensed; he had sensed no presence within the cave, but the words had come in a voice not his own.

They will soon be found, Kane. They have held him off, but the warlord grows angry.

The use of his name had him looking rather wildly around the cave, searching. He found nothing, although every corner was lit enough to see by the faint glow of the fire's embers.

Your tactics have worked, but they are too few. The warlord has brought in too many mercenaries from the far north, and longbowmen from the south.

Tal. It was Tal's voice, he could not deny it. If he'd known any of the common oaths of protection against sorcery he would have uttered it; but he'd never bothered to learn, since he'd never believed in such things.

Do not choose now to reverse your acceptance, Kane. Jenna is in danger.

Kane's stomach knotted. "She is . . . ?"

Alive. In body. But I cannot speak for her heart and spirit if her people are destroyed.

"Can you not help them?"

He couldn't believe he'd said it aloud, but his self-reproach ended abruptly when he got an answer.

I cannot. The spell of Hawk Glade is much stronger than any I've ever felt. My powers are useless here. I can do only the simplest things. Such as fire, and this.

Kane gritted his teeth and steadied himself. He shook his head, glanced around once more to make sure his friend wasn't simply sitting in the shadows, out of sight. The cave was empty.

"Tal?" he said, feeling foolish.

But it was gone. That sense of connection was gone, as was the voice, the voice he could not possibly have heard, but had.

It did not matter. He knew, as he suspected he'd known for days, that he could not go on like this. Jenna haunted him as nothing else ever had, not even the horror of his sister's death. He had been but a child, he could not have stopped that. But Jenna . . . if she were to die when he could have saved her . . .

He could not go on like this. He could not just leave

it like this, knowing she would die. She would die, because she would never, ever give up. It wasn't in her.

He had thought he would regain his peace when she had gone. He knew now he could not buy that peace at the cost of her life, even if the alternative was to lose his own.

It was not that he thought she would truly come back here. She would never leave her people, he knew that well. He had the fleeting thought that the old Kane would have made that the price for his help, that she stay here with him forever. And if she believed that the only way to save her clan, he believed she would agree, she loved them that much.

But the woman who stayed would not be the woman he had known. She would be but a hollow shell, for her heart would stay in Hawk Glade.

He had never fought without expecting some gain for himself, in either spoils or the regard for his warlord. Kane the Warrior knew no other way. But Kane the man knew the moment he rose to his feet that his decision was made. And that it was irrevocable. He was going to go to Hawk Glade. He was going to go back on his vow never to leave these mountains, and if Tal's warning came true, so be it. He might die, but if he did not act, he most surely would, because he could not bear another day of this. He either went to help her, or he went to the cliff Jenna had climbed and walked off the edge. Either choice was more bearable than living like this.

He began to gather his things. He packed by rote, an old habit long unpracticed but never forgotten, the collecting of the tools of war by a man long used to their use.

He hesitated only once, when he went to the back of the cave and knelt to dig with his small dagger. He reached a long, narrow bundle wrapped in deerhide.

He lifted it out. For a long moment he simply looked at it. Then he undid the wrapping and tossed it aside. His hands moved instinctively, one grasping, one pulling in a swift, smooth motion. Even in the dim light of the back of the cave, the silver blade flashed.

The sword of Kane the warrior was as deadly as it had ever been. He only hoped the man who held it had remained as sharp.

"You're certain of this?"

Cara's young brother nodded nervously. "Yes, I a-am," he said, flushing as his voice broke. "They have not moved."

A sad thing it was, Jenna thought, when this child has to forgo what should have been a time of games and learning to instead risk his too-short life to become a spy for them. Yet there were so few adults left, and they were all exhausted.

"Well done, Lucas. I thank you."

The boy's blush deepened. "Thank you, Hawk," he said, making a short bow as he backed away.

Jenna smiled a rueful, inward smile; she doubted she would ever grow accustomed to the bowing obeisance that came with her rank. No more than she would ever be comfortable in this long dress that had been her mother's, worn when she was faced with some complex decision. Jenna had donned it in the hopes some of her mother's simple wisdom might be imparted by the dress she'd worn as the Hawk. It was simple by some standards yet ornate by her own; trimmed with elegant stitchwork, it draped gracefully over her slender frame, the long sleeves coming to a point over her wrists. The only thing she truly liked about it was the color; a deep, rich blue given a faint sheen by the soft nap of the fabric.

"You have held them in place," the storyteller observed.

"Evelin has," Jenna corrected, giving the healer a grateful look. "Thanks to her potions, those who are still on their feet at all are too weak to move."

" 'Twas your idea," Evelin said, satisfaction in her expression despite her refusal of credit.

"Not mine. Kane's."

She thought she'd said it steadily enough, betraying nothing. Yet the storyteller turned his gaze on her, studying her as if she had screamed her heartache to the night sky.

She was a fool to dwell so much on a man who had been only too glad to see her go. His reluctance to see her leave had only been that he'd been certain she would die. She supposed he had seen enough of death, enough so that he did not welcome more, no matter who it was. The coolness with which he had let her go in the end proved there was nothing more to it than that. And proved that she was worse than a fool to think that Kane the Warrior, the mercenary fighter who had struck terror into the hearts and minds of countless of his victims, had any kind of soft spot for the desperate woman who had come to him begging help. She had eased his male needs for a space, that was all. She was no more to him than that.

"Yet you have carried it out," the storyteller said. "Since your return, Druas has gained little ground, where before he had gained by the league."

A chorus of cheers for the new Hawk broke out, and Jenna tried to hush them, embarrassed at the outcry. She felt she was doing so little, yet they looked upon her as if she were a miracle worker. The storyteller had told her it was only natural, that in their desperate straits they would look upon any small hope as salvation, but still, the burden weighed upon her.

She glanced at him now, wishing the old man would give her that look of reassurance she had come to depend on these past few days, that bolstering of spirit

that had often been the only thing that had kept her
going. But he was not looking at her, he was peering
off into the forest. She could not really see his face,
but she had the oddest feeling he was very pleased
about something.

" 'Tis true," Cara said when the last of the cheers
died away, hope renewed in her voice. "Since Jenna's
return, they have been lodged on the edge of the forest, unable to move. There are already rumblings
among them that the forest is hexed, or haunted by
spirits who do not welcome them. And many have
withdrawn from the forest to hide in the stronghold."

Jenna looked at her friend, who was beginning to
look more like her old self, although grief for her lost
family still shadowed her eyes.

"And how would you know this?" she asked.

Cara flushed. "I . . . overheard them talking."

A murmuring rippled through the gathering. "You
took a foolish risk, getting so close," Jenna said
sternly. "You know as well as I what happens to Druas's prisoners. Especially women."

"I was safe," Cara protested.

"You know we do not know exactly where the protection of Hawk Glade ends. You could have been
seen. Captured. We cannot afford—"

"—to hold any one life too dear."

The clan cried out, and as one whirled toward the
voice that had come ringing out of the night, Jenna
was beyond speech, frozen. The others reacted to the
shock of the unknown, harsh voice; Jenna was reeling
because she knew that voice all too well.

He strode out of the trees, came out of the darkness
looking like the shadows themselves had spawned him.
Clad in black from head to booted toe, he looked like
the legend come to life, larger than any mortal man,
tall, powerful, his expression cold, merciless. Even his
armor was black, not the polished metal they had

come to know and fear. With a long black cloak swirling around him, he looked like the blackest of demons, the stuff of myth, the man used to frighten children into behaving, and men into laying down their arms without a fight, for who could hope to fight such a devil?

Had she not known, Jenna would barely have recognized him. This was not the man she had known on the mountain, the man who wore simple leather leggings and tunic, the man who, for all his size, power, and experience had achieved a wry peace with the world. This was Kane the Warrior, and she realized only now that as fierce as he had seemed to her before, it was nothing compared to the reality of what he had been.

And her first reaction was pain that she had brought him to this. That because of her he had donned the implements of war once more. That because of her he had turned his back on his hard-won peace. That because of her he had left his sanctuary—

I . . . cannot leave here. If I do, I will die.

His words, Tal's prophecy, rang in her head.

She stared at him, stunned anew.

"Kane," she whispered, her heart twisting inside her.

She did not know what else to say to a man who had just offered up his life for them.

Chapter 16

She heard the awed gasps as she spoke his name, heard the murmurings, the rustling of movement as people turned to gape, then quickly averted their eyes, as if fearful of being caught staring at him. Except for the storyteller, whom no one had ever thought to question, no one unknown to them had ever found this glade. And although she did not know how Kane had discovered them, she could see that it only added to the sense of awe among the clan that he already had inspired.

They parted for him as if he were brandishing the sword that was sheathed at his side. He walked toward Jenna. She looked at him, eyes searching his face. She saw nothing but the cold, ruthless gaze of the legend. Not even recognition warmed his icy gray eyes. Nor did he speak to her when he came to a halt before the still-dazed gathering.

"If you wish to succeed," he said, his voice booming out over them all, his tone one Jenna had never heard from him before, even when he had been shouting his sharpest orders at her, "you must think of yourselves all as already dead. You await only the vultures to confirm it. If you can do this, some remnant of your clan may survive. 'Tis unlikely, but possible."

The murmurs came again. Kane cut across them like the sharpest of blades, effectively silencing them.

"No one life is worth anything, if you wish to save the whole. If you cannot accept this, your only choice is how you will die. You can continue and die, or surrender and die anyway. Either way, your enemy will have this place."

Jenna could not find her voice, she could only stare at him. Of all the others, Evelin was the first to recover enough to speak.

"You leave out the choice of escape," she said.

He turned on the older woman. Jenna saw the fear in Evelin's eyes as she faced the legendary Kane, but the woman stood her ground, and Jenna felt a surge of pride. And when Kane spoke, his voice was surprisingly gentle.

"You have left that too late. It is no longer a choice. I have seen how close they are. All exits will be cut off. All roads guarded, in all directions. And anyone captured will be tortured for what information they can give, and then killed."

"You sound very certain."

It was the storyteller, and Jenna watched Kane as he turned to look at the old man, wondering if he would see what she had seen, or if the resemblance to Tal was just some odd fancy of hers.

For the first time she saw a flicker of a change in his expression, saw his brows lower just a fraction, and she knew he had seen the likeness. But when he spoke, it was as if he had seen nothing.

"I am."

"How?" Evelin dared to ask.

Kane turned to look at her again. "Because it is what I would do."

It silenced them all, this dark, grim knowledge of who and what he was. Jenna saw him take in the reaction, saw the expression she thought already ice grow even colder.

"So you are saying," the storyteller said, his voice oddly casual, as if beginning one of his philosophical speculations, "that you and Druas are cut from the same cloth?"

Kane's head jerked around toward the old man. The others drew in audible breaths and shrank back. Even Jenna gave a little start; she had never seen Kane move that way, violently, as if involuntarily.

The storyteller never moved, despite Kane's towering, threatening stance.

"Druas?" Kane spoke the name lowly, harshly. "It is Druas you fight?"

"It is," the storyteller answered, his voice steady even in the face of Kane's fierce, sudden intensity. Jenna was proud of him, too, not in the same way she had been proud of Evelin but, oddly, in a somehow more personal way.

And then Kane turned toward her, and she wondered if she would be the one to quail before him.

"You did not tell me it was Druas."

Jenna gathered her wits and her will to answer him levelly. "I did not think it mattered. One vicious warlord is much the same as another."

Something dark twisted in the depths of his eyes, something that made her want to take a step back, and only sheer determination enabled her to stay where she was.

"You underestimate him," Kane snarled.

"And who would know better than you?" the storyteller said softly.

Again Kane's head came around sharply. This time he studied the storyteller at length, until Jenna wondered that the old man did not wither under the scrutiny. At last he turned back to Jenna.

"I would speak with you," he said, his voice abrupt

and ringing with command. He glanced at the storyteller. "And you. And whoever else you have of leadership left."

Jenna silently gestured at Evelin and Arlen to follow them, then led them all into her small cottage,
leaving the rest of the clan outside to whisper among
themselves in tones of shock and awe.

Inside, Evelin took the most comfortable chair when
Jenna insisted; she did so smothering a pang at the
sight of Latham's careful work. At her nod of permis-
sion Arlen sat as well; Jenna knew the man was weary,
he'd done much of her bidding in these days just past,
and she'd quickly come to trust him in these duties
that were far removed from the making of snares he'd
done before.

The storyteller moved to a darker corner of the
room, lifting himself to sit upon the edge of the table
there with an ease that belied his age, as if he had rid
himself of the stiffness she'd noticed since her return.
She herself kept to her feet, as did Kane.

She watched him for a moment as he stood beside
the hearth, an even darker, more ominous figure as
the flickering light of the fire danced over his somber
attire. The blackness was relieved only slightly by the
dull sheen of his light armor, and the much brighter
sheen of his dark hair. A tingling spread over her as
she remembered that thick mane of hair brushing over
her naked body as he taught her things she'd never
dreamed of, as she remembered her fingers tangling
in it as she cried out at the explosion of pleasure he
gave her.

He looked past her, as if he did not know her at all.

She thought of all she wished she could say to him,
ask of him, and knew she could speak none of it. Not
only because of the frigidity of his manner, but because she had no time to even make a fool of herself
with words she should not say and he would not want

to hear. Nothing mattered more than what they must deal with now.

And here, in the familiar surroundings, in the cottage that belonged to the Hawk, Jenna felt it was time to begin. She smoothed the soft fabric of her mother's dress. She was the Hawk now, she could wait no longer. But there was something she had to know first.

. She took a deep breath to steady herself, then turned to Kane. "What did that mean, that no one would know better than you of Druas?"

He turned to look at her, saying nothing. She met his gaze levelly, even though the flat coldness she saw there chilled her. Still he said nothing, but merely looked at her with that merciless unemotional expression. She sensed this was some sort of test of her will, and she knew she dare not look away. It took all of her nerve, but she held his gaze unflinchingly. Finally, in the instant before he spoke she thought she saw the tiniest flicker of salute in the gray eyes.

"It means," he said, his voice neutral, "that Druas is the warlord I fought for."

The sharp exclamation Jenna knew came from Arlen, the gasp from Evelin. The storyteller said nothing, and she turned to look at him.

"You knew this," she said slowly, with certainty, "when you sent me to him."

"I did."

"You dared send Jenna to the man who was the head butcher for the very warlord who seeks to destroy us?" Evelin cried out, rising to her feet and forsaking Jenna's proper title in her anger.

"I did." The storyteller's voice was calm, unruffled.

"Why?" Arlen exclaimed. "Surely you knew he would most likely kill her!"

Jenna held up her hand for silence. She got it; one of the benefits of being the Hawk that she appreciated.

"But he did not kill me," she said, not looking at

Kane but at the storyteller as she walked over to stand before him.

"No," he agreed unnecessarily.

She studied him for a moment, the weathered, lined face and the silver hair, the dark brows and the bland expression. But most of all the eyes, those intense, changeable eyes that could reveal the wisdom of the world or conceal it.

"You sent me to him not just because he was Kane the Warrior, but precisely because he had been Druas's right hand, didn't you?"

The storyteller smiled, as a teacher smiles at a particularly bright pupil. "How better to learn to defeat him?"

"Clever." The sharp comment drew all eyes in the room to Kane. He walked over to stand beside Jenna. "I presume you are her precious storyteller?"

The old man's dark brows rose. "Precious?"

"I head much of you in the time she was with me."

The old man smiled, winked at Jenna, and said to Kane, "Too much, I gather?"

"I grew weary of it, old man. But more, I grew suspicious. You know of things no man should know."

"I know what makes a good story," the old man replied. "And Kane the Warrior is one of the best. I made the effort to learn all I could of him."

"You told her how to find me."

"I am . . . familiar with the mountains. I knew where the place the tales describe must be."

"Does this matter now?" Jenna interrupted. "Do we not have more important things to speak of than what is past?"

"That's my girl, always to the heart of the matter," the storyteller said with a grin that took years from his countenance and made him look eerily like Tal. Jenna felt Kane's sudden stillness and knew he had seen it, too.

"Who are you?" Kane asked.

The storyteller winced, like a man realizing he'd betrayed something he hadn't meant to. "I am merely a storyteller. Ask any of the clan, they will tell you."

"These people may be content to take you at your word, but I am not," Kane said.

"No, you take no one at their word, do you? Who was it that taught you so completely to trust no one but yourself?"

Kane's brows lowered, and his jaw tightened. "Suffice that I learned it well and early. And I have rarely been wrong."

"Ah, but if you do not trust, you have no way of knowing if you could have."

Kane snorted. "You talk in riddles, old man." As if dismissing the subject, he turned back to Jenna. "What was said, is it true? You have held them where they are, on the edge of your forest?"

She nodded. "For several days. We have harried them at every turn, as you said. Loosed their horses, tainted their food and drink, stolen everything small enough to be easily carried."

"And left behind inexplicable signs, mysterious carved stones, footprints that could come from no less a creature than a bear that would tower over even you," Evelin added proudly. "Druas's men are half convinced the glade is full of evil spirits. And every night we make sure they hear noises that convince them even further. They've slept little since they set up their camp."

"They always were a credulous lot," Kane said, nodding slowly in approval. "Clever of you to play upon it."

" 'Twas the Hawk's idea," Arlen said, gesturing toward Jenna. "Because of her, Druas has even called much of his force back to his stronghold in the west."

Kane looked at her then. "The Hawk," he murmured. Jenna felt herself color. "You thought of this?"

She shrugged. "They were already wary of the forest, since they knew we had to be here somewhere yet were unable to find us. And then I remembered something . . . someone told me, about people fearing the unknown more than anything else. So I thought to take advantage of that."

"Someone?" Kane's voice was low.

"Tal," she admitted. "He spoke of it on the way down the mountain."

"So he *is* here," Kane breathed.

"Here?" Jenna gave him a puzzled look. "No. He told me he was going to see to . . ." She broke off, doubted Kane would like it if she phrased it as his friend had. "He said he was going back to the mountain. I've not seen him since. Only Maud."

Kane blinked. "Maud?"

"He sent her after me, I think. And I was more than glad of it. She's a very clever bird." She glanced at the others, who were looking at her rather curiously. She knew she could say no more of Tal's uncannily intelligent companion in front of them, so she hastened to go on. "She stayed with me to the edge of the forest, but she would come no further. She must have gone back to find Tal."

"But he is—"

Kane broke off, and she had the oddest feeling that he was thinking just as she had been a moment ago, that whatever he'd been about to say should not be said in company.

"I will need to see the lay of the land," he said, changing the subject abruptly. "And to see what you have done so far."

Jenna took a breath. "Why?" His brow furrowed. It took a great deal of effort to go on, but she got out the words. "Perhaps more correctly I must ask why are you here?"

"And," Evelin added, apparently getting over her awe, "how you found Hawk Glade."

"You told me how," Kane said, looking at Jenna.

"I?" she asked, startled.

"Do you not recall? The night you told me how he"—he jerked a thumb at the storyteller—"found you?"

Jenna's breath caught, and she prayed that the room was dark enough that the others could not see the color that rushed to her cheeks. She indeed remembered that night, when Kane had used his mouth on her for the first time, when he had taught her there were kisses more intimate than anything she had ever imagined.

"You told me he is a man capable of seeing what others cannot, patterns where others see only chaos. That he knew Hawk Glade was supposed to be here. When he arrived and it was not, he merely discounted the evidence of his eyes and kept coming."

"I never meant . . . 'twas only to try and explain how this place keeps us safe," Jenna said in embarrassed consternation.

"Never explain what advantage you may have to anyone not on your side," Kane said flatly. "If they do not turn it against you themselves, they will most likely sell it to someone who will."

She drew herself up then; she was the Hawk, and it was past time she started acting like it.

"And which will you do, Kane?"

For an instant he looked startled. "What?"

"I ask again. Why are you here?"

Jenna got the distinct feeling he was uncomfortable, although she thought it so unlikely she was reluctant to trust her senses.

Kane glanced around at the others in the room. "I would speak with your Hawk alone."

"No," Arlen said protectively.

"You shall not," Evelin said simultaneously, in much the same tone.

"I mean her no harm," Kane said, clearly restraining his anger with an effort; Jenna doubted he was often gainsaid in such a manner.

"It is all right," she told them.

"No!" they chimed together.

"Be easy," the storyteller, slipping off the table to walk over to the two. "He will not hurt her."

"You cannot be sure of that," Evelin protested.

"Had he wanted to harm her," the storyteller said mildly, "he had ample chance. Do you forget she spent the moon's cycle in his company? Come."

Reluctantly casting concerned glances back at Jenna, they let the old man usher them out. At the door, the storyteller glanced back over his shoulder at them, giving them both one of those intense, disconcerting looks of his, and then he walked out without another word.

Jenna watched as Kane stared after the old man.

"He looks like Tal, does he not? Or as Tal will look, many years from now."

Kane's gaze snapped back to her face. "So you see it as well?"

"I saw it in Tal from the beginning. So much that I asked him if his father still lived."

Kane blinked. "Does he?"

Jenna blinked in turn. "He is your friend. Do you not know?"

"I . . . no." He had the grace to look embarrassed. "I don't . . . I never asked. I've never . . . had such a friend."

As easily as that she was back to where she'd been on the mountain, aching for the man so many saw only as myth, the man who had never had a chance to become anything but what he had become, a man who walked alone, whose very name made others walk the other way.

"He said his father was long dead," she said quickly, fighting the unwanted emotion he seemed always to spark in her. "And the storyteller has no kin in the mountains. 'Tis only a fluke, it would seem."

"An uncanny one," Kane muttered.

"Yes. But no more uncanny to me than you walking out of the night. Why?" she asked for a third time.

"I thought that obvious."

"Is it? You told me you would never again take up arms. That you had buried your sword deep, never again to see light."

"I never meant to."

"And now I know you were once at the right hand of the warlord who wishes us all dead and out of his way."

"I do not deny that."

"But I am to believe you came here to . . . help us?"

He made as if to speak, then stopped. When he went on, she was somehow certain it was not what he'd been about to say. "You will believe what you wish."

"You told me you would die if you left your mountain."

His mouth twisted wryly. "That may yet be true."

She stared at him. "You still believe you might die, yet you came? Why?"

He looked at her for a long, silent moment, so long that she felt her heart take a quivering little leap. Not for her? Surely not for her? She didn't dare to hope for such a thing.

"I grew bored," he said at last, the cool dismissal in his voice at odds with the intensity of his eyes.

"Perhaps teaching you reawakened my interest in contests of this kind."

"No!"

Her cry startled her even as it broke from her. Kane looked at her, brows lifted as if in faint surprise at her reaction. She mistrusted the reality of the emotion; somehow it seemed Kane had utterly withdrawn, except for that moment when he had learned the name of the warlord they fought.

"I . . . did not wish that," she stammered.

"You came to me asking for just that, did you not?"

"Yes, but . . . I do not wish it now."

"Why?"

"I . . . understand now, why you abandoned that life. What it took from you. What it cost you. I do not wish to see you return to it. Bury your sword again, Kane. Go back to your mountain, where you are safe."

For an instant, no longer, she thought she saw a surprise in his face that was genuine, not a mockery of the emotion. Then the mask was back in place, that cool, uncaring expression the belied what she thought she had seen.

"Safe from what?" he asked, as if it were only an idle inquiry, not a matter of his own death. "Tal's prophecy, or Druas?"

"Both," she said. "Have you not thought that if Tal's prophecy is right, Druas may be the means?"

"I had not," he admitted. "But I was unaware it was Druas you faced until now."

"Then you must see," she said urgently. "If your intent was truly to help us, you must see that if Druas finds out that you have turned against him—"

"I turned against him long ago."

"You merely left him," Jenna pointed out.

" 'Tis the same to Druas. You are either his man, or you are against him."

Jenna did not question his words; she'd seen enough of Druas's brutality to believe them. "Then he will be truly angry should he discover you are helping us."

"He will be," Kane said with a negligent shrug of one shoulder, "incensed."

"Then you cannot risk it. You must go. We are holding them. We will continue, until they give up and choose another path to the north."

"They will not."

"But you said—"

"That was before I knew you dealt with Druas." Kane closed the slight distance between them with one long stride. "He will never give up. Nor will he turn away. He has set his course, and he will follow it. He will have his path to the north, if he has to cut down every tree of your forest. And he will not care if he cuts all of you down as well. In fact, he would take great satisfaction in it."

Jenna stared at him, unable to doubt the certainty of his words. "He is . . . even more evil than we had thought."

"He is."

"Yet you fought for him."

"I did. For years. I trained for it since I was twelve, fought for him since I was sixteen."

Her breath caught; so young?

"Do not foster any benevolent thoughts of me, Jenna," he said, speaking her name for the first time; he said it so coldly she could have wished he had not. "I was the perfect right hand for Druas's evil. I cared only for the goal, nothing for the method. Nor did I care for those who were left trampled in our wake. Druas gave me orders, I carried them out. I never questioned him. It was my place to see his wishes enacted. I did so."

His voice had taken on the quality of a lash, snapping, cracking as though impacting on flesh. And although his expression betrayed nothing but cold composure, Jenna knew instinctively that the lash was directed at himself. And she knew in that moment that no one could ever punish Kane the Warrior for what he'd done any more harshly than the man himself.

"Kane," she said, then stopped, afraid to go on when she had heard the tremor in her voice, echoing with the pain she was feeling for him.

"Stop," he hissed. "Do not squander your soft feelings on me. I do not deserve them."

She couldn't hold it back, the words tumbled out. "But you need them. More than any man I've ever known."

Kane recoiled as if she'd slapped him. "I have no need of anything from you, or anyone."

That was as clear an answer as she would ever get, Jenna thought. Whatever they had had, it had ended, completely and permanently, when their bargain had ended.

Jenna studied him for a moment, gathering her nerve; this meeting was truly testing her mettle. "If you need nothing from anyone, then why are you here?" she finally asked again. "Why did you not simply stay in your cave, apart from the world?"

His aloofness was quickly back in place. "I told you. I grew bored."

"I do not wish you to . . . amuse yourself here. Go back to your mountain, Kane the Warrior."

He lifted a brow at her tone. His glance flicked to the carved mantel above the fireplace, where the golden Hawk gleamed dully in the firelight; she should have realized he would have noticed it.

"Is this the Hawk, giving an order?" he asked.

"If you wish. 'Tis bad enough I have the blood of my people on my hands and my heart. I do not care to add the blood of an outsider, with no need to be here."

He shook his head. "It is my choice, Jenna."

"To risk your life? For people you say yourself you neither need nor want anything from? For a lost cause? You called it a fool's errand, did you not? 'Tis not like you to play the fool."

Kane looked at her, and again she made herself hold his gaze.

"You wear it well," he said after a moment, his voice quiet. "Command suits you."

"I have no wish to command. I wish only to save my people."

"Then you must retract your order, Hawk. With me, you might just have some small chance of surviving. Without me, Druas will crush you to the last, and not leave any trace that you were ever here in the process."

Jenna knew she could not tell him that the thought of him taking up arms, of him becoming again that which he had fought so hard to leave behind, hurt her nearly as much as the thought of her people being slaughtered by their vicious enemy. She could not tell him that she wanted him to stay simply because she was hungry for the sight of him, and hungrier still for the feel of him. She could not tell him that she wished more than anything that she could abandon the task before her, could shirk the responsibilities of the Hawk and run with him back to his mountain.

She could tell him none of that. He would not welcome it, nor could she humiliate herself so and still expect to function as she must. And the truth of his words were undeniable; with him, a man trained by, and well versed in the tactics of their enemy they might have a chance. And it might well be their only chance. What right had she to refuse, simply because

Kane's presence would wreak havoc with what tiny bit she had left of peace of mind?

She glanced at the golden hawk, the generations-old symbol of her office. She did not have the right. She should have welcomed him without question, without thought of the cost to him. Yet she had thought of it, second only to her dread for the clan. And if she were honest, in the first moments, she had thought of it foremost.

With an apology directed as much at the golden statue as anything, she made herself speak.

"I will consider revoking it," she said, "if you will honestly tell me why you are here."

He was silent for a moment. She wondered if he was debating what to say, or simply whether to answer at all. At last he spoke.

"I have many reasons. They are my own. But now that I am here, now that I know who you face, there is yet another reason I will give you. I have . . . reason to wish greatly for the defeat of Druas. And reason to want to be the one to bring him down."

It was his other reasons Jenna wished to know, but she knew he would not tell her. And it mattered not, not in the end.

She had no right to think about her own concerns. She had no right to place her own or anyone else's welfare above that of her people. She had no right to turn down his offer. Kane was their best, perhaps their only hope of survival. She had to accept what help he could give.

Even if it cost him his life. And what was left of her heart.

Chapter 17

It felt very odd to be among people again, Kane thought. Especially people like these, generally quiet, peaceful, and more than a little bewildered by what was happening to them. He'd never dealt with this kind before; he'd grown up among fighters, not villagers, and he'd been taught that the latter were most often stupid fools who generally deserved whatever fate befell them.

He soon became aware that the legend of his warrior prowess was well known to the entire clan, and his physical presence did nothing to dispel the whispers of superhuman strength and utter ruthlessness in battle. He'd not heard some of the more exaggerated claims before now, and didn't know quite how to feel that some actually seemed to believe he was immortal, except to wryly observe that it was quite likely he'd disprove that part of the legend fairly soon.

That he was helping them was apparently the crowning achievement of Jenna's short reign as the Hawk, and when she had announced to them that he would be acting as their general, the people had looked at her with almost as much reverence as they did Kane.

That they loved her over and above the reverence was something he could not help but see, nor could he miss the reasons why; she knew each of them well, and despite the heavy burden she carried, she never failed to greet each of them daily, and ask if there was anything she could do to help them. They responded with a familiar yet respectful devotion that was tinged with the same sense of awe they exhibited toward him. What was missing was the fear, and while it had always suited his purposes before to have people fear him, he found it oddly bothersome now to have them all watching him so warily.

All except the storyteller, who seemed only mildly amused by the entire situation. That alone intrigued Kane, and he planned to investigate that soon.

He had spent the past few mornings with Arlen, learning the boundaries of the glade, although Arlen explained with no evidence of doubt or self-consciousness that they did not know exactly where the protection ended. Kane had been a bit taken aback when, at his request to see where the enemy was, the man had strode to within sight of Druas's main encampment without making the slightest effort to conceal himself. Arlen had explained patiently that they would not be seen, as long as they stopped in the place he indicated.

He'd not been able to make out much at this distance, other than that, as he himself had instructed long ago, Druas's men had set his tents in a random pattern, so as to give no cover to any approaching enemy. He saw only a few men—Druas had indeed left a minimal force here—and they were too distant for Kane to tell if he knew them. He doubted he would; not many men lasted with Druas very long, and he was sure most of those he'd commanded would be long dead, either in battle or by Druas's own hand for some offense real or imagined.

When he'd told Arlen to carry on as they had been before his arrival, Arlen had nodded without hesitation; Jenna's declaration that his orders were to be considered hers clearly was being taken seriously.

Jenna.

His stomach knotted, and he tried to shove aside the tension merely the thought of her wrought in him; it was as useless a task as fighting the need to come here had been. And the nights since he'd been here had been a torture unlike any he'd ever experienced, even when he'd been captured by Druas's main rival and had discovered Druas was not the only one with unique approaches to convincing prisoners to talk. Fortunately he had managed to escape—killing only a single guard in the process, not the dozen the legend seemed to have progressed to—before experiencing more than a taste of it.

But he would have welcomed it over the hell of lying in his makeshift bed beneath the trees, aching beyond belief for the woman who lay in the small cottage mere yards away. The woman who had once warmed his nights with an ardor he'd never thought possible for him, and was certain he would never find again, in this life or any other. The woman who had taken his breath away when he'd seen her standing there, lit by fire, in a dress that clung to her body, turned her eyes an even more vivid blue, and her hair to pure flame.

He had thought of naming a price for his help, the same price he had demanded of her on the mountain. He had thought about it long and hard, and the temptation of sharing that sweet, hot passion once more had been a lure he had been hard put to resist. He wasn't even sure why he had resisted it, why he had decided against it, except that the seductive memories of that time on the mountain seemed marred somehow by how they had come about.

And, he thought wryly, the very real chance she would refuse him this time.

Now, as he walked through her village, he glanced around at the people who hushed at his passage. Would it destroy the homage they paid her if she were to take the infamous warrior she had brought here to her bed? Or would it somehow, in some strange quirk of man's mind and the power of myth, enhance it, as if they saw the joining of their precious Hawk and the one they saw as more myth than man as somehow fitting?

By the heavens, he was getting feebleminded if this was all he could think about when there was an army bigger than any he'd ever seen in all his years in armor somewhere out there, waiting. He picked up his pace, aware of the eyes fixed upon him in the same way he was aware of the movements of any around him when he was preparing for battle.

He didn't really know where he was going, he just wanted to get away from the staring. He purposefully avoided Jenna's cottage; she of them all he did not want to deal with right now. A smaller, even more modest hut caught his eye, the hut he'd seen the storyteller go into after Jenna had made her announcement that he was in charge. The door stood open, and he changed direction and headed that way.

He wasn't sure what the protocol was here, but he'd never paid it much mind before and felt no need to now. He called out a hail, and then stepped inside.

The old man sat at a small table, bent over a piece of parchment, a quill in his right hand. It looked like the feather of a hawk, and Kane caught himself wondering fancifully if it was from the original hawk that had led these people here.

"A moment, Kane the Warrior," he said without looking up, and without the slightest trace of surprise or curiosity in his voice.

"You expected me?"

The old man finished the line he was writing, then

lifted the quill from the page. For an instant he still touched it, running a finger over the soft feather as if the texture pleased him. Or as if in memory of something. Then he sat it down and looked up at Kane.

"I expected you sooner," he said.

"Did you?" Kane asked.

"I knew you would not long be able to resist your curiosity. Sit," he added, gesturing toward a stool like the one he sat on. Kane took it gingerly; it did not look particularly strong, but it held him despite his size.

"You know too much," he said abruptly.

"You underestimate your own fame. It spreads across the land, until there is not a man, woman, or child who has not heard of Kane the Warrior. You are legend."

Kane's mouth twisted. "I never sought it."

"I know. But you have it, all the same. 'Tis why these people accept you so readily. They know you are a man who knows what they do not, who can do what they cannot."

"They will learn to do it, or they will die."

"Yes."

He said it calmly, so calmly Kane's brow furrowed. "Who are you?" he asked again, then added pointedly, "I mean your name, not some clever dodging of my question."

"This from the man who goes by only Kane? I would have thought you would not require names from all you met."

Kane winced inwardly, the old man had stabbed true; what right had he to demand another's name?

"I am the storyteller here, nothing more," the old man said again, leaning back against the table.

Kane's gaze narrowed. "And what are you elsewhere?"

Something flashed briefly in the old man's eyes, and

Kane was reminded of the resemblance he'd forgotten until now. But today, in the light of day, he looked like nothing more than an old man, gray and weather-beaten. The resemblance to Tal was only in the eyes, and he supposed the sheer intensity there could make that so.

"I am but a traveler, a . . . scholar of sorts, I suppose you could call me."

Kane was not satisfied, but he had no time to dwell upon it, not with Druas camped on their toes. And the man's words brought something else to mind.

"You were not born here," he began.

"No. I came here . . . when Druas began his bloody rampage to the south."

Kane thought of asking where exactly he had come from, but guessed he would get yet another vague, parrying answer. Instead he asked, "Then you are not one of them. The Hawk clan, I mean."

"By birth, no. By philosophy? Yes."

"Philosophy." Kane snorted. "Perhaps you should use that as your defense. If you cannot fight them, bore them to death with impractical visionary notions."

To his surprise, the old man laughed heartily. "I know some old stories that would quite likely do just that. There's a tale of voyages in search of scholarly learning that goes on for days on end, and I promise you, 'twould at the least put you to sleep."

To his further surprise, Kane found himself laughing in turn. And when he voiced his next question, the challenging tone was gone.

"You are not one of them, so perhaps you can explain. Why do they stay? Why did they not pack up and leave when they heard Druas was on the march? They had to know they had no hope to defeat him."

"They know. They have always known. But they have known as well that this is their place of destiny. It is sacred to them."

Kane's lips tightened. "Their destiny is extinction if they persist."

The storyteller lifted a heavy brow, surprisingly dark beneath the silver of his hair. "You are saying you cannot help them?"

"I am saying one man cannot defeat Druas."

"They do not wish to defeat him, merely to . . . turn him."

"If it were anyone else, I would say it might work. But Druas has dug in now. You have made him angry. He will not be moved."

"You have seen this before?"

"Countless times. He is inexorable once his mind is set."

"Does he never encounter others who think they are also immovable?"

"Of course."

"You have seen this firsthand? When you were with him?"

Kane nodded, the old memories flitting around his head with the persistence of the flies that clustered on the bodies of the dead. He fought them off; he could not afford to fall prey to them now. He got to his feet and walked to the doorway, looking out at the village that was so unexpectedly peaceful.

"I saw those who fought him," he said at last. "Men fiercely determined to resist him. But they soon learned."

"And who taught them, Kane? Who carried out the lessons Druas ordered?"

He spun around on his heel. He stared at the old man, who met his gaze with the same courage Jenna did. There had been nothing of accusation in his tone, nor was there any in his weathered face.

"Who, Kane?" the storyteller asked quietly.

"I did," he spat out. "As well you know."

"I do," the storyteller agreed. "But I was afraid you had forgotten."

"What I did in that time," Kane said, his voice hoarse, "is not something I will ever forget."

The old man looked at him steadily, with that same compassion in his changeable eyes that he'd seen so often in Tal's. "Perhaps you should not forget. Perhaps even evil memories have some use, if they keep you on the new path you've chosen."

Kane sucked in a breath at the uncanny accuracy of the old man's guess.

"And perhaps you can turn them to some good use," the storyteller added. "If you are the force that made Druas immovable, then perhaps you will be the force to move him."

Arlen looked away guiltily, and Kane knew he'd been staring at the scar on his face. Imagining it the result of some huge battle or fight, he supposed. And he probably wouldn't believe the much uglier truth if told it, Kane thought. Arlen was a good man, but he showed the signs of having been raised in a place like Hawk Glade; he trusted too easily and could not quite accept the utter evil of the man they were fighting.

"The stronghold, how far is it from here?"

" 'Tis just outside the forest, to the west," Arlen said.

He watched from his seat on the fallen log as Kane paced before him. The shadows were long now, the growing darkness heightened by the thickness of the trees surrounding them.

"It was already there when our clan first arrived here, according to the story," Arlen went on when Kane did not speak. "Claren of Springwater, the old man who lived there, was the descendant of the man who built it, generations ago. He was a gentle soul. He and his wife and daughter often traded with us, game for grain." A shadow crossed Arlen's face. "They are dead now. Murdered, Mary and Regine raped and tortured. And Druas now lives in their home."

Perhaps, Kane thought as he looked at the sudden hardness of Arlen's expression, he was not so trusting any longer. He sat on the log beside the man who was as close to help as Jenna seemed to have.

"Describe it to me again."

It took a moment for the man to gather himself and go on, but when he did, it was in brisk, unemotional tones. He knew when there was no room for emotion, Kane thought approvingly. Or he had learned, in the harshest of ways.

The diagram Arlen drew in the soft dirt was much as Kane had expected; square, corner towers, flanking towers, battle parapets around the top of the walls, and an inner courtyard with the various structures necessary for the maintenance of such a household. It was not large, but the stone walls gave it strength, and gave Druas a great advantage.

"Did Claren not have fighting men of his own?" Kane asked.

"But a few. They died trying to hold Druas off. But they were older, and he had not had any need of renewing his forces. There has been peace here for generations."

A sharp retort, that anyone who thought peace could be kept without cost was a fool, leapt to his lips, but he held it back. He was not sure why, except that he saw no gain and felt no pleasure in further berating a people who had already had their concept of life ripped apart.

"What you said, when you came here," Arlen said slowly, "that we should think of ourselves as already dead . . . is this the way you lived as a warrior?"

Kane met the other man's curious gaze, seeing in his

eyes both genuine curiosity about something obviously foreign to him, and the wariness of asking anything at all of the legend. But he had asked, and Kane had to credit him again with more nerve than he had first thought.

"It is the way I lived all my life," he said.

Arlen shook his head slowly, almost sadly. " 'Tis a terrible way to live. Perhaps we have taken the protection of our glade too much for granted."

Kane gave Arlen a sideways look. "Jenna has spoken often of this protection. You all believe in it?"

Arlen looked startled, and it took a moment for Kane to realize it was at his use of Jenna's name. He wondered what the man would think if he knew that Kane the Warrior had taken far more liberties than simply using her given name rather than her title.

"Of course we believe in it," Arlen said hastily, recovering. "It exists. Countless times we have seen travelers pass us by without a look, when they could not have helped but see us were it not for the magic. 'Tis what keeps us safe. We can go to meet those we wish, and those who appear a threat we simply wait and let pass. They never even know we are here, they see only an impenetrable wood. It has ever been thus."

Something tugged at the fringe of Kane's mind, memories of the times on the mountain when he'd been certain he'd been spotted by those hunting him. Yet they had passed on as if they had never seen him. Their weapons had never been drawn, nor had they shown any sign of even suspecting he was there, when he knew they could not have missed seeing him.

Countless times we have seen travelers pass us by without a look, when they could not have helped but see us were it not for the magic.

Tal.

Tal had been with him each time it had happened.

Had Tal done something like this, had he used whatever his powers were to protect him? The thought, which once would have had him laughing in scornful disbelief, now made him feel an odd warmth.

"Who put the spell on this place?" Kane asked softly.

Arlen shrugged. "That we do not know. Legend has it that the first Hawk, who was also a healer, saved the child of a wealthy man, who offered her whatever payment she desired, including the services of his own sorcerer."

"And this place is the result?"

"So says the legend."

Arlen shrugged again, in the manner only a man who had grown up with a legend and therefore found nothing odd in it could. But his warm brown eyes turned troubled then, his distress visible even in the last dim light of dusk.

"But even the magic will not be enough if Druas does not change his course. What must we do?"

Kane resisted the urge to say there was nothing they could do, that Druas would have his way if he had to burn this entire forest to the ground. He wondered for an instant why he was suddenly compelled to be so careful about his own words, why he felt the need to protect these gentle people from the grim truth. He'd never done anything like it before, and he wasn't sure he liked it. He wasn't sure he disliked it either, and that bothered him even more.

"Have you any builders?" he asked.

Arlen's mouth went tight with pain again. "We had the best of builders in Latham, but he is dead."

He didn't waste time on useless condolences. "No one else?"

"He had an apprentice, Flaven, and I had worked with him now and then myself."

"If I draw you a plan, can you build a machine?"

"I . . . suppose," Arlen said doubtfully. "We built all the bows and crossbows you ordered. What kind of . . . machine?"

"A catapult." It was probably pointless, Kane thought, but they needed to be doing something, and this would serve as well as anything. And it might be of some use.

Arlen's expression lightened. "I have heard of such a thing, from the storyteller. I think we can do it."

The storyteller. Kane's mouth twisted. There was more, much more, to that man than met the eye.

"Good. And build some ladders, as well."

"Ladders?"

"The height of the outer walls."

Arlen sucked in an audible breath. "You mean . . . to attack?"

"I mean it to look that way," Kane said.

A slow smile spread across Arlen's face. "I see. I will get Flaven, and others to help. Shall I go now?"

Kane nodded, and watched the man hurry away into the darkness. He was so pitifully eager to be doing something, anything, Kane thought.

It was amazing that any of them had any spirit left at all, considering what they faced, and what they had already been through. Yet they did, they had never given up, had never lost hope. Perhaps he'd underestimated them, as he'd once underestimated their leader.

Jenna.

Just the thought of her sent a stab of longing through him, a wistful, tight feeling that was so much more complex than simple desire that it almost frightened him. He was barely used to dealing with any kind of real feeling; this was something far beyond his control and ken.

And surviving another night like those he'd ached through since he'd come here seemed beyond his endurance.

He got to his feet, and before he could stop himself he had strode across the clearing to her cottage. He thought he felt eyes watching him, but he no longer cared. Nor did he care when Jenna did not respond to his knock or call. He strode inside anyway; the people of Hawk Glade were too in awe of Kane the Warrior to question his right to speak to the Hawk at any time.

He came to a halt a step inside the door; she had not lit any of the lamps, and the hearth was cold and empty. The room as well was taking on the chill of evening. It took a second for his eyes to adjust to the darkness. And then he saw her, and pulled the door closed behind him.

The bed, simply made of rough-hewn logs, was barely visible behind a blanket that hung from a ceiling beam in one corner of the room. Even less visible was the small, huddled shape beneath the bedclothes.

She had insisted, he knew, on doing her turn at guarding the perimeter. Including the nighttime turn. No royal prerogative for the Hawk; she pulled her weight along with her people. He wasn't surprised; he would have expected no less from her.

He moved quietly to the foot of the bed and stood there looking down at her for a long time. She didn't move, just lay there curled up on her side, one slender hand beneath her cheek, her hair a spread of muted fire. His body tightened fiercely, and he fought the urge to slide in behind her, just to feel the soft warmth of her as he pulled her against him. He wouldn't have to take her, although he wanted to, just holding her would be enough.

And that disturbed him; never in his life had he wanted to simply hold a woman for the sake of holding her. But he wanted to hold Jenna. He wanted to hold her, protect her, ease the weariness from her eyes and the worry from her soul. He, who had not wanted anything for years but to be left alone, had wanted nothing to do with anyone, suddenly wanted to give to someone else the ease he'd never known himself.

And standing here in a darkened room, staring down at the woman who had somehow gotten past his inviolable guard, he could not even deny it. Not now, when she looked so fragile, not now, when he knew the weight of her responsibilities was wearing down even her fierce spirit.

Moving quietly, he laid a fire on the hearth and lit it. Once it was going he considered lighting a lamp, then decided not to; the fire threw off enough light. As much as he wanted, anyway. He picked up one of the chairs from beside the fire and carried it over toward the bed. He put it down close by, where he could see her face. He sat, and swung his feet up to the edge of the bed, settling in to wait. For what, he was not sure. He knew only that he wanted to watch her. Endlessly. And he could not find it in himself to deny that, either.

Chapter 18

Kane neither knew nor cared how long he sat there. All that mattered was that he could see the soft sweep of her lashes, the exquisite fairness of her skin. All that mattered was that he could remember, so very clearly, what it had felt like to hold her, to have her hold him in turn. It had begun as a bargain, yes, a cold, mercenary trading, he could not forget that. But neither could he forget that it had become much more. It had become a passionate, breathless, living thing that had grown between them. It had become a thing that did not die when the sun rose to end the sweet darkness, but grew instead with each day that passed between them, each time he saw anew her bright courage and dauntless determination.

And it had become the source of the unexpected sense of peace that descended upon him now, just from the simple act of watching her sleep. The peace he had so long sought but never found in his withdrawal from his old life, had never found in the high reaches of his mountain, seemed here for him, waiting only for him to accept.

It was too much to even think there was anything of redemption for him here. He'd never even dared to think of such a thing; the best he had ever hoped for was to find some kind of existence that would numb the memories. Even when he'd come here, knowing his death would likely be the result, he'd not dared to wonder if it would even help his cause in the hereafter were he to die trying to help her.

He thought he must have dozed, for he lifted his eyes suddenly to find Jenna awake and looking at him, and he wondered how long she had been watching him as he had watched her. She was sitting up, the bedclothes falling back, and Kane sucked in a breath when he saw that the firelight made her body a supple, curved silhouette through the cloth of the softly woven nightdress she wore.

Jenna's expression changed, and he knew she had read his own. For a long, silent moment she simply looked at him. His jaw tightened as he fought to hide the raw, clawing need that had swept over him. Once, he would have demanded she submit to him. He had demanded it, on the mountain, and despite having done it in the certainty she would run, he supposed some part of him had wildly hoped she would accept his bargain or he wouldn't have thought of it in the first place.

But he would not demand it now. He could not. Not of Jenna. That he had no interest in anyone else, and doubted he ever would have, did not matter. Nor did that little voice in the back of his mind which was telling him he had undergone some change that was more momentous than he yet realized, that he could not, would not take her by coercion.

Fool, he told himself scathingly. *What think you, that she would have you any other way?*

And then Jenna answered his unspoken question without speaking a word of her own. Silently she shifted in the carved bed, and drew back the bedclothes in a gesture that could only be one of invitation.

Kane's heart slammed into his throat and he couldn't breathe.

"The nights are cold, and I've . . . missed you, too," she whispered, and he realized just how much had shown in his face.

"Jenna," he said, sounding strangled, but amazed he could get it out at all.

She lifted her arms then, opening them for him. His feet hit the rough wood floor with a thud, and he was nearly out of the chair before he could stop himself.

"This is not . . . you do not . . ." He swallowed tightly and tried again. "You are free of our bargain."

It was short, sharp, and probably curt, but he could not help it. But Jenna seemed to understand, as so often she did.

"This has nothing to do with any bargain. It has everything to do with need. I should not allow myself to want you so, not now, not when I should be thinking only of my people, but I cannot help it. I have never stopped wanting you, since I left your mountain."

What little breath he had left rushed out of him as if she'd slammed that tiny yet powerful fist into his gut.

"You . . . want me?"

"I do," she said simply, her hands now in her lap, her fingers laced together tightly, as if she were trying to hide their trembling.

"Even . . . without our pact to force you to it?"

Something came into her eyes then, something soft and warm that made him fear she was pitying him. Then she smiled, a tiny womanly smile that made it impossible for him to think of anything other than what she was offering.

"I think," she said quietly, "that force quitted our agreement long ago."

He opened his mouth to deny it, but the words would not come. She was right, and some part of him knew it, some part of him that had wished for it to be true, some part that he had constantly tried to quash for being the height of foolishness. Whatever it had been in the beginning, what was between them had rapidly changed to something else, something he had no name for, because he had never known its like before.

And then Jenna lifted her arms to him again, and he was lost. Nothing mattered to him now, nothing except the woman who was holding the world out to him. Not even his own certainty that it would come crashing down around him before this was done mattered; he could no more turn away now than he could go back to the old bloody life he'd left behind.

Swiftly, trying to ignore the shaking of his hands, he shed his tunic and leggings. He straightened, ready to take the last step toward her, the step so short in actual distance yet seemingly across worlds and a lifetime. But he stopped when he saw Jenna looking at him, an odd expression in her eyes.

He'd never been more conscious of the scars that marked him, never been more aware of rigid heat that had had him ready for her since the moment the firelight had reminded him so potently of the body he had once held, caressed, and poured himself into with a passion that had stunned him. Was she repelled by the scars, had she merely hidden her reaction before, perhaps feeling compelled not to show it? Or was it the swollen readiness of his body, already letting slip a tiny drop that betrayed his urgency?

The air seemed suddenly warm and heavy, much warmer than a mere wood fire could make it.

"You are indeed beautiful, Kane the Warrior," she whispered.

He groaned, low and deep in his throat as a sheet of fire seemed to ripple through him like a wind-caught banner. It weakened his knees and it was all he could do to go down to the bed with any kind of control.

He grabbed her and hauled her hard against him, pausing only long enough to strip the nightdress from her body.

She was as lovely as he remembered. Lovelier, as if somehow seeing her here, in her own world, seeing the burden she carried so nobly, the extent and strength of the love her people bore her, had only added to the powerful hold she seemed to have on him. And the fact that she welcomed him eagerly, that she reached for him even as he reached for her, completed the spell.

"It has been so long," she said, and the note of eagerness in her voice made him shiver with all the need that had been building since the day she had left him. In that moment nothing in his life—or even his pending death—mattered more than this moment, with this woman.

It should have worried him, that she held him in such thrall, but it did not. He could not even think of it, not when he had her in his arms again, not when he could feel the soft heat of her, not when her breasts were pressed against his chest, not when his eager maleness was caught between her thighs, sending darts of heat through him every time she moved. He could only think that, whether or not he deserved it, he would seize this bit of heaven offered him, for he had little doubt it would be his last taste of it.

"Nothing else," he muttered against her hair as he levered himself over her. "Think of nothing but this, Jenna. Just for this time, put it all from you."

"Help me," she whispered. "Burn it away."

He knew it was she who would set the fires here, and he who would burn. He knew it from the way his pulse leapt and his body flexed involuntarily every time she touched him. She stroked his sides and he sucked in his breath. She arched her back to rub her breasts against his chest, and he twisted helplessly when he felt the twin hard points of her nipples. Her hands slid up over his back and then down to his waist, and he quivered. She grasped his hips and pulled him against her belly, capturing his rigid flesh in a hot, pressing caress, and a groan he could not stop escaped him. And when she parted her thighs and reached to cup his buttocks and urge him into her, he shuddered so violently he thought it might be over before it began.

He fought down the hot rising tide, although he knew it was only a temporary victory; Jenna was too hot, too fervent, too ablaze in his arms for him to hold back for long. But he had not had nearly enough of her, he wanted to touch every soft curve, probe every hollow, first with his hands, then his mouth. He wanted to taste her until she cried out under the on-slaught. He could not help the hold she had on him, but he could at least see that he was not alone, that she was there with him, as desperate, as needy as he felt right now.

He stroked her, caressed her, until she was fairly rippling under his hands. He followed the same paths with his lips, then his tongue, until he had the hot satisfaction of hearing her beg him to come inside her in the moment when he knew he could no longer wait.

He slid into her, wondering at how her body could be so welcomely slick and so sweetly tight at the same time. And then all he knew was the hot, coaxing friction of her as he began to move. In moments he was out of control; he who never, ever relinquished his mastery was wild, driving hard and deep, unable to stop, reaching, striving for the fierce, blazing release he had only ever found with this woman. And she was with him, clawing at him in a way that only made him wilder, matching him with her own passion, with a pure, clean honesty that made him, just for an instant, as he hovered on the edge of explosion, hope.

And then he felt it, the first hot clasping of that feminine flesh around him. His body answered hers, that hot tide sweeping through him, engulfing him. He drove himself deep once more, only vaguely aware of the harsh cry of her name that burst from him as his body bowed, his hips grinding against hers. His head began to spin, and he couldn't feel his hands, his feet, couldn't see, and he thought he should be alarmed but he was not, for Jenna held him, so tightly, with her arms, her legs, her body, and it was all right, it was safe, and he was home at last.

"You're leaving, then?"

Kane finished tucking the loaf of bread Evelin had given him into his pack before he looked at Jenna. When he did, he could read nothing in her eyes or expression.

He had left her at dawn, certain she would not wish her people to know he had been with her. To his dismay, both Arlen and one of the children, a tow-headed boy named Lucas, had been outside Jenna's front door. The boy had looked at him with the awe and fascination all the children seemed to give him, while Arlen had merely glanced at Jenna's door, then back at Kane, and blushed.

"Is the Hawk asleep?" the boy had asked innocently.

"I . . . yes," Kane answered, not looking at Arlen.

"Good. She was very weary," the boy said in a very solemn tone. "I'm glad you were there to guard her."

Kane had only nodded and hurried away, fearful of what Arlen might say, and wondering when he had become such a coward, running from a villager and a boy.

He glanced at Jenna now, wondering if she would speak of last night, of what had passed between them. He had thought the passion they had found on the mountain incredible; it had been nothing compared to what had gone between them here. She said nothing more; it was as if she had donned a mask that hid all that he'd once been easily able to read.

"Someone reported to you, did they?" he said at last.

"I am the Hawk. All that goes on here finds its way to me eventually."

She said it simply, with no trace of arrogance. And again he was struck with the oddness of these people; they loved and respected their leader, not feared her, they lived in peace, not strife, and most of all they respected each other, with even the inevitable disputes being handled in a calm manner that was unlike anything Kane had ever seen. And anything that could not be resolved among themselves, he'd been told, was taken to the Hawk, and the decision rendered then was final, indisputable. It happened rarely, but never had the decisions been anything less than fair, according to every member of the clan.

As far as he could tell, the position of the Hawk seemed more work than it was worth; constantly seeing to the needs of all while forgoing your own, seeing to the happiness of all before you saw to your own . . . and based on the grim tales he'd heard of the recent history of Hawk Glade, allowing everyone else to grieve for their dead while you kept on, doing what you must while your own tears remained unshed.

He wondered if Jenna had ever wept for her brother, for her mother. He doubted it. She would put the welfare of her clan far above any such relief for herself, above her own needs, above her own hopes. She had proven that by sacrificing herself for them, by surrendering her virtue to the one man she hoped would save them. They did not know that, but he doubted they would hold even that against her if they did. They loved her too much.

That in the process she had seared him so deeply

he feared he would never recover was something he
hoped she never guessed. He had perhaps come a long
way from Kane the Warrior, but he still felt no desire
to be shown the fool. Lusting after a woman far above
him in both position and purity of heart was one thing,
hoping for anything more was beyond a fool's game.

She was waiting for an answer, he realized, and hastened to speak. "I have given Arlen orders to follow
in my absence. I need to see this stronghold for myself, and get a better idea of the lay of the land around
it," he said as he closed up the pack that held the
food, "before I can plan any strategy that—"

"You're staying?"

Kane looked at her, puzzled at her startled tone and
the conflicting questions. Perhaps it was at last telling,
the weight of her position. He explained patiently.

"No, I am leaving. For a few days, four at most,
I think."

"I . . . thought . . ." She lowered her eyes. "Pay me
no mind. I am . . . weary, that is all."

He didn't doubt that; the dark circles beneath her
eyes spoke not just of last night, but of a string of
nights as sleepless as his own, though he doubted it
had been for the same reason, despite her eagerness
for their coupling.

He fought down the surge of heat that threatened
at the mere memory. She was the Hawk, with reason
enough not to sleep. And reason enough to turn even
to him in her need for a few moments' oblivion, and
a night of needed rest. 'Twas all it had been, and he'd
do well to remember that.

"I have learned all I can of your glade and the close
surroundings," he said quickly, in the manner of any
commander's report to his superior. "I must go further
afield now. It will take at least four days to learn all
I need to know, to see exactly where Druas's stronghold is, where the roads intersect, and where exactly

your forest meets the base of Snowcap. Arlen has told me, but it is not the same as seeing it—Jenna?"

She was staring at him so oddly he halted in his explanation.

"Why . . . are you telling me all this?"

He shrugged. "You are the leader here, 'tis your business, is it not?"

"I . . . yes. I just never expected to have Kane the Warrior reporting to me."

Kane's jaw tightened. He turned his gaze on her face. "I would ask one thing of you."

She seemed to sense his sudden tension, and only nodded warily.

"From the others, I expect it. I accept it. But not from you. Do not call me that."

"Call you . . . ?"

"Kane the Warrior. As if it were my given name. It is but a legend, a myth. I have no other name but Kane."

"I only speak of you as the others do."

"Yet you, of them all, know I am just a man. And not a very honorable one."

Jenna drew herself up, and when she looked at him then she was every bit the Hawk, the leader of her people.

"Were that really true," she said, holding his gaze with that directness that never failed to amaze him, "you would not be here."

She turned then, and began to walk away. Kane watched her go, his chest oddly tight. She moved with such grace, the gentle sway of her body heating his blood as it tightened the clamp that seemed to be bearing down on his heart. He had to lower his eyes.

He wished it were true, what she had said, but he knew it was not. If she knew the full truth about him, if she knew the horrors he had committed, she would not risk contamination by even speaking to him. What she had risked by touching him, and allowing him to touch her in turn, in intimate ways he'd never done with any woman, he did not care to think about.

"Kane?" He looked up. "I'll expect a report when you return."

Despite his inner turmoil, he nearly smiled at her nerve. No, Jenna did not have a cowardly bone in her.

"Yes, Hawk," he said obediently.

When she blushed at his tone and turned away, he did smile. The irony of it bit deep; he had smiled at pain before, had smiled at anguish. But never at his own.

She *was* weary, wearier than she could ever remember being. Had it been only the annihilation looming so close, she thought she could have dealt with it; just the knowledge she would die with her people gave her an oddly twisted kind of peace. But when Kane's utterly disturbing presence had been added, it was suddenly too much, and she felt as if she were going to fly apart into countless tiny fragments at any moment.

And when she had awakened alone, she had had a moment of sleepy wondering whether she had dreamed it all, and only the pleasant ache of her body and the faint marks she found on her skin proved to her Kane's presence had been very real.

Since their encounter the morning after he had come to her, she had not seen him again before he had gone, and she had spent most of her day trying to put him out of her mind, a fruitless exercise given the continuous murmurings among the clan, still amazed at the presence of a legend among them. Now that he was not immediately present, they all seemed to want to talk about him, and of course they came to her, as the one who knew the most of him. Even when she had first come home they had not been so inquisitive, as if they had not really believed she had found him, had not quite believed he was real until that night when he had strode out of the dark and stunned them all with the sheer power of his presence.

More than once she had had to resort to her power as the Hawk to avoid answering questions she could not, or would not answer. She could not speak of the personal things Kane had told her, the memories that haunted him. Nor could she ever speak of what had passed between them. Not, somewhat to her surprise, out of any sense of shame or embarrassment, but simply because the memories were too precious, too intimate to be shared with anyone, even those she loved most.

And then when she had seen him packing, the morning after the hot, tender night they had spent, she had thought he was leaving for good, going back to the sanctuary of his mountain, and that the idea stabbed a coldness through her as icy as Snowcap's peak, scared her deeply. For he would leave, she knew that. That Tal's prophecy seemed wrong meant nothing, not really; she knew he stayed on his mountain because he wished to more than anything. He would leave, and she would have to go on as she had before. She would have to bury deep her memories of sweet, hot kisses and caresses and a scarred, powerful body moving over her, filling a place she had never before realized was empty. Never again would she know what it was like to be mindless with pleasure, what it was like to hold Kane in her arms, to feel him grow as mindless as she and know in her female heart that she had done it. To hear him cry out her name, and cry out his in turn.

I have no other name but Kane.

His words came back to her unexpectedly. He had told her he had left the fighting life behind, and she could easily understand why. But he had never spoken of his name, of why he denied any family connection, of why he was known only as Kane to one and all. But then, a legend did not need anything more. And Kane the Warrior was a legend, no matter that he seemed to have no liking for the fact.

From the others, I expect it. I accept it. But not from you.

She was a fool to read something into those words, a fool to think he, too, remembered those moments in the dark with longing. She found herself blinking rapidly as she hastened through the village. She saw the respectful nods of the people she passed, and returned them with an effort.

She would be the Hawk, with all that meant. She would be their leader, and it would have to be enough. If, of course, anything survived for her to be leader of. And that, she thought, despairing at the ache that rose up anew, depended on Kane.

She saw Cara approaching in the growing shadows of dusk. Instinctively she dodged out of sight; cowardly it was, but she could not face her old friend right now. Even though she doubted anyone knew Kane had come to her in her cottage, sometimes she swore that Cara, with some female instinct, had guessed at least something of what had happened between them. And the longer Kane was here, the more curious Cara had become. Whenever they were together, even speaking only of plans, or the trials to come, Cara seemed to be hovering, watching. Although she was glad to see her friend taking some interest in life again, she could have wished it was something other than she herself who was providing the means.

"You look a trifle desperate, child."

Jenna stifled a yelp and spun around to see the storyteller watching her, that faintly amused expression on his face. She had, she realized, dodged behind his hut.

" 'Tis Cara," she admitted sheepishly. "She is far too curious about things I care not to talk about."

"Such as you and Kane?"

Jenna's lips parted for a startled breath as her eyes widened.

"Do not worry," the old man assured her. "He did not speak of it. But he spoke of you. And you of him. It is there in your eyes, and his. 'Twas not hard to see."

"Not for you, perhaps," Jenna muttered. "I have met my fill of mind readers of late."

The storyteller only smiled, but it was an oddly crooked smile, as if he were thinking of something far removed from Hawk Glade.

"You have a task ahead of you," he said gently, "if you wish to overcome what has passed."

She drew back slightly. "Do you mean Druas? Or Kane?"

For an instant the old man stared at her as she had looked at him when he had startled her so with his perception. After a moment he relaxed, shrugged, and said in that annoyingly vague way, "Both."

She opened her mouth to protest his ambiguity, then shut it again. There was no point in arguing it, he was right on both counts. And at this moment, when weariness threatened to overwhelm her, she wasn't sure she could win either battle, let alone both.

She heard a flurry of voices from the other side of the hut and wondered what small catastrophe had befallen them now. No doubt she would learn soon enough, when someone arrived seeking the Hawk.

"Where were you?" she asked, seizing upon the distraction of the fact that he wore his heavy cloak and that it bore the marks of travel; leaves clinging to the shoulders, and a dampness at the bottom.

The storyteller toyed with something in his hands before he shrugged and said, "I went to see a friend."

"A friend?" When the storyteller did not elaborate, she prodded further. "Outside the glade?"

The old man tilted his head, lifting a dark brow until it was hidden by a thick lock of his silver hair. "Are you asking as Jenna, or as the Hawk?"

She considered that for a moment. "Both," she said. "As your friend, for you have never mentioned a friend close by. And as the Hawk, because it is dangerous to venture beyond the protection of the glade."

His hands moved again, and Jenna saw that he held a feather, glistening black, between his fingers.

"You need not worry, Hawk. I would do nothing to endanger your people."

She drew back, looking at him curiously, "You are one of my people, are you not? 'Twas *you* I worried about."

The old man looked absurdly pleased. "I thank you. Not many worry about an old man like me."

"You are very special to me. As friend, and as the Hawk."

"You are very kind to an old fool."

Jenna laughed. "Do not try that doddering act with me, I know better. What you might lack in youth you make up for in wit, and well you know it."

The storyteller laughed, deep and booming. It was the laugh of a young man, and it made Jenna smile. She had heard such a laugh before, not so very long ago—

"Jenna!"

The cry came from the clearing in the center of the glade. It was Cara, but it was not the cry of a friend looking for her friend to taunt with hints and probings.

It was a cry of desperation.

Without another thought Jenna turned and ran. The moment she saw Cara's face, saw the horror that had again taken over her eyes, saw the tears streaming down her face, she knew it was no small catastrophe that had overtaken them.

Kane? Had Tal's prophecy been right after all? Please, she begged, not certain of who. Not Kane. He could not be—

"Lucas," Cara wailed. "They've taken Lucas."

Chapter 19

"He's all I have left, and they've taken him."

Jenna stared at her sobbing friend. Guilt slashed through her that her first thought had been of Kane. But as Cara clung to her, weeping, an old enemy flooded her; it was this feeling she had fought so hard, this feeling of helplessness.

Lucas. She remembered the day she'd come back, remembered the boy clinging to Cara's legs, his eyes wide and stunned and far too old in his childish face.

Fury rose in her, pushing the helplessness before it like the spring flood pushed toward the sea. She would not let this stand. She was the Hawk, and it was time she started acting like it. It was past time. She had nothing to guide her, no Hawk had ever had to deal with such things. But the clan, gathered round now, trusted her, trusted her to do what should be done, as they had trusted her family for generations. She would not let them down.

"Cara, please, you must calm yourself. Tell me how this happened."

"I . . . he wanted to show me . . . something he'd found. He was excited, Jenna, almost happy, and he's been afraid for so long, I could not deny him this. So I followed him. I tried to stop him when we neared the pond, but he insisted."

"But you know the protection of the forest ends there."

"I know, but all was quiet, there seemed to be no one around—"

Her voice broke and the sobs threatened again. Having just fought such a battle herself, Jenna recognized the echo of guilt in Cara's weeping. But she could not stop to soothe her now.

"Forget that," Jenna said, fearing she would never get the story if Cara broke down completely. "What was this thing he'd found?"

"A . . . puppy."

Jenna blinked. "What?"

"A puppy. A small, spotted one. It was trapped in the mud at the far edge of the pond. It was whimpering so pitifully, Lucas must have heard it from within the glade and followed the sound . . ."

"Go on. What happened?"

"I . . . went with Lucas to try and help it. 'Twas only when I looked closely that I realized it was not trapped, but tied there."

Jenna went still. "Tied?"

Cara nodded miserably. "I knew then it had to be a trick, and I screamed to Lucas to run. But it was too late, they came out at us. They'd been hiding all around the pond. They grabbed Lucas and threw him over one of their horses."

Jenna fought off the image of that already cowed little boy facing such terror yet again and tried to concentrate on the facts of what had happened.

"Did you make it to the protected woods? Did they not see you?" she asked.

Cara's tear-streaked face took on a puzzled expression. "No, they saw me. I know they did. Two of the men argued about . . . whether they should take me, too."

Jenna's forehead creased. 'Twas not like their

enemy to let a woman go, especially a beauty like Cara. "Why only Lucas?" she murmured.

"I do not know, except that one of the men said something about their orders. Oh, Jenna, he was so frightened, we must help him, we must!"

Orders? Jenna wondered.

"We will think of something," she told Cara, although she doubted her own ability to carry out that promise. She dared not look at the others, fearing they would see her doubts.

"He's just a little boy," Cara said, the tears beginning again. She looked utterly distraught, and Jenna put her arm around her.

"Cara, you must get some rest. Have Evelin fix you an herbal draft."

The healer stepped forward with a nod, and tried to draw the girl away. Cara resisted.

"But they will kill him. I just know they will. They kill everyone and everything."

"Exactly," Jenna said. "Yet they did not kill Lucas. Had they wished to, they would have right there. Nor would they have left you to report back."

This made sense even to Cara in her distress.

"What do you think, Hawk?"

It was the storyteller, watching her as a teacher watched a pupil taking a difficult exam. She only wished it were something so simple.

"There is a plan at work here, I think," she said at last. "And until it succeeds, I think Lucas is safe enough."

She saw the flash of a salute in the storyteller's intense gaze, and felt a rush of pleasure in his approval. She had another thought and turned back to Cara.

"What happened to the dog?" she asked, not sure why it mattered.

Cara shuddered. "They . . . drowned it."

Something cringed inside Jenna, although she did

not know why; she had expected this answer. Cara
gulped and continued.

"They took the rope it had been tied with and fastened it around a rock and threw it into the pond. I
couldn't . . . I didn't . . ."

"It's all right, Cara. I only wondered. There was
little you could have done without further risking
yourself. Go, now, with Evelin."

She watched as the healer led her shattered friend
away. How many times would she yet go through this,
see someone she loved, one of her own, devastated
by loss?

"And there you have the difference," the storyteller
said, "between a cold man and a vicious one, a man
who has locked his heart away and a man who has no
heart at all."

Jenna turned to look at him. "Another of your ob-
ject lessons?" she asked wearily.

"No. Merely an observation. But I think you have
already learned this one."

"Have I?"

"You know which one Kane is," he said, and then
left her there, pondering his words, the subject of
Kane for once less painful than what immediately
faced her.

She could not let this pass. If they had known
enough to set such a trap, and she had no doubts that
was what it had been, then they knew too much. They
knew Hawk Glade was here, even though they could
not find it. And if Druas was as Kane had described
him, he would not stop until he did. He would find
them, and because they had made it difficult for him,
he would make it as appalling and monstrous as possible for them.

And she suspected he had just made his first move.

She lay sleepless long into the night. Visions of Lucas's face haunted her. She remembered when the boy

had been born, and how his parents and both his sisters had doted on him, yet he had remained remarkably unspoiled, giving back as much affection as he got. She remembered when Cara's parents had been killed, early casualties of the battle they had not yet realized they were in, their bodies found on the path down from Snowcap, where they had ventured to show Lucas snow for the first time. Cara and her sister and Lucas had survived then, but now only Cara was left of them all.

"No!"

She sat up straight, her own protest ringing in her ears. She could not, would not accept it. She would do something. If she was right, and there was some motive to Druas stealing Lucas away, then she had to believe he was still alive.

And she had to do something. It was up to her; Kane had only been gone for two nights, and would not return—if he indeed returned at all—for two more. Besides, she guessed his ever-practical, ruthless mind would decide one small boy was not worth the risk.

We cannot afford to hold any one life too dear. . . .

He'd said as much, when he'd finished her sentence as he'd walked out of the night and stunned them all into silence.

You must think of yourselves all as already dead.

As much as she hated it, she knew he was right; only that kind of single-mindedness could possibly save the clan, and that some would yet pay the same price so many already had. But she could not accept that even the children must die. The adults, they had made their choice, when they had agreed to stay instead of attempting to flee, with Kane to lead them. But the children . . .

It was still dark when, decided at last, she rose and dressed quickly. She would go to the pond, she thought. She would go and see if perhaps there was some clue, some hint that Cara, in her frenzy, might have missed. Perhaps they had even left some message, some demand. Something. Anything. She could no longer just sit here and wait. Kane had counseled caution, but that had been before Druas had stolen a helpless child.

She hesitated, then picked up the small, lightweight crossbow Kane had made for her. She'd practiced with it until her shoulder ached, but now she hit her target more times than not, and it comforted her to carry it.

She felt no fear as she made her way toward the pond. Even in the darkness she knew her way; she knew every bit of Hawk Glade and the forest that surrounded it. It was only when she reached the pond that she would have to exercise due care, and it was for that moment that she carried the crossbow. She would not assume, as Cara had, that because there was no sign there was no one there; Kane had taught her too well for that.

When you least expect it you should most expect it, he had said, after one of his pointed lessons where, when she'd thought herself alone, he had startled her half out of her life by sending an arrow whistling past her ear to thud into a tree trunk barely a foot from her.

When she was within sight of the pond, when she could see the smooth surface of the water, she halted. She found a likely spot of cover and crouched behind it, waiting. It was a precaution she didn't really think necessary, her faith in the protection of the forest was unshaken, but Kane had taught her never to take anything for granted when dealing with a ruthless enemy.

She waited for a long time; Kane had taught her patience as well, and that quiet waiting often prodded an enemy into betraying himself. Of course, Kane had also once taught the forces she might be facing here;

she wondered if any of his teachings had been carried on after he'd gone.

And she wondered if the thought that had occurred to her during Cara's painful recital could possibly be true.

As the gray light of dawn began to push back the night, the pond became more visible. And still Jenna heard nothing. Nothing to indicate there was anyone here but herself. She held her breath, straining to hear, but there was no sound other than the steady beat of her own heart, and the occasional trill of an early-rising meadowlark behind her.

When it became light enough that she was sure she could not miss any sign left behind by the men who had taken Lucas, she rose slowly, loading a bolt into her crossbow and drawing the string back until it caught on the nut for the trigger. She stepped out from her sheltered hiding place. She was not sure exactly where she would lose the safety of the forest; it was one of the problems of those born in Hawk Glade that they did not see it as others did; for them the glade was always visible, so there was no way to tell how it appeared to others and where the invisibility ended.

She should ask the storyteller how it appeared to him, she thought suddenly. And if he still saw it as an outsider, perhaps he could help them mark the boundaries, so they would know for certain. She should have thought of that when he'd first arrived. She would ask, as soon as she—

They were there, at least a dozen of them, before she could react. She whirled to run, but found them behind her as well. Surrounded, she raised the crossbow to her shoulder, wondering if she could take at least two of them down before they were upon her. She searched the slowly approaching men, looking for some sign of rank. Just as she found it, an epaulet of ribbon on one man's shoulder, someone cried out, "Is it her?"

The man with the marking answered. "It must be. She matches what the boy said. How many can there be in these parts with hair the color of fire?"

Jenna shifted her aim coolly, centering the bow on the man's chest; the bolts Kane had given her, he had said would pierce even the finest armor if fired with enough power—or at close-enough range. She figured ten feet was close enough.

The man she aimed at laughed as he kept coming toward her. "She has the fire to match her hair, just as the boy said. We have the Hawk."

So she had not only walked into a trap, it had been a trap baited specifically for her. Jenna's stomach knotted but she fought it down.

"They may," Jenna told him, proud of the steadiness of her voice. "But *you* have nothing but the grave to face."

He stopped, hesitating in the face of her unwavering aim and unruffled voice. "Do not be a fool, girl. There are too many of us."

"I do not care how many others there are. I care only that you will not live past your next step. Or anyone else's next step."

"If you fire at me, you will be dead before your next breath."

"I do not think so," Jenna said, hoping she sounded more certain than she felt. "If your orders were to kill me, I would already be dead."

The man looked reluctantly impressed. "So she has a brain as well," he muttered. "A dangerous combination. I see why Druas wants her taken."

He moved as if to take another step. Jenna's finger tightened on the trigger of the bow. He stopped.

"If you kill me," he said, " 'tis the boy who will pay."

Jenna froze.

"Druas will kill him most painfully. He delights in it, you know. It would give him great pleasure. He needs only to have an excuse."

"Why has he not killed him yet, then?"

The man laughed. "Clever girl. Because he wants you, of course. If you come willingly, the boy will live. If you fight, he will die. But either way, he will take you."

She could fight, could perhaps even kill one or two of them. But she could not win, that was obvious. He was right about that. "Why should I take your word that he will not be killed anyway?"

"Because it is your only chance. He *will* die otherwise."

Kane had been right. She had thought with her heart instead of her head, and because she had ignored his warning, she was now faced with a decision that was really no decision at all. She had been unable to accept what he'd told her must be, and because of it, she was here, now, in enemy hands, with little hope of survival.

She lowered her bow, unfired; the bitterness welling up inside her made it far too heavy.

She had failed. She had failed at everything, failed her people, her family, her heritage, and in a strange way had failed Kane as well. Her people would die, and Kane would go back to his mountain alone, to live in utter isolation, probably to never remember the woman he had tried to help except as a hopeless fool who should never have left her precious glade.

Kane lay in the darkness, staring upward at the few stars that shone between the thick branches overhead. Sleep continued to elude him, although he rarely did more than doze lightly when he was on a foray such as this.

He'd been afraid his skills would have deteriorated too much in the years on the mountain, but they came back with a speed that surprised him. After the first day, it had been as if he'd never been gone, as if he'd never stopped this living on the edge, ever aware of his surroundings, expecting attack from any direction at any moment.

The only difference was that now, he found it hard to believe he had lived most of his life in this way. If nothing else, that simple awareness told him he had indeed achieved, at least in part, the transformation he'd been after. Tal was right, he'd been fighting within himself. He'd gone to the mountain to change, to leave his old life behind him forever, yet he'd fought the inevitable results of that change. He'd fought the gentling, the softening, thinking it wrong somehow, or impossible.

Yet how could a man such as he had been change, except to soften? He could certainly become no harder, crueler, or more ruthless than he had been. He began to understand what Tal had been telling him all along. He closed his eyes wearily.

"I wish you were here, my friend," he muttered.

He meant it. He could well use Tal's wit. And his magic, even if that was truly what it was.

'Twill take that to beat him, he thought. Even in his mind he did not name the enemy. For fifteen years, since he'd turned sixteen, he'd worn that man's armor, had fought for him, killed for him.

Slaughtered for him, he corrected in silent abhorrence.

And now Druas had others who would do the same, others drawn by his high pay, and willing to put up with his brutal discipline for the chance at spoils of all kinds.

His eyes snapped open; he could not risk sleep, not now, not with such memories stirring so near the surface. He had no wish to wake with a scream on his lips, betraying his position to anyone who might be nearby. He had no idea if he was back within the supposed protection of the forest, or even if he believed in it. Without Tal around to provoke him, he found it hard to believe he'd ever taken such nonsense seriously.

If you leave these mountains, Kane the Warrior, you will no longer exist. You will cease to be. I have seen it, and it is truth.

Tal's long-ago words, spoken on their first meeting, haunted him now. He'd stared at the man who would become his friend warily, wondering what kind of crazy man he'd encountered. Just the distant, unfocused look of those eyes was enough to rattle him, but the unshakable certainty of his voice had put the seal on it; he scoffed, he laughed, he shrugged . . . but he never forgot the warning. And in time, when he'd come to realize how rarely Tal was wrong, he'd come to believe.

So why, then, was he still alive?

"He didn't say *when*," he muttered to himself, wondering at the oddity of mixing reasoning with magic as he sat up, giving up on sleep for the moment.

He was too weary to deal with the paradox and turned his restless mind to more worldly concerns; the terrain he'd covered in the past three days. He had always had a knack for remembering ground once he'd walked it, and he now had a true picture of the forest in his mind, a grimly accurate assessment of the strength of the force that beset them, and thanks to a short exploration outside the forest after darkness had fallen tonight, he knew just how solid Druas's stronghold was; the situation was not encouraging.

After he had slipped past the few sentries that remained on the perimeter—Druas was indeed nervous, he thought with satisfaction, to have drawn so many

of his men back to protect his stronghold from the
threat he could not find—it had not been hard to find
the place. Arlen had said the stone-walled bastion was
the largest structure for five leagues in any direction.
Druas was following his old habits, taking over an
easily defensible place that had belonged to some
wealthy man he had murdered.

Kane had sat there, staring at the stone walls, thinking of all the times he had carried out Druas's orders.
He thought of what Arlen had told him about who
this man had been, that he had an attractive wife and
daughter. And tried not to think of what had happened to them; he knew they would have been turned
over to Druas's men as soon as the place was secured.

Druas himself had little interest in such things;
blood and carnage and victory and land gained were
his passion. Kane had also held himself above those
kinds of spoils; rape was not to his taste. The drive
for land seemed somehow easier to accept; that was
one reason it had taken Kane a long time to realize
just how evil Druas was. And how evil he himself
had become.

But it hadn't been until the day he himself had
nearly killed that child, the day when she had offered
herself in the hopes her small brother might live, that
he had finally recognized that he was no better than
the man he served, that he was perhaps even worse,
because he carried out the orders of a cruel, vicious
man when he knew they were vile. And the reason he
had done it would win him no mercy when it came
time for a final accounting.

Nor would the fact that he'd cast his lot against the
man now, Kane suspected. He'd done too much, and
come to this side far too late for that.

So why was he here?

He knew the question was pointless. He knew why
he was here. He was here because even risking the

fulfillment of Tal's grim prophecy was better than sitting in that cold, empty cave wondering if Jenna was dead yet.

He scrambled to his feet, knowing now that sleep was not going to come. And as long as he was awake, he decided he might as well be moving.

He took the course he would have taken had it been light. His sense of direction and memory of the terrain was a skill that had never failed him; he was as sure of his path as if he'd traversed it countless times. But for once he wished he was less certain; he would have welcomed having to concentrate every step of the journey. It would have kept his mind off other things he'd already spent far too long thinking about.

Once, as he walked, the faint rustle of wings behind him made him stop in his tracks. A winged night hunter brought only one thing to mind, Maud, and he looked around, wondering if Tal was about to appear out of the darkness. But neither the clever raven nor the more clever man materialized, and after a moment Kane kept on, smiling wryly at his own fancifulness. The memory of that night when Tal's voice had come to him in the cave had never left him. He'd been half expecting to see him since he'd arrived here. But Tal had said his powers were useless here, that the spell of Hawk Glade was too strong.

Only now did the significance of those words truly strike home to him. If Tal knew his powers were useless here, then he had been here. Perhaps even then, when his voice had echoed impossibly inside the cave.

Kane didn't know what unsettled him more, that Tal was quite possibly nearby and yet not showing himself for some reason of his own, or that he himself had begun to think this way, accepting his friend's mysterious capabilities as if he'd always believed in such things.

But he did know what unsettled him most; the sim-

ple fact that even this, the contemplation of his best
and only friend being some kind of sorcerer, was easier to confront than his thoughts of Jenna.

Cursing himself for a fool, he lengthened his stride.
As he went he forced himself to consider the limited
options left to them. He knew as well as he knew
anything that Druas would not retreat, that he would
not give up his plan to cut a path straight through the
forest rather than go around. The man was unyielding
and inflexible once his mind was set. And if he was
opposed, his bullheadedness only grew stronger. There
was no turning him away with resistance. Only richer
plunder had ever turned him.

He thought about this as he strode on through the
night, wondering what it would take to convince Druas
it was greatly to his advantage to change his plans.
There were no other plums ripe for the picking in this
vicinity, and Kane doubted if Jenna would approve of
solving their problem by intentionally passing it off to
other innocents anyway. Harrying their enemy into
passing them by was one thing; deliberately inciting
them to attack others instead was something else
again.

As he approached Hawk Glade in the light of dawn,
he was still turning over ideas in his mind, wondering
if there was some way to plant a rumor among Druas's
men of fabulous riches elsewhere, near enough to be
tempting, yet far enough away to ensure the safety of
Jenna's people.

He stopped abruptly, instinctively, as his eyes told
him he was about to collide with one or more of the
trees before him, all of them growing so closely upon
each other, their branches so intertwined, that passage
between them was impossible. The impenetrable thicket
stretched onward out of sight in the gray light of early
morning. Anyone in possession of their senses could

see there was no getting through, that this portion of
the forest would have to be circled.

Which meant, he supposed ruefully, that he had lost
possession of his senses.

For a moment he simply listened, not for any sound
from within the dense thicket, but for any sound from
outside it, any threat on the flanks or from the rear.
He heard nothing. When he was as certain as he could
be that it would not get him killed, he took a deep
breath and closed his eyes, he had not yet managed
the kind of faith that would let him do this with his
eyes wide open.

He walked forward, straight into the impassable
barrier of trees.

A moment later he heard the sound of voices. He
opened his eyes. The village was there, unchanged
since he'd left it three days before.

Or perhaps not. There was a knot of people gathered, even at this early hour, in the yard before Jenna's cottage. They looked disturbed. Worse, they
looked distraught. He spotted Cara, the pretty blonde
who was Jenna's friend; tears streaked the woman's
face beneath reddened eyes that looked as if she had
been weeping for days.

And then someone called his name, in such tones
of relief that he felt a shiver of foreboding.

" 'Tis Kane, come back! He will save her!"

Jenna.

He knew it with a certainty he did not, could not
question. He knew it just as he knew it was this that
had driven him to walk through the night to return
here. He fought the sickness that roiled inside him
and walked toward them.

"Where is she?" he asked without preamble.

For a moment they said nothing, but glanced at each
other somewhat fearfully. Cara began weeping anew,
and Evelin put an arm around the girl to calm her.

"Where is she?"

It was a demand this time, given in the tone of a man well used to instant obedience. Arlen drew himself up and faced Kane as a man facing execution.

"She is taken. Druas has her."

Chapter 20

Kane fought down the nausea that rose in his throat. Jenna, in the hands of the man who haunted him, the man who had made him what he was, a cold, ruthless soldier who never questioned orders, only followed them.

Don't blame him, he ordered himself sharply. *You're the one who went along. You're the despicable coward who couldn't stand up to him, wouldn't even try to stop him.*

"What will you do?"

Kane looked at Arlen, his expression betraying nothing of his thoughts. When he spoke, it was not in answer; he had no answer. Instead, he asked for the details of Jenna's capture. He listened impassively as it was explained to him. He did not even grimace as Evelin laid a long lock of fiery hair across his palm, explaining that it had been found near the pond, tied to the branch of a low-growing shrub.

" 'Twas left as proof Druas has her," the healer said.

"You're sure of this?" Kane asked, his voice flat, unemotional.

The older woman eyed him for a moment, then drew something out of the pocket of her smock.

"As certain as this can make me," she said, handing a narrow triangular strip of cloth to him.

Kane did not need to unfurl it to recognize it. He knew this pennant too well; he had carried it for a decade. Yet he let the small banner unroll anyway, staring fixedly as the emblazoned viper came into view.

Druas.

And then, heedless of his weariness after his sleepless night of travel, he ordered Arlen to show him the place where it had happened.

Arlen was frightened, that was clear. Whether it was of going to the place where the boy and Jenna had been taken, or of he himself, Kane didn't know. But Arlen drew himself up and nodded, and started off.

He was a good man, Kane thought as they left Hawk Glade and started through the forest. He was a good man doing his best in a situation he was not suited for; he was afraid, yet he had never shirked the dangerous tasks that had been assigned him.

This was true courage, Kane thought suddenly. His own much vaunted bravery had been merely the result of not caring overmuch if he lived or died; it was when you did care, when you feared death, and risked it anyway for what you believed in, that the true worth of a man came out.

Which proved, he supposed as he followed Arlen through the trees, that what he himself possessed, whatever it was, was something much less commendable. This was no surprise to him, merely another reason to despise what he was. Another reason to wish he'd had the courage to simply end it instead of running away and hiding.

Another reason he wasn't good enough to bow before the likes of Jenna, the Hawk. Her pure, noble courage was far too rare to be squandered on the likes of him. That she had paid the price he'd demanded of her without flinching, indeed with an innocent, honest response he'd never expected or known before—and certainly did not deserve—only made her more extraordinary . . . and he himself more contemptible.

But it was too late to undo the past. Nothing could change what had passed between them, and Kane admitted ruefully he would not even if he could. He would not give up those precious memories of nights spent cradling her in his arms as she slept, memories of losing himself and all the pain and self-disgust and bitterness in the glorious heat and sweetness of her body, memories of the odd sensation of pride that had overtaken him countless times as he had watched her determinedly set herself to learning what she needed to help her people.

And not for his own life would he give up the memory of the night she had invited him, free of the coercion of their bargain, into her bed.

No matter that he did not deserve any of it, he would keep those memories, treasure them as he'd treasured little else in his life. They would not keep him warm at night, but they at least would remind him it had once been possible to overcome even the fierce chill that held frozen what little he'd kept of his soul. It had been possible. With Jenna.

He fought off the swirling emotions; he had no time for such things. He'd never had time for such things, had indeed thought he'd successfully purged even the capability of feeling them. Until Jenna had come into his pitiful life and brought them all surging to the surface. Until Jenna had taught him he hadn't killed them, he'd only buried them alive.

He saw the glitter of water through the trees in the instant before Arlen began to slow down.

" 'Twas there that the boy was taken," Arlen said with a gesture of one hand that betrayed his nervousness with a tremor.

"And you're certain Jenna came here?"

"She loved the boy. 'Tis what she would do."

Kane's jaw tightened. Of course it was. He had to look away from Arlen's weary, tense face; the look of worry in the man's eyes reminded him too much of the kind of woman Jenna was, to inspire such love in her people. And it was then, when he moved his head, that he spotted the lone figure crouched by the edge of the pond.

His instant reaction was to tense; it was not like him to be so unaware of another's presence. But when he saw the morning light reflecting off the pond and glinting on the silver hair of the man beside it, he relaxed.

"Go back," he ordered Arlen. "I will return shortly."

Arlen hesitated. He shifted his feet nervously before blurting out, "We must do something. We cannot leave her in that butcher's hands."

"I know." Kane said it flatly, coldly. But Arlen apparently understood Kane's tone was not aimed at him, for he did not cringe away as most did when they heard it. Or else he had again underestimated the man's nerve.

"We will follow you, all of us. We know little of fighting, only what Jenna—I mean, the Hawk has taught us, but we will die to the last of the clan to save her."

"I know," Kane repeated, but this time his tone was low, soft, nearly wondering. "Go now."

This time Arlen obeyed, with a haste that betrayed his gladness to be away from this place. Kane did not watch him go; he had turned back to look at the motionless figure beside the pond. The old man did not look at him, although Kane thought he had to have realized he was here.

He wondered briefly if this was some sort of contest

of wills, if the old man was refusing to come to him, or simply waiting to see if Kane would come to him first. Kane found he cared little about the balance of power between them at this moment, and started walking. He spared an instant to think of the oddity of that idea, that there was a division of power between him and this old man. Yet he could not deny that there was something commanding about the storyteller, some sense of mastery that made the thought less improbable than it seemed it should be.

He came to a halt before the old man, who was still crouched at the water's edge, staring at the glassy surface as if the answer to all the questions of the universe were displayed there. He did not react to Kane's presence at all.

Kane was not used to being ignored, and he opened his mouth to speak. But something about the intensity of the storyteller's concentration forestalled him, and he held his tongue. That intensity, that focused intentness, reminded him of something, but before he could pin it down the man shook his head sharply, as if coming out of a reverie.

The storyteller showed no surprise at Kane's presence, so he had at least been aware of him despite his engrossment. He stood up. Not, Kane noted curiously, like an old man whose joints protested the long time in an uncomfortable position, but like a young man, easily, smoothly.

"She stood up to them," he murmured, still looking at the water. "Held them off by picking out their leader and drawing her bow on him. She has more courage than even I thought."

He spoke as if he'd witnessed it, Kane thought. Perhaps his storytelling again; had not Jenna said he spoke of great battles as if he'd been there?

"I should have been able to help her," the storyteller muttered angrily, glancing at Kane. "It's this spellbound place."

"Why," Kane said neutrally, "would you think you could have helped her, against Druas's men?"

The old man looked startled, and for a moment Kane wondered if perhaps he'd been wrong, that the storyteller hadn't been aware of his presence after all. Then the old man glanced down at his weathered hands, as if seeing them for the first time. The movement made his silver hair fall forward in front of his eyes, and Kane saw him look at it. His mouth twisted ruefully.

"This place is enough to make a man forget who he is," he said in a voice that matched his expression.

It was an odd thing to say, and not for the first time Kane had the feeling that there was much more to this old man than he or any member of the Hawk clan knew. And he had not forgotten that the storyteller had so far avoided answering any direct questions about his identity.

As if he sensed Kane's thoughts and wanted to head off any more of those questions, he asked one himself. The one Arlen had asked, the one Kane himself had not answered.

"What will you do?"

Kane still had no answer. He stared down at the glimmering sheet of water, as the old man had, but he did not expect to find any answer there. Unless he drowned himself in its cool depths, this pond held no solution for him.

His mind was lashing out, flogging him with accusation and guilt. He was Kane the Warrior, yet he stood here, pondering, while Jenna was in the hands of the man he hated most.

"Do you still have some . . . loyalty to Druas?"

Kane's head snapped up, his hand instinctively reaching for the hilt of the sword that hung at his side.

The old man didn't move, didn't even react, as if he hadn't seen the threatening motion. He merely watched Kane thoughtfully, assessingly. And something in those eyes stayed Kane's hand.

"I should kill you for that insult," he muttered.

"But you will not. For you know there was no insult intended."

He did know. He was not at all sure how he knew, but he did. He released the sword.

"What will you do?" the storyteller asked again.

"No doubt what I've always done, against Druas," Kane heard himself say in bitter tones. "Nothing."

"Always?"

A shudder rippled through Kane. He fought it, wondering why he had let such a thing spill from his lips to this man he barely knew. But there was something about him, as Jenna had said. . . .

"Always. I never withstood him. I followed his orders, carried them out even when they made me sick. Even in the end I had not the courage to strike him down, but only to run away and hide."

"But you found you could not hide from such things," the storyteller said softly.

Kane drew himself up; there had been enough of this foolish talk. "Some things should not be allowed to be forgotten. And some men never forgiven."

"Are you speaking of Druas? Or yourself?"

"Both," Kane said coldly.

"That explains it, then."

"Explains what?" Kane asked, a bit snappishly.

"Why you could not let go of the memories. You have not forgiven yourself. If you do not, they will haunt you forever."

Kane met the old man's wise gaze steadily. He said nothing. Understanding sparked in the old man's eyes, those eyes so like Tal's. For an instant, he wondered . . . But he had no time for such thoughts now. Jenna was in deathly danger. And he was to blame, as he was to blame for so much else.

"I see," the man said, as if he did indeed. "This is the punishment you've sentenced yourself to, a lifetime of torture, haunted by memories you cannot change."

"Those I have destroyed would find it too light a penalty."

"Perhaps." The storyteller gave him a look that was devoid of judgment, of censure, a look that held only a world of empathy and wisdom. "But there is one thing wrong with your deductions."

"Wrong?"

The storyteller smiled, a slight, gentle smile. "You," the old man said, "are not the one to pass final judgment, Kane the Warrior."

He said it like a benediction, and a shiver of odd sensation brushed over Kane. But before he could even acknowledge it, the man asked yet again the question Kane had no answer for.

"What will you do?"

His own thoughts about Druas came back to him, echoing in his head like Maud's harsh cries. There was no turning him away with resistance. Only richer plunder had ever turned him.

And suddenly the answer was there.

"There is only one way to save Jenna and put an end to this," he said slowly, suspecting that he'd known the answer all the time, but he had not wanted to face it. He felt more the coward than ever; it should have been obvious to him from the beginning.

"There is a way, then?" the storyteller asked, sounding more curious than anything.

"Druas is a man of . . . determination. He will never give up anything he has gained or hopes to gain. Unless it is to get something he wants more."

The old man studied him for a moment. "And there

is something Druas wants more than he wants this land?"

"There is one thing he wants above all else. Something he has been hunting down for years."

"Hunting down? It sounds as if he wishes it dead."

"He does," Kane agreed flatly.

The old man drew back slightly, looking uneasy for the first time. "And what is this thing he so badly wants to kill that you believe he might give up this battle for it?"

Kane drew in a long, deep breath, his mouth twisting bitterly.

"Me," he said.

Jenna stared at the man before her, not sure if it was his reputation or his appearance that was making her stomach knot. He did not look like evil incarnate; instead he looked like a twisted rendition of a fallen angel. He was tall, nearly as tall as Kane, and nearly as dark-haired for all that he was clearly twenty years older. His brows were thin, oddly, almost femininely arched, giving him a rather demonic air. But in fact he was probably more well favored than Kane, handsomer . . . until you looked into his eyes.

His eyes were pale, the irises rimmed oddly with a circle of black, giving them a frighteningly eerie look. But more unsettling was the fact that they were utterly dead. There was not a trace of human life or feeling in those eyes, as if the man had absorbed somehow the death he surrounded himself with.

She had thought Kane's eyes cold, remote, but next to this man's, Kane's were vivid with life. Even the pain she so often saw there was a sign of life, life that was missing in this man. And she knew in that moment that she and the storyteller had been right, that Kane was not beyond redemption. He only thought he was.

And she found herself clinging to that knowledge as if it would help her get through this, as if just the thought of Kane was powerful enough to give her the courage to survive. It was, somehow, and she fought her inner shaking to a standstill.

"You are not afraid," Druas said, those pale, eerie eyes fastened on her. He sounded intrigued, and that made Jenna nervous. She fought that down as well.

"Why should I be afraid of a man I merely find contemptible?"

To her surprise, Druas laughed. It was a sound as empty and lifeless as his eyes. "Brave words, when I hold your life in my hands."

"My life," she said with a shrug, "means little." Kane's words came back to her, and she added, "I consider myself already dead."

Druas drew back, staring at her. "Spoken like a warrior."

If only you knew, she thought. "Shall we save some time? I will not help you, nor tell you anything. Nor will my people give up. So do what you will, and get it over with."

Druas continued to stare at her for a long, silent moment. Then, thoughtfully, he turned and walked to the table behind him and poured something from a large jug into a silver goblet. He sipped, all the while watching her. He was an impressive man, tall, strong, commanding, imperiously handsome, and she began to see why he was so often victorious.

What she could not see is how anyone could serve a master with those eyes. What they held was worse than evil, even evil had a purpose, even evil cared about that purpose. What these eyes held was . . . nothingness. A vast, endless expanse of emptiness, that would suck up souls as easily as blood.

She felt a shiver that had little to do with the chill of the stone walls of the stronghold Druas had com-

mandeered for his use. She did not want to think of
what had probably happened to the prior owners. She
had been brought here bound and gagged, and left in
a cold, damp cell she supposed was below ground, for
how long she did not know. But when he had at last
had her brought before him, Druas had ordered her
released, had even offered her food and drink. She
had refused, despite the dryness of her mouth and
throat, and the urge she felt to wash away the taste
of the filthy cloth they had used to silence her.

A shout came from outside, followed by an answering shout and running footsteps along an upper battle-
ment as some sentry ran from his post to another.
Druas cocked his head, listening, but when nothing
more came, he turned back to her.

After a moment he walked over to her, offering
her the goblet he had drunk from. She turned her
head away.

" 'Tis not poisoned," he said. "As you saw, I drank
of it myself."

" 'Tis poisoned now, then."

Again to her surprise, he laughed. And again, it was
a soulless sound that chilled her.

"I see your fire matches your hair, as I was told."

Jenna went still. Told?

"Shall I tell you what else I know?" Druas asked,
his fingers tapping the side of the silver goblet. They
were blunt, the pads of his fingers seeming to swell
up over the short nails in a way that made Jenna think
of the brute strength of an animal. "I know that this
forest to the east is the reputed location of Hawk
Glade, which most take to be merely a legend. I know
that the clan who supposedly lives there is under the
protection of some magical spell that prevents outsiders from finding them."

"Everyone has heard such legends," she said easily,
thankful that Tal had told her of the commonness of

such stories about her home on the outside. "Even I have heard them. 'Tis common enough, stories of distant places, magical forests, that sort of foolishness."

" 'Tis said this clan has a leader marked by the possession of a golden hawk."

"Ah. So it is that you are after? Some piece of gold? It seems a small bit of plunder for such as you. Assuming it even exists."

Druas erupted into sudden motion, flinging the goblet against the wall. It barely missed Jenna's head, and the red liquid it held splashed across her tunic like blood.

"Do not play me for a fool," he ground out, fury now contorting his face into a vicious mask, and she thought herself the fool for ever thinking there was not pure evil here. "I know who you are, Jenna." Her breath caught at his unexpected use of her name, and he smiled viciously. "I know that you are the Hawk, leader of the clan of Hawk. And I know the magic that protects Hawk Glade is real, is the only reason we have not yet trampled your clan into dust."

"Lucas," she breathed.

"Yes," he hissed out. "The boy told me everything I wanted to know. Before he died. Slowly."

Jenna tried to bite back her cry of pain; Lucas's life had been so short, so full of pain and loss, to have died what must have been a horrible death at this man's hands . . .

"You have truly earned your reputation," she said bitterly.

"I have only begun to build my reputation," Druas retorted with smug satisfaction. "And my empire. I hold every bit of land between here and the sea. And before I am done, I will hold all to the mountains to the north and the plains to the south. No one will dare oppose me."

"You are overly confident," Jenna said, even know-

ing the likelihood of anyone strong enough to withstand Druas's might was very slim.

She heard another noise from outside, but Druas
did not seem to notice this time, he was too intent on
cowing her. "When I am through here, there will be
no one to oppose me. No one."

"Even you cannot defeat the magic of Hawk
Glade."

"Even the magic of Hawk Glade cannot withstand
the torch," Druas said.

*He will have his path to the north, if he has to cut
down every tree of your forest.*

Kane's ominous promise echoed in her ears; she
supposed burning or cutting made little difference.
And they did not know if the magic of the glade would
hold under such an assault. They knew so little of how
or why it had come to be. She wished Tal were here;
he knew of such things, he could—

"I will have this land," Druas said. "And you cannot stop me, even with some magic spell to hide behind." He leaned forward, pinning her with those
uncanny, dead eyes. "Nor can anyone else."

Kane, Jenna thought instantly. Did he know?
Heaven help them, did he somehow know that the
man who had turned on him was helping them? Had
poor Lucas let that slip as well?

How could he not have? she realized. He was just
a boy, and he had been more awed than any of them
by the great warrior's presence. It would have taken
little to get him to boast of it. Far less than what
Druas had no doubt done—

The sudden, heavy pounding on the oaken door
made her jump.

"Sir!" The door crashed open, and a panting, heavily armored man staggered into the room. "Sir, the
north wall is under attack! They are firing arrows

flaming with something that will not be put out. Several men have been injured."

"Arrows?" Druas exclaimed, his tone incredulous. "Against stone walls?"

"But they are . . . different, I tell you. They cannot be smothered, or doused. 'Tis sorcery, I swear! They just keep burning, and if you are struck—"

The man broke off at Druas's sharp gesture. "What action have you taken?"

"I've ordered all the standing guards but the four corners to the fray. I've rallied the rest of the men. They are arming themselves now."

"Get those guards back in place!" Druas snapped.

"But—"

"Are you too big a fool to see that this was meant to draw our attention to the north wall? Do it! And pull all the men from the inside corridors to the battlements and the towers."

"But that will leave the interior vulnerable—"

"Exactly as I wish it. Do not question me again!"

The man scrambled to do his leader's bidding. Jenna thought—hoped—Druas had forgotten her. But he turned back to her then, wearing a smile that chilled her to her soul.

"So. He comes."

She swallowed, wishing there was some other way to interpret that smile and those words. There was not. When he saw her reaction, his malevolent smile deepened.

"What the boy said was true, then. I disbelieved it at first, for I know Kane. He would never risk himself for a mere woman. But when the boy insisted it was true with his dying breath—"

"You bastard," Jenna hissed.

" 'Tis Kane who is the bastard. He and his whore of a mother are of the same ilk. He turned on me,

and I take that from no man. I will have his head
by morning."

He had planned this, Jenna realized with shock. He
had known Kane was here, and he had planned this.
The trap she had walked into had been for her, but
Druas had only wanted her to bait an even bigger trap.

"It was he you wanted all along, wasn't it?"

"Clever girl," Druas said. Then he smiled, that chilling smile. "I have removed even my own guards, leaving the way conveniently open for him. I wish to kill
him myself. With my own hands, as he deserves."

Kane, Jenna thought, pleading to all the gods at once,
even while doubting there were any powerful enough to
stop this man. Druas laughed, that frigid, dead laugh, as
he picked up the bonds he had ordered removed from
her hands and used them to tie her to the chair he
pulled out from the table that held the wine.

"And once Kane is dead," Druas said once she was
tightly bound, "there will be no one to stand in my
way. No one." He looked at her consideringly. "And
once he is dead, perhaps I shall have to sample the
woman he thought worth dying for. Perhaps she could
interest even me."

She ignored the threat and thought only of Kane.
She didn't doubt Druas was right; as well as Kane
knew his former leader, that leader would know Kane.
And the realization that Druas feared him warmed
her even as it doubled her dread for Kane.

He had come for her.

And he would die because of it.

And for the first time in her life, Jenna felt a pain
as strong as that she felt for the clan she loved. She
could no more bear to be the cause of his death than
she could bear to stand by and let her people die.

And she thought it a cruel joke that it was only
now, when it was too late, that she finally realized
what that meant.

Chapter 21

Kane pressed himself back against the cold stone wall. He heard the shouts, heard the sound of running footsteps overhead and knew that Druas had guessed Arlen's attack of the north wall was a diversion. He hoped Arlen had followed orders and had gathered his small troop and retreated by now.

He hadn't expected he would have long, a few minutes at most, but it had been enough to get inside unseen, over the east wall that had been momentarily deserted. Arlen might not be a born fighter, but he was a courageous man, and he'd held their attention long enough. Kane could only hope they could avoid capture by the men Druas would send after them. If they could just make it to the protection of the forest in time, they would be safe. He no longer questioned the fact; he knew it worked and at the moment did not care how.

He turned his attention back to his search. He knew nothing of this particular stronghold beyond what could be seen from the outside, but he had been in many others that Druas had taken, so he knew all he needed to find was the former master's quarters and he would find Druas; the man took the best as his due.

He moved down the shadowy corridor; Druas was as stingy with light as always. But then creatures like him did their deeds most easily under cover of darkness.

Kane did not exclude himself from that group. Now more than ever, he loathed himself for what he'd brought down on Jenna. For he had little doubt what had happened here. There was no reason they hadn't slaughtered both the boy and Jenna on sight. No reason but one; Druas had needed them for some reason of his own. And there was only one reason Kane could think of.

Druas knew he was here.

In a way, Kane thought as he checked room after empty room—Druas had already done his looting, it seemed from the bareness of the chambers—it was a relief. Five years ago he'd walked away, but he'd never really left it behind. It had never really been over. He had run, had hidden like some wounded wild thing, while Druas had searched for the warrior who had betrayed him. And he would continue to hunt, Kane realized now. That feeling he'd had of being a prisoner on his mountain was no less than the truth. And he would remain a prisoner as long as this man continued to hunt him. Which meant as long as he was alive.

He should have done this long ago. Should have confronted Druas, and ended it one way or another. But now Druas had Jenna and the thought that she might be the one to pay the price for his cowardice made him shudder. He fought it down; there was no place for emotion in this exigency. If he could not quash these distracting feelings he would have little hope of saving her. He had to be as cold, as ruthless as he had always been. There was no other way to deal with Druas.

But there was no way he could forget that it was Jenna's life at stake. And that if she lost her life because of him, he would be worse than dead. The memories that haunted him now would be nothing compared to the memories that would torture him if she died because of him.

He came to a turn in the corridor and stopped. He edged closer to the corner and peered down through the darkened hall. As he had suspected, a pair of heavy oaken doors marked a larger room. This room faced the south, and would get the benefit of the longer hours of sun to warm the stone in the summer; it was natural the master would choose this for his own rooms.

And the absence of any guards, here and anywhere else inside the stronghold, told him as clean as if it had been shouted from the battlements.

Druas knew he was coming.

He had always known Druas would want to kill him with his own hands. It was his way with traitors, and he took great pleasure in it. And in bringing the betrayer to his knees first. There was nothing Druas liked better than having a man beg for his life; it made the taking of it so much sweeter, he was fond of saying.

He knew all the begging in the world would not satisfy Druas when it came to himself. And he had a good idea of what it would take to satisfy the man's thirst for vengeance. Men who had only been enemies had received easy deaths compared to what Druas reserved for those rare few who betrayed from within.

He would no doubt have something bloodily inventive in mind for the man who had betrayed him the most, his right hand, his most trusted ally.

It was no more than he deserved, Kane thought, and started down the dank corridor. He made no effort at silence; it was pointless now. Nor did he hesitate at the heavy doors; he merely kicked one open with a heavy thrust of his foot. It crashed back against the inner wall.

He saw Jenna first, tied and helpless, saw her eyes
wide with fear and regret and sorrow. And something
else he dared not name, something that leapt to life
in the vivid blue the instant she recognized him.

"Welcome back, Kane the Warrior."

The voice was the same as it had ever been, cold,
lifeless, soulless. He did not look at the man he had
once followed, had eyes only for the woman who had
made him see he was not the same, although the
knowledge had come far too late to save him.

But perhaps not too late to save her.

"Let her go," he said.

"What? No greeting after all these years?"

"Let her go, or we have nothing more to say."

Druas laughed again, and this time there was a note
of triumph in the glacial sound.

"So 'tis really true, what the boy said. Kane the
Warrior, brought to his knees by a mere woman."

"Let her go," Kane repeated, "and you can have
what you really want."

"Kane, no," Jenna whispered.

Druas glanced at her for a moment, but not long
enough for Kane to move.

"Interesting," Druas observed dispassionately.
"How did you manage that?"

"She has nothing to do with this."

"True," the pale-eyed man agreed. "She and her
little clan are merely a nuisance I shall soon be rid of.
I was simply curious as to how you, of all men, had
managed to charm such a fierce one. Has she a pen-
chant for your kind of cruelty?"

"Little you know of him," Jenna said, but subsided
when Kane looked her way and gave a slight shake
of his head.

"Even more interesting," Druas said.

There was a clatter in the hallway, and four armored
men appeared in the doorway. Druas glanced at them.

"Stay in the corridor, await my call. And close the door," he ordered. "I shall deal with this."

One of the men protested. "But, sir, there are men gathering—"

"Can you not even deal with such a puny threat as this pitiful clan of farmers and gatherers? Close the door! And do not set foot in here again unless I order you to!"

Hastily they did so, and Druas turned back to his study of the man who had once been his best warrior.

"Let her go," Kane repeated. "I am the one you want."

"And I have you," Druas said. "I see no reason I should let her go."

"I am here," Kane corrected. "But I have not surrendered."

Druas's thin brows rose. "You are saying you would, if I let her go?"

"I would."

"Kane, no! You cannot!" Jenna's cry ripped through him like a broken, rusty knife. He did not dare look at her. He was aware she struggled against her bonds, but as long as she said no more he concentrated on his deadly enemy.

"You would give yourself up to me, knowing what awaits you?" Druas asked in obvious fascination.

"Only when I know she is safely away."

"So 'tis really true. Kane the Warrior, enslaved by a female. Is she so very good in the carnal arts to have bewitched you so?"

Kane's jaw tightened. There was no safe answer to such a question; Druas did not indulge himself often, and he did not want him to take an idea that Jenna should be the exception.

"Let her go, and I will hand you my blade."

"But I will have you anyway," Druas pointed out.

"My men are within call, and even Kane the Warrior cannot overcome such a force."

Kane lifted one shoulder in a negligent shrug, as if his words meant little to him. "Perhaps. But it would be easier for you without a fight."

Druas studied him for a moment. "And perhaps worth it, to see you so humbled."

"You will see nothing until she is safely away."

Druas looked thoughtful. Kane did not move, knowing that if he dared even glance at Jenna he would lose his concentration, and Druas would be on him in a heartbeat.

"I make you a different offer, Kane. One I have never made to any other man. I do it because of the bond between us. And because no warrior has ever quite taken your place."

It was an astonishing admission from such as Druas, and Kane was instantly wary.

"I want nothing from you," he said.

"Not even your life?"

Kane's eyes narrowed as he studied the man who had ordered his life for so long. "Is that your offer?"

"Only in part. I trust you will take this as symbol of the value I put on you. I will give you back your life . . . and your position."

Kane stared, genuinely startled. Never had Druas shown the slightest mercy, never had he taken back one known to have betrayed him. They had all died, slowly, painfully, at Druas's own hand.

"You have reason to look well surprised. You surprised me once, Kane, when you became the greatest of warriors. I have never given a man a second chance. Yet I give it to you. Rejoin me, and we will build an empire like no other ever seen."

Kane heard a smothered sound from Jenna, a sound of pain, of hope, of resignation, he could not tell. He

still did not look at her. He could not. It was all he
could do to speak her name levelly.

"And Jenna?"

"My generosity does not come without price,"
Druas said. "I cannot have the warrior at my right
hand bewitched."

"So the price for my place with you regained is her
life," Kane said, keeping his voice even with an effort.

"She is merely a woman, replaceable in your bed,"
Druas said. "Although I confess, I am surprised you
allowed one to become so important to you. I
thought"—Druas gestured toward the scar on Kane's
face—"I taught you better. Perhaps it is part of this
magic?"

It was magic, truly, Kane thought, but not the kind
Druas inferred. It was something more powerful than
any spell Tal or his like could ever cast. And something Druas would never understand.

"She lives," he said coolly, "or you die."

"You're hardly in a position to threaten me," Druas
said. "Did you think you found that hallway empty by
chance? I knew you would come. You always had that
stubborn streak of honor, no matter how I tried to
crush it. But my guards are now merely awaiting my
order to take you."

"But you will die before they lay a hand on me. I
promise you this. And you know I can do it."

For an instant something flickered in the eerie pale
eyes. "They would hack you to pieces."

"So be it."

With a sharp sound of protest, Jenna struggled violently against her bonds, the chair she was tied to
scraping loudly across the stone floor. Neither man
looked at her.

"You can have what you want at little cost," Kane
said softly. "It is me you hate, not her. She means
nothing to you."

"But she clearly means a great deal to you," Druas said thoughtfully. Kane suppressed a shiver when he realized the man was trying to think of a way to use her against him. And of the ways he would come up with, given time.

"She is merely an excuse," he said. "This should have been done long ago."

"Stop it!" Jenna shouted. "I am not some pawn to be scrabbled over by a couple of dogs! I will not let you do this, Kane, give yourself up to this butcher!"

"You have two choices," Kane said swiftly, before she could say any more, draw any more of Druas's attention to herself; he was already looking at her with far too much interest. "Release her, and live. Or die."

"Either way, you die," Druas pointed out.

"Yes. But you will be deprived of the pleasure of killing me yourself. Slowly, as I'm sure you've planned these five years past."

Druas said nothing for a long moment. Then he smiled, a bone-chilling smile that made Kane want to strike him down right now, before he could unleash any more evil on the world.

"I will let her live, in exchange for your surrender."

Kane let out a breath. "Done."

"Damn you!" Jenna cried out, "You have no right to do this, Kane! I do not want your sacrifice." She looked at Kane, her eyes alive with a fierce pride and courage that made Kane want to take her in his arms and shelter her forever, simply because she did not need it.

"We will speak of rights," Druas said ominously, "after I have your sword, Kane."

"Release her."

With a shrug, Druas drew his small dagger from his belt and strode over to slash through Jenna's bonds, first her hands, then her feet. It was his mistake; as he bent to cut the rope that bound her ankles, Jenna grabbed the pottery wine decanter and brought it down hard to shatter against his head. In the same instant she brought her knee up hard and fast, hearing the satisfying crunch as she broke his nose.

His scream of rage echoed off the walls as he went down to his knees. But he swept one arm back and caught Jenna around the waist, dragging her down with him. Imprisoned by his considerable bulk, she could do nothing but pummel his powerful chest uselessly.

This was not what he would have tried, but Kane took the chance she'd offered and struck swiftly with the hilt of his sword, knowing he didn't dare use the blade when Jenna was so close. Druas fended off the blow with one metal-gauntleted forearm. Only then did Kane see he had brought his dagger across Jenna's throat, drawing blood from the pale skin. The sight stopped him cold.

"Drop your sword or I'll slash her throat right here," Druas ordered, his voice sounding muffled by the blood pouring from his nose.

"Kane, no! Don't let him win!"

She meant it, he knew she did. She would truly die rather than let him hand himself over to Druas. As he would die rather than leave her in Druas's hands. Something stirred in the back of his mind, some realization he knew was important. Yet he also knew he had no time to dwell upon it now. Druas was tightening his hold, and blood was welling from the fair skin beneath his blade, the skin that was softer than anything he'd ever touched. And there were noises coming from outside the stronghold's walls, shouts, rumblings, footsteps; something was happening.

"Now," Druas snapped. "Before I change my mind about our bargain."

Kane's sword clattered to the stone floor. Jenna whispered something low and harsh. Druas got to his feet, dragging her with him, his eyes never leaving Kane.

Druas shouted toward the doorway, and the men who had been waiting, no doubt weighing Druas's orders to stay out against the sounds they heard from inside, burst back into the room.

"Sir, there is something afoot outside—" The words stopped, all eyes widening at the sight of their leader's bloody face and wine-soaked hair. At Druas's sharp order the man who had spoken took Kane's arms and yanked them behind him, tying his hands together tightly.

Druas gave a deep, satisfied laugh despite his bloody nose. Then he shoved Jenna toward one of the other men.

"Tie her to the bed," he ordered. "It's where I'll want her, later."

Jenna kicked out furiously, and the man trying to restrain her howled in pain. Kane swore, jerking free of his captors for an instant before they scrambled to restrain him.

"So you've taken to betraying your own word, Druas?" Kane spat out.

"I have not. I promised only that she would live. She will. But she will live as my whore. And you, Kane, will watch as I make use of her. 'Twill be my parting gift to you, before I skin you alive."

"You will not," Jenna said coldly as the man pushed her to sit on the foot of the bed, and struggled to bind her to the bedpost. "I will die first."

"Noble, but wasted," Druas said. "I am glad I thought of it. It is most fitting, that he watch the Hawk turned into a whore, and that you watch Kane the Warrior die, slowly, screaming."

"I change my mind," Jenna said. "I will kill you first."

Druas laughed. "I do believe I will enjoy this." He

glanced at Kane. "I salute your choice in women, my—"

"Sir!" The clatter of booted feet echoed ominously in the corridor. A man wearing an insignia of rank at his shoulder pounded breathlessly into the room. "Sir, we must secure for an attack! A mighty force approaches!"

Druas glared at the man. "A force of weaklings armed with nothing more fierce than burning arrows—"

"No, sir. 'Tis a real attack, not those simple clanspeople. I don't know where they all came from, but there are scores of them, mounted, armed, and they are riding this way. They came out of the forest as if out of nowhere, a huge force! 'Twas a sight to behold, in the moonlight—"

"Enough!" Druas whirled on Kane. "This is your doing."

Kane shook his head, knowing he must look as puzzled as he felt. "I know nothing of this. You've made enemies enough, perhaps they've joined together."

"Sir, you must hurry," the man urged. "They have a huge machine, the master of arms believes it is a catapult of some size."

Druas growled something low and obscene, then turned to his officer. "Rally the rest of the men. I will come see this army of yours for myself." He picked up the sabre Kane had dropped, then glanced back at its owner. "I cannot risk your escape," he said.

Kane knew what was coming, tried to dodge, but he was held fast by the two men and could not evade the blow. Druas's heavy metal-clad gauntlet caught him on the temple, and everything went black.

Jenna wrestled with the rope that held her, although her wrists were raw to the point of bleeding. Kane lay frighteningly still where he had fallen, his hands still tied tight behind him, and from here she could not even tell if he was breathing.

Panic welled up inside her; he could not be dead. Not Kane, not so simply, by a single blow from the likes of Druas. It just could not be.

She yanked at her bonds again, ignoring the pain in her wrists as she was ignoring the alarming noises from outside. And ignoring the chaotic tumbling of her thoughts, a much harder task. Kane had been willing to give himself up to a certain, painful death in exchange for her freedom. She did not know what to think of that fact, knew only that she could not, would not let him do it.

If he was still alive to argue the point.

Her throat tightened, and stinging moisture pooled in her eyes. She cursed herself, tears were a useless luxury she could not afford now. She swiped at her eyes with her forearm, all she could manage, tired as she was.

The motion brought into her field of vision a slight gleam coming from the floor beside her feet. She leaned forward. It was a shard of the pottery decanter she had shattered over Druas's head.

She stretched out her legs, and captured the fragment between her feet. Twisting until she could barely breathe, pulling until she thought her arms would part from her shoulders, she managed to bring her feet up to the bed. She edged the piece to one side and let it drop on the coverlet. Shifting to her side, and thankful for the thickness of the feather coverlet that made it possible, she pressed the side of her leg downward until she caught the shard between her knees. Swiftly she doubled up her legs and caught it in her teeth, then transferred it to her hands, praying all the while not to drop it.

The edge was hardly knife sharp, but it was the best thing—the only thing—she had, and she sawed away

until her wrists ran red with blood from her efforts.
Each passing moment seemed an hour long, and with
every sawing motion of her hands she knew they were
one step closer to death. She could hear the sounds
still echoing outside, and although she'd never been
in one, she could not doubt these were the sounds of
battle. She sawed harder.

When the rope at last parted, she stared for a split
second, unable to quite believe it. But then she was
moving, kneeling beside Kane's inert body.

He was alive. For a moment that was all she knew
or cared about, that rise and fall of his chest, the
steady thump of his heart beneath her fingers.

She rose quickly then, searching the room. Tossed
in a corner she found, of all things, her small crossbow;
she supposed Druas had found the little weapon amus-
ing. But that was of no help to Kane at the moment,
and she looked on. She found no kind of knife, and
was about to begin the laborious sawing with the bits
of pottery when she saw the corner of her small quiver
protruding from under the rushes strewn on the floor.
She grabbed it up; the feathered bolts relied more on
force than sharpness, but they were still sharper than
the pottery. And they meant she was armed, as well.

It took her only half the time to saw through Kane's
bonds. She rolled him onto his back, and welcomed
the low groan that came from him. Blood trickled
down the side of his face, following, oddly, the path
of the old scar. She again fought back tears, trying to
think. If only Kane would awaken, if only he would
tell her . . .

"What would he have you do?" she whispered to
herself.

Even as she asked it she knew. And she picked up
the small bow, loaded a bolt in the groove, and
notched the bowstring, ready for firing. Only then did
she go to the earthen pitcher on a low table across

the room. She found a small amount of water in the bottom, poured some of it out into the goblet that matched the one Druas had hurled at her. The rest she used to soak the corner of the coverlet from the bed, and wiped it over Kane's face.

After a moment he stirred, his dark, thick lashes fluttering as his eyes flickered open. He stared at her blankly for a moment, the normally clear gray cloudy and confused. He tried to move, and winced.

"Don't try to move yet," she said softly.

He blinked, then focused on her face. "Jenna." It was a warm sigh, both pained and wistful, and the sound of it tightened her throat unbearably. Then she saw awareness come rushing back to him, saw the moment when the sounds from outside registered on his trained mind.

He sat up abruptly, weaving a little as a wave of dizziness took him. She reached out to steady him, but he had already recovered.

"Druas," he said in a hissing tone as cold as his speaking of her name had been warm.

"He hasn't come back. Perhaps he will not, if this force is truly as great as they say."

"He will come back," Kane said grimly, "if he has to crawl, if he has to let every one of his men die to do it. He will let nothing stop him from killing me."

"He would let his entire army die just to execute one traitor? That does not make sense, Kane."

Kane laughed, short, sharp, and very harshly. "It does, when you consider who the traitor is."

"He hates you that much?"

"He does. More than any other man who has ever turned against him."

Jenna studied him for a long moment, bits and pieces of things said and seen whirling in her mind. Old scars and unprecedented offers and dead puppies and murdered children . . .

"You were more than simply his right hand, weren't you?" she asked finally, very gently.

He met her gaze then, and she knew by the way he looked at her that her knowledge of the truth was clear in her face. He turned his head, averting his eyes as if he could not bear to look at her. When he spoke at last, his voice was a twisted, broken thing.

"He is my father."

Chapter 22

"Tal," Jenna muttered as she helped Kane get to his feet, "is doing a mightily poor job of keeping his promise."

"His promise?"

"Never mind," she said. "But I would like to know where your magical friend is, now that we could truly use his help."

She busied herself, once he was steady enough to stand, with gathering up her small bow and the quiver. When she straightened, she saw him watching her, his face expressionless.

"How did you know?"

She knew what he meant, and knew better than to even try to pretend she didn't. She let out a short breath. "Many things."

"We are . . . so much alike?"

The self-loathing that had crept into his voice startled Jenna. "No!" She shook her head fiercely. "You are nothing alike. It was not that, nothing like that. It was only things you had said, and his methods . . . and perhaps my hope that there could not be two such evil, cruel men. And that I could think of no other reason for him to hate you so much than if he felt you had betrayed more than simply his trust."

"His blood."

She nodded. And then something else came to her. "And his name," she said softly. "You did not simply leave him, you left . . . everything. You turned your back on what he was, what he tried to make you . . . even on his very name."

"I could no longer bear to carry it. He has turned the name of Druas into an depraved, poisonous thing."

"So you are known only as Kane by your choice. Not simply because the legend is of Kane the Warrior."

His mouth twisted. "Such repute will do us little good here," he said, clearly not wanting to discuss it any longer. The noises from without were growing louder and closer, and his tone became ominous. "And if we do not get out of here, it will not matter."

He glanced at the small openings in the south wall, big enough to let air in, and arrows out, but not much more. He walked over to the heavy oaken doors, inspecting them carefully.

"He had them locked, and barred from the outside, after he . . . struck you."

Kane only nodded and continued his inspection.

"He is . . . the one who gave you that scar, isn't he?" she asked.

Kane's hand moved reflexively up toward his cheek. He stopped the motion and continued to study the doors without speaking. But Jenna knew he had answered as clearly as if he had said it; it indeed had been his father who had sliced his face open and left him with the mark he would carry for life.

" 'Twill not be easy. They are solid," he muttered, pressing a hand against the closest door.

It swung open.

Kane dodged back, clearly startled. Jenna stared.

"I heard them bar it, I know I did," she said.

"I do not doubt you," Kane said, never taking his

eyes off the unexpected opening into the apparently deserted corridor outside. "He would be a fool not to lock us in."

"But how—"

"I do not know. Most likely it is a trap of some kind. But no more than this room is."

"Then we are . . . going?"

He looked back at her. His eyes held that flat, emotionless look she had seen when she had first come to the mountain. She had almost forgotten it, and she did not care for its return. It spoke too clearly of a man who considered himself beyond feeling. Beyond caring. Beyond redemption.

"Will you trust me enough to come with me?"

Her brows furrowed. "Why would I not?"

"You know whose spawn I am now."

Jenna stared at him. "You think I would . . . turn on you, for that?"

"It would take less, for some."

"To repudiate you because of something you had nothing to do with?"

"You are the Hawk for the same reason."

"Only because my people have not found cause to replace my family."

He blinked. "What?"

" 'Tis all it would take. A simple vote. If enough felt we were not doing what was best, a new Hawk would be chosen."

"I . . . did not know."

"And I did not know you thought me of that ilk, to turn upon you so easily," she said, making her pained disappointment with a cool tone. "Now, are we going?"

He hesitated, as if he'd heard the hurt in her voice, but in the end he only confirmed, "We are."

The strained exchange pushed aside with an ease Jenna envied, he turned away from the beckoning doorway, his eyes darting about the room. He quickly gathered up anything he thought likely to help; flint and stone, tallow candles, a polished bit of metal that had no doubt served as a shaving mirror for the deposed owner. Seeing what he was doing, Jenna ran to the trunk that sat against the wall by the bed and pulled it open. She pulled out items of clothing, then a woman's shawl. She seized it and lay it out on the bed. Swiftly he dropped the things he'd collected onto the cloth, then knotted the corners together around his belt.

"See if there is anything else of use in there," he said with a gesture at the trunk. "And something to cover your hair."

Then he walked back to the open doorway, as warily as a wolf scenting the lure yet instinctively sensing the snare.

Seeing the point of hiding the hair that stood out like a beacon, Jenna dug into the trunk and found a small, rough-woven cloth in a dark shade of blue. She quickly bound her hair, covering the now tangled mass as best she could. She returned to her search of the trunk, but found nothing but more clothing, and then a belt. She thought perhaps that might be of some kind of use, so she pulled at it. It came out of the tangle of cloth she'd made, and only then did she see that she had found more than a simple belt. She rose quickly and hurried over to Kane.

"I found a dagger," she told him.

He glanced at the small knife with its bejeweled handle. His mouth twisted. "A lovely woman's weapon," he said. "But of little use."

Jenna glared at him. "And who would a woman have cause to use such a weapon against, but a man?"

In the space of a moment he looked startled, then thoughtful. And then one corner of his mouth twitched upward as he said ruefully, "Would that this blade were as quick and as sharp as your mind." Then, in an entirely different tone, and with his jaw set, he added, "Bring it. You may have need of it."

Mollified, Jenna strapped the belt on over her own, and watched as Kane edged forward. He peered into the darkened hallway. He reached down to his left and came up with a thick, heavy board of the kind that barred other doors in the stronghold.

"It appears to have slipped free," he said.

"But you don't believe it," Jenna guessed from his tone.

"It seems a bit . . . convenient."

She could not disagree with that, and kept close behind him when he started down the dank corridor. He kept the piece of wood in his hand; it was not much, but even a club was better than nothing. And Jenna guessed that Kane the Warrior could make even that a formidable weapon.

Kane seemed to know where he was going, and Jenna was of no mind to question him. Her mind was reeling with the realization that the man they faced, the man who had brought such suffering to her clan, was Kane's father. She understood much now of why he had been the man he was, and admired even more that he had found the courage to leave it behind, to turn his back on the evil that he had truly been innocently born into.

"Wait," Kane said suddenly.

"What—"

She broke off as he held up a hand for silence and turned his head as if listening. They were, she guessed, beneath the parapet walk on the south wall. The sounds of fighting were clearly heard here. And from the sound of it, Druas's men were not happy with the way things were going.

Kane swore, low and harsh.

"I told Arlen to retreat as soon as I was inside,"

he muttered. "And not to come back." He glanced at her. "I should have guessed he would not leave until you were safe."

"He is loyal," Jenna agreed. "But I would hate for him to die for my sake."

"Then we'd best give him some help."

Jenna looked at the club he held, his only weapon. "How?"

"The same way you held Druas in place for days on end, Hawk."

He did not say the title with the respect and deference her people did. But he did say it in a way that made her feel more than all their obeisance ever had. As if he approved of what she'd done. As if he were proud of her. As if he cared.

Keeping to the shadows, Kane moved toward the inner wall, looking, Jenna guessed, for a passageway to the inner courtyard. They reached the curved wall of a flanking tower, and he found what he wanted. He pulled the door open slightly, then paused, listening.

Jenna's breath caught as she heard Druas's voice; it sounded as if he were right over their heads.

"—have you found?"

"There has been much damage to the north wall, sir. I fear a breach is imminent."

Druas swore. "Who *are* they?"

"They wear a badge, sir. A raven."

A raven?

Kane glanced at Jenna and saw the same thought in her eyes. Tal? Could it be?

"I know no one with such a preposterous insignia who could raise such a force," Druas said, clearly losing patience.

"Still, they are here, and they are gaining ground," the man insisted. There was a pause before the man said in odd tones, "And they cry the name of Kane the Warrior. The men fear it is he who leads them."

"It is not Kane," Druas said.

"But the men have seen a huge man, astride a destrier as dark as the night—"

"It is not Kane! He is dead . . . or as good as."

Kane pulled back into the tower and closed the door. Swiftly he unknotted the cloth at his waist, and handed Jenna the flint and the candles. She took them, then gave him a questioning look.

"We need to draw their attention to another flank. There is more wood here than you might think. Set fire to what you can find. There should be straw to be found in the bailey. If not, use the rushes from the floors. They should be dry enough this late in the year."

Wide-eyed, Jenna nodded.

"Watch the smoke from your first fire, and work your way upwind, if you can. The smoke will be thick enough, trapped inside the walls."

She nodded again. "And you?"

"I will do what I can," he said simply.

"Kane, if it is Tal—"

"Even he will need help." He took in a deep breath. "He told me once that magic is an illusion, and it was foolish to be afraid of an illusion." He looked upward, where the sounds were still echoing, the shouts, the running, the occasional cry as a man was struck down. "An illusion, no matter how clever, is not going to win this battle. Now go. And when you have done all you can, get out. There is a postern in the west wall, take it and get to the forest as fast as you can."

"But you—"

"Do not worry about me. Get yourself out. Your people need you, Jenna."

She grabbed his arm. "We need you, too."

He looked down at her, and what she saw in his eyes—acknowledgment and resignation—took her breath away.

"I will make sure of one thing," he said. "You will no longer face Druas."

He did not say, "If it costs me my life," but Jenna heard the words as clearly as if they had been spoken.

"Kane, please—"

"Go. Time is short."

She knew he was right, but she hated leaving so much unsaid between them. She also knew the worst thing she could do right now was give him the declaration that was in her heart to carry with him. She sensed somehow that even Kane the Warrior, that man who admitted no emotions, had his limits, and that he was near them now.

"Live," she said fiercely, with all the command of the Hawk ringing in her voice. "We have too much to say."

"Go," he ordered in turn.

In this, the order of Kane the Warrior held more weight than the Hawk, and she turned to go.

"Jenna?"

She looked back at him, her breath stopping at the sound of his voice, as if her name had been wrenched from him by some force he had tried mightily to resist.

"I . . . Thank you."

And then he was gone, leaving her to wonder what he had been going to say. And to try and quash the hope that she knew she was a fool for harboring. Especially since it was likely neither she nor Kane would survive this night's work.

Because she had no intention of leaving him here to die alone.

Jenna coughed as she ran, thinking how much worse this would have been had she not followed Kane's advice and worked upwind, even in the slight current of air moving inside the walls of the stronghold.

No one seemed to notice her as she moved in the

shadows. She'd not dared risk trying to keep the candle lit, so had had to rely on the flint and what straw or tinder she found or could carry with her. She'd ignited whatever looked likely, as swiftly as she could. And soon she heard the shouts of the men as they realized something was wrong within as well as without.

When she'd reached the kitchens, she'd found the rooms empty of men and full of wooden tables and chairs. As swiftly as she could, she dragged several into a large pile against an inner wall. She lit one of the candles, and set it to burning where the flame would, she hoped, eventually set the whole heap afire.

She saw wounded men being carried down the ladders that led to the battlements. She thought of burning them, too, but settled for simply removing the ladders whenever she could without being spotted. She used the small dagger to slice through the leather strips holding them together, then pulled them apart, rendering them useless even if somebody should find them. It wasn't much, she thought, but it might slow them down.

When she could find nothing left to burn, she set herself to her next task. And it was not getting herself safely to the protection of the forest, as Kane had ordered. She ran back to the south wall, where she had already seen there were few men left fighting. She wrestled with one of the ladders she had removed and hidden intact for this reason, raising it again to the parapet walk, and scrambled up.

The moment she was on the walk, she loaded her small crossbow. She ran forward in a low crouch, thankful for once for her size, which allowed her to keep in the shadows, and the hours of training Kane had forced upon her. Only when she reached the flanking tower did she look over the wall, toward the north. What she saw stunned her; it appeared dozens

of men, all mounted on powerful warhorses, their
armor not gleaming silver in the moonlight but as
black as Kane's, rode back and forth at will, seemingly
impervious to the arrows rained down on them by
Druas's men. From where she stood she could see the
men behind those armored riders, her clan, loading
and firing the catapult more rapidly than she would
have thought possible. And she saw a rank of archers,
sending waves of flaming arrows toward the walls,
arrows that burned with an unearthly light.

*They cannot be smothered, or doused. 'Tis sorcery,
I swear!*

The excited babblings of Druas's man did not seem
so demented now, and Jenna became more certain
that somewhere in this was indeed Tal's fine hand.

She started forward again, dodging men who
seemed too hurried to notice one small, silent, dark
shape hidden by shadows. She reached the corner
tower safely, pausing to listen to the odd, clanging
sounds from within. She found the arched entryway,
but the moment she stepped inside she came up hard
against a man hastening out. They both careened back
out onto the parapet. He seemed more startled than
anything, but she took advantage, as Kane had taught
her, of his heavy armor and weight, and her small
stature; she used her body to take him at the knees,
and he went over the edge with barely a cry.

She stepped back into the round tower room. And
sucked in a sharp breath at what she saw, the answer
to the clanging she in her ignorance of such things
had not recognized.

A wide shaft of moonlight lit the scene like some
sort of devil's dance. Two tall, strong men, evenly
matched in size and strength, one with hair shorn
battle-helm short, one with hair flowing in a dark
mane down his back, each doing his best to hack the
other to pieces with heavy blades. These were not the

graceful blades like Kane's slim sword, they were heavy, brutal broadswords of weight and killing edges. Nor was the fighting graceful; it, too, was heavy and brutal.

Sweat poured off them both, and she wondered how long they had been at it, how long father and son had been locked in a battle she knew would be to the death.

She watched as if entranced as the fight went on, fighting the urge to cover her ears to muffle the clanging of metal on metal. It seemed she could almost feel the vibration of the blows as they were struck. Once Kane staggered, and she held her breath; no matter how evil or powerful she had always thought Druas, she had never imagined anyone could overcome Kane, and the thought that this might have a different outcome than she expected only now occurred to her.

And if Kane died, that left her to deal with Druas.

Her own words echoed in her head. *I will die first.*

Then Kane's words, his odd tone and the set of his jaw as he spoke of the dagger she'd found came back to her.

Bring it. You may have need of it.

And she suddenly knew what he'd been thinking. She might well need that dagger, to use upon herself if both of them failed to take Druas down.

Druas. She still thought of him in that way. Kane spoke of him in that way. As Druas, not his father. Although she could not doubt the connection, it seemed too awful to be real, and she couldn't bear to think of what Kane had had to endure as the son of this man. What he still had to bear. And she realized now that what she had seen in his eyes when he had learned it was Druas they faced was hatred. A pure, raging hatred for the man who had betrayed his own son from the day he was born.

The men passed out of the silvery light, made eerier

by the smoke from the fires she'd set, then back into
it again as Kane pressed the attack and Druas fell
back. Jenna, crouched in the shadows, staring as if
spellbound. They were so alike in size, build, and
quickness. And so very different in mind, intention,
and heart. She knew that as well as she knew her own
name, no matter that Kane did not believe it.

Would he believe it, even if he killed Druas? Would
that gain him the peace he thought beyond his reach?

Even as she thought it, she knew it would not. He
was not his father, who could, she knew without
doubt, strike down his own son with little more feeling
than as if he were killing a helpless puppy. No, he was
Kane, not Kane the Warrior, but the Kane he had
become on his mountain, the Kane she had come to
know, the Kane who had loved her with passion and
held her tenderly, a man who sought only peace, and
to leave behind the horrors of his father's kind of life.

No, it would not give him peace, for the torture was
not from his father, it was from within himself. And
patricide would only increase the agony, and she could
not bear to think of him in more pain.

*When I first came here, I feared he might seek a
permanent end to his pain.*

Tal's words haunted her now more than ever, for
she could easily see this becoming the last blow that
would send him in search of that final respite.

She would not let it happen. She could not. Not
even were it to save her clan, she could not let him
pay such a price. She had no time to analyze what
that meant, she could only accept that somehow this
man, this warrior who carried scars beyond believing,
scars far worse than those that marked his powerful,
beautiful body, had become as important to her as
her people.

Kane slipped, as if he had stepped on water-slick
stone. Druas struck from the side, hard and swift.

Kane took the blow on the ribs, where Jenna knew the opening in his lightweight armor left him vulnerable. Jenna heard his grunt of pain. He went down to one knee, clearly stunned.

She straightened in the instant that Druas raised his sword. He lifted the heavy sword above his son's head. Jenna saw his face in the moonlight, a face twisted by a hatred unlike anything she'd ever seen before. She could not doubt for an instant that this was to be a death blow. She stepped away from the wall. She lifted the small bow to her shoulder.

And then Kane moved, with a swiftness that took her breath away. He launched himself from the knee he had feigned collapsing to, and drove his full weight into Druas's belly. The man staggered back, his intended blow glancing off Kane's black armor. The force of it was proven as the weapon bucked in his hands and Druas lost his grip on it. It clattered to the stone floor. And Druas stood unarmed before the son he'd been ready to kill.

"Do it," the man hissed when Kane merely stood there, his sword held before him, between himself and his father, as if now, far too late, it could protect him from the evil. "You've betrayed me from the day you were born of that whore. So finish it."

"If she was what you say," Kane said in a tone that was oddly conversational, "then why did you ever acknowledge me as your son?"

Druas spat something out Jenna could not hear.

"Because you know she was not," Kane said. "You cannot have it both ways. Either she was a whore, and any man could be my father, or you know you are, and she was not. You acknowledged me, so you know—"

"I acknowledged you because I hoped you would have more of my blood than hers," Druas said, fury distorting his voice. He moved oddly, a sort of sideways twitch, and Jenna's brows furrowed as he ranted on. "Because I thought you might become a worthy successor, heir to my empire."

"Your empire," Kane said bitterly. "Built on the blood of innocents."

Druas laughed harshly. "You pious hypocrite! You spilled most of that blood."

"Aye. Except my mother's. And my sister's. I was too young to stop you then. But I will stop you now. It is the best I can do to atone for that."

Kane lifted his sword. He seemed to shudder, as if the weight were suddenly too much. Druas moved. Jenna saw the glint of silver in the man's right hand. Saw the dagger he'd pulled streak toward Kane's unprotected throat as Kane's hands tightened on the hilt of his sword.

It would not give him peace.

She raised her bow and fired.

Chapter 23

Kane stared as his father suddenly grabbed at his neck. The malevolent pale eyes were staring, first at Kane, then at something past him.

"You!"

It was a hissing, gurgling sound as blood spurted from between his fingers, fingers that were grasping the crossbow bolt that protruded from between them.

Only then did Kane see Jenna step out of the shadows near the wall and into the shaft of moonlight that came through the small window. She reached up and tugged away the dark scarf, letting the red fire of her hair tumble free as she strode toward them, looking to Kane's stunned eyes like an avenging goddess come to earth.

"Yes," she said, her eyes fastened on Druas, who had sagged to his knees as his life pumped away. "I am the Hawk, and I claim your life for my clan. For those you have murdered. For my family. For the children. Even for the animals. But most of all, for your son."

Druas gurgled as Kane's breath caught in his throat. His father was dying, the tormentor of his childhood, the creator of the thing he had become, was dying, but he could look only at the woman before him. Even when he heard the faint thud of Druas's lifeless body at last slipping to the floor he could not look away from her.

"Jenna," he said, and could say no more.

Her eyes shifted from the dead man to Kane's face. And when he saw her eyes, when he saw the fierceness that still glowed there, he knew she was the Hawk in more than just name.

"You *are* the Hawk," he said softly. "And you have your vengeance. As you said."

Her gaze seemed to narrow as she looked at him. "I meant what I said," she told him pointedly. "*All* of what I said."

He knew what he referred to, but he couldn't believe she meant it as it had sounded.

"It is better this way," she said softly, as if she'd read his thoughts. "Better that it was I who killed him. 'Tis why I came back. No matter how evil, he was still your father. That would not sit easy upon your soul."

Kane was stunned. She had done this, had come back when she could have escaped to safety, had killed a man, for a reason such as that? For him?

"He . . . was not worth the cost to *your* soul. One more stain on mine would make little difference."

"Even the strain of patricide?"

" 'Twould be hard to make my soul any blacker."

"The storyteller once told me that the path to hell is the path to redemption, if you walk the other way."

Kane shook his head slowly. He doubted there was anything that could earn him redemption, but it was a tempting thought. And it warmed him that Jenna thought him worth it.

And it stunned him anew, what she had done. She had killed a man, not just for her own powerful reasons, but so that he would not have to live what was left of his life with the knowledge he had killed his own father.

"The storyteller," Jenna breathed, turning her head

to the window, where the moonlight poured in silver pure. But Kane knew she was thinking of what was happening outside in that unearthly light. Druas's men fought on. And so did the Hawk clan.

"Will they quit, now he is dead?" she asked, looking at Druas's body.

"Most will. But they must learn of it first."

"How?"

"I will deal with that. You must get out of here. Go back to the south wall, you should be able to slip out unnoticed."

He saw her answer in the stiffening of her spine and the warning flash in her eyes before he heard it. "I will not. There is fighting yet to be done—"

"And you would be the perfect hostage," he pointed out. "Get out, get back to the forest. Druas's men will give up eventually, when they realize he is dead."

"But you—"

He cut her off. He could not bear to think that she would risk herself for him yet again. "It is your people who matter, Jenna. They are brave, Jenna. Foolhardy, but brave. They would fight to the death for you, to the last one standing. Is that what you wish them to do, thinking you are still held here?"

He knew it was the one argument she could not meet. He could see the inner battle in her tight, troubled expression.

"Go, Jenna. They need you."

She drew herself up, looking once again every bit the Hawk. "I will see you when it is done."

It was not a question, it was a command. Kane did not speak. He could not lie to her, and if he spoke the truth, he knew instinctively she would not go.

After a moment, she turned and left the tower, back toward the south wall as he'd told her. Kane watched her go, and as she was about to disappear from his vision, he whispered softly, "Good-bye, Jenna."

When she was gone, he took a deep breath. He felt the pull, the tearing in his side. He ignored it, and knelt by the sprawled body of his father. He tried to lift him, but the pain that shot through him quickly told him he would not be able to. Quickly, he stripped off the man's heavy armor and tossed it aside. Then he levered the literal dead weight over his shoulder, his jaw clenching as the pain ripped through him again as he tried to stand.

I will see you when it is done.

He only wished it could be true. Even if it were only to truly say good-bye, he wished he could see her again. But he knew it was not to be. Tal's prophecy would come true. But first he had this to do, to show Druas's force that they fought for a dead man who would neither pay them nor brutalize them again. He had to hold on long enough for that.

And judging by the pain in his side, and the warm wetness steadily pumping from the wound there, it would be the last thing he would ever do. But as long as Jenna was safe, he didn't care.

He would be dead, but Jenna would survive. It was enough. It was all he had.

Jenna slipped through the shadows, toward the sounds of shouting and of the dull thuds of heavy stone on stone. The catapult she had thought at the time a waste of effort was doing its job well, it seemed. And the smoke was rising from inside the walls, adding to the chaos. She allowed herself a smile, then dodged behind a thick stand of old birch trees as a man shouted from the wall nearly over her head. She heard Druas's name again and again, and it was clear the men were beginning to become aware they had not seen their leader in some time.

She worked her way forward, until she could see the streaks of the arrows burning with what appeared to be merely normal fire now. And, it struck her suddenly, the mounted warriors had vanished, leaving not even torn and trampled earth behind them to mark their presence. It was puzzling, but she kept on, until she saw a familiar figure calling for the archers to unleash yet another volley.

"Arlen!" she called.

He whirled, giving her a startled look. Startled, but no more, Jenna thought, but before she had time to dwell on it, he spoke.

"I thought you were with Kane."

"I was."

He glanced around, clearly puzzled. "Where is the horse you rode? You could not have returned so quickly on foot."

Her brow furrowed. "Horse?"

Arlen stepped toward her, worry suddenly erasing the puzzlement from his face. "Are you hurt? Your head—"

"I am fine," she hastened to assure him. "But, Arlen, I must tell you—"

A roar went up from the men working the catapult. " 'Tis Kane!" they shouted, pointing.

Jenna turned. She looked upward to where the men were pointing and gesturing wildly. And her heart nearly stopped at what she saw.

Kane, silhouetted against the moon, his cloak swirling around him, his hair whipping in the wind. In his arms was an unmistakably limp body, and Jenna's heart began to race to catch the missed beats as she realized what he was doing.

"How did he get up there?" Arlen said, bewildered. "He was here, astride that huge warhorse of his, just moments ago." He looked at Jenna. "You know, you were with him. How did he get you out so quickly?"

She blinked, momentarily distracted. "What?"

"We thought you still captured, when you rode out on that white steed, your hair like fire even in the moonlight. 'Twas a sight I'll never forget—"

"Arlen, what are you talking about?"

"I—"

The sudden hush cut him off as effectively as the roar of the men had. Jenna's head snapped around as her eyes sought Kane once more. He was lifting the body he held, and then it was flying, through the moonlight, twisting, to land in a broken heap, in view of all on the ground and upon the walls. And Kane's voice boomed out, loud enough to be heard by all.

"Your leader is dead. You fight for nothing. Halt, and you will be allowed to leave alive. Continue, and you will die to the last man." He paused, and in that moment Jenna knew she was seeing the man who had struck fear into the hearts of countless men, the man who had been as fierce as the ones he faced now. "I am Kane," he said, his voice lower now, but no less powerful, "and you know I will keep my word. Whichever way you choose."

Even from here Jenna could hear the murmurings from the parapet, the cries of shock and fear and false bravado.

"You have until dawn," Kane announced.

And then he was gone, vanished from the parapet in a swirl of dark cloth and rising smoke, like the demon some called him. 'Twas only a trick of the light and the thick haze from the fires she'd set, Jenna knew, but it was eerie nevertheless.

Druas's men seemed stunned, and the rain of arrows from the walls that had halted with Kane's dramatic appearance did not resume. She heard the jubilant exclamations from around her as she began to walk among her people, fearful of what she might find. Yet all seemed accounted for, all seemed upright and well, if tired and shaky in the aftermath of a battle they had never expected to fight.

And all of them, she came to realize in consternation, seemed to believe they had been led into this battle by two people, two mounted leaders who had exhorted them to fight as they never had, who had inspired in them a determination that would not be beaten. Two leaders, astride a black warhorse and a graceful pure white steed, a dark warrior and a fiery Hawk.

Kane and Jenna.

Who had been locked up inside the stronghold until a short while ago. But everyone of her clan believed Kane had miraculously rescued her from Druas's clutches within minutes, and that they both had returned in time to lead the assault. It was a sight none of them would ever forget, they all said.

A sight Jenna well knew they could not have really seen at all.

It was then that Jenna began to search again. This time for two men with changeable eyes, both of whom were far too clever. She wasn't certain who she wished to find first, the storyteller or Tal, but when she found them, she would have the truth out of them both. In plain words, no more obscure evasions, no more enigmatic allusions.

And then she would deal with Kane. And if he did not come to her, she would find him.

She returned to Evelin, who was still tending to the few minor wounds that had been inflicted on the clan. She had lit torches as clouds rolled in, obscuring the moon. Jenna shivered, although it was not really cold.

"Where is the storyteller?" she asked the healer.

Evelin looked up from the bloody splinter she had just removed from the hand of the man who had been loading the catapult; it seemed the most serious of the slight injuries.

"I have not seen him," she said. Then, forehead creasing, "Now you speak of it, I have not seen him since just after you were taken. Kane spoke to him then, but that was the last time anyone saw him, I believe."

"Have there been any strangers about? A young man, fine-featured, with dark brows, and silver-shot hair?"

Evelin looked blank. "No. Why on earth would a stranger be here amid a battle?"

" 'Tis a long story," Jenna said, and left the woman to her work.

No one else she asked was of any more help. She knew Tal was here, he had to be, it was the only explanation for what had happened here. And she had the feeling that if he did not wish to be found, he would not be. But the storyteller—

"Jenna!"

She turned as Arlen came running up to her. As if suddenly remembering himself, he tipped his head and reported respectfully, "They are leaving, Hawk. Many of them, at least. Under cover of the darkness, now that the moon is hidden, out the back of the stronghold, where we have no men. Shall I send some to stop them?"

She nearly smiled at the man's assumption that they could stop them, even now. Victory was a heady thing, but Druas's men were still hardened veterans of battle, and Jenna knew it was only the presence of Kane that was convincing them it would be wise to leave. But she would not deprive Arlen of his pride; he had earned it.

"Let them go. It will be as Kane promised. If they wish to leave, they will be allowed."

Arlen looked almost disappointed, but he nodded. "Where is Kane?" he asked.

"A question I would like answered myself," she muttered. "Has no one seen him?"

"Not after he tossed Druas like the offal he is. But Flaven said he saw someone on the rise, over there."

He gestured toward a small knoll between the stronghold and the forest. It would give a good view of the entire area, and she thought it likely Kane might have gone there, to the higher ground, to watch and be sure his orders were obeyed. She nodded at Arlen and headed that way.

She only became aware of her own weariness when she began to walk to the top of the rise; it was not a great slope or a great height, yet she found it tiring. The air felt oddly heavy here, and the further she went, the greater effort each step took.

The clouds sailing across the sky cleared for a moment, and in the spill of moonlight she saw a limp form at the crest of the rise. She could see only that it was a body, lying at a grimly awkward angle that suggested she was in no danger, yet she gripped the hilt of the small dagger she'd taken from the stronghold.

She tried to run, but it was oddly difficult. Still, it was only a moment before she was close enough to see more clearly, and a cry of protest rose from her when she saw the familiar dark robes of the storyteller.

She did run then, fighting the odd lethargy at every step. She dropped to her knees before the motionless, hooded body, reaching for his shoulder to turn him over. A sharp cry stayed her hand. Startled, she looked up. She stared at the glistening black bird who was bobbing her head furiously.

"Maud?" Jenna whispered in disbelief.

She heard a low groan then, and yanked her attention away from the bird to the old man who lay, thankfully alive, before her. She rolled him over gently. The hood of the robe fell back, and in the momentary moonlight she saw his face. His hair.

It was Tal.

It came to her in a rush, with a certainty she could not deny. Tal was not related to the storyteller. He *was* the storyteller.

He groaned again, and she saw his lashes flutter. She lifted him slightly, cradling his head on her knees.

"Tal," she whispered urgently.

His eyes opened. He looked up at her. Blinked. Lifted a hand. Touched her arm.

And smiled. "Jenna."

"Are you hurt?"

"I . . . no. Just . . . tired."

Relieved, Jenna's questions burst from her. "What happened? How did you get here? Where have you been? Is this your doing?"

He chuckled, or tried to; it was a mere ghost of his usual laugh. "At my best . . . I could not keep up with . . . that torrent of questions. And I'm not . . . at my best, at the moment."

"Talysn ap Bendigeidfran I will have a straight answer from you," she said warningly.

His mouth quirked as she managed to say his name without stumbling. "Been practicing?"

"Do not try to divert me, I—"

"You used my name," he said suddenly, trying to rise, as if this realization disturbed him.

"The only name I know," she corrected pointedly, "storyteller."

He fell back against her knees, and as moonlight shifted over his face she saw that what she had thought merely the effect of the stark light were indeed dark shadows circling his eyes. He looked beyond tired, he looked exhausted unto collapse. Which is apparently what he'd done.

He lifted one hand, grabbed a lock of his own hair, and pulled it before his eyes.

"Drat," he muttered.

Jenna remembered that day on the mountain with Tal, when the shadowy light had given an oddly silver cast to all of his hair, not just the streaks of gray at his temples, and had made his eyes look the same misty green as the storyteller's when he was deep in concentration, that day when the resemblance to the storyteller had been so pronounced. And he had said it was merely the light.

And now she knew it was much more. He *had* been grayer, that day. Because he hadn't quite made the change back from the storyteller's silver to his own mixed locks.

"Forget something?" she asked mildly.

Tal glared at the dark strand of hair. "I was . . . busy."

"Too busy to remember who you were pretending to be?"

He eyed her warily. "You're going to make me pay heartily for my little deception, aren't you?"

"I think," she said, " 'tis Kane who will exact a hefty price."

Tal's mouth twisted wryly. Then, abruptly, all trace of any emotion except fear vanished from his face. Before she could stop him he sat up, his eyes wide, his breathing labored.

"Kane," he said, and the sound of his voice struck terror into Jenna's heart.

"What is it?"

Tal tried to stand, but could not. Jenna scrambled up barely in time to catch him as he fell to his knees.

"Damn," he swore, shaking is head. "That vision, holding it for so long, it was too much. I can't even move."

"What about Kane?" she urged, grabbing Tal's shoulders. She was worried about the wizard, and the awful fatigue in his face, but she loved Kane. And she did not even hesitate to admit it now, although she'd been avoiding the knowledge for a long time.

"You have to find him," Tal gasped out. "He's . . . hurt. Bleeding." He closed his eyes, his breath coming in gulps. "I can't . . . the battle . . . took all I had . . . I . . . had to leave the head of the snake . . . to you."

Jenna moaned, barely managing not to shake him. She knew he was trying, she could feel it in the shudders that swept through him beneath her fingers.

"Where is he, Tal?"

"I can't . . ." His brows lowered as he closed his eyes tighter, straining. "Someplace . . . dark. Enclosed. Stone."

"Inside? He's still inside the stronghold?"

Tal shuddered violently. "Heaven . . . help him, he's dying and I can't . . . reach him. I can't help him."

"No!" Spurred by the despair in the wizard's voice Jenna shook him, hating herself for it; he looked like death himself, but only he could help her save Kane. "Where, Tal? Where is he?"

She felt yet another shudder ripple through him. And then he lifted his head. She saw in his eyes a fierce golden glow, like that of a fire in the last moments before burning out.

"I'm sorry, Tal," she whispered. "I know you're tired, but I cannot spare you this. Kane's life—"

"Maud," he said.

She blinked, and then drew back as the raven cried an answer. Tal looked at the bird, who stared back at him. He gave a low, odd-sounding whistle. The bird cried out again, sounding for all the world like a protest. Tal whistled again, sharper this time. This time the bird took flight, beginning to circle slowly overhead.

Tal looked back at Jenna. The glow was extinguished in his eyes, and Jenna wondered just what she had cost him.

"She will . . . help you search. Hurry," he said. "There is . . . little time."

"Tal—"

"Go. And be . . . careful. I cannot protect you."

He said it as an order, no less commanding for being whispered as if with the last of his strength, and she obeyed; something about this man made it impossible to do otherwise.

The moment she got to her feet, Maud voiced a cry and flew toward the stronghold. She left the wizard there, wondering if she was leaving him to die, alone. But he had given her no choice, if indeed there had ever been one.

In the tradition of a people who had once done the same, she followed a bird's flight. And she supposed she could be forgiven if, in the eerie light of the moon, this bird looked more hawk than raven.

Chapter 24

Maud led her to the south wall, where she had exited under cover of darkness and the distraction of the battle. There the bird circled tightly, like a hawk who had spotted her prey. It occurred to Jenna then that Kane would no doubt go to guard the armory there, to be sure that Druas's men did not raid it in an effort to wipe out the small clan that had defeated them as they departed.

She saw no one as she went and wondered if indeed Druas's men had all fled before Kane's ominous promise of retribution if they did not. She would not be surprised; few would dare gainsay a legend. Especially Kane, as he stood towering above them all, handing down his ultimatum with all the authority of a legend come to life.

But she knew all too well that the legend was a man, a man who could bleed and die as any other man. With Tal's words haunting her, she ran through the darkened corridors.

She found him, on the floor beside the barred iron door of the armory. She ran to him, dreading what she would find. She dropped to her knees, terrified she would touch him and find him cold and lifeless beneath her fingers.

He was pale, and cold, but not unto death; she

found a faint, fluttering beat at his throat. She bit back a cry of relief. Hastily she took out the remaining candle and despite her shaking hands managed to light it. The warm glow did little to brighten the grim sight before her; Kane looked worse than Tal had, his eyes deeply shadowed, his skin with a distinct gray tinge, his breathing barely perceptible.

She began to search him for signs of a wound. She found cuts, far too many of them, but nothing that seemed capable of having brought him down. It was not until she unfastened the heavy black armor that she found it. The left side of the tunic he wore beneath the armor was saturated with blood, and his leggings all the way down his left leg to his knee. It flashed through her mind, that blow he had taken to the ribs from his father's sword. She had thought, when he had surged back into the fight, that the armor had taken the blow, that it had been a feint, that going to his knees, it did not seem possible that he could have gone on with a wound as severe as this one.

But that's what legends do, isn't it? she thought bitterly to herself as she peeled away the cloth from the ugly wound. It was long and deep, and she knew it was beyond her limited medicinal skills.

"Jen . . . Jenna?"

His voice was faint, wondering, and her gaze snapped up to his face.

"Kane," she whispered urgently, as if her worry could somehow give him strength. When she reached out to touch his cheek, his brows rose slightly, as if he were startled at the contact.

"You are . . . all right?"

"I'm fine. Not even a scratch."

He looked puzzled. "Then I . . . I'm alive?"

She realized he hadn't been certain until he'd felt her hand on his face. "And you're going to stay in that condition," she said fiercely as she began to fold the scarf that had held the candles into a pad.

"I thought . . . it would be over . . . by now."

He looked a little bemused, and she knew he didn't mean the battle. "Over?"

"The . . . prophecy. I didn't realize . . . would take so long."

Every ounce of spirit Jenna still held within her rebelled. "You are *not* going to die! I don't care what Tal said."

That she'd seen undeniable proof of Tal's powers tonight did nothing to lessen her ferocity. There had to be an answer, Tal would not have been so anxious to find Kane if he were only to die anyway. She could not believe that.

"I don't . . . mind," he said softly. "As long as you . . . are all right."

"Stop it—"

". . . meant to be, Jenna. You know . . . that." He let out a labored breath. "I am . . . at peace. At last." He closed his eyes.

"No!"

The dark lashes lifted, and Jenna winced at the weariness in his eyes. "Tal . . . was right," he murmured. "Let it be."

"Don't speak like that," she ordered. It made her shake, his composed acceptance of the death he thought certain. He had expected this, she realized. He had expected to die, just as the prophecy had predicted. He had believed it, every step of the way, and he had come anyway. He had not just risked his life for her and her clan, he had given it away, knowing he was doing so, from the moment he left his mountain.

Fighting her trembling, she pressed the folded scarf against his side; the bleeding was only a slow seeping now, but Jenna feared that was only because there was so little left. A sound of pain escaped him before he could stop it, and she apologized for hurting him. He gave the barest shake of his head.

"Arlen, and the others?"

"All are well," she said, watching the pad slowly turn red with frightened eyes.

"Druas's men?"

"In retreat, running from Kane the Warrior like frightened children."

"It is done, then," he said, and his eyes closed.

Fearing he meant more than the fight, Jenna spoke sharply. "Oh no, it is not. We have much to talk about, Kane. And I will never forgive you if you deny me that."

She thought, just for an instant, he smiled. But then his head lolled to one side, and her heart leapt to her throat. Only when she had reassured herself that his own still beat did she leave him and go for help.

Jenna shifted her position to ease the ache in her back, but she did not move. She had not left Kane's side since they had brought him here, to her cottage in Hawk Glade, where he lay in her bed, racked with fever and barely breathing.

For three days now she had kept vigil beside him, taking heart at Evelin's promise that every day he lived brought more hope, and losing it every time she fancied a change for the worse in his already pale face, every time she dozed and awoke with a start, and it took a moment for her to be sure he still lived.

Arlen had reported the stronghold deserted now, Druas's body lying unclaimed before the breached wall. Coldly she had ordered it buried. "I don't want it poisoning the animals," she said, never taking her eyes off the man that brutal, amoral savage had some-how fathered.

When Arlen came back to report it done, she had sent him to search for Tal; a fruitless effort, she was certain, and she'd been unsurprised when the hunt yielded no results.

The others came one at a time, to pay tribute to the man who had saved them, and to the leader who was clinging to the hope that they would not have to mourn him.

On this fourth night, Kane lay so quietly Jenna was afraid to look away from him. Before he had seemed to fight the fever, sometimes thrashing so much Evelin feared he would bleed again. But now he just lay there as it grew worse, as if too weak to even fight, until even Evelin looked grim as her herbs and medicines failed one after the other.

When he suddenly spoke, hope seized her. But she soon realized it was the ravings of fever, broken sentences that either made no sense—or too much. He spoke of battles fought, of blood and carnage seen, until Jenna felt her stomach roil. He spoke of the dark evil shadow that dogged his life, the father he had turned his back on in sickened loathing.

And in the end, he spoke of the woman who had come to him on the mountain. The woman who had made him wish he was not already damned. Who had made him wish he knew how to love. And then he said her name, in a tone unlike any she'd ever heard from him, a loving, sorrowful tone that brought tears to her eyes she'd thought long cried out.

Please, she pled. *Please, he's been through so much. He has done cruel, hard things, but surely he has earned a chance at redemption? He walked away, he left the brutality behind, and he has spent years living quietly in peace, hurting no one.*

She did not know who she was begging. She did not care, and directed her pleas to all the gods her people had once worshipped, and a few she had only vaguely heard of. Or one who was above them all, if there was such a thing.

It was not his fault, what he was, she moaned inwardly. *His father made him that way. He has tried so hard, he has changed so much, don't let it all be for naught.*

Kane grew still again, and his breathing even shallower. She could almost feel him slipping away, and when she reached out to grasp his hands they were so cold she cried out her fear.

"No, Kane, hold on!" Tears began to streak down her cheeks, and she turned her eyes heavenward as she choked back her sobs. "Please! I do not ask for myself, although I love him. If the only way he can live is to go back to his mountain, I will take him there. I will leave him there if I must, live without him if I must, but please, he must not die."

She heard an awful, rattling sound from Kane's throat. Terror gripped her. She tightened her grasp of his hands, knowing she was losing him.

"Damn you, Tal, this is your doing, he'd fight if he wasn't so convinced you were right."

She regretted the words the moment she'd said them. Tal had done much to save her people, and at great cost to himself, nearly his own life. It was not his fault that Kane had decided to ignore his warning. For her. It was not his fault if his powers, whatever they were, could not save him.

She moaned, aloud this time, unable to stop it. "Why can you not save him, Tal? If you can make such a promise to me, that my blood will never die, why not him? Why not the man you call your only friend?"

Brokenly she begged the man she was not sure she would ever see again.

"I wish you would take your promise back! I care not if my line ends with me, but Kane . . . Take your promise back, and give it to him. Give it to Kane."

Her tears overcame her, and she lowered her head

to rest on her hands, still wrapped tightly around Kane's.

She felt the gentle touch on her shoulder, and an odd sort of strength flowed through her. Only once before had she felt such a thing, the day she had become the Hawk. When the storyteller had sent her that look of support so strong it was almost tangible. She jerked upright.

Tal was sitting cross-legged beside her. He looked almost recovered, although shadows still darkened his eyes, eyes that were that misty forest green tonight. His hair was caught somewhere between his own dark locks and the storyteller's silver, giving him the look of both. And he moved as they both did, in that graceful, tightly knit way that seemed so natural to Tal and so amazing in the storyteller. But now that she knew, she wondered that she had not realized they were, not related, but the same man.

"You sensed it, Jenna, all along."

"And you," she snapped, "can quit reading my thoughts and do something to help him!"

His mouth quirked. "You are doing that, Jenna. Just do not let go of him."

Kane was breathing quietly again, but still far too shallowly. But he was breathing. She looked at Tal.

"Who are you?"

"You know my name. You even pronounce it tolerably well."

"I am in no mood for your evasions, wizard. You helped my people, and for that I am grateful. I am even grateful to see you alive. But if he dies—"

"Jenna—"

"Why did you not help him?"

Tal sighed. "I could not do both. I had not the strength. So I chose what I thought Kane would have wanted." He gave her a sideways look. "There are limits to what I can do, you know."

"No, I don't. I don't even know who—or what—you are, you hide it so in vague words and hints."

"Wizard will do," he said with a shrug.

"Not storyteller?" she asked, her voice biting in spite of her efforts to control it; she was more than grateful to Tal for his help, but terrified that Kane was dying, and that put an edge in her voice she could not stop.

" 'Twas necessary, Jenna. Your people were at war. They would naturally be suspicious of any stranger."

"Except a doddering old man who was no threat?"

He nodded. She eyed his dark hair, again seeing how it had taken on more of the old man's silver.

"You need to practice your disguises," she said.

His mouth twisted wryly. "It's this place, I swear it. The magic here plays havoc with anything I try to do. All the time I was here, I could do only the simplest of things. It took all my concentration simply to keep up the guise of the old man. Maud won't even fly into this place."

"I wondered where she was." Jenna looked thoughtful for a moment, almost thankful for the distraction, although a large part of her attention was always fixed on Kane, watchful for any sign of a change. "When you sent her after me, she stopped at the edge of the forest."

Tal nodded. "She is wary of spellbound places."

"Yet she stays with you?"

"That's different. She is under the same spell as I."

Jenna blinked. "What?"

Tal sighed. "It is a long, unpleasant story, and one I'm sure you do not wish to hear right now. Suffice it to say I once long ago made someone very angry, and Maud and I have been paying for it since."

Jenna glanced at Kane, and found him unchanged. She looked back at Tal. "And will you ever have paid enough?"

Tal's changeable eyes narrowed. "Probably not enough to ever break the spell, unless I finally find the one who cast it," he said. "But I do not think we are speaking of me any longer."

She did not deny his perceptive—or magical—guess. "He has paid a great deal for his past," she said softly. "Must he give up his life for the peace he seeks?"

She saw the glint of that golden glow deep in Tal's eyes. "You said you wished I would take back the promise I gave you and give it to him. Did you mean it?"

She did not question how he knew, nor did it frighten her; whatever Tal was, he was not evil, no matter what others might think. There was great darkness in him, she knew that, and from what he had just said, she knew his life had not been easy, but there was no malice, no malevolence in him. So she answered him honestly.

"I meant it. Can you do it?"

"Not . . . exactly."

She looked at Kane, saw the faint sheen of sweat on his brow, the shallowness of his breathing. He appeared barely alive, and her heart twisted painfully inside her. She had to look away.

"What can you do, then?" she asked, looking instead at the wizard who sat so calmly beside her.

He smiled at her then, a lovely, soft smile that took her breath away. Tal was indeed a beautiful man, and it amazed her yet again that she could be immune to him simply by the sheer power of her love for Kane. She hoped someday Tal would find a woman who would love him for all that he was, who would look past the things that frightened people so and see the brave, generous, honorable heart.

"I can give you rest," he said quietly, reaching out to touch her cheek.

She needed rest, she admitted, the weariness was

suddenly almost overpowering. But she could not sleep, not when Kane was so weak, so near to leaving her forever.

"He will be here when you wake," Tal promised softly.

Jenna yawned, fighting the need to go to sleep right now. She forced her eyes open, and stared at Tal. His eyes glittered oddly, in a way she'd never seen before, even as changeable as they were.

Tears? she wondered. Surely not. Wizards didn't cry, did they? And he had promised Kane would be there, it could not be that . . .

"Tal? What is wrong?" she asked, her voice already heavy with the sleep she was resisting.

"A woman once looked at me the way you look at him," he whispered. "She paid the price for what I did as well. And I can never atone for that."

In that moment, Jenna saw in the wizard's face the man he had been, and the man he was now, a man almost beyond retrieval, and who knew it. Her heart ached for him, and for a moment Tal closed his eyes, as if it had shown in her face and was too much for him to bear. Then he opened them again, and the golden glint was even stronger.

"Thank you," he said. "Now rest."

In that moment her head became too heavy to hold up. She lay down upon Kane's chest, taking some small comfort in the sound of his heart, even though the beat was alarmingly faint.

"Rest, Jenna." Tal's voice was lulling, soothing. "You have earned it. You both have. Kane will have his peace. And you will both reap the harvest of your own courage."

She murmured something, or tried to. She heard Tal say something, very softly, something that sounded like good-bye. And then the blackness, dark, warm, and mercifully free of dreams, enveloped her.

*   *   *

Jenna awoke slowly, coming up out of the dark depths of a healing sleep like a small trout swimming toward the morning sun. She did not know how long she'd slept, only that it was long enough that sunlight came through the windows of her cottage, and that Kane's chest felt even harder than usual beneath her cheek.

It was harder. No, it was not Kane's chest she felt.

She sat up sharply, her hands shaking as she reached out to touch him, dreading what she might find. But he still breathed, his heart still beat . . . was it even stronger now? Was he truly warmer, or was it merely wishful thinking on her part?

She did not trust herself to judge, and thought to call Evelin. But before she could make the thought action, she realized what she had been resting on, although she did not know where it had come from, how it had gotten wedged beneath her head while she slept.

It was a book.

She knew it only by hearsay; she was familiar with scrolls and the like, but this kind of thing was unknown to her people. But the storyteller had spoken of them, of volumes that lasted much longer than the fragile parchments, generations, volumes oddly bound with a protective cover that held pages in place for easy reading, that—

The storyteller.

Tal.

She stared down at the heavy tome. It was covered with what felt and smelled like leather, although it was stiffened somehow. The color was deep, rich, and dark blue. The pages looked thick and heavy, and were edged with gold that glinted in the morning light in a way that reminded her of the glint in the wizard's eyes; she was more sure than ever that this had some-how come from him.

She inspected the volume carefully. There were no markings on the outside, nothing to hint at what it held. But the most overpowering thing about it was that it was . . . warm. Not in the way she would have expected had it truly rested beneath her cheek for any length of time, but in an odd way that made her, hold-ing it, somehow feel warmer. And she couldn't define the strange sense of peace that seemed to have over-taken her. Peace, and a gentle easing of tension and strain.

Kane will have his peace. And you will both reap the harvest of your own courage.

Tal's words echoed in her mind. Yes, it had come from him. She could not doubt that now. And as if in confirmation, something else he'd said came to her, in Tal's voice, as clearly as if he were there and had spoken the words again.

But there must be a way for those who are the last of the line to know, to understand what they must do to assure it continues. Something to guide them along the right path . . .

A guide.

She looked at the book more closely.

The pages were of parchment, made heavier and stif-fer by the gilt of the edges. The inside of the cover was lined with an even heavier parchment that also made up the first page, a paper marbled with an un-usual design in shades of blue that blended with the color of the cover. A design that seemed to change as she looked at it, to flow and fluctuate, until she almost thought she was seeing something more than a ran-dom design, thought she was seeing images there, shadowy figures of people, seeming to move as she looked. She felt an odd light-headedness, shook her head sharply, and the pattern settled down into a merely intriguing flow of lines and ripples.

Wizard's work for sure, she thought, but she felt no fear. She could not fear anything that had come from Tal.

She turned one of the parchment pages. It was blank, but the next page was filled with lines of an ornate, elegant script, in the written language of her people. For an instant she simply admired the grace of the writing, but then her gaze locked on the top line, and she froze.

The page was headed with a variation of her name, in a bolder version of the same script. And Kane's name was set beside it, in the same bold hand.

"Jenna Hawk," she whispered, liking the sound of it. Simple, clean, minus the pretension of her title.

Kane was listed only as Kane. No explanation, but then, legends did not need explanation. When she read on, her brow furrowed. Unfolding there was the story of her clan, bits of history no one outside knew, not even the storyteller.

But Tal would know. She read on.

Tears began to pool in her eyes as she read the stark, unflinching account of the horrors that had befallen them, and in reading the account Jenna saw how futile their efforts had been, how foolish to think they could match such a force as Druas. She read of the deaths, so many deaths, and pain welled up anew at the loss. Her mother, her brother, Latham, Lucas, all the others . . .

Her fingers tightened convulsively on the binding, and she felt another rush of that odd warmth, as if someone had touched her with a gentle hand, just to assure her she was not alone. It was so strong she lifted her head quietly to look around, half expecting to see Tal again. But the cottage was empty, quiet, as she had ordered it when Evelin had told her there was nothing more she could do, nothing anyone could do but wait for Kane to heal or die.

She looked again at Kane. Hope leapt in her chest; he *did* look better, she was almost certain. And he was warmer, she knew he was. As warm as the book felt to her, she thought, wondering if there was some connection. Yet she hesitated in summoning the healer; she did not want to hear, or see in those wise old eyes that she was fooling herself.

Drawn inexorably, she looked back at the book, at the story written there. It told of her search for Kane, the arduous journey, and his initial refusal to help her. And heat crept up to her cheeks as it told of the bargain they'd struck, including the price Kane had demanded and she had paid. She had realized Tal would no doubt know this as well, but it was still disconcerting to see it written so plainly. Only the fact that the book also said that the price had become more of a joy than an obligation kept her from closing the book in embarrassment.

She smiled at the account of her first encounter with Tal. The book made her part in his escape sound much more pivotal than it had been; she realized now he had never needed her help at all. But the words praised her courage to the skies, and her kindness and gentleness far beyond human capacity for such things.

She read on, and in a few moments had the answer to what she had suspected; the final battle, where the wizard she had saved returned the favor to her clan, creating the vision of a huge armed troop, and of herself and Kane to lead the battle. She remembered what it had cost him, as well, remembered what he had looked like when she had found him afterward. No, she could never be afraid of him, wizard, sorcerer, or whatever the world called him.

The next passage was of Kane, of his daring, his bravery, and the way he had risked his life for her and her people, and she read swiftly, hoping to find some proof that Tal had done as she asked, that he had taken back the promise he had given her and given it to Kane instead. Instead, she found again Tal's promise as if it had been given to her, that her line would never die, and in fear she lifted her head and looked at Kane.

Her breath caught. His eyes were open, and he was watching her.

And then, slowly, he smiled. He looked bemused, as if he were surprised he was still here. But what showed in his eyes above all else was the love behind that smile, in these moments when he was too unsteady to try and hide it.

And Jenna knew the joy had only begun.

Chapter 25

"Kane . . . Hawk?"

He said it tentatively, uncertainly. The offer was so very tempting, to stay here, to become one of the Hawk clan. But it would also be unbearable, to be so close to her and not be able to—

"Do you not see?" Jenna asked, cutting off the painful thought. " 'Tis what Tal's prophecy really meant, not that you would die, but that the man you were would be no more. That it is Kane Druas who will die, the moment Kane Hawk is born."

"I . . ." Kane stooped and shook his head in bewilderment, slowly; his strength was still limited, and he was still feeling a bit dazed. As much from all Jenna had told him as from his injury. He felt like a man within reach of the sun, needing the warmth so desperately, yet fearing the inevitable burn.

Finally he decided on a question he thought safe enough. "Tal . . . was here?"

"He was." Her expression changed, saddened. "But I do not know if he will come back. I . . . have the sense that this"—she held up the book—"was a parting gift."

She had told him the whole incredible story when she had explained about the appearance of the mysterious book. And when she had read the writing it held to him, and he had been forced to admit there was no way Tal could have known much of it save magic of some sort. And he'd had to believe the tale of the vision Tal had created; he'd seen the mounted warriors himself, had heard the clan speaking of him and Jenna leading the battle when in fact they had been locked inside the stronghold walls. He'd admitted in his head that Tal had such powers, but only then had he at last admitted it in his heart.

It was when she told him of finding Tal after, appearing near to death himself, that he had realized it did not matter what Tal was, only that he still and would ever call him friend. And he had sought reassurance that Tal had survived, that she had seen him since that time, alive and well.

He looked now at the book his friend had left behind.

"I . . . hope it is not meant as good-bye," he said quietly.

"As do I," Jenna said. "He is an extraordinary man, but I think he carries many secrets and too much darkness for one soul, and he needs friends who will not hold against him the simple fact of what he is."

"I . . . do not."

"I know. And so does he, Kane. He knew the battle you fought was with yourself more than he."

"He truly said . . . good-bye?"

"I cannot be sure," Jenna said, her expression troubled once more. "I was so very tired, I might have dreamed it."

Evelin had told him how Jenna had refused to leave him for days, refusing to sleep or even eat more than crumbs while he lay near death. And he could not deny the look on her face when he had first opened his eyes to her; it had been pure joy, and it had thawed the last frozen bit of his heart as the sun thawed the winter ice on the forest pond.

But it seemed so impossible, that such a treasure should be within his reach, that he had bit back the first words that rose to his lips. Perhaps she was just grateful that he lived, he'd told himself. She would feel the same for anyone who had helped her save her people.

And anyone who had done so would have been welcomed by the clan as well, he told himself now. The offer had been from the clan, not Jenna herself. He would do well to remember that.

"The book," he said, not liking the turn his thoughts had taken, even though he knew it had to be the truth. "He said it was a . . . guide of some kind?"

She nodded. "He promised me my descendants would always walk the world. And that there would be a guide to show any who were the last of the blood what must be done to assure this."

"Your . . . descendants," he said, lowering his eyes.

Children. Jenna's children. Who would have children after them, who would also have children, on down through eternity. He did not doubt it would be so; Tal did not make promises lightly. So the Hawks would go on, the children of this woman who had proven herself worth both the title and the reverence that came with it. They would be the children of royalty, in spirit as well as fact.

And they would be fathered by someone deserving. Someone as fine of heart and spirit as Jenna herself. Someone who had earned the right to become her mate by living a life worthy of her.

Someone he hated even without knowing who he was.

"Is the thought so awful to you?"

He looked up at her words, sensing the sudden tension in her. "What?"

"Descendants. Children. Is it such a repellent idea?"

"No," he said hastily, realizing his feelings must have been reflected in his expression. "You will have . . . many, I'm sure."

As he spoke the words something tore inside him, hurting as badly as the stabbing blow his father's sword had delivered. Even imagining them together, Jenna and whoever he would be that would father those descendants, made him sick inside.

Oddly, Jenna looked relieved.

"Then what is it that makes you . . . scowl so?" Jenna asked. "Is it that you do not care for taking the Hawk name?"

He struggled to keep up with her; he was weary, and emotions he'd never felt before were making it difficult to think clearly. " 'Tis not. It is a fine name, a name to be proud of. Certainly better than that which I carry from birth."

"Then perhaps you have some idea it is not fitting that Kane the Warrior take the name of a woman?"

He shook his head; he was feeling a bit dizzy again. "Jenna, I am honored that your clan would consent to have me among them, more so that they would allow me the name. 'Tis . . . more than I deserve, but . . . I cannot."

She drew back, her eyes narrowing again, and all the tension he'd sensed before rushing back.

"Cannot . . . what?"

"Stay."

She looked away abruptly, lowering her head as if staring at her hands folded in her lap were her sole task in life. The wavy mass of her hair fell forward, masking her face from him.

"It is . . . me, then?" she asked, her voice oddly tight.

He was surprised at her perception, but then realized he should not have been; she had always seemed to have a knack for sensing, not his thoughts, as Tal did, but his feelings. Almost as uncanny a talent, really, since he understood them so little himself. But this he understood.

"I . . . could not do it, Jenna," he said softly. "To live here, to be so close to you, and not . . . I could not watch you with those children who will come, watch them with their father and wish—"

"Watch them with their father?"

Jenna's head had come up sharply, and she looked at him. She had been weeping, he realized in shock as he saw the wetness on her cheeks. He stared at her, utterly lost now, wondering why on earth she was crying now, when it was all over, her people were safe, and he would soon be gone and her life would be her own once more.

"How can you watch them with their father," Jenna said slowly, "when you would *be* their father?"

Kane gaped at her. "What?"

"Heavens above, Kane, what did you think I meant when I asked if you would take the name Hawk?"

"I thought . . . I know you . . . the clan, they're grateful, and—"

"Gratitude?" Jenna leapt to her feet. "There is nothing of gratitude in this! I offer you *my* name— not the clan's but mine, the name given to me by the wizard who promised my blood would live for eternity—and you believe it is gratitude? Then you do not know me at all, warrior. Did you learn nothing during my time on the mountain? Do you truly believe I am a woman who would offer herself forever out of *gratitude*?"

Kane's head was reeling, and for a moment he thought he would not be able to speak at all.

"Jenna, I . . . please, I cannot think clearly. I know you can't mean you . . . want me, but what do you—"

"Oh, Kane," she said, her voice suddenly full of remorse as she sat on the bed beside him and grabbed his hands. "I'm sorry. You truly did not understand, did you? Of course I meant for you to join with me, to become Kane Hawk, not merely Kane of the clan Hawk. Our holy man is lost to the war, but Evelin can perform the ceremony, she has the right to accept our pledges to each other."

Kane closed his eyes, then opened them and struggled to draw in a breath that was somehow very hard in coming. "You want to pledge yourself . . . to me?" he asked in astonishment.

Jenna looked stricken. "I just . . . assumed you knew. When you woke up, you looked at me with such love, I thought . . ." She broke off, paling slightly. "But perhaps I was wrong? Is that what makes you hesitate? If you do not love me as I love you, then that I must accept. 'Tis the only reason I could accept."

"I . . ."

He stared up at her, unable to quite believe that it was all before him, all he'd never dared hope for, never even dared think of, waiting for him to simply reach out and take it. But then he remembered that moment in the stronghold, when Jenna would have died rather than let him hand himself over for his father's torture.

"Are you . . . sure I am alive?" he asked, hearing the wonderment in his voice even as he saw Jenna react to it, saw the tears begin anew.

"I have done this all backwards, haven't I?" she said softly. "And I have assumed too much. I love you, Kane. I loved you before I ever left your mountain, before you came here and handed your life to fate for my sake. But if you do not love me in the same way, I—"

She broke off when he moved suddenly, turning his hands beneath hers to grasp her slender fingers.

"I . . ."

He had to suck in a breath and try again.

"I do not think I know . . . what love is, Jenna. I don't know if I . . . am even capable of it. But if it means anything to you . . ." He hesitated, and the rest came out in a rushing spate of words. "I admire and honor you above anyone I've ever known, your heart, your kindness, your courage, I like nothing more than to watch you at the simplest of tasks, I hunger for the taste of you more than my next breath, and it ripped my heart out to watch you leave that day on the mountain, and all that mattered to me during the battle was that you would be safe . . ."

He swallowed tightly, thinking what he had to offer her a pitiful substitute for the real love she deserved. But she held his hands so tightly, was looking at him so steadily, so lovingly, that he knew he had to give it all, however poor it might be.

"I hate the thought of you with another man even more than I hate the thought of living on without you, and I want, more than I've ever wanted anything, even the peace I've searched for for so long, for those children to be mine, when I've never even dared think of such a thing . . . if those things can make up for the love I cannot give you, they are yours."

"Oh, Kane, you big, witless idiot!"

Kane blinked. Tears were streaming down her face now, but she was smiling in a way that made the tightness in his chest ease, and her tone was so full of joy and delight that it belied the words she spoke.

"In heaven's name," she said, "what do you think love is?"

Kane put his sword down next to the small Hawk dagger they had retrieved from the stronghold. He looked at the shelf which also held the book and the golden Hawk. He no longer felt the need to bury the sword again; it was a reminder now, but no longer a goad.

He fingered the spine of the book, feeling as he always did when he picked it up, the same odd sense of warmth and welcome Jenna said she felt every time she touched it. Whatever spell or incantation Tal had used, it was a powerful one.

"You still miss him, don't you?" Jenna said from behind Kane as she slipped her arms around his waist.

"I do," he admitted.

"So do I. I hope he finds what he searches for and comes back to us someday."

"You still believe he is looking for whoever . . . bewitched him?"

Jenna stepped around to stand beside him. " 'Tis the only thing that makes sense. He said the spell would last until he found the one who cast it. I think he seeks out places of powerful magic, such as Hawk Glade, in the hopes it will lead him to the one who made him what he is."

Kane nodded slowly. Then he opened the book he held, to look once more at the exquisite drawing that had emerged on the first page, which had been empty when it had first appeared. It was as clear a portrait as he had ever seen, and although he did not like looking at himself in it, he loved to look at Jenna, and never ceased to marvel at the fact that she was his, in the eyes of the world as well as in his heart; the ceremony Evelin had conducted barely three moons ago had made it so. He was Kane Hawk now, mated to the Hawk, and Kane Druas no longer existed.

And Jenna had slowly drawn the last of his father's poison out of him, convincing him slowly but inexorably that he could be free of the taint, that the evil had been stopped, that he had in essence stopped it when he had walked away from the monster that had sired him. He felt reborn, clean in a way he'd never known, and as the ugliness left him, the void left behind was quickly filled by Jenna's unquestioning and unending love.

". . . and so begins the history of the Hawks, and so will it continue in an unbroken line into all eternity . . ."

Jenna read the now familiar words in the tone of a ballad. The lines detailing their own joining, the union of Jenna the Hawk and Kane the Warrior, had appeared the morning after the ceremony, along with the intricate drawing of the newly pledged couple. While it had been startling, it was certainly no more so than anything else that had happened, and they had accepted it with wary wonder.

"I wonder," Jenna said thoughtfully, "why it did not tell of our joining until it was done?"

Because even a wizard cannot force love, my friends.

Kane nearly dropped the book, and Jenna stifled a cry as Tal's laughing voice echoed in the room. They both looked around, but they were alone in the cottage. Kane, having been through this before, recovered first.

"You are all right?" he asked. Jenna smiled at him then, as if pleased that had been his first thought, rather than to question how what they had heard was possible.

There was a pause, until Kane began to wonder if the connection was to be that brief. Then, in Tal's infuriating way, a nonanswer came back.

I am as I have been. But you have things to do.

"Tal—" they both began in irritated unison.

Turn the page, came his voice again. *And be well, my friends.*

Jenna opened her mouth, then closed it. She looked at Kane. He tilted his head slightly, then nodded at her.

"He is gone." He sighed. "Perhaps forever, now."

"I will remember and pray for him always," Jenna said softly. "All of us will."

Kane felt a tightness in his chest, worry for the man who had for so long been his only friend. "He needs it more than any man I know. Now."

Jenna smiled, and he knew she had not missed the significance of that last word; once he had needed her prayers more than any man living, and she had given them, and her love freely.

"I love you," she said suddenly, urgently.

Kane's mouth softened into the smile only Jenna could get from him.

"And I love you," he said; it came almost easily now, but never, ever lightly. Never without full knowledge of the wonder of it, the power of it.

It was a moment before he remembered Tal's words and turned a leaf in the book, to what yesterday had been a blank page. He was not really surprised when it was no longer blank, it had happened before, but when he read the words that had appeared his breath caught. His gaze shot to Jenna, who was looking up at him, her face shining with joy.

"You have built weapons all your life," she said softly. "Can you now build the one thing that most signifies hope for the future?"

"I . . . what?" he said, feeling a bit stunned by the news he could not doubt.

"A cradle," Jenna whispered.

He pulled her into his arms. "I know nothing of cradles," he said against the warm fire of her hair. "I know even less of . . . fathers and children, as they should be. But I will learn, Jenna. I swear to you I will learn."

"Our son, and his brothers and sisters after him, will be a fortunate child to have such a father," she said, hugging him back so fiercely he reveled in it.

"And it will happen," he said in awed wonder. "It will go on, and on. Always."

"And our love will be the beginning."

Kane stared down at her, saw the courage and heart and spirit of the woman he held so clearly that he wondered anew at the pure glory of having her love. It was a love so pure and strong it would indeed carry down the years, and in that moment he believed that even the family to come generations from now would feel it.

If you feel it half as strongly as I do now, you will be blessed. She is a woman worthy of founding a dynasty, he said to himself, wishing he could send the thought down to these unknown children so far down the years.

Then he felt the warmth of the book he still held.

And he knew that he need not worry. For all the generations of Hawks would know of her, and of their heritage. And he knew with a certainty that he could not question that Jenna Hawk, with her fiery hair and fierce heart and courage, would be the pride of them all.

And our love will be the beginning, she had said.

And there will never be an ending, Kane promised her silently.

And so he stood there holding the woman who had made his most impossible dreams come true, Kane the Warrior wept, and they were tears of joy.

Epilogue

"He will be as big as his father," Jenna predicted as she prepared the bedding in the cradle.

For one who had professed to know nothing of such things, Kane had produced a perfect, smooth-rocking cradle. And whenever she handed him his son, as she just had, the man who had once struck fear into the hearts of scores of men at once looked more fearful than any of them ever had.

He also, holding the baby with terrified care, made her want to cry, as did many things in these emotional days. But the sight of Kane, tall and powerful and scarred, holding the tiny, perfect child, never failed to move her almost unbearably. She grew to love him more each day, and the occasional battle he still fought with his past only made her love him more, for he fought with such determination she knew he would win; he treasured both her and their son too much not to.

The baby cooed and grabbed a lock of his father's hair, tugging happily. Kane grinned, a little sheepishly, not yet used to the power this tiny bit of humanity had over him. This man who had brought a needed bit of wildness back to Hawk Glade was soft clay in the tiny hands of his son. A wave of love swept over Jenna, so strong she had to turn away for a moment.

It was then she noticed the empty place on the shelf below the small window.

"It's gone," she said.

"Yes," he said, his voice very quiet. "I noticed this morning. I didn't speak of it, you were so weary."

"And my temper has been . . . unsettled of late," Jenna said, knowing the strain her pregnancy had put on them both.

"Has it?" Kane said innocently.

She tried to glare at him and failed utterly when he broke into that grin again; the expression that had once been so rare was more common now, but no less precious to her. As precious to her as the memory of the night he had held her so sweetly when she had at last allowed herself to grieve for the loss of her family. The night when, she was certain, they had conceived their son.

"We knew it would happen," she said finally.

They had, the book had explained it; after the entry that had appeared the night of the baby's birth had come the lines explaining the volume would vanish now, until the next time it was needed. The next time there was only one Hawk left in the world. And then their story would be added, chronicling the renewal of the line, and again the book would disappear. And on it would go, forever.

It was an odd, if heady feeling, to think of the book reappearing time and again, to be read by people yet unborn, but connected to her in a direct bloodline. Would they be proud, those children to come?

She looked again at Kane and their son, who was already asleep. When he was old enough, they would tell him the story, she thought. And perhaps, someday, he would tell his own children. And they would tell theirs.

But this one thing I can give you, Jenna. Your line will continue. You will be the beginning, and your heart, your soul, your courage, your blood will continue in an unbroken line, forever. Should fate step in and reduce your line to but one, it shall still go on. I promise you this.

She watched as Kane laid the baby in the cradle with tender care. And when he straightened and looked at her with the love he no longer tried to hide, she needed no wizardly prediction to tell her that the Hawks to come would be proud.

She could then only wish them the kind of love she had found. But that was up to them. Even a wizard cannot force love. And love, she thought as Kane picked her up and laid her on their bed, was a force more powerful than any other.

And when he came down beside her and pulled her close, she was suddenly sure that the Hawks would forever know that.

And the Hawk held her warrior, with no thought of the lineage begun, but only of the love that would live on forever.